STAR WARS
BATTLEFRONT II

INFERNO SQUAD

BY CHRISTIE GOLDEN

STAR WARS

Star Wars: Fate of the Jedi: Omen
Star Wars: Fate of the Jedi: Allies
Star Wars: Fate of the Jedi: Ascension
Star Wars: Dark Disciple
Star Wars Battlefront II: Inferno Squad

STAR TREK

Star Trek Voyager: The Murdered Sun
Star Trek Voyager: Marooned
Star Trek Voyager: Seven of Nine
Star Trek: Voyager: The Dark Matters
Trilogy, Book 1: *Cloak and Dagger*
Star Trek: Voyager: The Dark Matters
Trilogy, Book 2: *Ghost Dance*
Star Trek: Voyager: The Dark Matters
Trilogy, Book 3: *Shadow of Heaven*
Star Trek Voyager: No Man's Land
Star Trek Voyager: What Lay Beyond
Star Trek Voyager: Homecoming
Star Trek Voyager: The Farther Shore
Star Trek Voyager: Spirit Walk,
Book 1: *Old Wounds*
Star Trek Voyager: Spirit Walk,
Book 2: *Enemy of My Enemy*
Star Trek The Next Generation:
Double Helix: *The First Virtue*
(with Michael Jan Friedman)
Star Trek: Hard Crash (short story)
Star Trek: The Last Roundup

WORLD OF WARCRAFT

Lord of the Clans
Rise of the Horde
Beyond the Dark Portal
(with Aaron S. Rosenberg)
Arthas: Rise of the Lich King
The Shattering: Prelude to Cataclysm

Thrall: Twilight of the Aspects
Jaina Proudmore: Tides of War
War Crimes
Warcraft: Durotan
Warcraft: The Original
Movie Novelization

STARCRAFT

The Dark Templar Series, Book 1:
Firstborn
The Dark Templar Series, Book 2:
Shadow Hunters
The Dark Templar Series, Book 3:
Twilight
Devils' Due
Flashpoint

ASSASSIN'S CREED

Heresy
Assassin's Creed:
The Official Movie Novelization
Blackbeard: The Lost Journal
Abstergo Entertainment:
Employee Handbook

RAVENLOFT

Vampire of the Mists
Dance of the Dead
The Enemy Within

ORIGINAL NOVELS

On Fire's Wings
In Stone's Clasp
Under Sea's Shadow
Instrument of Fate
King's Man & Thief
A.D. 999 (as Jadrien Bell)

STAR WARS
BATTLEFRONT II

INFERNO SQUAD

CHRISTIE GOLDEN

Based on characters and story developed by
Motive Studios, EA, and Lucasfilm for Star Wars Battlefront II

DEL REY • NEW YORK

2018 Del Rey Mass Market Edition

Copyright © 2017 by Lucasfilm Ltd. & ® or ™ where indicated. All rights reserved.
Excerpt from *Star Wars: Phasma* by Delilah S. Dawson copyright © 2018 by Lucasfilm Ltd. & ® or ™ where indicated. All rights reserved.

Published in the United States by Del Rey, an imprint of Random House, a division of Penguin Random House LLC, New York.

DEL REY and the HOUSE colophon are registered trademarks of Penguin Random House LLC.

Originally published in hardcover in the United States by Del Rey, an imprint of Random House, a division of Penguin Random House LLC, in 2017.

This book contains an excerpt from the book *Star Wars: Phasma* by Delilah S. Dawson. This excerpt has been set for this edition only and may not reflect the final content of the forthcoming edition.

ISBN 978-1-5247-9682-2
Ebook ISBN 978-1-5247-9681-5

Printed in the United States of America

randomhousebooks.com

9 8 7 6 5 4 3 2 1

Del Rey mass market edition: April 2018

This book is dedicated to the "real" Inferno Squad:
T. J. Ramini, "Del Meeko,"
Paul Blackthorne, "Gideon Hask,"
and especially Janina Gavankar, "Iden Versio,"
who reached out to me with such enthusiasm to
learn more about this book and about Iden Versio,
a character we both have come to love and admire.

THE DEL REY

STAR WARS™

TIMELINE

THE DEL REY

STAR WARS

TIMELINE

A long time ago in a galaxy far, far away. . . .

STAR WARS

BATTLEFRONT II

INFERNO SQUAD

CHAPTER 1

The firm control of one's emotions was an unspoken criterion for those who would serve the Empire. One did not gloat, or cheer, or weep, or rage, although cold fury was, upon occasion, deemed an appropriate reaction to particular circumstances.

Senior Lieutenant Iden Versio had been familiar with this stipulation since she was old enough to understand the concept. Even so, now, at this hour of the Empire's unequivocal and absolute triumph, the young woman raced across the gleaming black surface of the Death Star's corridors with her helmet cradled in one arm, trying and failing to smother a grin.

Today, of all days, why shouldn't she smile, at least when no one was watching?

When her orders had come to serve on the space station—which a scant few hours ago had reduced an en-

tire planet into rocky chunks of glorious rebel *rubble*—
Iden had endured resentful, sidelong glances followed by
murmurs pitched exactly too softly for her to catch. But
Iden didn't need to hear the words. She knew what the
others were saying about her. It was nothing more than a
variant on what had always been said about her.

*She's too young for this position. She couldn't have
earned it on her own.*

She got it because of her father.

The self-righteous mutterers would have been startled
to discover the degree to which their assumptions were
wrong.

Inspector General Garrick Versio might well be one
of the highest-ranking members of the powerful and se-
cretive Imperial Security Bureau, but Iden had gotten
nothing out of the joyless task of being his daughter.
Every honor, every grade, every opportunity she'd had,
she'd fought for and obtained *despite* him.

She'd been primed for the military academy while
barely more than a child, studying at the Future Imperial
Leaders Military Preparatory School on her homeworld
of Vardos, located in the Jinata system, where she had,
literally, been bloodied. There, and afterward at the Imperial Academy on Coruscant, Iden had graduated top
of her class, with honors.

All that felt like a mere prelude to this moment. For
the last several months, Iden had been part of a small,
elite TIE fighter unit aboard what was arguably the pin-
nacle of Imperial design—the massive space station
known as the Death Star. And she was rather unprofes-
sionally excited.

Even as she tried to rein in her enthusiasm, she could

sense that others hastening to their own TIE fighters shared it. They betrayed themselves with the surging tattoo of booted footfalls, their upright positions, even the brightness in their eyes.

It wasn't new, this happy tension. Iden had seen it bubbling under the surface after the first test of the station's capabilities, when the Death Star's superlaser had targeted and obliterated Jedha City. The Empire had landed a one-two punch in a handful of seconds. It had destroyed not only the rebel terrorist Saw Gerrera and his group of extremists known as the partisans, but also the ancient Temple of the Kyber, held sacred by those who secretly hoped for the return of the disgraced and defeated Jedi. Jedha City represented the first real demonstration of the station's power, but that fact was known only to those who served on the Death Star.

For now. To the rest of the galaxy, what had happened at Jedha was a tragic mining accident.

Things had happened with shocking speed after that, as if some galactic balance had suddenly, drastically, been tipped. The superlaser was again employed at the Battle of Scarif, this time wiping out an entire region and several rebel ships trapped under Scarif's shield along with it. Emperor Palpatine had dissolved the Imperial Senate. His right hand, the mysterious caped and helmeted Darth Vader, had intercepted and imprisoned secret rebel and now former senator Princess Leia Organa. The Death Star's director, Grand Moff Wilhuff Tarkin, had used the princess's home planet of Alderaan to demonstrate the true breadth of the power of the now fully operational battle station.

As nearly all on the Death Star had been ordered to

do, with their own eyes or on a screen, Iden had stood and watched. By their treasonous actions, the rebels on Alderaan had brought destruction not only on themselves, but on the innocents they always seemed so keen to protect. She couldn't get the image out of her head: a planet, a world, gone in the span of a few seconds. As, soon, would be virtually all the Empire's enemies. In a very, very short time, the galaxy would receive an implacable and thorough understanding of just how useless resistance would be. And then—

Then, there would be order, and this ill-thought-out, chaotic "Rebellion" would subside. All the extensive hours of labor, all the credits and brainpower spent on controlling and dominating various unruly worlds could, at last, be turned to helping them.

There would, finally, be peace.

The event would be shocking, yes. But it had to be, and it was all for the greater good. Once everyone was under the auspices of the Empire, they would understand.

And that glorious moment was almost here. Tarkin had located the rebel base on one of Yavin's moons. The base—and the moon—were but a few moments from oblivion.

Some of the rebels, though, were not going to go quietly.

These few had taken to space and were presently mounting a humorously feeble attack on the gigantic space station. The thirty Y- and X-wing fighters the rebels had mustered were small enough to dodge the station's defensive turbolaser turrets, zipping about like flies. And, like flies, this nominal, futile defense would be casually swatted down by Iden and the other pilots in ship-to-ship combat, as per orders from Lord Vader.

Within the span of seven minutes, Yavin's moon and all the rebels it had succored would be nothing more than floating debris. On this day, the Rebellion would be no more.

Iden's heartbeat thudded in her ears as she all but jumped down the ladder into her fighter, sealing her flight suit and pulling on her helmet. Slender but strong gloved fingers flew over the consoles, her gaze flitting over the stats as she went through the preflight checklist. The hatch lowered, hummed shut, and she was encased in its black metal belly. A few seconds later she was swirling in cold, airless darkness, where the distinctive scream of her vessel was silent.

Here they came, now, mostly the X-wings—the Rebellion's answer to TIE fighters. They were impressive little single-occupant vessels, and they skimmed along close to the surface of the station, a few of them misjudging the distance and slamming into the walls around the trenches that crisscrossed the Death Star's surface.

Suicide, Iden thought, even as she knew the term was just as often applied to those who flew TIE fighters. You either loved the small starfighters or you hated them. A TIE fighter was fast and distinctive, with its laser cannons quite deadly, but it was more vulnerable to attack than other vessels as it wasn't equipped with deflector shields. The trick was to kill the enemy first—something Iden was better at than anyone else in her squadron. Iden liked that everything was compact and immediately to hand—flight controls, viewscreen, targeting systems, equipment for tracking and being tracked.

Iden listened to the familiar beeps of the tracking equipment as it targeted and locked onto one of the X-wings. She swung her vessel back and forth with easy familiarity as the enemy ship frantically jigged and jagged in a commendable, but ultimately useless, effort to evade her.

She pressed her thumbs down. Green lasers sliced through the X-wing, and then only pieces and a flaring sheet of flame remained.

A quick count on her screen told Iden that her fellow pilots were also efficiently culling the herd of rebels. She frowned slightly at the tiny, ship-shaped blips on her screen. Some of them were veering off from the group, going deeper in toward the Death Star, while others seemed to be trying to draw the TIE fighters away from the station. Iden's gaze flickered to another ship, a Y-wing—one of those enemy vessels that always looked to her like a skeletal bird of prey—and she went in pursuit, rolling smoothly and coming up on its side. More streaks of green in the star-spattered blackness, and then it, too, was gone.

Her gaze now lingered on the more suicidal of the enemy fighters, watching as they dropped into the trenches. As far as Iden knew, no one in her six-pilot squadron had been told *why* the rebels had adopted this peculiar tactic of flying through the trenches. Iden had grown up with nearly everything—from what it was her father actually *did* for the Empire to what her mother was designing that day, even what was for dinner that night—being on a need-to-know basis. She had grown accustomed to the situation, but she would never like it.

"Attention, pilots," came the voice of her commander,

Kela Neerik, in Iden's ear, and for a brief, beautiful instant Iden thought her squad commander was going to explain what was going on. But all Neerik said was, "Death Star is now six minutes out from target."

Iden bit her lip, wondering if she should speak up. *Don't. Don't,* she told herself, but the words had a life of their own. Before she realized it, out they had come.

"Respectfully, Commander, with only six minutes until the entire moon's destruction, why are we out here? Surely thirty one-person ships won't be able to do anything resembling damage to the Death Star in that amount of time."

"Lieutenant Versio"—Neerik's voice was as cold as space—"don't assume your father's position gives you special privileges. We are here because Lord Vader *ordered* us to be here. Perhaps you'd like to put your question to him personally when we return to the station? I'm sure he'd be delighted to explain his military strategy to you."

Iden felt a cold knot in her stomach at the thought of a "personal" conversation with Lord Vader. She'd never met him, thankfully, but she had heard too many chilling rumors.

"No, Commander, that won't be necessary."

"I thought not. Do your duty, Lieutenant Versio."

Iden frowned, then let it go. She did not need to understand the rebels; she needed only to destroy them.

As if they sensed her renewed resolve, the rebel pilots suddenly upped their game. There was a brief flash at the corner of Iden's vision, and when she turned to look, she realized with sick surprise that the debris hurtling off in all directions was black.

Iden didn't know who had just died. TIE fighters were so uniform as to be practically indistinguishable from one another. Their pilots weren't supposed to think of their ships in the warm, fuzzy way the rebels were reported to do. A ship was a ship was a ship. And Iden understood that, as far as most in the Empire were concerned, a pilot was a pilot was a pilot: as expendable and interchangeable as the ships they flew.

We all serve at the pleasure of the Emperor, her father had drilled into her since she was old enough to comprehend what an emperor was. *None of us is indispensable.* Iden had certainly seen Imperial ships shot down before. This was war, and she was a soldier. But *indispensable* be damned.

The half smile she'd been wearing during most of the combat vanished, and Iden pressed her lips together angrily. She veered, perhaps a touch too violently, to the right and targeted another X-wing. In mere seconds it exploded into a yellow-orange fireball.

"Gotcha, you—" she muttered.

"No commentary, Versio," warned Neerik, her voice rising a little; more hot than cold, now. "We will be having the honor of Lord Vader joining us momentarily. He and his pilots will be focusing on the hostiles navigating the meridian trench. All remaining units are ordered to redirect their attacks to the rebel ships on the magnetic perimeter."

Iden almost shouted a protest, but stopped herself just in time. For some reason *still unknown to the squadron,* this perplexing tactic by the rebel pilots was clearly of great concern. Lord Vader wouldn't trouble himself with appearing personally to take care of it otherwise.

Almost everything Iden knew about Darth Vader was pure speculation. The exception was a single revelation on the part of her father, in one of those rare moments when he was feeling less taciturn than usual with his only child.

"Lord Vader has great power," Versio had said. "His instincts and his reflexes are uncanny. And . . . there are certain abilities he possesses that our Emperor finds to be of tremendous value."

So yes. Vader was head and shoulders above the rest of them—literally and figuratively. But it wasn't Vader's friends who were dying in this battle, and Iden burned to be the one to make the rebels pay.

With a huffing sigh that she was certain was audible, she swerved from tailing the X-wing, frowning as red laserfire came perilously close to her fighter's fragile wings. That was on her; she hadn't been focusing.

She corrected that oversight immediately, zooming away from the station toward a pair of Y-wings that was, successfully, attempting to get her attention. Any other time, Iden would have enjoyed toying with them—they were decent pilots, although the ones in the X-wings were superior—but right now she was too irritated to do so.

She targeted the closest Y-wing, locked onto it, and blew it to pieces. Watching the fragments of the starfighter hurtling wildly was some small compensation for the deaths of her fellow pilots.

"Death Star is two minutes to target. Be aware of your distance from the planet."

Ah, so that was why Neerik was giving the count-down. Iden had to give the pilot of the other Y-wing credit for courage, albeit of the foolish kind; the ship was now racing *away* from the Death Star at top speed. Were they heading back to Yavin's moon, nobly choosing to die with their base, or were they just trying to evade her?

Not happening, Iden thought, and continued her pursuit. She got the vessel in her sights and fired. She didn't slow as the ship exploded, but simply pulled back and looped up and over the fireball and debris, snug in her crash webbing, and smoothly dipped the TIE fighter in front of the second Y-wing for the perfect shot.

The pale moon-shape of the Death Star loomed behind the vessel, its gargantuan size making the rebel ship look like the toys she'd been allowed to play with as a child. The Y-wing was making for Yavin as fast as it could, swerving erratically enough that Iden frowned as she tried to get a lock on it.

A sudden scalding brightness filled her vision.

Temporarily blinded, Iden hurtled wildly, her TIE fighter tumbling out of control. As her vision returned, she realized debris was coming at her as intensely as if she had suddenly materialized inside an asteroid field. Her focus, always powerful, narrowed to laserlike precision as she frantically dodged and swerved, maneuvering around the biggest pieces and wishing with all her being that TIE fighters had shields.

Iden pivoted and tumbled, breathing the mercifully still-flowing oxygen deeply and rhythmically. But she knew in her heart it was just a matter of time. There was too much debris, some of it the size of a standard escape pod, some of it as small as her clenched fist, and she was right in the thick of it. The smaller pieces were pelting her TIE fighter already. Sooner or later, one of the big chunks would hit her, and both Senior Lieutenant Iden Versio and her ship would be nothing more than smears on what was left of Yavin's moon.

Somehow, she'd wandered too close to the Death Star's target and had gotten caught up in the chaotic sweep of its destruction—exactly what her commander had been warning her against.

But how was that possible?

"Mayday, mayday," Iden shouted, unable to keep her voice calm as she desperately dipped and dived to avoid disaster. "This is TIE Sigma Three requesting assistance. Repeat, this is TIE Sigma Three requesting assistance, do you copy, over?"

Silence. Absolute, cold, terrifying silence.

The inevitable occurred at last.

Something struck the TIE fighter, hard. The ship shuddered, tumbled off in a different direction, but did not explode. A piece of one of the sleek, fragile wings flashed across Iden's field of vision and she realized that control of the vessel was out of her hands.

Others would panic, or weep, or rail. But Iden had been raised to never, *ever* quit, and now, at this moment, she was grateful for her father's implacability. The ship was careening and, as she could do nothing to stop it, she took a few seconds to observe.

The prospect of her own violent and, possibly, painful and prolonged death was something that held little fear for her. But what she saw in those seconds struck terror down to her bones.

It was the blue-green moon of Yavin. And it was completely intact.

Not. Possible!

She thought of the dreadful silence on the comm. And now that she knew, now that she had wrapped her brain around something that was not supposed to happen, that no one had ever imagined *could* happen, she recognized some of the pieces that she was trying so desperately to evade.

They were of Imperial construction.

Imperial.

Pieces of the greatest battle station that—

A single short, harsh, disbelieving gasp racked her slender frame. Then Iden Versio clenched her teeth against a second outburst. Pressed her lips together to seal it inside her.

She was a Versio, and Versios did not panic.

The destruction of the Death Star was the brutal and irrevocable truth that the impossible was now possible. Which meant she could survive this.

And she was going to.

Iden clawed her way back to control and assessed the situation with a bright, sharp, almost violent clarity.

The impact of the debris strike had, fortunately, served not only to damage the wing but also to push her toward the moon, and without the pull of the Death Star to counter it, the gravity of Yavin's small satellite was greedy. She couldn't direct her trajectory, but she could manage it. Iden went on the offensive—a preferred tactic—but this time not against a rebel vessel. This time, her enemy was the debris that hurtled toward her.

She spun toward the moon's surface, targeting anything in her path and blasting it into rubble. This sort of thing was second nature, so she let part of her mind deal with how to manage the process of reentry, a controlled crash, and ejection.

There would then be avoiding capture, stealing a vessel, and absconding with it, presuming she landed on Yavin's moon in one piece.

There it was again, that frisson of bestial, primitive panic, closing her throat. Iden swallowed hard even as cold sweat dewed her body—

—*beneath the uniform of an Imperial officer*—

—*beneath the helm of a TIE fighter pilot*—

—and again took a deep, calming breath. The oxygen was finite, but it was better to use it now to help her focus than later as she panicked.

Iden was, as far as she knew, the sole survivor out of over a million victims of this act of rebel terrorism. She *had* to survive, if only to honor those who hadn't. Who hadn't chased the foe in an impulsive act that ought to have been a mistake, but instead had gifted her with a chance to live.

She would find a way back to Imperial space ready to continue the fight against the Rebel Alliance for as long as it took to eliminate every last one of the bastards.

Her jaw set and her eyes narrowed with determination, Iden Versio braced herself for a bumpy landing.

CHAPTER 2

"She . . . she's *what*?"

Lieutenant Junior Grade Gideon Hask, twenty-seven, tall, elegant, the sole living member of a proud family of high-ranking Imperial officers, was usually poised and cool, just as he ought to be. Never sudden in his movements unless swift, decisive action was called for, his voice was well modulated and resonant. A voice, Gideon always thought privately, that was made for giving orders.

But now that smooth voice betrayed harsh joy as it cracked on the last word.

He had been summoned with no explanation to the Federal District of Coruscant's Imperial City by Inspector General—no, Hask corrected himself, there had been a promotion in the last few days—*Admiral* Garrick Versio. The admiral was at this moment frowning ever so slightly in disapproval at Gideon's lapse in professional demeanor. But for once, Gideon couldn't care less.

"I said," Admiral Versio repeated with a slight hint of impatience, "Senior Lieutenant Versio is alive."

Gideon swayed, ever so slightly, and had to catch himself on a corner of the gleaming black desk behind which sat the admiral—and his best friend's father.

Iden's alive.

"How the hell—" At the admiral's arched eyebrow, Gideon took a moment to recover. He released his grip on the desk and straightened, taking a deep breath. "How is that possible, sir? We were informed that everyone aboard the Death Star was killed."

A mere three days after the inconceivable disaster, the destruction of the mightiest weapon the galaxy had ever known, the Empire was still reeling. No one admitted it, of course. And it was easy to take all that disbelief and shock and grief like a piece of clay and mold it into hatred and cold fury. Revenge—no, nothing as petty as that; *justice* for the deaths of hundreds of thousands—was the focus now. The dead were to be avenged and honored, not grieved.

Except . . . Gideon *had* grieved for Iden, privately, and on his own time. He had encountered the Versio family when he had been sent to Vardos to attend the Future Imperial Leaders Military Preparatory School. Vardos was an illustrious and staunchly Imperial world located in the Jinata system. The system had been praised throughout the Empire for its efficient control of its worlds. Garrick Versio himself had been the one to bring the planet into the Empire when he had been a young man. He had done so successfully and without violence, and the population loved both him and the Empire. In many aspects, Vardos *was* Versio.

Gideon, a native of Kuat, had been orphaned at age ten when a rebel infiltrator had detonated a bomb at the planet's shipyards. His parents had died in the blast. Gideon had grieved when he'd lost them, too—also privately, and on his own time, alone in his room in the now too-large house on Kuat, during the handful of days it took for his legal guardian to arrange for his enrollment in the school.

The guardian had deemed the school an adequate substitute for parents. It was not, of course, but over time Gideon had learned to appreciate that it had forced him to mature, taught him invaluable skills. And . . . it had connected him with Iden. Though she was several years behind him, he'd been tapped to keep an eye on her while he was at Future Imperial Leaders, and had come to respect her. She was definitely a Versio, fiercely determined and excelling even at a young age. Later, they'd found themselves at the Coruscant Imperial Academy at the same time—and this time, Iden was the one keeping Gideon on *his* toes.

This shared history made them less than friends—because, as the school's headmaster, the Aqualish Gleb, had instilled in them, young Imperials did not make "friends," they made "allies"—but more than colleagues. Gideon and Iden had an intense but respectful and strangely amiable sense of competition. She had consistently bested him, but that didn't lessen the amount of regard he had for her. Her excellence only spurred him to his own. Like the pair of siblings they were not, they jostled for recognition. It had smarted when she received the coveted appointment to the Death Star while he, five years older and more experienced, had to be content with the TIE squadron aboard the *Advance*.

Until just this moment, Gideon had viewed that appointment as Iden's death sentence. He was both unable and unwilling to share his torment with anyone; nearly everyone he knew had lost friends or family on the Death Star, and no one seemed to be as devastated as he. Gideon had wrestled with the enormity of the hole Iden Versio had left behind in his universe. To have lost the only regular presence in his life for over a decade, and in such a manner, had shattered him more than he could have anticipated.

And now this revelation had restored him with the same unexpected force. Iden was alive. That suppressed joy made it all right that Admiral Versio sighed heavily and said, an edge to his deep, rumbling voice, "*Of course* everyone who was physically on the station died in that tragic event. But Lord Vader, Lieutenant Versio, and a handful of others were *not* on the station. She was in her TIE at the time."

Carefully, Gideon said, "Then there is one thing to be grateful for, in the midst of this tragedy."

"I have to admit I myself was very pleased to hear the news."

The confession surprised Gideon—it was definitely out of character. But he did not acknowledge it, instead asking, "What happened?"

"According to her report, Lieutenant Versio's TIE fighter was damaged in the explosion. She maneuvered it to a crash landing on the surface of Yavin's fourth moon, ejecting safely before impact. She eluded detection and relieved the rebels of one of their hyperspace-capable vessels. When she reached Imperial space, she immediately identified herself. She's been fully debriefed and is recovering on Hosnian Prime."

Gideon was smiling by the time the admiral had finished, but then, catching himself, he forced his face to return to a carefully neutral expression. *Of course that's what Iden would do.*

"Quite impressive, and a testament to your training, sir," he said.

"Not all that impressive," Versio demurred. "Lieutenant Versio reported that there was a lot of celebrating going on." The admiral's voice dripped with contempt. "There's not too much honor in eliminating a handful of drunken guards."

Although he'd known Admiral Versio his whole life, Gideon had never seen him effusive about anything except the glory of the Empire, so he shrugged off the older man's downplaying of the scenario. The rebels, with their shocking, sickening victory, had suddenly proved themselves a force to be reckoned with. Gideon couldn't imagine they would drop their guard and drink at their posts at any time, even when they'd struck a major blow against their enemies. He knew that Versio knew this, too, and that the admiral was simply being . . . well . . . the admiral.

He had mentioned that Iden was "recovering," which meant she'd suffered injury.

A thought occurred to Gideon. He hesitated, but had to ask. "Does . . . has her mother . . ."

"Zeehay Versio has been informed." The clipped tone of the words was a warning, one Gideon knew to heed.

The Versios had divorced when Iden was five, and Gideon had never met her mother. Iden didn't talk about her much, though Gideon knew they stayed in touch. The last time Iden had mentioned her, Gideon recalled, his friend had let slip that Zeehay was unwell, but had said nothing about her since. Zeehay was a premier artist at the Coalition for Progress and, until her recent illness at least, traveled to various worlds, designing inspirational Imperial posters tailored to appeal to each culture. There was no one Gideon admired more than the man he stood before at this moment, but he couldn't fathom what it must have been like to be married to him, especially given Zeehay's artistic nature.

Iden had gotten her mother's coloring—warm, light-brown skin and black hair—and curiosity, but her strong jaw and strong personality had come straight from her father.

"Thank you for letting me know, sir," Gideon said. "But . . . I'm fairly sure you didn't request me from the *Advance* just to tell me Lieutenant Versio is all right."

"No, I didn't, but we will discuss that here in my office tomorrow at oh nine hundred. Lieutenant Versio and two others will be joining us. I've had quarters prepared for you at the Diplomat. Please head there directly and speak with no one. You're dismissed, Lieutenant."

Usually, Gideon would salute and depart, but there was something else he had to ask. "Sir? Would it be possible for me to talk to Iden?"

Versio's gray eyebrows lifted. "I said, she will be joining us tomorrow morning."

"I know, sir, but . . . if it's permitted, I'd like to speak to her."

Versio analyzed him for a moment, then nodded. "Very well, I'll send you the coordinates. You may contact her once you reach your quarters."

Gideon didn't need to ask. He knew the conversation would be monitored.

Everything was monitored when it came to dealing with Garrick Versio.

Under ordinary circumstances, Gideon would have been assigned visiting officers' quarters at the barracks, but it was clear that whatever the admiral wanted to discuss with him and his daughter, it was top secret—as were the identities of the *two others*.

He certainly didn't mind the change of venue, relaxing in the comfort of the VIP shuttle that ferried him to one of the highest levels of the city-world, 5120, a short distance from Versio's office at the Imperial Security Bureau headquarters in the Federal District.

The lift opened onto a floor with a single entrance. Clearly at some point in the hotel's illustrious past, others had appreciated the value of near-total privacy. A guard stood beside the door, rigidly at attention.

"Your identification, sir," the man said briskly. Bemused, Gideon handed him his code cylinder. The guard scanned it with a small, handheld device, then stepped up and pressed his palm against a square reader affixed to the door. It hissed open onto cool darkness.

"Welcome, Lieutenant Hask. I'll be outside," he said. "Com me if there's anything you require."

"Thank you," Gideon replied, and stepped inside. The enormous suite lit up to welcome him. It was luxurious but also austere. The far end of the room was composed entirely of reinforced glass. Gideon knew the topmost level of the hotel was above the planet's cloud layer, but this floor was located beneath it, revealing the bustle of Coruscant outside.

The only splashes of color in the otherwise stark black-and-white room were in the artworks. Recruitment posters from years past had been carefully framed, and Gideon found himself looking at images of proud young men and women, stormtroopers, and Imperial officers set against the stylized backgrounds of various worlds. Gideon was not an art aficionado, but he spared a moment to wonder if this was Zeehay Versio's work. The young girl gazing up raptly at the stars in one painting certainly looked like Iden.

His bag slung over his shoulder, Gideon walked through the main room with its black-and-white couches, chairs, and table, and selected a room at random. He whistled softly as the door slid open. The room was, by military standards, enormous.

"Nice," he murmured, "very nice." He dropped the bag on the neatly made bed and headed for the holoprojector perched on the small table. He entered the coordinates and waited for what seemed like forever but was in reality only a few seconds.

She appeared before him, miniature and gray-blue, but even in holographic form it was easy to see that her face was swollen and there was the ghost of a bruise on her temple.

Her eyes widened. "Gideon!"

She always called him by his first name, except under professional circumstances. That wasn't true with anyone else, not even her father. And Gideon had long since gotten used to being called Hask by everyone else. His first name was theirs, between them.

"Iden!" He found himself grinning. "I never thought . . . I *just* heard. I'm . . . I'm so glad to see you."

She smiled weakly. "I'm glad to be seen."

"Are you all right?"

She sobered. "A bit battered and bruised, but the bacta tank fixed the worst of it. I'm trying to get a little rest, but honestly, I can't sleep."

It hung between them; the thing they couldn't talk about, probably shouldn't talk about . . . but needed to.

Gideon waited patiently. Iden had been closer to it all than he had. She was sitting up in a medcenter bed, propped up against the pillows, and was obviously holding the holoprojector in front of her in her hands. She looked away for a moment, then back at him.

"Over a million people. So fast. Gone, just like that."

He nodded mutely and tried to reach for the positive. "But *you're* not gone. You're lucky to be alive."

She started to give him one of her wry smiles, then winced a little; the gesture clearly hurt. "Sure."

"Don't do that," Gideon snapped. "You *are*. And I'm glad, and your parents are, too. I saw the admiral today, and he even said so." A slight exaggeration, but true as far as it went.

Iden brushed it off. "I mean . . . think about who we lost. The repercussions are going to be pretty horrifying. Some of the Empire's top people were on that station. Grand Moff Tarkin. Colonel Yularen. So many good men and women. The Empire would have been better off if others had made it instead of me. I'm just a TIE pilot."

Iden sighed and rubbed at one of her eyes with the heel of her hand. "At least Lord Vader survived."

"Well, you did, too, and I'm glad. I know you, Iden. You'll work to make sure your survival means something."

He leaned forward, folding his arms on the small table. "So. Tell me what happened. How you got out."

Light-years away, still in a medcenter bed, bone-weary and sick with guilty grief, Iden permitted herself to be distracted. She told him about the crash, how she'd been injured but had been able to fashion a splint out of debris. How she'd walked several klicks through the thick, unnervingly green press of the jungle. She'd eluded detection, save for a single rebel, but she had dispatched him before he could raise the alarm. Then she'd slipped into a cargo ship and headed for the nearest Imperial system.

"Not too exciting," she said. "First aid, walking, taking a ship, and recovering here. No space battles."

Don't boast, her father had told her. *Accomplish. Then let others notice and react appropriately.*

"Nope. Nothing remarkable. Just sneaking onto a major rebel base and stealing a vessel right underneath their noses," Gideon pointed out. "And," he added, somewhat more somberly, "surviving the Death Star."

Iden felt herself retreating inward. She didn't want to see it, to think about it, because she didn't want to lose control. Senior Lieutenant Iden Versio couldn't afford to do that, not in front of anyone—even Gideon.

"Did you hear how the rebels did it?" Gideon asked.

He was usually good at reading her, but Iden knew from experience that it was difficult to see expressions and body language on a hologram. She resigned herself to a discussion.

"Something about stolen plans to the station," she said.

"More than just that. Iden—it's awful." He looked down for a moment. When he lifted his head, despite the distortion of the small size and color of his face, Iden saw that his eyes were blazing with fury she suspected had been too long buried. "One of the scientists who helped design the Death Star . . . he built it to be destroyed."

Iden stiffened. "Explain," she said coolly.

"He'd been planning for this to happen all along. Years. He built an instability into the reactor. There was a small thermal exhaust port below the main one, along the meridian trench. The damn thing was only two meters wide. The shaft led directly to the main reactor system."

Iden twitched as a scene flashed before her eyes: the X- and Y-wings heading straight for the trench, dropping down, moving along it, dropping—

"Proton torpedoes," she said. It had to be. The shaft was ray-shielded. Because any sane attacker would try to fire lasers.

"Exactly! How did you—" He bit off the words. "Sorry."

She waved in annoyance. "Go on."

"Well, it turns out a direct hit started a chain reaction."

"And the Death Star blew up from within." Iden shivered. *That's why the rebels were sending in such small ships. That's why they were heading for the trenches. And we who were on our comfortable, impregnable station, or in our fine fighters—we thought they were just grandstanding in a final gesture of defiance—*

"Rumor has it the plans were stolen from Scarif," Gideon continued. "That's why the battle was fought."

"But they died, didn't they?" Iden's voice was harsh. "The rebels? On Scarif?"

"Yes. They were able to transmit the plans to—"

"But they *died*?"

Hask blinked at her intensity, but replied, "Yes. They died."

"Good. I'm glad. They should have died. They should *all* have died for what they did. But Senator Organa escaped." She uttered the name of the traitorous princess like an epithet, then took a deep breath. "Gideon—she was on Yavin. While I was there."

Now Gideon caught on, and his strong-featured face grew sympathetic.

"Yes, she was," he agreed cautiously, "and your job was to get out of there alive, not execute every rebel in the place. You were wounded, Iden. Pretty badly, if I can see it even now—and in a holo. No one just hops into a bacta tank for a quick splash."

She found herself smiling. She hated that Gideon knew her so well . . . but it was a comfort, too.

Still, the warmth of her affection for him faded, the cold knot of hate growing inside her.

"We're going to get them, Gideon." It wasn't a statement. It was a vow. "We're going to make them pay. We're going to crush this Rebellion. We're going to get justice for this—this terrorist act."

He smiled—the cold, thin-lipped smile of absolute calculation that Iden usually didn't like to see but now welcomed. "Oh yes, indeed we are. And I have a feeling you and I are going to get to be part of it."

"We damn well better be."

CHAPTER 3

Lieutenant Commander Del Meeko piloted the *Lambda*-class T-4a toward the silver-gray-brown ecumenopolis that was Coruscant. Once, it had been home, but he had not returned for a very long time. The sight of white clouds coyly offering glimpses of a world composed almost entirely of the artificial was nostalgic, and curiously comforting. Which was good, because ever since he'd gotten the mysterious summons, the former chief engineer of the Star Destroyer *Implacable* had been more than a little on edge.

He'd reported for duty this morning, bleary-eyed as always before that first cup of caf, to find his crew awaiting him in Engineering. Lieutenant Naylyn Bashan, his immediate subordinate, had told him there was a message for him in his office. "Top priority," she'd said, almost blurting the words. She and the rest of Engineering did their best to not look alarmed, and Meeko, of course, had also done his best to also not look alarmed. All of them knew that after the destruction of the Death Star nothing, absolutely *nothing* was going to be the same, and they were all prepared for the worst.

Admiral Dayun's face, always florid, had been outright flushed as he spoke.

"You're to be reassigned, Del," he had said, using the chief engineer's name instead of his rank and thus revealing how much the information had thrown him. "Admiral Garrick Versio requested you specifically."

And that was, apparently, all Del was going to get. In the relative privacy of the shuttle, Naylyn had asked variants on *what the hell is going on*. Del had nothing to tell her. So instead, they'd told stories about their first time on the ship, and the ritual of practical jokes to which "nerf meat"—newcomers to the team—were always subjected. But now, with Coruscant filling their viewscreen, they fell silent.

Then Naylyn spoke. "Del . . . do you think this has anything to do with you having been stationed on Scarif?"

Del forced himself not to wince. Earlier in his career, he'd been a soldier, not an engineer. He had begun Imperial service as a stormtrooper, and had seen his share of battle. Later, he had served as a shoretrooper on the Imperial base that was once considered a working holiday. Most of the friends he'd made during that time had still been stationed there when the rebel attack occurred.

None had survived it.

"I've been asking myself that," Del admitted. "But I can't think why. That was a long time ago."

"Lots of rearranging going on," Naylyn said, then added, after clearing her throat, "Lots of positions to fill."

"I serve at the Empire's pleasure," Del said, and while it was the expected reply, it was also true. "I've no idea what this is about, and if I did—well, I could tell you, but . . ."

They chuckled together at the ancient joke and the mood lightened. Del maneuvered the shuttle down, skimming along the white clouds pierced here and there by duracrete skytowers, their gleaming reinforced glass windows catching the light. Below that layer, the vessel entered the often dangerously speedy flow of busy traffic that constantly crowded the space above the capital world of the Empire.

Their destination was Imperial City, specifically the section that had, until recently, been called the Senate District. But there was no Senate any longer. When the shuttle was within a few kilometers of the area, two smaller ships materialized seemingly out of nowhere.

"You are entering a restricted area," came a clipped, cold voice. "Identify yourself and prepare to be rerouted and boarded."

Del and Naylyn exchanged glances. "This is vessel 4240-C, of the Star Destroyer *Implacable*. I am Lieutenant Commander Del Meeko, my copilot is Lieutenant Naylyn Bashan. Our authorization code is—"

"Authorization code is irrelevant. Sending coordinates. Reroute immediately."

Something was wrong. Del remained calm as he said, "I've been ordered to report to Admiral Garrick Versio."

There was a pause. A long one. Then: "Authorization code?"

Del gave it. Another long pause. Then: "You are cleared to proceed. We will provide escort. Head to these coordinates."

The coordinates appeared on the console, and Del entered them. As he punched in the last number, he permitted himself to exhale. The two ships dropped to either side of the shuttle, one slightly ahead, the other a bit behind.

"Kriffing hell, Meeko, it looks like you were right about having to kill me!" Naylyn exclaimed, her eyes wide. "That name was like a magic word out of a folktale or something."

"Yeah, well, I am definitely a hero in my own mind." As the shuttle drew nearer to the restricted area, Del glanced at the great dome and wondered what it would be called, now that there was no Senate in the Senate District. He wasn't about to inquire.

"We're going to miss you, Del," Naylyn said.

"You'll make an excellent chief engineer," Del reassured her. "I mean, *now* you will. You were pretty slipshod when you arrived, but I trained you well."

That got the desired eye-roll out of her. He smothered his own grin. Wisecracks weren't regulation, but Del let his team indulge in them. They knew well enough how to be serious—deadly serious—when the time came.

Sobering slightly, he said, "I'll miss you all, too." One wasn't supposed to get overly attached to one's team, but Del did. He got attached to lots of things, and one of the most challenging lessons he'd had to learn was how to curb his natural friendliness.

But his time in Engineering was done, and soon, the mystery of just what Admiral Garrick Versio wanted from Chief Engineer Del Meeko would be solved.

Del only hoped the revelation wouldn't be something he'd regret.

The young woman was diminutive, both small and slight, and the chair in which she sat, as her eyes darted rapidly from one screen to the next, came perilously close to engulfing her. But she had grown used to it, and she swiveled and turned as necessary.

Short, neatly trimmed nails tipped the small fingers that flew over the controls. There was a tiny, nearly invisible earpiece in her right ear, through which a musical language of clicks and whistles came. Most would find any or all of the situation distracting, but the young woman had learned to master it. Her eidetic memory ensured that a brief perusal of an item was all that was required.

"Lieutenant?"

Lieutenant Seyn Marana's gaze went toward the one screen in the room that had been dark a moment before. The face of Jastin Vrayn, her assistant, was laced with an expression of confusion and a flicker of concern.

"Yes, Ensign?" Seyn replied, returning her attention to the half-dozen screens and the words scrolling across two of them.

"There's a message for you. It's coming from Admiral Garrick Versio. Security level two."

Admiral? That was new. But then, so much was new, since the destruction of the Death Star. Seyn had barely left this room since the word had come, shocking everyone and overturning everything she had believed and hoped and trusted was real. She knew of Versio, and had worked on some cross-faction cases for him. She had never met him, never interacted with him, and was surprised that he knew her name.

And level 2—that was the top clearance she had. Whatever it was, it was big, and would require her full attention. Seyn rapidly hit buttons to pause the vidscreens, then took a deep breath.

"Security level two in place. Patch it through."

Jastin's pleasant face was replaced by the gruff, almost grizzled one of now Admiral Garrick Versio.

Seyn listened. Her eyes grew wide.

And she began to smile.

At oh eight fifty, Iden Versio and Gideon Hask strode into the admiral's private conference room, shoulder to shoulder. One of Admiral Versio's favorite phrases was *If you're early, you're on time. If you're on time, you're late.* Both Gideon and Iden had internalized the message.

Iden wore her black TIE pilot's uniform, but did not bring the helmet to the meeting. Gideon was clad in the smart gray-green gaberwool of his officer's uniform, his cap removed and tucked under his arm.

Oddly, it was the first time Iden had ever visited her father at his place of work. When she was growing up, he'd had an office in one room of their house, but she had seldom been allowed in there, either. This new office was located on the top floor of the Imperial Security

Bureau headquarters, and it was as cool, efficient, and without embellishment as the man himself. There was no art on the smooth white and durasteel walls, no rugs on the mirrorlike surface of the floor, nothing but data-pads and equipment on the tables.

They were greeted by an impossibly perfect lieutenant, a young man about three years older than Iden with blond hair, green eyes, and startlingly white teeth. "Good afternoon, Lieutenants. Please follow me."

The meeting room consisted of a black table, six chairs, a small table to one side, and an entire wall devoted to consoles. It had two occupants already. One was a dark-haired man with a friendly-looking face whom Iden guessed was about ten years her senior, wearing the same uniform as Gideon. He was tall and broad-shouldered but not bulky.

The other was a young woman, petite but sitting with perfect military straightness in her chair. Her light-brown skin and short black hair was set off by the crisp white tunic that marked her as being affiliated with Intelligence in some manner. Her eyes were dark brown with an epicanthal fold, and her fresh face betrayed her youth; she looked right out of the Academy, if not younger, and Iden spared a moment to wonder at how she'd already achieved the rank of lieutenant. Both rose as Iden and Gideon entered.

The young woman saluted. "Lieutenant Seyn Marana, Naval Intelligence," she said, her voice a pleasant, girlish treble.

"And I'm Lieutenant Commander Del Meeko." The man's voice suited his face: friendly, but not effusive.

"Senior Lieutenant Iden Versio," Iden said, returning the salute, "and this is Gideon Hask, Lieutenant JG."

"Excellent," came the admiral's brisk voice as he strode into the room, commanding and receiving their full attention. "You've all met. No need to waste time on pleasantries, then. At ease. Take a seat."

The four young officers obeyed and turned to look at the admiral expectantly. He had offered them no refreshment, and indeed Iden knew the members of the little gathering could count themselves fortunate they had been invited—or, rather, ordered—to sit.

Versio's dark eyes roamed over each of the faces turned toward him, settling on Iden's. The stern visage gentled, ever so slightly.

"Lieutenant Versio," he said, "I'm glad you could join us."

Iden felt a quick flush of warmth. Gideon had been right. Her father *was* glad to see her.

"Thank you, sir," she said.

That was, apparently, enough sentimentality for the admiral. He turned to again address the entire gathering. "I direct your attention to the holoprojector in the center of the table."

Iden went rigid.

She suspected what they were about to see. And she realized it had been she who was responsible for it being here.

Gideon glanced at her, one brow raised in question. She shook her head almost imperceptibly.

Iden watched along with the others, stone-still. The only part of her that moved was the quick pulse of the vein in her slender throat. She saw the battle unfold, again, heard the sound of orders being issued. The count-down. The flash of light, the chaotic careening of her ship.

She forced herself not to look away, but out of the corner of her eye she registered the reactions of her fellows. Meeko's face displayed shock. Marana's eyes were wide and her lips parted slightly. Even Gideon had turned a shade paler, and she could tell he was forcing himself not to glance over at her, to illogically confirm with his own eyes yet again if she was all right.

Her father, mercifully, ignored her completely.

"I believe we all know what this is," Versio said, pausing and then deactivating the hologram. "This recording is currently being analyzed and evaluated as one of a handful recovered from ships that were out of the direct blast area."

Iden was grateful he didn't single her out, but from the sidelong glances of Meeko and Marana, she suspected they knew anyway.

"This was a dark day for our Empire. A very dark day. But, as you can imagine, and perhaps already know, we are working on plans for retaliation against the Rebel Alliance on every level open to us. We're doubling down in areas where we have, perhaps, been a trifle lax. For instance, we control the major media throughout the galaxy, but we've rooted out over two dozen smaller pirate transmitter stations. We commandeered them to broadcast the execution of several high-ranking prisoners, and then destroyed the stations. There are still a few operating out there, but not many, and we anticipate that soon there will be no more difficulty from the media.

"You are aware the Senate was dissolved. We are presently in the process of arresting all members, including some who served in years past, and confining them in the Arrth-Eno Prison Complex. They will remain imprisoned until we can assess the level of participation each has had with the Rebel Alliance. We're reaching out to possible sympathizers among the rebels' numbers, seeing if we can't coax them to join the right side.

"We have plans from the very grand to the very intimate. And the latter is where the four of you come in. There's a particular front in this battle that I have suggested be addressed, and I have been given authorization to proceed."

Iden's father was using *that voice*. *That voice* meant something very big, very significant, and very personal to him was going on. That he was including her in it made Iden feel proud—but it also put her on high alert. She sat erect in her chair, her eyes on her father, her breathing slow, and listened.

"Our glorious Death Star was destroyed by something very small indeed—a tiny flaw, implanted by one man who single-mindedly betrayed the Empire over the course of years. One person, in an X-wing fighter, hit a target only two meters wide."

He squared his shoulders. "We were arrogant," he said, and only Iden—and, perhaps, Gideon—knew what that admission cost him. "We paid a terrible price for that. And we will not make that mistake again.

"The grand scale, which is, of course, the ultimate vision of our Empire, is being attended to. But the little things . . . they, too, need to be addressed. And sometimes, the fewer who do so, the better.

"The contribution that one small team can make when it comprises the best of the best is, I believe, both overlooked and invaluable. The distillation of individual accomplishments and skills into a smoothly functioning unit will be something the enemies of the Empire will not be prepared to guard against.

"After careful evaluation, I have decided that the four of you represent the finest the Empire can field."

It was quite a statement, and they all knew it. Versio clasped his hands behind his back and walked in a predatory circle around the rapt group as he regarded each of them in turn, his eyes searching, laserlike, and piercing, as if trying to plumb their very souls. Gideon and Iden were used to that level of scrutiny, but familiarity made it no less intimidating.

The admiral's gaze settled on the tall man. "Del Meeko. You worked your way up through the ranks, first as a stormtrooper, then a shoretrooper, then a TIE pilot. You have received several commendations for courage under fire. Your commanders have made notations that you excel at whatever you turn your hand to, but you seem to be particularly gifted with repairing everything—from armor to droids to engines." Versio smiled thinly. "Your captain did not part with you with good grace."

Meeko was smart enough not to break eye contact with the admiral. Garrick didn't appreciate it when those he spoke to did so, deeming it disrespectful. *If I'm standing in front of you, I'd damn well better have your complete attention,* Iden had heard him say more than once. But the mechanically inclined TIE pilot did fidget slightly in his seat as he inclined his head in appreciation of the words.

"Seyn Marana," Versio continued, turning to the petite young woman. "You possess the gift of eidetic memory, which has served you well throughout your career. You graduated top of your class at the Imperial Academy of Uyter a full year early—and with honors. You speak . . . twenty-seven languages, is that correct?"

He paused to let her answer. In that sweet voice, the very young lieutenant replied, "Twenty-nine, sir."

Versio's eyebrows rose. "Twenty-*nine*," he said, his voice a gravelly purr. "I stand corrected. You can read and write seven more—it is seven, yes? I'd hate to be mistaken a second time."

The girl—Iden couldn't help but think of her that way; clearly Seyn was barely into her twenties at best— seemed to be seriously reconsidering her earlier quick correction of Versio, but she replied, "Yes, seven, sir."

"Seven. You are also a master cryptologist. And a superior shot who can take out a foe at over five kilometers."

Iden regarded the "girl" with considerably more respect.

Now Versio turned to Gideon. Iden, who knew him so well, saw her father's expression soften with pride. "Gideon Hask. First in his class at Coruscant Imperial University. Served with valor aboard the *Mandate*, receiving a battlefield promotion and the Crimson Star for exceptional performance against the enemy.

"And finally, Iden Versio. Graduated top of her class at Coruscant Imperial University, with honors. One of a handful of survivors of the Death Star, where she had held the record for most verified kills in battle—and has the melancholy honor of never losing that title.

"Your mission will be to recover information, artifacts, or individuals that could prove harmful to the Empire if they fall into the wrong hands—or if, perchance, such information has already fallen into the wrong hands. You'll be cleaning things up, as it were. We've just borne witness to the level of damage that can be inflicted upon our Empire when such pivotal information is used against us. We cannot, must not, *shall not* allow this to happen *ever* again. Is this understood?"

Everyone replied quickly in the affirmative. The admiral nodded.

"You will do as you are instructed. No questions. We need to recover anything and everything, anyone and everyone, who might pose the slightest threat to the Empire. You are all accustomed to being part of something larger than yourselves. To being a part of a vast machine. But this unit will be a microcosm of only four. You'll be performing the majority of your duties without direction from me—in fact, there may be lengthy periods of time when you will not be in contact with me at all. It is imperative that you learn very quickly how to work together smoothly and efficiently. You'll find that a great deal of weight will be resting on your shoulders."

Iden's heart began to slam slowly against her chest, but she gave no sign of it. It wouldn't do to register how thrilled these words made her feel. Responsibility was exactly what she wanted. The team as a whole, it seemed, would be given a great deal of it—but she wanted more.

"Now," her father continued, "while I will be the one evaluating your performances and assigning your missions, I will not be your field commander. That challenging role will fall to one of you. Your strengths are so unique and varied, it's difficult for me to tell which of you will stand out."

Iden's face grew hot. She did not know if it was from anger . . . or mortification. How could her father say this? Had he not monitored her behavior her entire life? What more did he need?

He went to a side desk and picked up four datapads, passing them out. "So, I have decided how that process might be made easier. Your task is twofold. On those datapads is information on your first mission. You will be permitted to do further research on your own. First, by oh nine hundred tomorrow, I want a proposed mission outline from each of you. All the information you'll need is here. I'll use it to evaluate who will oversee this initial endeavor. You will work with that individual fully and completely, is that understood?"

Murmurs of "Yes, sir," went around the table.

"Good. Second—your leader's position will only become permanent if the mission goes well."

Iden accepted her datapad without comment, though inwardly she was still burning with fury and shame. He knew what she was capable of. And still, he thought one of these others might be a better choice. And the nature of this test? Really? The best of the best had to write an *essay*? What was next, bed without supper if the proposal wasn't accepted?

Almost, as it turned out. "You will be escorted from here to your shared suite at the Diplomat. You will not leave, but your meals will be provided. Impress me, Officers. Show me how you think. Make your plan so solid, so worthy, that I cannot help but select it. Any questions?"

It was always best not to have questions with Garrick Versio, but Seyn didn't know that yet. "Sir? Are—are we free to discuss among ourselves? Share what information we have?"

Get what information we don't *have?* Iden thought uncharitably, then chided herself for the thought. Honestly, if she was as neck-deep in Naval Intelligence as she appeared to be, Seyn had the least to gain and the most to lose by such sharing. Meanwhile, Iden thought, as her heated emotions began to dissipate, sharing could help her. She'd have to present the best plan of the four. Had to. If her father was going to assemble a team, Iden couldn't bear to simply serve in it.

Garrick considered. "Yes. You may share."

The girl smiled, and for a moment Seyn looked so young that Iden wanted to protect her more than she wanted to fight alongside her. She dismissed the thought. Seyn's youth surely belied a lot of strength. Garrick Versio would never want anyone on "his team" who wasn't strong. After all, they were the best of the best.

That logical conclusion meant that the quiet Del Meeko also had something special to offer. And of course, Iden knew Gideon well enough to know how much he brought to the table.

"Any other questions?" There were none. Versio nodded. "Dismissed."

The four got to their feet, saluted, and turned to go. At the door, though, Gideon hung back, considering, then asked his new commanding officer, "Sir? Does this unit have a name yet?

The faintest of smiles quirked Versio's lips. "It does," he replied. "It's a promise to the rebels.

"It's called Inferno Squad."

CHAPTER 4

The four members of the freshly minted Inferno Squad stood together silently in the lift as it hummed upward, the awkwardness of the meeting only exacerbated by the task set before them. Finally Meeko, who stood beside Seyn, leaned toward her and asked, quietly, "Are we being recorded in the lift?"

"Images only in this one," Seyn replied. "Hotel security needs to know who enters and exits the building, but there are a lot of secrets discussed in this lift that people don't want overheard."

He nodded, brow furrowed in consideration, then said, "Well then . . . given our assignment, anyone else think *Hot Seat Squad* would be a better name than *Inferno*?"

Everyone stood frozen, mouths slightly open. The moment stretched on. Seyn shifted position. Del cleared his throat. "Sorry," he said. "Just trying to lighten the mood."

More silence, then Gideon gave a single, very slight, snort of laughter.

Iden was not in a mirthful mood, but at another time she might have joined Gideon because it was absolutely, positively true. Her father loved to put everyone—especially his only child—in the hot seat whenever he could possibly do so.

Gideon had stayed here the previous evening, so he didn't bat an eye at the fact that their suite amounted to an entire floor, and that there was a guard posted at the door. Iden took it in stride as well, but the other two members of Inferno Squad seemed surprised. Meeko, who'd worked his way through the ranks, looked uncomfortable at what clearly struck him as lavish quarters.

For her part Iden had simply hoped their room would be located at one of the uppermost levels, above the cloud layer, where the sun would set peacefully and the night would be untroubled by activity at all hours, but they had no such luck.

"Iden, isn't this your mother's work?" Gideon asked, indicating the posters. Iden knew her old friend meant no harm, but inwardly she winced, especially as there was a print of YOUNG IMPERIALS CAN REACH THE STARS. The other two already knew her father was Admiral Garrick Versio, their commanding officer. They didn't really need to know that her mother was someone significant, too. She wanted this unit almost desperately, but she wanted to earn it. She didn't want anyone to think nepotism was alive and well in the Versio family.

"I think so," Iden said, trying to sound nonchalant. Marana looked impressed and peered again at the signature.

"I have to say," Del said, shaking his head, "these are by *far* the nicest quarters I've ever seen. Too bad we can't just relax and enjoy."

"No," Iden snapped, more sharply than she had intended, "we've all got quite a lot of work to do tonight. And we should get going on it."

"Of course you're right, Lieutenant," Del said formally. "Are these rooms assigned?"

"I was here last night, and I took that one," Gideon said, pointing to the door on the far left. "But I don't mind moving if need be." He turned to Iden. "Lieutenant?"

Iden regretted shutting Meeko down. She was irritated with the situation, not with him—in fact, she was quietly grateful that he had redirected attention from the boldly colored art adorning the walls. "No, that won't be necessary. Everyone just pick whichever one you'd like."

She headed for the one nearest her, looking around as the doors hissed open. The bed looked comfortable, but Iden didn't miss the fact that it had been made with perfect, precision corners, and she found herself smiling. Even when occupying a luxury apartment, the military was the military.

"Lieutenant Versio?" Meeko's voice, warm with surprise and pleasure. "Look what I found!" He stood in the doorway brandishing what looked like an old bottle of wine. "Right on the bedside table."

Iden glanced at her own nightstand and noticed a

single, elegant, fluted glass. She picked it up and went back into the communal room. The others had found their own glasses.

"I didn't know your father had it in him," Gideon said casually, ducking into the food prep area and rummaging about for something with which to open the bottle. Del bore the celebratory beverage to the main table.

I need to say something to Gideon later, Iden thought, but for now she simply corrected him. "The *admiral,*" she said. "He's our commanding officer from this point on. We need to refer to him as such."

"That must be difficult, since you're his daughter," Seyn said, stepping up to the table and setting her glass down.

"I don't find it difficult at all," Iden said stiffly. "Both my parents serve the Empire, and Admiral Versio ran a military household. He's my father, yes, but he's the admiral."

"Even in private, the Versios use their titles," Gideon said, giving Iden an apologetic look as he added, "And Lieutenant Versio is quite right to do so. Sorry."

Gideon emerged with the opener and handed it to Del. As he prepared to open the bottle, Iden noticed for the first time what type it was.

Alderaanian wine. Toniray, to be precise.

As always, Iden found herself wishing that the rebels hadn't made the destruction of Alderaan so necessary. The Death Star had destroyed an entire planet. Yes, it had been a rebel hotbed, a positive nest of treason. But surely not everyone who had died had hated the Empire. The destruction of the Death Star hit closer to home, as she had lost people she knew, but at least there had been no civilians on it. No children.

The child of a rebel may be a child yet, but we must look to the future. It will grow up to be an enemy. And our enemies must be destroyed. Words from her father, spoken to her long before she had heard of a Death Star. And there was truth in them.

Seyn, who always seemed to be studying everyone, followed Iden's gaze. "Oh my," she said. "Hang on, Commander Meeko. We might want to sell that bottle and make a small fortune."

Gideon glanced at the bottle Del was holding. He let out a low, soft whistle. "Maybe a not-so-small fortune." Then he grinned. "No, go ahead, Commander. Let's celebrate the birth of Inferno Squad with a bottle of rebel tears!"

The carbonation created a loud pop and the glorious teal liquid bubbled out rapidly, overflowing and creating a mess before Hask grabbed one of the glasses to catch it. And then the glass, too, overflowed, and everyone laughed.

The tension eased. It was just a bottle of wine.

Meeko handed out sticky, wet glasses to everyone. He had poured because the bottle was in the room he'd just happened to select, but now he paused. The leader of this nascent squad ought to be the one to make the toast, but there was no leader. Not yet.

You've done neither me nor the team favors, Admiral, Iden thought. If this little contest her father had devised had been meant to unify them, it would end up doing the opposite. Team members shouldn't be competing against one another, like dogs for scraps. The suddenly awkward pause stretched on for a moment, then Iden stepped into the breach.

"Well, we probably shouldn't drink too much of this since we've all got homework to do," she said, and that got another small laugh. Apparently, she was not the only one who felt that this assignment smacked of Academy classroom homework. "But we should make a toast, at least. Here's to a successful first mission—and many more thereafter!"

"Hear, hear," Meeko said, and clinked his glass against hers. Their eyes met and she gave him a slight nod, indicating he could make a toast as well.

"Um . . . well, I toast Admiral Versio, for having the good sense to select all of us for the squad."

More clinks of the delicate stemware, then Meeko turned expectantly to Seyn, who stood next to him. She rattled off something in a guttural, deep-pitched language punctuated by the sound of her clacking her teeth together. They all looked at her warily. Like most Imperials with a good education, Iden herself knew two or three of the more common languages in addition to Basic, but this was nothing she recognized.

Seyn suddenly grinned. She looked about twelve years old.

"That's a traditional toast of the Ahak Maharr. It means, 'May we rend the flesh of our enemies, and drink their blood as we do this liquid before us.'"

There was a long pause while they stared at her, and her grin widened impishly.

"Damned if that isn't the best toast I've ever heard," Gideon said. "I'm going to make you teach it to me, Seyn."

"I'll try," she said, "but it's difficult to pronounce Ahak Maharr if you don't have tusks."

"Then I'll just have to do my best," he said, giving her one of his charming smiles. He lifted his own glass and looked around. "That's a hard act to follow, so I'll keep my toast simple. Here's to Inferno Squad. May we live up to our name."

They all drank. The liquid's bubbles tingled against Iden's tongue, sweet and playful. She didn't drink much, as she never drank on duty, and she was on duty most of the time. When she wasn't, she was exercising or sleeping or studying—doing everything to be even better at tasks she had usually already mastered. *If you don't hone your edge, you'll lose it,* her father had warned.

She looked at her new teammates. Del Meeko and Seyn Marana, the two "outsiders," were relaxing and chatting easily, already soothed by the alcohol. Gideon Hask, child of impeccable heritage, looked as though he had been born with a glass of fine wine in his hand.

Let them chat, and laugh, and bond, Iden thought to herself. *Let them have a second glass.* She understood her father well enough to know that nothing he did was accidental or incidental. The room, the view, the alcohol, the "game" of having one of the four finding the bottle in a room they had selected entirely at random—he had chosen these things as carefully as he had chosen the four team members.

Versio knew his daughter as well as she knew him, and he knew she'd be hungering for the leadership position. She'd let herself be distracted by her own emotions, but now she'd figured it out. Oh, this was a test all right, but not about who had the best mission plan of attack—

which, Iden mused, her father had likely already drawn up himself. No, the test was here, was now, to see who would be alert, observant, and on task even when there were new people to get to know, comfortable surroundings, and good food and beverage.

So Iden set down the half-full glass of the expensive and now exceedingly rare vintage, and went to order something to eat. It was going to be a long night, and Iden knew she needed to be sharp—and she needed to learn. Her father had put together a good team—and she would use them to her advantage.

When she finally sent her mission plan off to her father and placed the datapad down on the bedside table, Iden was mentally exhausted but too keyed up to sleep. Even when she turned out the lights with a word and pulled the covers over her, the overly stimulating, colored illumination from Coruscant traffic trickled into the room, just as she had ruefully anticipated earlier.

Iden had trained herself to fall asleep quickly, easily, and soundly almost on command, waking alert and attentive. But tonight, she found sleep elusive. There was a knot in her stomach that was all too familiar; one she'd hitherto managed to chase away with adrenaline rushes and intense duty shifts.

Her father had often ignored her throughout her career. But now his eyes were on her.

And Iden Versio would not—*could* not—fail.

Iden had set the room's controls to wake her early with gradual natural light, but before the illumination had gotten to level three of ten the smell of caf had teased her fully awake. As much as she longed to immediately grab a cup, she stepped into the shower and then dressed in her uniform before heading to the kitchen.

Meeko was there, sitting at the shiny black table sipping at a cup and thumbing through his datapad. He, too, was already dressed for the meeting that wasn't for another two hours. He smiled a greeting and nodded toward the pot.

"Good morning, Lieutenant," he said. "Please, help yourself."

"Thanks." She returned to the table with a cup of caf and a slice of buttered cuanut bread and sat down with her own datapad, reviewing what she'd sent her father. He'd expect her to defend her plan.

"I'm betting on you or Hask," Meeko said conversationally.

Surprised, Iden turned to him. "What makes you say that? You've got several years of experience over both of us."

He mock-grimaced. "Hey, come on, I'm only ten years older than you."

"Oh, that's several," Iden said, then added more seriously, "And you've seen a lot more combat than I have."

Del sobered at her words. "That's true, but a leader needs to be more than someone who knows how to fire a blaster."

Iden turned fully in her seat to regard him, holding the warm mug in her hands. "You received commendations for courage under fire. And you were chief engineer of a Star Destroyer," she said. "You made a lot of important decisions."

He shrugged. "I'm good at what I do, but that doesn't

mean I should be leading this squad. I understand that, and it doesn't bother me."

Iden wanted to argue with him. She'd listened last night as he'd spoken, and watched his previous reticence evaporate once he began discussing technical approaches to problem solving, compared notes on expanding the limits of what everyone thought droids were capable of doing, and persuasively argued how to minimize casualties. Del Meeko knew his field inside and out, and how to weaponize it. A leader needed to know what Del knew. And had the circumstances been different, she realized, she might have accepted the choice of him as leader. He wasn't the attention-seizing, sharp-tongued individual that Iden was used to seeing in positions of command. There was something about him that she trusted already.

But she also suspected that he was right. And the circumstances *were* what they were. Her father was commanding this squad—and Iden could not bear to see anyone else in the position.

"Well," she said uncomfortably, "we'll just have to see."

"No offense, Meeko," Gideon said as he entered the kitchen, "and I admit droids are damn handy, but they're no substitute for a living being when life-and-death decisions have to be made. And which of you do I have to thank for having caf ready?"

"That would be Meeko," Iden said.

Gideon threw the older man a bright grin and raised his steaming cup. "See? Life-and-death decisions."

"I've seen Gideon before caf a time or two, and he's right," Iden said. "Life and death."

Meeko smiled, taking no offense at anything that was

being said, and her opinion went up another notch. He appeared to be one of those rare creatures—a calm, high-ranking Imperial officer with a sense of humor and little ego. It was enormously refreshing.

In a few moments, they were joined by Seyn. She would have passed any surprise inspection. Not a single strand of her short black hair was out of place. Her white jacket was spotless, and the crease in her trousers was almost sharp enough to cut. Her boots were polished to nearly a mirror sheen.

"Good morning," she said politely.

While they were all in their uniforms, there was something about Seyn Marana's perfection that undid Meeko's easy banter and the unifying smell of caf. Without even bringing up the subject, Marana had just reminded the other three members of Inferno Squad how very important what happened later that morning would be. Iden's spine straightened, and, almost like a droid, she felt herself shut down as she gave the NavInt officer a polite greeting and let her eyes focus again on her report.

There was no more chitchat. They broke their fast in silence, lost in their own thoughts.

The four stood rigidly at attention in Admiral Versio's office as he entered precisely at oh nine hundred. "At ease, and take your seats," he instructed.

They obeyed. Iden folded her hands in front of her and lifted her gaze to her father's face. Waiting patiently, as she had done for the last two decades.

And, as he had done for the last two decades, Garrick Versio got right down to business. "Your reports confirm my opinion that I chose wisely in selecting each of you. You also confirmed my suspicions as to how each of you would respond.

"Del Meeko." The engineer regarded his commanding officer steadily. "Your report relied heavily on the usage of droids and innovative technology. Seyn Marana—yours, on your own intelligence-backed knowledge of the situation. Gideon Hask, your straightforwardness is both simple and effective."

Iden's heart rate surged with both dread and anticipation. Her plan was sound. It would work. He had to select it. She tightened her fingers, hoping no one would notice.

"Everyone else prepared an excellent main course. You, Iden Versio—you gave us a meal."

Iden didn't let her gaze waver as he continued. She didn't dare make an assumption either way. "You took a bit of this, a dollop of that."

Relax, Iden, he does this all the time, she reminded herself. Versio was fond of uttering opinions in a certain tone of voice that conveyed irritation and admiration both. She was never sure which side of the line he'd come down on.

"Some would call that good. Some would not. In the end, none of you is offering to set a table. If you burn a roast, you eat something else. But here—you're performing a complex mission, and if you perform it badly, someone might well die. You *all* might well die."

He looked at them each in turn. "There is no single right plan. There is no foolproof recipe for success. There is only the best *chance* of success. And Lieutenant

Versio's option is, I think, the one that offers that best chance. So for now, for this mission—she will be the leader of the squad."

He turned to his daughter and indicated the wall to the left. All the screens were currently blank. "Lieutenant . . . you have the floor."

Iden could barely believe it. Faint as the praise had been, obvious as he had made his uncertainty, and laced with qualifiers as it was, Versio had named his daughter as leader of Inferno Squad.

Iden Versio rose, straightened her jacket, and strode to the wall screens. She entered a code and turned to her team.

Her team.

"I've sent my proposal to each of your datapads. Call it up and follow along with me. This is what we're going to do."

CHAPTER 5

"I really dislike dresses," Seyn grumbled.

She was currently clad in an exquisite one that was—according to Iden's research—the height of fashion among high-ranking Imperial society. With a high collar and long length, the pale-purple shimmersilk gown was perfect for the joyous but still formal occasion. Seyn's short hair was styled with a gem-studded band; other jewels adorned her ears. The only thing that didn't look poised and elegant was the girl's annoyed expression.

"I think you look better in them than I do," Iden offered. She didn't care for dresses, either, much preferring her uniform, and was glad she could pass this task off to Seyn. Admiral Versio's daughter might be recognized in this type of a gathering, but no one knew Seyn.

"I think," Gideon said, smoothing his elegant black

tunic, "that we both run the risk of drawing too much attention by being so attractive."

"He always like this?" Seyn asked.

"Usually," Iden said.

"I still think my plan would have been better," Gideon said.

"*Your* plan involved pretending to be a bounty hunter," Del said.

"Exactly," Gideon replied.

The task the team had been set that night two weeks ago was fairly straightforward. Moff Jaccun Pereez, like many in power, liked to indulge his pleasures. For him, these were drinking and gambling. Unfortunately, the one didn't do much to improve the other, and Pereez was finding himself with mounting debts. Intel had reported that one evening, Pereez was bragging about "knowing things" that would soon make those inconvenient debts "go away."

"Even with a moff," Iden had said during her initial presentation to her team—*her team*, she thought, and suppressed a smile—"words are just that. His debts are sizable. He wouldn't get those kinds of credits just for things he could tell someone when he was in his cups. He's got to have something concrete—visual blackmail material, data, security secrets, something like that—on someone close to the Empire. Who, we don't know, and it's better that way. Our job is to recover whatever it is Pereez is thinking about selling."

The other members of the squad had offered plans that focused on their own strengths and experiences. Gideon, ever eager for action, had suggested simply adopting the guise of a bounty hunter and strong-arming

Pereez for the information. Technology-minded Del had recommended setting up recording devices in the moff's mansion. Seyn wanted to analyze everything the Empire had on Pereez and confront him with the information that he was not getting away with anything. She'd taken the idea a step further as well: They could easily present the moff with forged documents that implicated him in much worse things, just in case he should change his mind later.

Iden had listened, and done her own research on the man himself. The Empire needed Pereez right where he was. By all accounts he was a cheerful, affable leader, and the people of Arvaka Prime were very fond of him. Any hint of scandal or disgrace could create instability in the sector. A weak heart meant that a dangerous confrontation—say, with a bounty hunter—might cause his death, which was also not the preferred outcome.

They needed to get into his home, where he certainly kept his valuable information close at hand.

And fortunately, the moff himself had extended an invitation to visit. Or at least they could make it look like he had.

Inferno Squad's first mission would be crashing a wedding.

Now all four stood in the docking bay as the technicians went through the final check on the nondescript, sleek shuttle that would doubtless have several counterparts ferrying guests to the elegant mansion on Arvaka Prime. In contrast with the elaborately dressed "wedding guests," Del and Iden wore the dark-gray uniforms of private shuttle pilots. Unmarked armor was stashed away in the back.

Iden looked at the members of her team, wanting to say something perfect but having no idea what that might be. So she kept it brief and to the point.

"We all know what we're doing, and we've trained for this. We've done test runs on our equipment. We know the schedules. We also know that while plans can be perfect, what happens outside of meeting rooms isn't. But that's part of it, too. Whatever happens, we'll handle it. Because that's what we do. Anyone have any questions?"

Everyone shook their heads. Iden could feel their eagerness to be under way.

They were all ready.

"Then let's go."

"'Moff Jaccun Pereez requests your presence at the wedding of his daughter, Famma, to the rising young star of the Empire, Commander Yendiv Bensek,'" Gideon recited as the shuttle landed a few hours later.

"Once again, Seyn, your forgeries are astounding," Iden said. "And Gideon, just remember, the bride pronounces it *Fa-MAH*, not *FAH-ma*. Del, how are we looking?"

Del had his eyes glued to the second console in the vessel. "All screens are operating perfectly." Strings had been pulled to get Del onto the decorating staff the bride-to-be had hired. Yesterday for six hours he had been able to conceal tiny, state-of-the-art recording devices throughout the moff's mansion. He'd even tinkered with one of the regular droids to give the squad "eyes" they could control while Seyn and Gideon were inside.

"And your earpieces?" Iden inquired, referring to the

tiny devices inserted deep into the ear canals of the "wedding guests."

Gideon tapped his ear and grinned. "We'll hear every whisper," he assured her.

Iden took a deep breath. "Okay," she said. "Good luck. If all goes well, we'll rendezvous here in two hours."

Gideon rose and offered his hand to Seyn. "Shall we, darling?" he said as she picked up the wedding gift.

"Don't lay it on too thick," Seyn warned as the ramp extended, but she did take his hand.

The day could not have been more beautiful. The moff's official residence was large and sprawling, but somehow managed to be quaint at the same time. Iden had said something to the effect that it was built to replicate the architecture of centuries past, but all Gideon needed to know was its layout—which Seyn had been able to acquire.

Flowers of every shade imaginable bloomed, and the warm air was heavy with fragrance. If the house had been designed to look like one from long ago, the massive gate encircling it was distinctly modern. Gideon made note of where the controls were. Casually he angled his body so that the tiny cam embedded in the Imperial symbol on his chest could send the information to Del.

"Perfect, Lieutenant," came Del's voice in his ear.

Seyn, who despite her protests appeared to have been born into a life of formal gatherings and gowns, held the wedding invitation in one gloved hand. She handed it to a guard flanked by a stormtrooper.

"Lady Dezara Monay," she said, introducing herself with a dazzling smile. "This is my guest, Brixx Gavan."

Lady Dezara Monay was an entirely fictional construct, although one Vezzin Monay was a distant relation to the groom. The connection would stand if they were suspected. Seyn had concocted histories for both Dezara and Brixx, elaborate enough so that they could make small talk if cornered by guests, simple enough to remember. Gideon half expected problems right at the outset, but Seyn's grace and ease were apparently as convincing as her forgeries. "Oh," the guard said, her expression changing. "I see you're one of our VIPs, my lady. The wedding will be held in the grand ballroom, but you and your guest may go upstairs to observe the ceremony from a special viewing area."

A droid hummed up to them, ready to scan them and the wrapped gift for weapons. Seyn eyed it with annoyance and the guard immediately said, "Cancel scan. Apologies, my lady, our droids are sometimes too efficient. I hope there's no offense."

"Not at all," Seyn said. "Moff Pereez is fortunate to have such diligent guards."

Serving droids milled about the green lawn area, where some guests, appreciative of the sunny weather, were enjoying drinks and canapés. "One of those serving droids is ours," came Del's voice. "Sending it to you now so you'll know which one."

Sure enough, one of the GG-class serving droids began rolling toward them, its tray filled with small goblets of rich red wine. Gideon took careful note of the droid, noticing it had a small scratch along its tray, and he and Seyn each snagged a goblet, nursing the drink as they examined their surroundings for a moment before heading inside. Seyn leaned over the droid for a moment and ordered, "Shadow Moff Pereez."

The droid booped, swiveled, and rolled toward the main entrance. Seyn and Gideon followed a moment, nodding pleasantly to the stormtrooper standing next to the large double doors. Two troopers and a guard so far. They stepped into a vast foyer with a high, arching ceiling and marble floor. The alcoves along the white walls were filled with art; the room itself, with chattering guests. To the left and right were other rooms— a hothouse garden and a study filled with more art and old tomes.

"Don't let the books fool you," said Iden. "Or the art. Pereez isn't an aficionado of any of it, but he likes how it all looks."

A formally dressed young man awaited them. He looked both excited and tired, but his smile seemed genuine.

"Welcome," he said, reaching to shake their hands. "I'm Sind Reloran, one of the groomsmen. And you are?"

"Lady Dezara Monay and Brixx Gavan," said Seyn. Both she and Gideon were wearing gloves. First, because they were in fashion this season, apparently, and second— no fingerprints. "Can I trouble you to take this, please?" She held out the gift to him. "It's sunfruit liquor. For the bride and groom, of course, but I know that Moff Pereez appreciates the finer things. He might want to make a toast with it today, so let him know, please?"

The groomsman's eyebrows had risen when she mentioned sunfruit liquor, and he accepted the gift, handling it carefully. "I'll see that he gets it," he said. "In the meantime, there's food and drink being served in the sun parlor, on your right. Don't miss a chance to look into the library—the moff has a collection of actual old *books*. Don't see that every day. Down the hall there's an area for the guests; there's a restroom right there. Will you be watching from the upstairs viewing area in the connecting hall?" At Seyn's nod, he continued, "There are staircases that will take you there. Thank you so much for coming!"

Gideon shook Sind's hand and clapped him on the shoulder. "I've never seen a book collection," he said to Seyn. "Let's take a look."

They had the room to themselves; despite the novelty of antiquated tomes, most of the guests seemed to prefer to congregate in areas that provided refreshments and high-ranking Imperials with whom they could mingle. Again, Del's voice came in his ear: "The books on the end, on your right. Second shelf."

While Seyn stood guard, casually looking around, Gideon followed Del's directions. "You're looking for a red one. The title is *Ancient Keltrian Poets: Masters of Alliteration*."

Gideon almost choked with laughter, but he bit his lip and forced it down. "That's, ah . . . not going to be a popular one."

"That's why I picked it," Del said. Gideon found the tome—a surprisingly thick one; the ancient Keltrians must really have enjoyed their poetry—and removed it. Nestled behind it was a tiny piece of technology the size of Gideon's thumbnail: a security code descrambler.

"Del, let's always be friends. That way when you

come visit, I'll never have to worry that you're hiding all kinds of things I'd never find."

Del's laugh was surprised and genuine. "Deal," he said.

"The bait's been taken," Seyn murmured. Gideon slipped the descrambler into his pocket and replaced the book on the shelf, then went to Seyn. He followed her gaze and saw an older, rotund man with a pleasant expression speaking with the groomsman he and Seyn had passed the gift to. Now the gift was passing into Moff Pereez's eager hands.

"You really think he'll drink before the wedding?"

"Our dossier says he's likely struggling not to rip open the box right this second," Seyn said quietly. "A rare alcohol? Two things he can't resist. We don't absolutely need him to, of course, but it'll be an additional distraction."

The liquor was genuine enough, rare and expensive and delicious. But ten milligrams of deraformine had been mixed in with it. Seyn had called it the life-after-death drug. At certain concentrations, the reaction mimicked death so perfectly that the average person would not be able to tell the difference. It was occasionally used among agents as an exit strategy from an assignment. It worked—provided the "body" was recovered intact and whisked to safety or a medical droid wasn't summoned. The risk was high, but sometimes a fake death was the only chance to avoid the real thing. Smaller amounts merely rendered the victim unconscious and posed little danger.

"Inferno-One," said Seyn, "Del's serving droid is

shadowing Pereez. Notify us once our host begins drinking."

"Copy," Iden said.

"Let's go and see the view from upstairs," said Seyn. Threading their way through the crowd, they made their way to an open area with two sets of stairs on either side, a fountain containing brightly colored fish in the center, and a uniformed guard. *Two troopers, two guards,* Gideon thought.

The fountain bubbled loudly while Seyn showed the guard the invitation, and he cleared the pair to go upstairs. Only a few people were up there now. They would start showing up closer to the time of the wedding. All four of the team had seen the layout of the house, and Seyn of course had memorized it. On that level there were four bedrooms, including the master suite with an attached sitting room and office. The office would be the first place they searched.

"The wisest thing would be to keep incriminating documents and other items offsite, but easily accessible," Seyn had said during the planning stages of the mission. "The second-wisest thing would be to place them somewhere no one would think of looking. But people are generally foolish about such things. They fall back on habit, laziness, familiarity, or a false sense of security. The odds are that he has a safe in his personal office and he keeps the materials there."

They would have time to look elsewhere, as the wedding wasn't going to start for well over an hour, but Gideon didn't even want to entertain the idea of failure. Two of the bedrooms on the floor were standing wide open, in case anyone needed to use the facilities. They were probably guest rooms: While tastefully decorated, they were too tidy and lacking in personality.

The master bedroom and a fourth room flanked the viewing area, a temporary cluster of chairs on a three-level dais. Below was the grand ballroom, beautifully decorated and awaiting the ceremony. "The decorators did a marvelous job," said Gideon.

"Thank you," Del replied.

"Inferno-Two and Four, alert. He's started," Iden interrupted.

Seyn gave Gideon an I-told-you-so look. "Copy that. How much?"

There was a pause. "He's on his third shot."

"If he keeps drinking like that, he's going to be down within ten minutes," Seyn said, clearly alarmed. "What room is he in?"

"Right now, the library, with a few others. He's saying he'll save enough for the toast later. Odds are when he collapses they'll shut the door to everyone but family and a physician, if there's one in attendance. The rest will be herded into the sun parlor or maybe even taken outside and detained until it's clear he's out of danger."

"So two choices," Gideon said. "Get the data now, or get it and then get detained for who knows how long, and possibly get discovered."

"We're going with plan A," Iden said.

"Give us a countdown," said Seyn. To Gideon, she said, "Come on. We've got one shot at this."

Gideon glanced down as he and Seyn went to the bedroom door. The guard was still at the bottom of the stairs near the fish fountain. After a few long seconds, the descrambler entered the correct code and the door slid open.

They hurried past the enormous bedroom, the dressing room, and the lavish bathroom into the office on the other side. Several artworks covered the red-painted walls. Gideon paid them no heed as he removed them, one by one. And there it was—a wall safe. Smaller than he'd expected, but then again datachips and holorecorders didn't take up all that much room.

"We found the safe," Seyn said.

"Good," said Iden. "It's been three minutes. He looks fine still."

Seyn put the descrambler on the safe. Seconds ticked by. She and Gideon exchanged glances. Then they heard a soft click, and the door swung open.

Inside were pieces of jewelry worth tens of thousands of credits and a holorecorder. "Got it," Seyn said.

"Wait," Gideon cautioned. "It could be anything. We should check."

"He's right," Iden said. "It's been almost five minutes, but check. If it's blackmail material, it might not be pleasant, though."

Gideon put it on the desk and pressed the button. To his shock, he saw the most innocent thing possible: a younger and thinner Moff Pereez holding his baby girl and singing her a lullaby.

He clenched his fist and almost brought it slamming down on the desk in frustration, but remembered the guard on the stairs. "Who the hell keeps something like this in a safe? And *where* the hell is the blackmail material?"

Seyn kept shaking her head. "No, it should be in

there. He'd want it close at hand. He wouldn't store it offsite."

"Five minutes. He seems to be looking sleepy," Iden said. Her voice was flat, as if she was controlling it with an effort.

Gideon looked around almost frantically. "Where do we even start?"

"His daughter," said Del. "He keeps a holo of himself holding her when she was a baby. It's that important. He'd want to keep something else important where he would never forget where he'd stashed it."

Gideon's eyes fell to the painting that had covered the safe. He had propped it against the wall when he'd set it down.

The image of an angelic little girl peered up at him. Seyn stood beside it, and now she dropped down to her knees and felt around the back.

Her eyes lit up as she brought forth a datachip. "*Now* we've got it," she said.

"Great—now get out of there. Our moff isn't looking too healthy."

She didn't need to order it twice. Seyn stuck the chip in the bodice of her gown while Gideon replaced the painting over the safe. As they started down the stairs, Iden's voice in Gideon's ear said, "He's down. Get out of there now!"

Even as she spoke he could hear some distressed murmurings and the voices of the guards telling everyone to stay calm. Gideon hoped the one at the foot of the stairs hadn't been alerted yet, but then he saw the man raise a hand to his ear and nod.

Seyn was ahead of Gideon on the stairs as the guard

moved to block their path. She paused on the step right above him. "I'm sorry," the guard said, "but there appears to have been an incident. We're going to have to ask you to—"

Seyn clenched her hands into fists, twisted her body slightly to one side, and slammed the guard's jaw with the most beautiful uppercut Gideon had ever seen. The man's head snapped back and he started to fall, but Gideon darted forward just in time to grab him before he toppled down the stairs. Seyn's breathing was quick and she grimaced, holding her hand.

"Thanks for catching him," she said.

"Thanks for knocking him out," he replied.

Gideon and Seyn shoved through the crowd just as people were about to start panicking, made it to the lawn, and were heading toward the shuttle when someone shouted at them to stop.

They exchanged glances. Seyn kicked off her high heels and they sprinted toward the nondescript shuttle, jumping onto the ramp as it was retracting. The vessel lifted off just as they fell into their seats.

When they'd made it to hyperspace, Iden let out the breath it felt like she'd been holding for two weeks. "Congratulations, Lieutenant," Gideon said. "I think we can safely say Inferno Squad has just completed its first mission successfully."

"You two did a fine job down there," Iden said. "And that was some quick thinking on your part, Commander Meeko. About where Pereez might be keeping the chip. Where *is* the chip, by the way?"

Seyn fished it from her bodice and handed it to Iden. "I feel a little bad for the moff now," she said, "putting him and his family through a scare on his daughter's wedding day. He really seemed to love the girl."

Something inside Iden twisted sharply at the words. She couldn't fathom her own father holding her when she was a baby. She couldn't recall any physical affection from him at all. And the only "portrait" that was ever painted of her was the one her mother did, in the YOUNG IMPERIALS CAN REACH THE STARS poster.

"We did what we had to in order to complete the mission, Lieutenant," she said. "And we always will."

CHAPTER 6

After the success of their first mission, Iden felt emboldened to ask for everything she felt her team truly needed: unfettered access to certain classified information, top-notch weaponry and equipment, and various specific materials.

"Reasonable requests, if expensive," Versio had mused as he perused the extensive list. "Will that be all?" Uncertain as to whether he was being serious or sarcastic, Iden had replied in the negative. "Well, there *is* more," he had said. "First, you'll all be getting promotions, so congratulations, Captain Versio. Second, I have a ship ready for you. I've instructed the rest of the squad to meet us there. Feel free to bring a bag of personal items if you like, as I'm assuming this will be your new home for some time to come."

There had never been room for anything sentimental

in Iden's life that she could recall. Her "bag" had been packed within five minutes.

The *Corvus* was a *Raider*-class corvette, sleek and gray and roomy enough at 150 meters long to accommodate a sizable crew, handpicked by Admiral Versio. For now, there were only two: a pilot, Adiana Caton, and copilot, Weston Morro. They seemed to be both professional and personable, and Iden anticipated no problems with them.

The *Corvus* was, Iden mused, the sort of vessel that would please everyone on the team. It had a hyperdrive and three engines for Meeko to tinker with, and was armed with ion cannons, dual heavy laser cannons, concussion missiles, and turbolasers. It had also, Versio assured the squad, been gutted and completely remodeled with the most up-to-date computer technology.

"You'll take it on your next mission," the admiral said, walking with Iden as she familiarized herself with the vessel. They had reached the cockpit to discover that Gideon was already ensconced there, going over the controls with an expression of satisfaction on his face. "And on any other missions when it is an asset rather than a liability. And of course, as time goes on, we'll get you a full crew."

"I thought Inferno Squad was a small, tightly knit unit," Iden observed. The pilot in her was excited about the opportunities afforded by the *Corvus,* but she did not like the idea of having several more people involved in what was supposed to be a unit comprising the four "best of the best."

Her father, as always, read her thoughts. "Meeko may enjoy repairing things, but he's not a simple technician. You'll want him with you when it comes to fighting. You're all superb pilots, but you won't necessarily be available to fly all the time. A well-trained crew that does what it's told and no more will be a help, not a hindrance. Don't worry, they won't steal your thunder." The last word was almost, but not quite, sneered.

Iden bit her lip. She wouldn't rise to the bait. Gideon, too, pretended not to have heard. Fortunately, Meeko provided a distraction as he entered with a smile on his face. "Hello, Admiral Versio, *Captain* Versio." His smile widened even further as he emphasized her new rank. "Look what I found," he said.

Hovering behind him, humming slightly, was a small droid about the size and relative shape of an overturned soup bowl. It was glossy black, with a single red photo-receptor front and center, and four smaller black ones on either side and below along its gently curving dome. Four articulated legs ending in pincers dangled in the air.

"That's an ID9 Seeker, isn't it?" asked Iden.

"An ID10, actually," Meeko said. "Fresh out of the factories. And I'm going to customize it for our next mission."

"You seem pleased, Agent Meeko," Iden said, trying out the title that all of them had now earned. "How about you, Agent Hask?"

"Very much so," Gideon replied. "Our pilot may not get to do much piloting if I have my way. Also, Captain Versio—if anything happens to you, that puts me in charge, right?"

"Stick to 'Agent.' Don't practice saying 'Captain' in the mirror just yet," Iden shot back playfully. This was an old, old joke between them, and hearing it trotted out was comforting.

"Admiral Versio," came Seyn's voice. "I've just finished a cursory perusal of the data banks. I'm . : . if I may say so, stunned. We are the beneficiaries of your experience, sir, and I'm grateful."

"You may, all of you, show your gratitude with success in your missions. I'll contact you with your next assignment. In the meantime, you should dedicate yourselves to knowing every centimeter of this vessel." With a nod, but not another word, he strode down the ramp, leaving the team to gaze after him.

"So," Meeko said, with his usual gift for breaking the tension, "it looks like the rest of us got our birthday presents." He tapped the droid on the top of its hovering frame. "What is it you want, Captain?"

Iden snapped her gaze from the retreating form of her father to Del's open visage. "I just want to train."

And so she did. While Meeko busied himself with the droid, Hask piloted the *Corvus* as often as he could get away with it, and Marana sequestered herself going over the most up-to-date intel, Iden trained with a single-mindedness of purpose.

She had recovered from the injuries suffered on Yavin 4, but she was stiff from enforced inactivity. She had lost her edge. She wanted to recover—no, *surpass*—her normal range of motion, speed, and strength as soon as possible.

She ran and worked with trainer droids in holographic battle simulations, pushing herself hard, eating meals designed less for taste than to perfectly suit her body's needs. She flew the *Corvus* both with Gideon, Caton, and Morro as copilots and solo, taking it through its paces until she knew its movements and moods as well as she had known those of her TIE fighter. She practiced with all the weapons that the team would have access to and went hand-to-hand with anyone and everyone who was willing to spar with her. At night, she would fall into her cabin on the *Corvus* exhausted and bruised, then sleep the sleep of the dead and wake before dawn to do it all again.

And when Admiral Versio contacted them with their next mission, they were ready.

The missions were generally not long-term. Most, like their first, could be conducted in the span of a few well-planned hours. The majority, also like their first, hit closer to home than Iden had expected. Del, too, seemed a bit disillusioned by the lack of character displayed by some fairly prominent Imperials.

"I hadn't expected so many to be so willing to bite the hand that feeds them," he'd lamented once as they themselves fed quite well on a meal he'd seemingly conjured from nowhere.

"I'm not surprised," Seyn replied. "You work in Intel long enough, you see a lot of things."

"Not everyone can handle power wisely," Iden said.

"I'm more than ready to go against the rebels," Gideon had said.

"We all are," Iden said. "But after their success with the Death Star, the Rebel Alliance is going to be extra careful with their secrets—and make it harder for those willing to share them with the Empire. Besides—we're doing a lot of good weeding out the bad eggs in our midst. Without Imperial treason, the Death Star would still be intact and the war won. I'm sure the admiral will turn us loose against rebel scum soon enough."

Iden was right. The call came . . . but it was not at all what they had been expecting.

The partisans?

Iden had accompanied her team to her father's office, excited to learn that they would, at long last, get to strike against the rebels. But the partisans? She glanced at her fellow squad members, all of whom looked as stunned as she felt. *Not all,* she amended almost at once. Seyn alone did not appear to be surprised.

"Sir," said Gideon slowly, "it was my understanding that all of the partisans were destroyed during the mining accident on Jedha."

Oddly, Iden's father looked pleased at the comment. He turned to his daughter. "Agent Versio, everyone in your team has level-four security clearance. You may speak freely."

"Yes, sir," Iden replied. She knew what he wanted her to say. "The incident at Jedha was *not* a mining accident. It was the first test of the Death Star. The site was selected for several reasons, one being that the destruction of Jedha City would eliminate Gerrera and his partisans."

Versio nodded perfunctorily and turned his attention to Seyn, an eyebrow raised. She cleared her throat.

"That's partially correct," Seyn said. "While we have confirmed that Saw Gerrera himself and many of his colleagues did indeed perish on Jedha, we have evidence that there were several individual partisans who were not on the planet at the time."

"Sir?" It was Del, who did not usually speak up at these meetings. "The partisans were never a major threat. They were always Saw's group, and their methods were too extreme for the Rebel Alliance. Even if there are some of them still out there, surely they'll just die out."

"As you say, Agent, they were always Saw's group. We had anticipated we'd seen the last of them with his death; perhaps a final, bloody skirmish here or there as they ran about, directionless and furious. That's not been the case."

He looked at them with a grim expression. "A group has arisen to fill the void. They call themselves the Dreamers."

Gideon scoffed. "Pretty name for a terrorist group," he said.

"Dreams. Hope. These are the things that those on the losing side cling to. These Dreamers identify themselves clearly as *Saw Gerrera's partisans,* and they seem to have sprung from nowhere. They're no longer limiting their fanaticism and viciousness to the random bombing or sneak attack here and there. They know things. Secret things. Codes, and names, and dates of events that a handful of suicidal followers should not be able to know. They are targeting with surgical precision."

Iden thought she hated rebels, but as she listened, she felt a cold knot in her stomach at the picture her father painted. Violent, almost sadistic terrorists, unencumbered by the Rebel Alliance's so-called morality, were apparently in possession of highly sensitive Imperial information.

There would be no moral high ground here for these Dreamers to claim. Just blood, Imperial blood, and buckets full of it. It didn't matter to "Saw Gerrera's partisans" whether it came from moffs, or laborers, or children.

"So . . . Saw Gerrera is now a martyr," said Meeko. "The fewer they are, the more they feel like everything they do counts. They're going to double down on the violence, and if, as the admiral believes, some kind of sensitive material has fallen into their hands, they're going to exploit it as much as possible while they're still alive to do so."

"Meeko is absolutely right about the nature of these terrorists," Versio said. "We need to recover whatever information has fallen into their grubby, blood-soaked hands. Once we have that, they will once again be reduced to an angry, impotent handful of soon-to-be-extinct malcontents. But to do that, we need more information about them.

"Apparently, the recent escalation of violence has turned the stomach of at least one of their members. We have a lead on a defector—not from the Dreamers, unfortunately, but from a smaller, less organized group. At this point any information from any partisan is helpful."

He pressed another button and the holographic image of a Sullustan appeared in the center of the table. "This is Bokk Naarg. He fought alongside Gerrera since before the formation of the Empire. He claims to have been having doubts about the partisans for some time, and now finally sees the futility of the cause. He wants to throw in his lot with the side that will win. He claims he has information on where the Dreamers have been getting their intel."

"And you believe him?" asked Gideon, a slight hint of doubt in his voice.

"I believe our agent, who's been meeting with him for some time now, and I'll say no more about that. Their task is done. Ours . . . yours . . . is to extract Bokk and bring him in. We need to know everything he knows. And I do mean everything. Any further questions about the importance of this mission?"

There were none. Iden felt a flutter of excitement. This was big—their biggest job yet. They could be making a real difference.

"Good. Now, Captain Versio . . . what is your plan?"

Every briefing for every mission ended this way. After the admiral had outlined the objective, he turned to Iden and challenged her to create a plan on the spot.

Every time he did so, Iden had felt the familiar sinking, the tightness of the worry that this time, this mission, would be the one that went wrong. The one she'd fail.

And every time, she shoved that thought deep down inside her mind and shut the door on it.

"First, I need to know what Bokk's contact knows," she said.

The extraction would transpire at the Tellik Station and trading post. Located along one of the major hyperspace lanes, it was nominally controlled by the Empire, but riffraff of all varieties stopped here to repair, rest, and refuel. There was a stormtrooper presence, and Imperial ships came and went frequently. But nobody appeared to look too hard at anything.

The *Corvus* docked without incident in Bay 47, allegedly to put in for refueling. When Caton and Morro shut down the engines, everyone was silent for a moment.

"Well," said Iden. "Here we go. Our first shot at the rebels. Lieutenant Hask"—she allowed herself to smile at her old friend—"you have the honor of getting things rolling."

"With pleasure," he said, returning her smile. Over the last few weeks, Gideon had stopped trimming his hair and shaving. His normal spit-and-polished appearance was now just untidy enough to look like he was a civilian pilot—perhaps one who sometimes ferried dubious cargo.

He turned to his "copilot"—what Meeko called his masterpiece, the revamped seeker droid. "Follow," he instructed. The droid bleeped and buzzed acknowledgment, gathered its legs beneath it, and accompanied Gideon as he strode down the ramp.

Everyone on the *Corvus* was silent, watching through the droid's feed as it and Gideon made their way through the crowded station to a place called the Singularity—a watering hole/club where the drinks flowed freely, deals were made, and a variety of pleasures were enjoyed. The décor seemed to be inspired by the club's name—the walls and furnishings were black-hole dark, and the establishment's front was a wide opening that narrowed and grew dimmer as one went deeper inside. Some of those cloistered in the heart of the Singularity looked as though they had been there for some time—and were not eager to leave.

Perhaps it was this architectural choice, or perhaps it was mere coincidence, but the Singularity was also one of those rare places where the Empire looked the other way if some crewmembers of the various Imperial ships chose to "relax" in ways that weren't strictly approved.

"Of course we know about the Singularity," Seyn had informed them when the meeting site was floated. "We are aware of several Imperial officers who are regulars. We've been gathering information in order to blackmail them if we ever need to bring them in line."

Iden winced a little as Hask and the ID10 entered the club. Loud, arrhythmic music pounded, and the singers—a pair of round-bodied, stick-legged Pa'lowick—had screechy, ear-rupturing voices coming from tiny mouths at the end of stalklike muzzles.

"No wonder people like to do shady business there," Iden commented. "You can't hear anything."

"Droid," Del said, "mute music." The droid booped and, thankfully, filtered that particular cacophony from the rest of the audiovisual feed.

Now that Gideon was in position, it was Iden's turn. She rose and picked up her white helmet as Del slid into her vacated seat at the console.

She'd never formally served the Empire as a stormtrooper, but as a TIE pilot she was used to helmets, and she had spent plenty of time in one of the plastoid uniforms over the last few days—training to move easily inside it as if she'd been a trooper for years. Everything was standard issue so as not to blow her cover; everything except the heads-up display inside the "bucket." It had been reconfigured to show the same images that the droid was transmitting to the *Corvus*.

"Report, Inferno-Two?" she said quietly.

"This looks like a good place," Gideon said. He had been surgically fitted with the same tiny, plastoid ear device he and Seyn had worn on their first mission. Any sentence with the word *good* in it meant that all was going according to plan. A sentence with the word *rough* meant trouble, and *stinks* meant danger.

"Copy that," Iden replied. "I'm taking up position."

She looked at the two who would be staying with the ship. "Be ready for anything," she said.

"You too, Captain," Meeko said, and Seyn added, "Good luck."

Iden donned her helmet, picked up her blaster, and descended the ramp, moving with the typical casual-but-alert movements of a stormtrooper on patrol. While the space station wasn't exactly crawling with stormtroopers, they were a common enough sight that no one spared her more than a quick glance.

Iden began her circuit of the area—a wide-enough range so as not to attract attention, but close enough to sprint to the Singularity if firepower was needed, or back to the docking area if a quick escape was required instead.

So far, the mission was eight minutes old, and nothing had gone wrong.

So far.

Gideon Hask was in high spirits. Hitherto, he'd served the Empire by blowing rebels out of the sky while piloting his TIE fighter, but this was different. Everything about Inferno Squad was different. The missions always held the possibility of exploding into danger and violence without warning, just like the fighting he had been more used to. Unlike going into battle, though, there was also a chance of that not happening at all. It kept you on your toes, and Gideon found he loved it.

He was less excited that, yet again, he was playing second to Iden, someone five years his junior. At least this time he was the one to make contact with the rebel deserter while Iden "patrolled" in her white armor. Really, the successful outcome of this mission rested squarely on his shoulders. He'd have to make sure Bokk trusted him, and that the encounter came off as casual and genuine to any observers.

Initially, though, assigning this mission to Inferno Squad hadn't made much sense to Gideon. He'd been the one to ask right away why they were going in instead of the Imperial who had already established a connection with Bokk. If the partisan informant genuinely wanted to get out so badly, surely he'd feel safer escaping under the wing of someone he knew and trusted.

"NavInt says the agent has many more contacts than this one," Seyn had replied. "Over a dozen things are in play. We can't risk having his cover blown. If he refers the informant to a 'trusted friend' and things go wrong, he's still got plausible deniability. I don't think you appreciate how convoluted espionage can be—or how many people are involved in it in one way or another."

That had rubbed Gideon the wrong way. He respected Seyn's unique skill sets, but she certainly could be arrogant.

Through the original Imperial agent, Bokk had been told to look for a human wearing a worn brown flight jacket with exactly three patches on it. Gideon, of course, had seen several images of Bokk: an older Sullustan with a scar-covered injury to his left eye.

Inferno Squad's second in command settled in, sprawling comfortably at a table near the back. When the serving droid came up to him, he requested a Bespin Breeze, then casually looked around the place. Del had ascertained where security's recording devices were located and had hacked into them. He could stop them recording at any point if need be.

Representatives of at least two dozen different species milled about. While the Empire worked with native species on planets under its purview, his immersion in the Academy and then on a Star Destroyer meant he'd had extended interactions with few. Now Gideon found the variety of individuals enjoying themselves—or at least pretending to—at the Singularity an entertaining spectacle. There were several near-human species represented— Twi'leks, Pantorans, Mirialans—but others who were distinctly not.

When the drink came, the droid unobtrusively scanned it for toxins. When it beeped to pronounce the beverage safe, Gideon took a sip.

"Any sign of him?" Iden's voice in his ear.

At that precise moment, Gideon's eye fell upon a figure working his way through the crowd. "Good drink," he said.

"Copy that," Iden replied. But even as his commanding officer spoke, Gideon realized something that threatened to render the situation not "good" at all.

Bokk had not come alone.

Accompanying him were three females and two males—a pair of Mirialans, two Pantorans, and a Togruta. These companions were dressed in alluring outfits and wearing chunky pieces of jewelry that looked to be made from inexpensive but brightly colored stones or beads. They were young and attractive and looked like they had come here to have fun. Their arrival was greeted with approval; clearly, they were regulars.

Gideon debated saying something like *Bet things can get rough in here from time to time,* but he didn't need to. His team had visuals.

Perched now on Gideon's shoulder, the droid made a series of quick clicks.

Back in the *Corvus,* Del swore under his breath. "Bokk's brought friends, and the droid reports they're armed," he said. "Their jewelry's fake—it's made with explosives that will detonate on impact."

"Dammit," Iden muttered. The Sullustan deserter was supposed to come alone, and Inferno Squad had anticipated being halfway back to Coruscant shortly thereafter. "Seyn, did any intel suggest Bokk might try to set us up?"

Iden wondered if this was a suicide mission. Once, the partisans had been so focused on killing Imperials, they regarded civilian casualties as merely an unfortunate side effect. But they'd always protected their own hides. That had changed with their leader's demise. According to the intel her father had shared with Inferno Squad, several partisans had already demonstrated that they would be happy to follow Saw as long as they took Imperials with them.

"The jewelry is a new wrinkle," Seyn said. Her voice was tight. "We haven't heard of that before. We know that suicide attacks are becoming increasingly common. I don't know if that's the plan here; jewelry clasps can easily be 'broken' and fall off, or be left in a restroom. Del, have the droid home in on that Mirialan's face."

The droid obediently did so. Sweat was gathering along the side of the Mirialan's hairline, and her nostrils flared with rapid breathing.

"That's not good," Meeko murmured.

"Quiet, Inferno-Three," Iden snapped.

A boisterous table of humans, their clothing too shabby for their shaved cheeks and military-styled hair, shouted out to one of Bokk's younger companions and waved.

"Some of your flagged-for-blackmail Imperials?" Del asked Seyn. The Mirialan waggled her fingers at the humans and said something to her companion, one of the Pantorans.

"That one is still playing the game," Seyn said, translating as fast as the ship's computer could have. "Right now she's talking about a party later on and who they're going to bring. I don't know if her friend is in on Bokk's plans to get out."

Gideon couldn't tell, either, but he didn't like it. When Bokk's single good eye met his, Gideon lifted his glass and waved the Sullustan over, as if they were old friends. Bokk waved back and said something to the Pantoran who stood at his side. The younger alien laughed and playfully linked her arm through Bokk's as they moved toward the table together.

Damn.

"Been awhile, old friend," Gideon said. "Buy you and your companion a drink?"

"Whatever you're having is fine, old friend," Bokk said, his voice raspy.

That was the code phrase; whatever was going on, Bokk still wanted out. Or wanted Gideon to *think* he still wanted out. Gideon gestured to the serving droid and said, "Two more Bespin Breezes." It bleeped and scurried off.

"They're all nervous," Del's voice said in Gideon's ear.

So was Gideon, but he was more excited than nervous. "Kind of a *rough* place for you," he said to the young woman, hoping the code word would be picked up by his team.

The Pantoran laughed. "Don't you worry about me, sweetheart."

Was that a threat? Even as he pondered whether to move to the next level of code, working in the word *stinks* to imply that he had a bad feeling about this, Bokk leaned over and whispered in his ear.

"Sharima wants to get out, too," he said, pitching his voice so softly that only Gideon could hear.

Gideon . . . and the droid.

"Only room in the cockpit for one other pilot," Gideon said as the serving droid rolled up with their drinks.

Now it was the Pantoran's turn to whisper as she

leaned in and pretended to flirt with him. "Both of us, or none."

"We should abort." Seyn's voice.

"Negative," was Iden's response.

"Inferno-One, we should abort *right now*." Seyn's words were urgent—and against protocol.

"What's in it for me?" Gideon replied to the Pantoran, pitching his voice equally softly.

Sharima lifted one hand and toyed with her white hair, drawing his eye toward her bracelet. What looked like the bracelet's clasp was in fact a tiny datachip.

"This," the Pantoran said.

"What's in my head, and what's on the chip," Bokk muttered.

Seyn didn't like any of this one bit. Gideon should have tossed some credits on the table and walked out. All her instincts, honed by her specialized training, were screaming at her that they were walking into a trap.

Her gaze flickered to the multiple streams of conversation going on around Gideon and the two apparent deserters. Some threads were already translated; some she did herself.

—*someday I'm going to get me a place on some little planet*—

—*more than your life is worth to cross a buckethead*—

—*never, ever gamble with a Gammorean*—

—*price of grain is climbing so high*—

—*Never seen him here before. Both of them?*—

It was the male Pantoran. Seyn closed her eyes and

focused, listening with her entire being, catching the two voices over the inane chatter of club attendees.

—*Are they trying to recruit him?*—

—*talking to Bokk*—

—*Looks Imperial to me*—

Seyn's eyes snapped open. "Inferno-Two, they've made you," she said. Iden spoke even before Seyn could draw breath for a follow-on comment.

"Inferno-Two, I'm heading your way. I'm closing this down. Get out of there. *Now!*"

CHAPTER 7

Gideon heard his commanding officer, but he disagreed with her assessment. She might be able to *see* what was going on, but she couldn't necessarily put it together the way he could, and he had an idea.

Out of the corner of his eye, Gideon saw the other three partisans get to their feet. They were good; their body language conveyed nothing out of the ordinary. If it hadn't been for Seyn's translation—

"Okay," he said to Sharima, "but I'm getting the datachip first."

"No way," said the Pantoran. "You'll get it when Bokk and I are both on the ship."

Gideon kept his eyes on the bracelet's "clasp." He hoped the droid—and therefore Del—had, too. Del seemed like a very intelligent and observant man. Gideon hoped the former engineer had figured out what he himself had.

"I think your friends might have something to say about that," Gideon drawled, "and I don't want them detonating their bombs before you have a chance to give that chip to me."

Everything happened at once.

Both Sharima and Bokk looked over at their approaching companions. Even as their eyes widened, there came the distinctively distorted shout of an armored stormtrooper. "Stop right there!"

Quick as a thought, the droid sprang from its perch on Gideon's shoulder and extended its pincers. Two of them snipped through the wire upon which the bomb-gems were looped. A third slender, mechanical arm snatched the chip and retracted, secreting it somewhere inside the droid's metallic innards. The fourth was reaching to catch the seven miniature bombs as they tumbled toward the floor, but Gideon was faster. He grabbed them in one hand before they hit and closed his other hand tightly around them.

Bokk and Sharima had risen, and Bokk was staring in openmouthed horror at Gideon. The other two partisans were yelling something, and had almost reached Gideon's table.

"Go!" he shouted to the droid. It rose straight in the air and zipped over the head of the now wary patrons toward the front of the bar.

A stormtrooper stood there, blaster raised. Gideon was almost certain it was Iden.

Almost.

He sprang onto his chair, then the table, knocking over the Bespin Breezes, and then he, too, was racing out of the Singularity toward the corridor.

As his feet hit the metal flooring and put distance between him and the erupting chaos of the Singularity, Gideon flung the small, brightly colored, lethal orbs behind him just as he heard the scream of blasterfire.

Then, suddenly, a plastoid-gloved hand seized his arm, yanked him forward, and shoved him farther away from the explosion that momentarily deafened him. He landed hard, and for a horrible second he couldn't breathe. Then he was hauled to his feet by the stormtrooper—*no, Iden, Iden who'd blocked the worst of the blast with her own armor-covered body*—and they were racing down the corridors. Gideon's lungs hurt from breathing the overheated air, his whole body hurt, but he ran.

More beings pelted past them, fleeing the blast. Others surged toward them, including a cluster of actual stormtroopers. "Rebel bombing, back at the Singularity!" Iden shouted. Two of them clattered to a halt, obviously confused that she was running in the opposite direction.

Iden waved them on, gesturing at Gideon, whom she still gripped tightly. "I got this! Go, go!"

Through her heads-up display, Iden saw the ID10's careening journey as it zipped along through the corridors at high speed, dodging the panicked throngs and largely ignored. Then the little droid was safely in the ship.

Iden found herself staring into an almost alarming close-up of Meeko's concerned face.

"What happened?" Then he amended at once, "Never mind, just grunt if you're both okay!"

"Yeah," she managed. Relief spread over Del's face like a sunrise.

"Thank goodness! We're monitoring the response to the bombing. Lots of panic, but no one's onto you. I'm doing some editing on the security recordings, and Caton and Morro have the *Corvus* ready to leave the second you two get here."

"Copy that," Iden gasped. Meeko's face disappeared and the droid turned its photoreceptors to the console. It was hovering above Seyn who was, as promised, working frantically at the console. The younger woman glanced up at the droid, and Iden saw worry furrowing her brow; then Seyn returned her attention to her task.

They were almost there.

Seyn tensed. "Inferno-One, you've got company coming behind you."

"Damn!" Iden blurted, furious. She and Gideon rounded a corner and found the corridor beautifully empty.

They stumbled into the hangar to see the ramp was down. Waiting for them was Del Meeko, lean and lanky and thin-lipped with intensity, standing with a blaster at the ready.

"Trooper, halt!" cried a voice behind Iden.

There was no time for this, no time to explain to the poor grunt just doing his job that she was cleared, no time to do anything but shove Gideon forward to run to the ship by himself while Iden whirled, switching her blaster to stun, to hold off her "fellow" stormtroopers.

She fired directly at them. They staggered backward, some of them falling. She kept firing circles of blue energy as she went up the ramp, and Del did the same. The ramp retracted and the door slammed shut. Iden and

Del tumbled into seats beside Gideon and grabbed for the crash webbing.

"Go, go!" Iden shouted to the pilots, and the *Corvus* rose, hovered for a second as it continued to be bombarded with lasers, and then escaped to open space.

Ten seconds later, white light streaked past and they were in hyperspace.

Failed. I failed.

Iden yanked off her helmet and whirled on Gideon.

"What the *hell*, Hask?" she demanded, cold fury making her voice shake. She hated that, and fought to get herself under control. "You deliberately disobeyed a direct order!"

Gideon looked stunned at her outburst for a second; then his black brows drew together in a thunderous frown of his own.

"This mission turned toxic the instant Bokk showed up with an entourage." Seyn's normally girlish voice was acidic with disapproval. "We should have aborted immediately. Now we've attracted undue attention and possibly jeopardized one of our key agents!"

"Your agent is fine," said Gideon. "No one will connect him with this, now that—"

"Now that everyone's dead?" Iden finished. "Was that what you were about to say? Dammit, people, our job was not that hard! Get one person to safety without being noticed. Now *he's* dead, his *friend* is dead—"

Gideon cut her off. "Yeah, that's right. Five partisans are dead, casualties of their own violence when their terrorist bombing went terribly wrong. That means it's very likely that the Dreamers are the only ones left!"

But Seyn wasn't buying it. "Irrelevant! *This* mission

was to extract Bokk and obtain information from him. And now he's dead, and we're no better—no, no, we are *worse* off than we were before. By any measure, it's a failure." Her eyes flashed. "Initial security recordings indicate that two of our potential Imperial blackmail victims were wounded in the blast as well. We are very fortunate they weren't killed."

Our contact's dead. Gideon killed him. Seyn's right. By any measure, it's a failure.

"Captain Versio?" It was Meeko, sounding a little sheepish. "I may not agree about how this went down, but . . . we may *not* have blown the intent of the mission."

Iden stayed silent for a moment, hardly daring to hope. Then she said to Meeko, "Did I see what I think I saw there—before Gideon decided to unleash hell?" Gideon's lips thinned at the comment.

"Droid, show us what you got," Del instructed the ID10. It had fastened itself securely to the *Corvus*'s bulkhead for the jump to hyperspace. Now it bleeped, detached itself, and floated over to Meeko.

It extended one of its arms. In its metallic pincers, it grasped a datachip the size of Iden's pinkie fingernail.

Carefully, Iden took the chip, holding it by the edges, and handed it to Seyn. The younger woman was silent; then she turned and inserted it into the console.

Letters from a variety of alphabets, including pictographic ones, along with numerals flashed rapidly along the screen. "It's encrypted, of course," Seyn murmured, almost to herself, "but . . . you may be right. We may not have Bokk—but we might have some of what he knew."

Gideon and Iden regarded each other. "Apology accepted," Gideon said at last.

"Oh, I'm not apologizing," Iden replied stonily. "To *any* of you. Hask, you disobeyed a direct order and put yourself, your commanding officer, and the rest of the team in jeopardy."

She looked over at Seyn. "Marana, you did not suggest that we abort the mission—you demanded it. Twice.

"Meeko, you aided Gideon's disobedience when you decided to have your pet project snatch the datachip and abscond with it," she finished.

Everyone was quiet. Iden ran a hand through her sweat-damp hair and sighed.

"And . . . as it turned out, Seyn, you were right," Iden admitted. "The situation *was* dangerous, and we should have gotten out right away and planned a second rendezvous. Gideon—you retrieved a datachip we hope will prove to be full of useful information, and by your actions we've eliminated five known partisans. And Del—your quick thinking got us the chip before said partisans decided to take matters into their own hands."

There was a long, awkward silence. "Permission to speak freely?" Gideon asked after a strained moment.

"Go ahead."

"Thanks. For the ap—" He broke off and amended, "For the acknowledgment."

Iden smiled thinly and nodded. She took a deep breath. "Now we just have to present this to Admiral Versio in a way that looks like we are still a smoothly functioning machine."

The droid—an *actual* smoothly functioning machine—booped in what sounded like sympathy.

· · ·

As it turned out, while Admiral Versio was not at all happy with how things had gone down, he surprised Iden with his final opinion at their debriefing in his office.

"Anyone can craft the perfect plan for how a mission should go," he told them. Iden's stomach tightened. "But the execution is something else again. I've spoken with Bokk's contact—he was surprised to learn that Bokk had changed the terms of the deal. If he, who had worked with the Sullustan for months, had not expected the, ah . . . twist, you could not be expected to."

Iden blinked. She had not anticipated such magnanimity from her father. Whatever else he'd learned must have pleased him greatly.

"As it had always been the intention to terminate Bokk once he had revealed his information, I believe we lost very little. What was on the chip was extremely useful. And the entire . . ." He searched for the word. ". . . turn of events during your mission might work in our favor."

Iden waited. It might not have been a disaster, but it was bad enough. It wasn't perfect. So she waited for him to single out the others for their responses. Waited for him to give the position of leader to someone else.

He did not.

After a moment, she said, "May we be informed about what you learned from the chip, sir?"

"In due time and as it pertains to your mission, Captain," Versio said. He sat down at the head of the table. Iden blinked. It was the first time—ever—that her father had sat down in a professional meeting. He folded his hands.

"I've made the decision to expand Inferno Squad's responsibilities in order to best utilize the information we have obtained on the partisans," he said. "As you will recall, I described the squad as being cleaners. Tracking down and recovering sensitive information, informants, defectors, and so on, usually with quick, precision attacks or incursions. For instance, your recent mission to the Tellik Four station, both planned and how it actually unfolded, was a military extraction operation. Despite the complications, you succeeded.

"You'll still be cleaners, but your next mission is going to be reminiscent of your first one. If all goes well, this could mean the end of the Dreamers in a single swoop."

The four exchanged glances, but they all held their tongues.

"As was discussed earlier, the Rebel Alliance has a mostly unified front, while the partisans have always preferred to operate in one or two small cells, with little or no connection. The most recent intel says that with the explosion on Singularity, the Dreamers is the sole remaining functional partisan cell. I've already told you that the Dreamers have likely obtained what could be potentially devastating intel. The information on the recovered datachip, among other things, appears to confirm this."

There wasn't any murmuring. Not quite. But the room was filled with swift intakes of breath and the creaking of chairs as their occupants shifted.

"It might seem that the logical thing would be to simply go in and destroy it. While that would indeed wipe out the enemy in one attack, we'd also be destroying our chance to discover *how* the intel has fallen into the partisan hands, who knows about it, and who controls the data flow. And so that means we need Inferno Squad to not just extricate information, but infiltrate the Dreamers."

Iden caught movement out of the corner of her eye. It was Seyn. She did not look at all comfortable with this statement. Truth be told, Iden wasn't, either. But she had learned not to question. Just to do, succeed, excel.

That was what Versios did.

"Any questions before I go over your specific assignments?"

"I have one, sir," Seyn said. "We have agents trained precisely for this sort of thing, and we've even attempted to infiltrate the partisans before. Why is Inferno Squad being sent instead of another ISB agent?"

A smile quirked the admiral's lips. "Do you think you aren't up to it, Lieutenant? I can certainly replace you on the squad if so."

Seyn stiffened. "Of course I am, sir. But I'm wondering why you think this team is a better choice."

"You've answered your own question, Lieutenant. ISB has indeed sent in agents before. None of them was successful. We can't afford to fail this time. I have nothing but respect for the brave agents of the ISB. The partisans—especially the Dreamers—are a military group, not a corporation or a governmental organization. Any agents sent in would also have to be trained to operate a variety of weapons and vessels. You will all see a lot of action, and you'll be asked to do things you might find distasteful. Up to and including possibly having to actively participate in attacks against your own people to protect your cover."

Iden blinked. That hadn't occurred to her. The Empire was certainly not overly compassionate. It understood sacrifice and duty—unlike the rebels. But this quietly horrified her.

Then she thought about the partisans, who had shown up at a bar wearing bombs disguised as jewelry, and hardened her heart. She *did* understand sacrifice. If she had to kill some Imperials to save the rest—to save all of what the Empire stood for—she would do it.

"Considering all that, I feel this assignment is a superb opportunity to showcase all that Inferno Squad is capable of."

And then Iden understood. She'd seen this type of behavior from her father before. Whatever was on that chip was something Garrick Versio thought he could turn to his advantage. Inferno Squad had been his brainchild. Its success . . . Iden's success . . . would be his.

She was conflicted. On the one hand, he was using the team to climb his way higher up in the eyes of the Emperor. On the other hand . . . he thought enough of her to involve her in his continued rise to power.

His eyes, almost reptilian in their flat coldness, roamed over the four of them. "If anyone feels they cannot complete this mission as I have outlined it, please speak up now."

There was silence.

"As I thought. Now to the details. The datachip revealed the following." Versio began to tick points off on his fingers. "First, it confirmed our suspicions that the Dreamers have indeed acquired sensitive information. The group is led by a man known only as Staven. We had apprehended Staven and, until Saw's death, he was rotting in a prison cell. Somehow he managed to escape, and he has apparently kept himself quite busy gathering hardcore recruits who were passionate about Saw and his mission."

"Anyone else named other than Staven?"

"No, unfortunately. That might have been Bokk's contribution, had he survived."

Iden tightened her jaw. Her father continued. "We do, however, have the names of a few notable Dreamer sympathizers; and finally, we know the Dreamers' next target."

Iden schooled her face to remain calm, but inwardly her heart leapt. She knew that the others struggled similarly.

"We've run all of this data by Intel, and it looks sound as far as we are able to determine," Versio continued. "The one thing we don't know, however, is where the Dreamers are based. Which means we'll need to convince them to take us there." Versio allowed himself a slight smile at their confusion. "Here's how this is going to work.

"The Dreamers are planning an attack approximately two standard weeks from now. We're going to let it proceed unhindered."

Versio had not exaggerated his warning to them. The

very first thing they would be doing in this infiltration mission would be allowing people to die. Versio directed their attention to a holoprojector in the table. A space station that looked like it had been haphazardly thrown together rather than deliberately designed turned slowly in the center.

"This is Otor's Hub," Versio said. "It's located in the Ojostor sector of the Outer Rim. It's a popular way station for travelers."

"So, sort of like Tellik Four?" Meeko asked.

"Tellik Four is a fairly straightforward refueling and repair station, and operates formally within the auspices of the Empire. This place is far more unsavory. Most of its merchants deal in the black market—or the slave market. There is a small cluster of merchants there who do a bit of spying for us on the side. They know to notify us if a person of interest patronizes their shop, or if a certain item crosses their path. It's a loose association, but a useful one. It turns out that the Dreamers have discovered our involvement with these merchants, and they've decided to put an end to it."

"That sort of enterprise isn't really in keeping with the data leak you're concerned with, sir," Gideon said. "It seems more personal than political."

"It does, and it likely is," Versio agreed. "But the partisans have ever been ones to smart against a perceived insult and hold grudges. *That* is entirely in keeping with their operation. I regret the necessity of sacrificing these merchants. They've been useful over the years. But I'm certain others will spring up to fill the vacuum."

Iden was nodding, relaxing a little. She had no problem with the idea of money-grubbing black marketers on the receiving end of Dreamer "justice." Much preferable to the thought of sacrificing Imperial lives.

Versio continued. "There's one merchant who's mentioned specifically by name. A Dug, even more unpleasant than most of his species, known for dealing in antiquities—mostly fake—and information—mostly true. We will approach this Rudaga and inform him that Lieutenant Marana is one of our agents. She will pose as his slave. People will grow accustomed to her presence at the shop, so she won't attract any attention the day of the attack. He'll teach the lieutenant enough about the business so the partisans won't suspect her."

Versio now spoke directly to the youngest member of the group. "You have an eidetic memory, and I've spoken with your superiors. Apparently, once you see something, you can replicate it, and you've done so on a few occasions previously."

"Yes, sir."

"Then you will claim you've been trained in forgery by your master. It's a valuable skill for the Dreamers to have. That and your sad story of mistreatment by your master will make it likely the Dreamers will take you with them once they've eliminated their targets."

The admiral slid a datapad over to her. "Your bio is here. Memorize it. And, as I'm certain you anticipated, we're going to have to do some work on you before you go. Per our standard operating procedure in these cases, everything we do, we'll undo at the completion of your assignment."

Iden was confused. Seyn seemed to know exactly what

Versio meant, but Iden was at a loss. So, too, it seemed, was everyone else on the team.

"Excuse me, sir," Gideon ventured, "but what do you mean, *work*?"

It was Seyn, not the admiral, who answered. "He means that my body is going to be altered to corroborate my cover story. It's commonplace for undercover operations like this one."

She seemed calm, almost clinically detached from her words. With growing unease, Iden found herself speaking up. "Altered how?"

"As she is purporting to be an escaped slave, Lieutenant Marana will need to display visible signs of abuse," Versio said in the same neutral, professional tone he might use to discuss his caf preference. "The question is, do we want to make it appear that the injuries have been accumulated from long-term mistreatment, or recent? Scars, brands, calluses on her hands—that sort of thing."

That sort of thing.

"I see," Iden said. "Understood."

The thought of any member of her team having to be mutilated in order to fulfill the mission made her uncomfortable, but Iden did understand. Everything rested on them being able to convince the partisans that they were sincere. And no one knew that better than Seyn. If anything, the youngest member of the team would have suggestions as to how to make her own scarification more believable.

"Once we're done with the meeting, there's a specialist I'd like you to consult with. You can go over the options together. Shum Laudor, perhaps you know him."

"We've not met, but I've seen his work. It's entirely convincing."

"Good." Versio turned to the two young men. "Now. Another useful thing we learned from the chip is that the Dreamers have a fairly regular supplier of food and often weapons. We have a plan for getting you aboard her ship, and she'll take you right to them. The two of you will be posing as a pair of brothers."

Iden had to admit that it made sense. Both had dark hair, brown eyes, and similar features, although Gideon's skin was paler. But they were hardly alike in demeanor. She was an only child, and had only the vaguest notion of how brothers would interact. The two men in question exchanged glances, then hid bemused smiles.

"Your particular challenge will be to cultivate an extra layer of believability to convincingly pass as siblings. For the next week, not only will you live together in the same unit and share the same room, you'll eat all your meals together, train together, and rehearse your stories together. By the time you're done, you should feel as though you truly do have a brother."

"I have two brothers," Del said confidently. "We'll be fine."

"I expect no less, Agent. If you do your jobs right and convince her, she'll take you with her. If you don't, make no mistake, she'll execute you on the spot."

"How charming," Hask said.

He'd mistaken the brother approach for lightness on Versio's part, and Iden knew at once that it was a mistake. Versio narrowed his eyes. "She's a pirate, and her reputation is quite terrifying. Her group is called the

Blood Bone Order. I've included information on your datapads. I suggest you read it. Thoroughly."

He passed them their datapads. Gideon accepted his without further comment.

"Hask, you will present yourself as the pilot of the pair. Meeko, you're the technician. Simple is always best, and remember, any lie is more effective if it holds some truth in it. Your droid will accompany you. Give some thought to what would serve a rebel group well, and tailor its upgrades to that."

They both replied, "Yes, sir," at the same time. Iden straightened in her chair and looked at her father with a calm, expressionless face. Seyn was to be a slave and have her body scarified for the role. The men were being drafted into a pirate's crew.

What horror did her father have in store for her?

"Now then," Admiral Versio said, "as for your commanding officer . . . I have saved the best for last." Iden tensed. Versio turned to the rest of them. "Iden will be leaving us shortly. She is to be stationed on a new Star Destroyer."

Iden felt the blood drain from her face. "Sir?"

"Don't worry. You're taking different paths to get there, but you'll all eventually rendezvous. Dismissed."

Iden waited as the others filed out. Del cast a concerned glance back at her. Then the door closed, and she was alone with her father.

"What do you have in mind for me, sir?"

"As I said. You'll be stationed on a Star Destroyer."

"I don't understand."

"There was one final piece of information on that

chip. The Dreamers themselves are emotionally rallying behind their founder, Saw. They want to realize his vision. But Saw is gone, and his name can no longer be used as the public face of the 'true partisans.' They need a new one. We're giving them yours."

CHAPTER 8

"The things we do for the Empire," Gideon said, sighing melodramatically.

"I hear you," Del said. "I mean, fighting and dying is one thing, but stowing away in this death trap of a ship? Do you think we'll get hazard pay?"

"If we get out of this alive, I think we could make an excellent case for it." He grinned at Del, who returned it.

Despite their feigned—okay, *slightly* feigned—complaints about their cramped quarters and steady diet of *delicious* ration cubes, things had gone well so far. True to his word, Admiral Versio had seen to it that the two "brothers" were constantly in each other's company. Del had been a little worried initially. He and Gideon did not seem like two people who would naturally gravitate toward each other. In the end, though, the shared adventure aspect bonded them.

The plan was simple, but there were many places where things could go wrong. Success hinged on greed, timing, and luck. Fortunately for the moment, the "brothers Farren" would be able to contact the admiral should something go awry—if, for example, the wrong group of pirates ended up attacking the ship.

A large handful of credits delivered by one of the Empire's many shadowy figures convinced a Devaronian smuggler name of Kurjak to take on a large, force-field-protected container. No questions asked. It was to be delivered to Eriadu, the end of the smuggler's run, where someone would be waiting to receive it in six days' time.

Someone indeed would be waiting to receive the container—provided the ship, known as the *Fast Friend,* actually made it to its final destination. Research had concluded that the ship's path would take it into dangerous space where Lassa Rhayme, the cruel leader of the Blood Bone Order, was known to strike.

"It seems funny to say, *With luck, we'll be captured by pirates,*" Del had commented as they prepared for the journey.

"Better than having to go through the whole ordeal a second time," Gideon had replied, and Del had to admit he was right.

The three of them—Del Farren, Gid Farren, and the droid—spent almost the entire journey in the container, sneaking out during times when the crew slept in order to grab some exercise and visit the restroom. They'd swapped battle stories, tales of their childhood, and reminiscences of girls they'd known all too fleetingly. The Empire was a demanding master, and there was little time for personal relationships.

"We're living on borrowed time, people like us," Del had said one evening. He had loaded up the droid with games and holovids to while away the time, and they were currently playing a travel version of dejarik.

"You've borrowed more than I have," Gideon had replied.

"Thanks for the reminder, baby brother."

"Seriously, retirement is just around the corner. You need someone to settle down with."

Del shook his head. "Nope. Wouldn't be fair. You?"

"Nah. I've got my eyes on a command." He moved a piece. The tiny holographic creature emitted a small squeal of delight as it destroyed Del's.

"Does Iden know?"

Gideon laughed. "Yes, she does."

Once again, Gideon had evaded a serious answer. Del noticed that his "brother" was closemouthed about his childhood, opening up only when it came to his time at the Future Imperial Leaders Military Preparatory School on Vardos and, later, at the Academy. Del knew he'd lost his family to a rebel bombing at a young age. It wasn't surprising, then, that Gideon seemed almost hungry to hear stories about Del's family and two older brothers, who also served in faraway positions in the Empire. Gideon struck Del as someone who was eager to connect with others yet pushed them away simultaneously. There was an edge to his humor, a coldness that Del supposed came with the tragedy that had struck him so young.

"And now look at you," Gideon had said. "You've risen higher in the ranks than anyone else in your family!"

Del had laughed at that, gesturing to the three-square-meter compartment lit only by the blue holographic glow the ID10 emitted. He picked up the ration cube.

"I'm living like the Emperor himself!" he had said. They'd both laughed, then suddenly quieted. Even here, even now, one did not joke about the Emperor.

They were halfway through the fourth day and were slowly running out of things to talk about. During a long silence, as they sat in the darkness to conserve their light, Del said, "I wonder if we *are* going to have to do this all over again."

"I desperately hope not. I'd rather face the torture droid than six more days in a container with you."

Suddenly a screeching klaxon sounded. Gideon activated his glowrod and the two looked at each other excitedly. They waited a moment to see if it was a false alarm, but when the earsplitting sound continued and the ship rocked violently, they had their answer. Del deactivated the force field and they leapt out, grabbing their packs and their blasters. The ID10 rose behind them, providing light for the two to navigate their way around towering crates of illegal goods.

Another barrage of cannon fire caused the old ship to shudder. The pair were knocked to the floor. Just as they clambered to their feet, there was a sudden blaze of orange and yellow flame—and then everything, including Del and Gideon, was being drawn toward the suddenly gaping hole in the hull.

ID10's metallic arms shot out, its pincers grabbing the two by the collars of their jackets. The other pair of arms fastened themselves firmly to the bulkhead as the smaller containers of ill-gotten gains were sucked out into space. Just as Del was convinced that one highly modified ID10 droid and two hapless humans would be next, the pressure stabilized and normal gravity returned.

The droid released them. Gideon looked at it with surprise and respect. "Strong little guy," he said.

"I reinforced his joints and added a magnet," Del said.

"Good thinking," Gideon said as he and Del slumped against the bulkhead and looked toward where the hole had been.

Their domicile of the last four days had plugged it. Astonished and gleeful, they looked at each other and started to laugh.

The smuggling compartment was locked, but that had never been a problem. Over the last four days, the droid had opened and locked it for them on request. At this moment, their goal was to stay alive long enough to surrender themselves to the Blood Bone Order and, now that the fighting had begun, they were determined to do what they could to help the pirates take the ship. The two Inferno Squad members hurried through corridors drenched in blood-red lighting, pausing to blast any member of the crew unfortunate enough to come across them. The droid, too, went on the offensive, attacking with electroshock prods.

They emerged onto the bridge, where, despite sparking and sometimes smoking consoles, the smugglers were doing their best to fend off the pirates.

"Looks like the cargo area was hit!" one of them shouted over the din.

The captain shouted a long string of something in

Huttese, following it up with, "Make them pay for the lost cargo!"

The pirate ship fired again. Del and Gideon stayed out of sight, watching and waiting. The droid fastened itself to Del's back.

"Direct hit on the engines!"

The screen on the main console suddenly flickered to life. The figure was only a third of a meter tall but imposing even at that diminutive height. It was a Pantoran female, with blue skin and a long braid of lighter-hued hair. She wore a black jacket, boots, and snug-fitting pants. She had a blaster in one hand and what looked like a cutlass in the other.

"I am Lassa Rhayme, captain of the *Opportunity* and head of the Blood Bone Order," she said in a clear, strong voice. "Prepare for either boarding—or becoming target practice. Which'll it be?"

The two humans looked at each other, grinning. Gideon gave Del a thumbs-up.

Kurjak drooped in defeat, sighing deeply. Rhayme put a hand to her ear, an exaggerated look of confusion on her tattoo-free, beautiful face.

"What's that? Target practice? Sounds fine."

"No!" Kurjak retorted. "We surrender! Damn you, blue-skinned devil."

"Devil, am I? Look who's talking! All right, I'll think about it." The pirate captain smiled, and her image disappeared.

It was all over after that.

By the time the *Opportunity* had planted the grappling harpoons and hauled the ship close enough for boarding, Gideon and Del had either eliminated or trussed up the crew of the *Fast Friend* and were awaiting the pirate's arrival. Lassa Rhayme liked to call herself a pirate queen, and while it was undoubtedly self-aggrandizing, reports claimed that she was always among the first to board a captured ship so she could terrorize the crew herself.

They heard the clank of the boarding tube connecting. Del glance over at Gideon. "Think she'll give us a chance to speak?"

"Don't know," Gideon replied. "I do know if we meet her with blasters blazing we'll be cut down without a second thought, so let's hope she'll listen."

"I'd rather be fighting than hoping."

"Me too," Gideon said. "Ready?"

"Ready." Del placed his hands behind his head.

Gideon pressed the controls to unlock the door, then stepped back quickly, imitating Del.

The door opened, and the striking black-clad, blue-skinned Pantoran of the hologram, Lassa Rhayme, the pirate queen of the Blood Bone Order, stepped onto the ship. Two of her crew followed her.

She was much taller than Del had expected—almost as tall as they were, and neither Imperial was short. Her braid, as it turned out, was lavender, and her golden eyes looked vibrodaggers at both the humans.

"You're mighty obliging," she said. "Usually someone has a death wish along about now."

"We do have a request," Gideon said.

She rolled her eyes. "Fine, I'll kill you quickly," she said, and lifted the blaster. Another Blood Bone pirate emulated his captain and aimed his blaster at Del.

"No, don't! We're partisans!" Del shouted quickly.

Lassa froze. "Cover this one," she said, and the pirate stepped forward, smirking as he retrained his weapon on Gideon.

The pirate queen's arm shot out, grabbed Del by the collar, slammed him up against the bulkhead, and pressed the tip of her blaster to his forehead.

"Start talking," she said, "and you'd better hope I like what I hear."

"We're partisans," Del stammered.

"You said that, go on."

"I'm Del Farren, and that's my brother, Gid. We were part of the Nebula cell. We were at the Tellik Four station when the Singularity bombing happened."

The golden eyes didn't waver. "I heard about that bombing."

Del wondered how much she knew about the logistics of the situation. In their haste to depart after the event, he almost hadn't taken the time to edit the security recordings. He was profoundly grateful he had. "Our cell had been compromised. Some of us volunteered to do a suicide bomb attack. The rest of us were going to join the Dreamers."

"Why Tellik Four?"

"We knew what ships were coming in. We knew the habits of some of the Imperial officers. They went to that bar often. We figured we'd kill who we could while causing a distraction. Some of us would die so we could escape. Try to make our way to join the Dreamers. Bokk said we could trust you."

Admiral Versio had pointed out that in any recordings of the event, Gideon and the droid would show up. He would be seen talking with known partisans. He would also be seen flinging bombs over his shoulder as he fled out of the bar, but thanks to Del's hacking, there were serendipitous bursts of static that had obscured anything that might give them away. And as there was no one left of the cell to dispute the claim, it stood as compelling support to their story.

The question was, was it going to be compelling enough?

Lassa Rhayme frowned, glancing from one to the other. Finally she said to one of her people, "Take them. I'll verify this. In the meantime, let's haul some cargo."

Del and Gideon were taken none too gently aboard the *Opportunity,* where they were put in a small holding cell. They were given water but nothing else, and their packs and the droid were confiscated. Del wasn't worried. He'd made some adjustments that would bury anything related to Inferno Squad unless a certain code was entered. Unless the pirates were exceptional hackers, the information was safe. Going on the assumption that they were being observed and listened to, they spoke little, and when they did, they made sure they said nothing to jeopardize their story.

Their time as undercover operatives had well and truly begun. Del just hoped that it would last longer than a few hours.

At last, the door was opened. The man who had trained his blaster on Gideon filled the doorway. His weapon was in its holster at his hip.

"Lassa wants to see you," he said. "Follow me."

Lassa awaited them in a large, comfortably decorated

cabin. There was a bed, a trunk, a table and chairs, and a sideboard with glasses and a bottle of amber liquid.

She looked them up and down as they entered, then nodded to her crewmember that he could go. The two men stood quietly, waiting.

"Sit," Lassa said. They sat. She poured three glasses and set two of them down in front of her captives. Or were they guests, now? Raising her own glass, she said, "To absent friends."

They drank. It was whiskey, and it burned warm and sweet as it slipped down Del's throat.

"I only met Bokk once," the Pantoran said, leaning back in her chair and putting her boots on her table as she rolled the empty glass between her fingers. "I'll bet he was glad to die doing something he believed in. With any luck, we all go that way. Making a difference."

Del's eyes slid over to Gideon's, whose face was carefully neutral. Lassa didn't miss the glance, and she emitted a soft, throaty laugh. "So you're thinking those are strange words coming from the leader of the Blood Bone Order, right? Would it surprise you to learn that I let that horned sleemo and what crewmembers you didn't blast go on his way—after lightening his load, of course?"

Another exchanged look, then Gideon nodded slowly. "We thought you'd kill them all. It's what all the stories about you say."

Lassa reached for the bottle and refilled her glass, waving that they should slide theirs over for the same treatment. "Don't you know, darling boys," she purred, "that stories are fiction? Oh, I've taken my share of lives—but always to save my own, or those of my crew. I just like to let people *think* I'm going to skin them alive.

It makes capturing ships so much easier, and poses much less damage to cargo."

Del was dumbfounded. Gideon started laughing. "Well," he said after a moment, "you certainly fooled us. And good Captain Kurjak, too."

Del smothered a smile at his last memory of Kurjak, hurling insults as Rhayme's pirates tied him to his command chair. He wondered if the Devaronian had figured out that he could escape.

Gideon took another drink of the whiskey. "This is excellent, by the way."

Lassa cocked a pale-lavender brow. "Partisans generally don't know much about fine alcohol." There was no trace of suspicion in the comment, but Del wondered.

Gideon nodded. "My brother and I don't know about vintages or cask-whatever, or things like that. We just know when something isn't swill."

"Oho, this is definitely not swill. Aged Tevraki whiskey. Very good stuff. But I break it out on rare occasions. Like saying goodbye to old friends." Her good humor faded, replaced by wistfulness.

"I knew Saw, back in the day. Never knew his sister, Steela. Wish I had—she'd have made a fine member of the order. She might be still alive today had she . . . Well." She swirled the amber liquid in the glass. "Let's just say you partisans sure like to burn through your numbers."

It was a good opening and Gideon took it. "Empire likes to do it even more than we do," he said darkly. "That's why we fight. And we'll keep fighting with the last breath in our bodies."

"We all fight in our own ways," she said.

Maybe it was the whiskey—Gideon had been right, it was excellent, and it was strong, too—but Del piped up and said, "If you don't like killing . . . why are you helping us? Why not help the Rebel Alliance, or stay out of it all together?"

She nodded. "Fair question. It's because I'm sentimental." Her gold eyes glinted with a hint of amusement, and her smile was warm. Del had not been prepared for how attractive she was. Nor had he been prepared to admire her quite so much. She reminded him of Iden—strong, take-charge, beautiful, smart. . . .

He frowned a little. Iden? Why was he thinking about her? *Oh yes,* he thought, *it's definitely the whiskey.*

"I've been around awhile. I've seen a lot of things. I know when things are simmering, ready to boil over. When something's going to disappear and never be seen in the galaxy again. The partisans are becoming extinct. You were dying out when Jedha happened. The Rebel Alliance—they're growing. They don't need me." She smiled an almost motherly smile. "You do."

The answer seemed to surprise Gideon, and by this point, as he drained his glass and held it out for more, all Del felt he could safely do was stay silent. After a moment, Lassa said, "And so, that is a very long answer to your question, Gid. And the answer to another question as well. Yes, I will see that you get to Jeosyn safely."

Jeosyn. At last, Del thought, they had name for the Dreamers' base of operations.

"I'm heading there with some supplies for the Dreamers, so it won't even take long." Lassa smiled slyly. "But I bet you knew that."

Del grinned sheepishly. Gideon said, "Bokk knew."

"Very good. But as you've got no way of paying for your transportation, I'll have to take it out of you in work. I have a couple of bunks open for you, and some clean clothes you can wear. But first"—she wrinkled her nose delicately—"you both need a bath."

CHAPTER 9

"Hey, Iden, wait up!"

Captain Iden Versio had captivated Tarvyn Lareka from the moment she showed up on the *Determination*, dressed in TIE pilot black, wrapped in Imperial legacy, and crowned with the rare aura of a Death Star survivor. When she was in a room, she owned it, even if she stood quietly at attention like all the rest of them. Hers was not a common beauty, but stemmed from her straight back and fierce dark eyes. And, Tarvyn had to admit, her smooth, warm-hued skin and lustrous black hair also helped make her unforgettable.

Of course, conspiracy theories had abounded as to why Iden Versio had survived when so very many others had not. *Double agent,* someone had whispered. *Force-user,* others said. Her dad arranged for her TIE to be modified, still others said. But anyone who watched her pilot her vessel could see that it wasn't anything other than damn fine skills that had saved her life. In fact, it was the thing that had edged Tarvyn from simple respect to . . . well, kind of a crush, he supposed. He'd never seen such ability. Watching her fly was more like watching an aerial performance than a regular military maneuver.

Which was why he was having a hard time coming to grips with what had just happened.

It had been a skirmish, not a battle, fortunately; one of many that the *Determination* had encountered in its patrols in the Mid Rim. But something about Iden had been off today. While the Empire had defeated the small handful of foolish rebels, Iden had missed shots she should have been easily able to take, and had been slow in coming around at times. He'd overheard their team leader dressing her down, and watched out of the corner of his eye as Iden's cheeks had flushed, though her beautiful face remained as implacable as ever.

Now, as they were heading back from the debriefing, Tarvyn wanted to catch up to her and find out why her game was off.

Maybe something was wrong. Maybe he could help.

She didn't slow, and he had to break into a jog to reach her, taking the time to awkwardly smooth the stubborn tuft of hair that never wanted to obey. He fell into step beside her. She gave him a quick glance, then lowered her head, almost like a reek about to charge, and kept going.

"Iden," he began, but she cut him off.

"I'm fine."

She obviously wasn't, and she had to know it. He

wanted to reach out and take her arm, but knew the gesture wouldn't be welcomed. So he simply said, "You don't seem fine. You missed at least two clear shots, and that's not like you."

"I took out two others."

"Yeah, but I took out *three*, and we both know my count beating yours is not normal."

He grinned, and he saw her start to smile. "Well," she admitted, "you're right about that. I just . . ." She glanced around at the other crewmembers striding briskly past them and lowered her voice. "I just . . . everything changed after the Death Star, you know."

Tarvyn nodded, sobering. He did know.

"I started thinking. About everyone we lost. And I got so angry. And then . . . then I started thinking about Alderaan. I mean—" She brushed a sweat-damp lock of hair from her high forehead. "The rebels attacked a battle station. With no civilians, only people who had signed up to be there. We attacked a *whole planet* that didn't even have defenses."

Tarvyn felt himself grow pale as she spoke, and this time he did reach out to grasp her arm. Gently, in warning.

"This is a bad place to talk," he said. Indeed, heads were already starting to turn in their direction. Others couldn't hear the conversation, but they could see the look of distress on Iden's face—a sure sign, if anyone knew her, that there was something gravely amiss. "We're off duty in two hours. Meet me at the bar. We'll talk more, okay?"

She nodded, and quickly composed herself. Another

thing Tarvyn admired about her. He'd been told his whole life he wore his heart on his sleeve. He blamed his fair coloring—it betrayed him constantly.

"Two hours," she said. "See you then. And Tarvyn?"

"Yeah?"

She smiled. His heart flipped over. "Thanks."

He watched her stride away on her long legs, head high, as if nothing in the world was wrong. But there was, and she'd confided in him.

Tarvyn understood that some people were having a harder time adjusting to the loss of the Death Star than others. Iden was clearly upset. He wanted to help—and he thought he knew how.

He was seated at a table in a little alcove in the back by the time Iden had arrived. They'd both changed into fresh uniforms, and since she was off duty Iden had unpinned her hair from the neat bun she usually wore; it fell loose about her shoulders.

He'd already ordered and was sipping a beer. Iden flagged down the serving droid and ordered a whiskey, neat. They were silent until the droid returned, then they sent it on its way.

Tarvyn waited for her to speak first. "I probably shouldn't have said anything to you," she said.

"No, no," he assured her quickly. "I'm glad you did. Really. I . . . what happened to the Death Star . . . you're not the only one who was shaken up. And I can't imagine how strange it must be to have survived that."

She grimaced and took another sip of the amber beverage. "No," she said, "I don't think anyone can. I can't stop thinking about it. I can't stop seeing Alderaan, either." She lifted dark eyes to his. "Tarvyn . . . we shouldn't have done it."

Tarvyn froze in his seat, his heart thudding rapidly. "Go on," he said.

"I mean . . . the rebel base? Fine. Destroy the Rebellion and the criminals. They brought everything on themselves. But an entire planet?" Her voice rose, and Tarvyn placed a hand on hers to remind her to speak quietly. She didn't pull away. "A lot of hostile, dangerous rebels died that day, there's no doubt about that. But a lot of other people did, too. People who didn't agree with the Rebellion. People who maybe even didn't know what was going on. Children. Resources, animals, plants found nowhere else in the galaxy—all for a display of power. And now we're hunting those few who were offworld for no reason other than that they've had the misfortune of surviving the death of everything they loved."

Tarvyn sat, stunned. It was worse than he'd feared. Iden was identifying with the other "survivors." He was glad he'd asked her to talk. He could get her help.

He squeezed the strong hand that still rested beneath his own. Iden took it as a sign to continue.

"I don't want to be part of mass murder," she said simply. "When I saw Alderaan, a place that offered no real physical threat to the Empire, just—just blown to pieces . . ." She shook her head. "Then the Empire came after those who hadn't even been on the planet. Those poor people are being hunted down like animals. This is wrong, Tarvyn. The Empire says it wants to *help* people, but instead it's erased an entire planet filled with them.

How can I have seen that with my own eyes and be able to look myself in the mirror ever again?"

Tarvyn stared at her, trying to mitigate his horror at her words. "Iden—"

But it was as if the emotions had been pent up inside her and now spilled forth in a flood. "The Empire must be swept away. It needs to go. And you know what else? I think the partisans were right. I think violence is the only thing the Empire really understands. It certainly knows how to utilize it against helpless people."

"Iden?" Tarvyn said gently, his heart full of pain for her. "This isn't you. You're just . . . confused. I'm going to help you, Iden. Others will, too. You'll see."

Her eyes widened suddenly, and her gaze slid away to the rest of the bar. Watching. Worried.

With his other hand, the one that wasn't placed over Iden's, Tarvyn clicked off the recording, then transmitted it to their commanding officer. A few seconds later, it vibrated in his hand and he read a message: *Coming. You did the right thing.*

"It's going to be all right," he said. "I promise. I remember: Right after the explosion, Commander Udrai took our squadron aside. He told us that if any of us felt troubling thoughts, to come forward and ask for help. It's normal to feel like that, and especially since you survived it—"

Iden jerked her hand back and clenched it into a fist. "Tarvyn . . . what have you done?"

He felt bad about having deceived her, but it was for her own good. "I recorded this conversation, and I just sent it to Commander Udrai."

Iden bolted upright, knocking the chair over. She looked around, wild-eyed—an animal in a trap. The distinctive *tramp tramp* of stormtrooper boots could be heard even over the bar's music.

Apprehension spurted through Tarvyn. Commander Udrai had said he was heading over, to take Iden to see someone. To talk. To heal her. Why were there stormtroopers? He rose, too, stepping forward and holding out a hand.

"Hang on a minute, guys, there's some mistake. Iden and I are going to see Commander Udrai. We were just leaving."

"Stand aside, Lieutenant Lareka," came the clipped voice of the lead trooper. "Captain Iden Versio, you are under arrest for sedition. Please come with us."

Iden's fist was still clenched. For an awful, wonderful moment, Tarvyn honestly thought she was going to fight them. Then slowly, with visible effort, Iden relaxed her hand. She did not resist as two of them stepped beside her, one on each side, seizing her wrists and snapping a pair of stun cuffs on them. Then they grasped her upper arms with their armor-covered fingers and escorted her from the premises.

Just as she was almost out the door, Iden looked over her shoulder. The look of haunted betrayal in her eyes was like a blaster bolt to his heart.

"Lieutenant," said the remaining stormtrooper. A hand closed hard on Tarvyn's elbow. "I'll need you to come with me."

Tarvyn felt the blood drain from his face as he stared into the black sockets of the trooper's helmet.

What have you done? Iden had said.

What, indeed?

"The daughter of renowned Admiral Garrick Versio of the Imperial Security Bureau and famous artist Zeehay Versio may be a traitor to the glorious Empire," holo-journalist Alton Kastle stated, with just the right amount of horror in his smooth voice. *"Captain Iden Versio has been recorded as spouting lies about the Empire and inciting violence, denouncing the brave subjects of the Death Star battle station who lost their lives while she survived. This is not in keeping with the behavior of the highly decorated captain hitherto, but the words are damning.*

"She is slated for an immediate court-martial. Hero of the Empire Admiral Nasha Garvan will prosecute, while the specialized legal-analyst droid HM-12 will provide proper defense as required by Imperial Navy law."

Lieutenant Jha Eka, assistant to Admiral Garrick Versio, stared, mouth open in an unprofessional, unconscious expression of shock, as the story unfolded. Then he swallowed and straightened his gaberwool jacket. The admiral needed to be told about this, and Eka could not imagine that his reaction would be pleasant.

Still, Eka knew his duty.

Versio was eating his lunch, a meal of steak, brightly colored roasted vegetables, and cuanut bread, as Eka rushed in without knocking.

"Sir," Eka began, his voice tense and strained, "your daughter—"

The young man fell silent as he realized his employer was already watching.

His back to Eka, Versio simply held up a hand. Eka remained quiet and breathed deeply, attempting to recover his composure during what, surely, had to be the worst public relations disaster the admiral had ever had to navigate.

Both men watched as images of Iden flashed on the vidscreen: Iden in stun cuffs. Iden surrounded by stormtroopers. Angry crowds surging toward her as she was roughly shoved into a shuttle. Only after Kastle had assured the viewers that the HoloNet would "continue to follow this shocking, developing story" did the admiral wipe his mouth with a fine linen napkin and, still without turning, speak.

"There's a datapad and a personal holoprojector on the corner of my desk. I imagine you're going to be swamped by journalists. The datapad is for you, the hologram for them—and that is all you are to give to them, for the moment. Need I remind you, you are to say nothing to anyone about this unless I instruct you to."

Eka blinked, stunned. Damn, but the admiral was a model of calm control. The lieutenant was embarrassed at his own earlier distress. "Of course, sir."

"Thank you. That will be all."

Even though he had been dismissed, Eka lingered. "Sir, I—is there anything you need?"

"If there is, I'll ask," Versio said calmly. "And Eka?"

"Sir?"

"Never, ever enter this room without knocking again."

"Of course not, sir. Apologies, sir."

． · ·

The door closed behind the chastened assistant. Versio continue to watch the "breaking news," finishing his meal as they played Tarvyn's recording over images of Iden shamed and in stun cuffs, and smiled slightly.

CHAPTER 10

As Seyn diligently practiced her forgery skills in a dusty corner beneath a chunk of fake white Muunilinst marble, she suspected, not for the first time, that Rudaga was a little bit too happy to have a "slave" to do his bidding.

The merchant was a sly, singularly unpleasant Dug who emitted a strange odor reminiscent of old cheese. His species had a long snout from which dangled thin, fleshy tendrils, and a squat body. More unusual was the fact that they walked on their arms and used their feet, which had long, dexterous toes, the way most other beings used their hands. He had been working with the Empire for as long as there had been one, he liked to boast. "Got the shop cheap back toward the end of the Clone Wars," he told Seyn one evening. "The former owner had been sniffed out by the Jedi for dealing in black-market items. Fortunately, the Republic eventually became the Empire, and what it gained in worlds it appeared to lose in scruples." Then, seeming to recall exactly to whom he was speaking, he amended quickly, "Well, at least when it comes to little things like the black market."

"Information is a useful commodity," Seyn had replied. "Sometimes the Empire must get its hands a little dirty for the greater good."

She'd done her research on him, of course. Rudaga had been useful, as far as it went. But lately his tips hadn't panned out, and some of his sources had turned up dead, so he was quickly becoming a liability. She suspected he wouldn't be terribly missed. The shop was filled, if not with actual antiques, at least with things that were certainly old, some of which smelled as bad as the merchant who sold them.

There was nothing resembling station security, as there had been on Tellik IV, which was officially managed by the Empire. Here, each merchant had to hire their own thugs, and Rudaga was no exception. The pair of Trandoshans who guarded the Dug and his merchandise were brothers. They were ugly, and crude, but while they may have made comments in their own language—which Seyn understood perfectly—they did so under their breath, and they did not overtly harass her. It suited her well enough. They wouldn't be around too much longer, anyway.

Versio had sent a few fake spies Rudaga's way, to lend Seyn's cover story some verisimilitude. He had been careful, though, to not select anyone who would recognize her. The "spies" accepted the datachips she gave them and dutifully carried them back to NavInt. If they were foolish enough to attempt to break the code, they would receive false "information." Few thought of Seyn as someone with a sense of humor, but she was terribly amused by all of this.

The day came at last. Seyn had spent extensive hours in simulators, and excelled in live-fire exercises, but her field experience was limited. She was looking forward to transitioning from the dim rooms with dozens of vid-screens to a place where she could actively participate. Things were going to be quite different—starting in approximately—

She heard the sound of blasterfire and screaming.

Now, she amended.

Even as she scrambled to get out of her alcove, the Dug's foot shot out and dragged her from it.

"Seyn! What's going on? Is this part of your cover?" He anxiously shifted his weight from one hand to the other.

She waved him furiously to silence. "Yes, yes!" she hissed. "You'll be fine." Until this moment, her world had been one of calmness, coolness, calculation, and focus. Now her heart was beating so *fast.* "This is all under control. Go and wait in your office, this will all be over in a moment. And take your Trandoshans with you; my contact is very skittish."

He grunted and hurried off to hide like the coward he was, his old-cheese odor lingering in the air for a moment. One foot waved to his bodyguards, and they followed him into the office.

Seyn wrinkled her nose. Yes, the galaxy was going to be much better off without him.

Outside, the screaming increased. Seyn took a deep

breath, remembered the helpless, frightened slave girl she was trying to be, and stumbled forward with such false panic she tripped on an old statuette of the Voolu-karian fertility god Kuk'waibi. Kuk'waibi's stone Spear of Desire stabbed her arm. It would leave a mark. Good. She used the sting to bring tears to her eyes.

She went to the front of the shop, looking around as if in wild terror, but in reality assessing the situation.

They were coming down the main corridor now. There were three of them: a male Kage, a Twi'lek fe-male, and a human male. Seyn was quite certain they knew exactly what they were doing. This group was vio-lent and willing to sacrifice themselves if necessary, but they were far from stupid. Some of the shops they ran straight past. Others, they paused and fired into. Still other shops exploded as small, blinking devices were rolled inside.

Seyn had to time her move just right. It was a risk—partisans of any stripe didn't care about collateral dam-age to the civilian population, but they were skilled. She had to trust they wouldn't fire randomly or decide to kill someone just for the hell of it.

They were three shops down . . . two . . .

Now.

Seyn ran out of the antiquities shop, sobbing, shout-ing and pointing back the way she had come, "He's hiding in the office!" Her arms were bare, so they could see the bruises and the freshly made injury courtesy of Kuk'waibi, and the neckline of her threadbare tunic re-vealed a slender throat encased in a shock collar.

"Move!" shouted the Kage, his pale-red eyes blazing and his skin the gray color of stone. He didn't slow his speed, leaping clear over her, hitting the corridor, and rolling to his feet in a staggering display of acrobatic athleticism.

Seyn was running out of the line of fire in a pattern that would bring her around behind the oncoming rush of Dreamers. She was barely clear when they started firing, stepping in closer until they had reached the office door.

If Rudaga and the Trandoshan guards screamed, the sound was drowned out by blasterfire. Once they were satisfied that Rudaga would never send another message to the Empire, the Dreamers moved on. As they turned and headed down the corridor toward their next targets, the Twi'lek, a female with rich teal coloring and striking purple eyes, paused long enough to give Seyn a searching glance. Her eyes lingered on the shock collar.

Then she followed her fellow rebels. And so did Seyn. She raced after them, not begging them to take her, not yet. Just running with them, and standing back, and picking up pieces of debris to throw while the others used their blasters and their bombs. The smell of smoke and burnt flesh filled her nostrils and caused her to cough.

How the human heard the sound over the cacophony, Seyn didn't know. He spared her a quick, angry glance from hard eyes.

"Get lost, kid," he shouted. The dismissal was amusing, considering the speaker was obviously not much older than Seyn.

"Take me with you!" Seyn cried. "I hated Rudaga, I hate everyone here. Please!"

They didn't reply, so she kept following, kept out of

the way—and kept helping them. Finally, they seemed to have finished what they had come to do. Behind them, they left a trail of debris, fire, people wailing in fear and agony, and alarms wailing in belated, useless warning—

—and bodies. Lots of bodies.

Seyn had memorized the layout of the station down to some of the finest details, and she knew that Docking Bay 32 was up ahead. This time, instead of Dreamers creating corpses as they went, the floor in front of them was littered with the dead. Someone had cleared their retreat path. The three partisans and the human Imperial agent didn't slow, simply leaping over the bodies and continuing on.

They had to be close to their vessel at this point. Again, the Twi'lek glanced at Seyn. But this time, she shouted, "Get over here! Hurry!"

Seyn hurried, sprinting toward them and moving behind the Twi'lek. The human tossed a grenade back down the corridor the way they had come. It exploded with much more power than the ones they had used previously, and the resulting pile of rubble provided an effective block against any pursuit. Seyn allowed herself an elated grin. This role she was playing, this Seyn the Slave—surely she would be ecstatic.

There were two final bodies, sprawled at the entrance to the docking area proper. The human entered a code and the doors slid open. Awaiting them on the other side was a ship, a little worse for the wear, but still spaceworthy. The portal to open space had already been opened, but a faint glow of blue light indicated the presence of a magnetic field.

The ship's ramp was down. Standing on it and waiting for the Dreamers, as Meeko had waited for Versio and Hask at Tellik IV not so long before, was a gray-furred, elderly Chadra-Fan. Barely a meter tall, with enormous ears and a snub-nosed muzzle set in a batlike face, he peered, blinking shiny black eyes in shock, at Seyn, smaller than any of them except for himself, tagging along behind them.

"Piikow!" the Twi'lek shouted. "We have to get a collar off!"

"Oh dear," Piikow said, his ears twitching nervously. "We don't really . . . hm, hang on!" He ducked out of sight as the partisans began to clatter up the ramp.

A hand closed, hard, on Seyn's arm, yanking her off her feet and spinning her around. It was the young human.

"Not you," he said. "We'll try to remove the collar, but that's it. You're on your own."

Seyn stared at him, the horror in her eyes not entirely feigned. A firm embracer of redundancy, she'd had two different backup plans, but both were useless now that she was sealed on the wrong side of the collapsed corridor. If the Dreamers refused to take her with them, the plan would fall apart. She'd be able to get out of the station safely, of course; the Empire would see to that. But too much would be public knowledge, and the Dreamers now knew her face. The mission would be compromised. She would have to sit it out—and Seyn couldn't bear that.

"Please, no!" She put everything into the words. "I'm trapped here now; they'll think I helped you!"

"You should have stayed out of it." The human was

implacable, but even as he spoke the Twi'lek clattered down the ramp. She carried a small tool.

"She comes with us," the Twi'lek snapped.

"But—"

"My mission, my rules." The beautiful teal-skinned woman leaned down and gazed into Seyn's eyes. "What kind of collar is it?"

"Explosive," Seyn said. "It'll go off if I leave the station or if it's removed improperly. Can—can you get it off?" The decision for Seyn to wear the collar was a risk, but a slave without one would be too suspicious. It was a safe bet that the partisans, who were constantly forced to improvise, would be able to remove the collar. And if not, Seyn always carried the key with her. If worst came to worst, she could claim to have stolen it but not know how to use it.

"Oh no, no, we're not doing this!" the man said. "Dahna, you could kill us all!"

"No, no," the Chadra-Fan insisted in his warbling, raspy voice. "That's not how this works. It will delay the explosion, but not stop it, so you'll have to hurry!"

"Got it," Dahna said. She pressed the device to the locking mechanism on the collar. It whirred and hummed. Then there was a soft snick and the lock opened.

Quick as a thought, the Twi'lek grabbed the collar, sprinted back to the door, opened it, and flung the collar back down the corridor. She quickly closed the door, pivoted, and raced to the ship. "Nadrine, get us out of here!"

The ramp was already being retracted as Seyn ran up it, dropping the now-unnecessary collar key. Then it slammed shut behind her and she was on the ship, diving for a seat and fastening the crash webbing as a fifth member of the crew, a tall human female with reddish-brown hair, was hitting buttons. Beside her in a cockpit clearly never designed for a Chadra-Fan sat Piikow, his tiny legs dangling as he operated a small handheld device.

"Magnetic field down in three, two—" he counted.

The ship lifted off, hovered.

"One!"

The glow that outlined the starfield disappeared. Faster than Seyn had expected, the ship surged through into the star-spotted darkness of open space.

Behind them there was an explosion from the corridor, and bright light from the portals flooded the cabin. The ship rocked but kept going. A heartbeat later the tiny dots that were stars turned into streaks of white as the partisans and their new ally made the jump into hyperspace.

Everyone, it seemed, let out a collective breath.

Then Dahna spoke. "Kaev, you're still new, so I'm going to cut you some slack." The young human partisan seemed startled, and glanced at Seyn before opening his mouth to respond.

Dahna cut him off. "Never, ever question the leader of a mission. Whatever they do. If they say shoot, you shoot. If they say die, you die. And if they say take along the slave who's just fought on your side to the best of her ability, guess what, you do that, too. Are we clear?"

"The explosion—"

"Are. We. *Clear?*"

Seyn had to admit, she'd held a stereotype of Twi'lek females as soft and kind. The one taking down the now subdued human was nothing of the sort. She was a goddess of righteous anger, fierce and yet in perfect control, and the twitching of the long, graceful lekku that fell from either side of her head was ominous rather than pleasant.

"Yeah," Kaev said. "We're clear."

"Good. Okay, everyone divest." They freed themselves from their crash webbing and got to their feet. All wore nondescript gray flight suits, which they began to unfasten. Seyn watched in surprise. Flight suits weren't the most comfortable gear, but usually crews wore them until they reached their destinations.

She became even more confused when they pushed their hands down the necks of their shirts.

"Um," Seyn began, and then fell silent when Dahna brought something out and showed it to her.

It was a small orb, similar to the explosive jewelry that Bokk's partisans had worn at the Singularity. This one, however, and the others the two males were retrieving from beneath their clothes, wasn't painted or otherwise disguised as a clay bead. A small piece of what looked like black metal was attached to each one.

Dahna held out her other hand. In it was a detonator.

Seyn stared at the explosives, then up at Dahna. "We wear them all the time when we go on a mission," the Twi'lek said quietly. "In case something goes wrong— we don't want to be caught and tortured by the Empire. And sometimes we know we're on a one-way trip going in."

"I see," Seyn said. She knew the partisans didn't shy away from suicide bombings. She hadn't known that every mission had the potential to become one.

The Kage gathered up the personal-sized bombs and took them back to another part of the ship for safekeeping. Dahna seemed to shake off the solemnity of the divesting.

"There, that's done. I don't know about the rest of you, but I always get hungry after one of these runs. Anyone else want anything?"

A chorus of nos greeted her, except from Kaev, who decided to stay sullenly silent.

Dahna went to a compartment in the ship's bulkhead. She removed two ration cubes, a container of nutritive milk, and a single spiky, slightly bruised meiloorun fruit.

"Go easy with that," the Kage said as he returned to the main cabin. "We're getting low on—well, everything."

"Don't worry. *Opportunity* should be arriving soon," Dahna replied.

"It had better. If it doesn't, the Empire won't have to worry about us. We'll have starved to death."

"We'll be fine. Even that growing boy of yours," Dahna reassured him as she helped herself to the rations and walked over to where Seyn sat. Seyn let her eyes flicker up, then down.

Dahna sat down beside Seyn and handed her a cube, the milk, and the meiloorun. Seyn accepted the milk and cube, but shook her head at the proffered piece of fruit. "Thank you," she said, glancing at the Kage, "but this is plenty."

Dahna smiled a sad, bittersweet smile. "I know those words," she said. "Those are the words of a slave. Want to know how I know?"

Looking up at her cautiously, Seyn nodded.

"I was a slave myself. Ever since I was an adolescent. The man who took me and half my village said he liked how I *danced*." Dahna spat the word, then laughed humorlessly. "He'd never seen me dance."

She looked over at Seyn. "You ever have to 'dance' for your master?" When Seyn shook her head, Dahna nodded, looking a little relieved. "Well, thank goodness for small favors. What *did* you do for him?"

Seyn suspected the query came from a genuine place of concern—one slave to another. But by the way the others were listening now, she also knew there was a deeper layer to the question. They had just—to the best of their knowledge—risked their lives to free her and had taken her with them. They wanted to know what she might have done to help the Empire, and also could do for *them*.

Slavers, rebels—they're all the same, she thought, and answered, with what she hoped was the proper beaten-down shyness of a former slave, "I know Rudaga was into some pretty bad things. Spying for whoever paid him. The black market. When he found out I knew how to read and write Basic, he put me to work in his shop. I helped him with numbers, cataloging—that sort of thing."

But the actual former slave was shaking her head. "Honey . . . it's all right. I know you did more. You had to have done more, or else he'd just hire someone and pay them starvation wages."

Seyn feigned hesitation, looking around at the faces that were now turned toward her. Except for Kaev, who was still stinging from Dahna's upbraiding, they seemed more curious than suspicious.

"I have a steady hand and a sharp eye," she said. "He put me to work forging. Letters, documents—you know, certificates of authenticity. Things to make stolen goods seem to be legitimate. Things like that."

Now even Kaev was looking thoughtful. "Do you know languages?"

Seyn shook her head. "Only Basic and Huttese. My mast—Rudaga wanted to make sure I couldn't eavesdrop on some of his conversations. I'm sorry."

"No need to apologize. When we get to the base, we'll see just how good you are at forging," Dahna said. "I know you're ashamed of what you had to do, but now you can turn that skill to something worthwhile. Something that matters. Do you know who we are?"

"No. I just know you killed Rudaga and others who were helping the Empire. So I'm guessing you're rebels."

"Of a sort," Dahna said. "We call ourselves the Dreamers. We're what's left of the real partisans—people like Saw Gerrera. I'm sure your master must have known about us."

Seyn nodded solemnly, and Dahna continued. "What you saw back there . . . we do things like that a lot. And sometimes we do things that seem cruel, but they're necessary. I think I can arrange for you to stay with us, if you would like to. Otherwise, we can take you somewhere safe."

Seyn bit her lip and looked around. "You saved me," she said. "I want to repay that. I'll stay with you, if you'll have me."

Dahna looked around at her crew for a minute, the tips of her lekku twitching as she pondered something. "Kaev, Ru—you should go take a look at that new tool that got us our newest recruit. Piikow, you were telling me you could use it to do the same thing on thermal detonators, right?"

The Kage and the human, of course, could see right through the Twi'lek's request, but the Chadra-Fan clearly didn't. "Absolutely!" Piikow's furry face was filled with enthusiasm. "Let me show you the schematics."

All three rose and went to the front of the cabin, allowing their commander and the "new recruit" some privacy.

Gently, Dahna took Seyn's hand and placed the fruit in her palm. "It was awhile before I told anyone," she said quietly. "I felt ashamed. It took the Mentor to show me that none of what happened to me was my fault. Maybe Rudaga didn't make you dance." She indicated Seyn's bare arms. "But I can see the marks. He wasn't a gentle master. Did you ever try to kill him?"

The words and the soothing, gentle voice in which they were uttered were such a bizarre juxtaposition that Seyn lifted her eyes from her plate.

"No," she said. Even though the entire story was fake, somehow, these words stung. Seyn was fond of this "character" she'd created. She didn't want Seyn the Slave to look like a coward. "But . . . I wish I had."

"Don't."

The Twi'lek was full of surprises. "Why not?" Seyn asked.

"Because that kind of killing is personal. And when it gets personal, it gets ugly, and some of that ugliness spills onto you."

She wasn't looking at Seyn as she spoke; her eyes were distant, unfocused. Seyn had debriefed enough agents to know that expression. It tended to hang, like a miasma, only around those who knew from experience what they were talking about.

"But . . . isn't what *you're* doing personal?" she inquired. "Killing people, taking their lives—I mean, that seems personal to me."

It wasn't personal at all. But it seemed like the sort of thing Seyn the Slave would have asked.

"You can't think of it like that," Dahna said. "You have to remember what we—and now you, too—are fighting for. We're fighting to end what happens to people like you and me. Oh, the Empire doesn't come out and endorse it officially, but I have danced a time or two for those who wore command caps. The Empire knows it happens, and they just don't care."

Her lovely face was hard as she continued. "They don't care about anything except themselves and that horrible, *evil* man who shuts himself away from everyone. They don't care about the billions whose worlds they've destroyed to get their metals, or their kyber crystals, or whatever the hell it is they're looking for this week. They don't care who dies or who lives. It's all for the glory of the Empire, honey, and don't you forget it."

"I won't," Seyn said earnestly.

And she wouldn't, either. The treasonous words were emblazoned in her memory.

Smiling at Dahna, she bit into the meiloorun.

CHAPTER 11

It had been years since Iden had visited her home-world. She'd always assumed that, one day, she'd return. Eventually. It was not a place with the happiest of memories; better things had happened to her at the Academy and during the months she'd been assigned to the Death Star's TIE fighter squadron. Vardos was where she had been born, in a comfortable, gleaming apartment in one of the high-rising buildings in the capital city of Kestro. It was where she'd lain awake at night, listening to her parents argue. Where she had kissed her mother goodbye as Zeehay Versio had left for a new assignment on Coruscant, and then to other worlds seemingly as often as Iden changed her uniform. Where Iden had been raised—more by Headmaster Gleb of the Future Imperial Leaders Preparatory School than by her own parents—studying human and alien anatomy before she was ten to know the most vulnerable place of attack.

Where she had killed for the first time, at age fifteen.

Her brief time on the moon of Yavin had been Iden's first experience with anything resembling a place that wasn't almost completely covered with duracrete and transparisteel.

She looked down at the city of her birth through the shuttle's windows as the vessel descended; at its orderly roads, all of them leading to the Archive, the world's most secure and valuable building. How odd and upside down everything was, Iden thought. When she'd imagined returning, she had seen herself doing so in triumph. She'd dared visualize parades along the city streets, perhaps with father and daughter participating side by side in positions of honor. The streets would be crowded as the planet welcomed the return of its favorite son, the man who had brought them under the benevolent and protective wing of the Empire, and its best-loved daughter, the hero of the Empire.

There were crowds gathering at the base of the Archive, all right. They were, as Vardosians always were, orderly; there had never been a riot here during Iden's lifetime. But the crowds had not come in anticipation of a parade. They had come hoping to get a glimpse of the traitor.

The shuttle settled down on the building's roof. One of the two stormtroopers who had been sent to "escort" Iden rose and strode to her, towering over her as she sat with the crash webbing on.

"Hold out your hands," he said brusquely. He, his companion, and nearly everyone else outside of Inferno

Squad itself were under the impression that she was truly a traitor, and while the trooper wasn't rude—Iden was still, after all, Admiral Versio's daughter—his contempt for her was evident in both the tone of his voice and the disapproving frown that wasn't yet hidden by a helmet.

Wordlessly, looking up into his cold eyes, Iden stuck out her hands. The second stormtrooper watched, his blaster trained on her, while the first one snapped a pair of stun cuffs on her wrists.

"You know how these work, right?"

"Yes," she said, coolly. "Of course I do."

"Got a big crowd out there," the other was saying. "We deliver her to J-Sec and then we wash our hands of her. They get to handle this from there. Blasters on stun."

"Copy that," the first one said. Just before he put the bucket on, slipping into the comfort of plastoid uniform anonymity, he said, "Anybody else, they'd execute. You . . . you get a job." He shook his head in disgust and put the bucket on.

As Iden followed him down the ramp onto the roof of the Hub, she was glad that she'd seen them both set their blasters to stun. Even so, she felt a phantom, anticipatory itch between her shoulder blades.

Gleb was waiting for her, clad in the familiar uniform Iden remembered from her childhood: dark-blue shirt and trousers, with a wide maroon belt. The uniform wasn't Imperial. It was unique to Vardos, denoting the wearer as someone who had been granted certain powers and rank in the eyes of the Empire, but who, obviously, wasn't an official member. The uniform was also distinctly non-Aqualish in design, and that was deliberate. Its lines gave Gleb the profile of a stocky, rather dumpy human—if one could get past her four red eyes and two enormous tusks.

Gleb stood at attention, waiting for Iden to be escorted to her. She had one three-fingered hand openly on her weapon, even though she was flanked by several armed Jinata Security officers. There were others gathered on the large rooftop: prominent Imperial officers and high-ranking representatives of the primary nonhuman species. Above, getting the best angle possible, hovered a cam droid broadcasting the drama live to the HoloNet.

"Iden Versio," Gleb said, speaking through the gold-colored translator around her thick throat. She spoke loudly, for the benefit of the broadcast and the crowd. "It has been a long time. How low the mighty have fallen."

"Hello, Major Gleb," Iden said. "Please allow me to thank you for the opportunity to work for you."

Gleb narrowed her top set of blood-colored, glittering eyes. "It was only as a favor to your father. Although you have dishonored him tremendously, his great love for you believes that you can redeem yourself with hard work. Perhaps you will remember some of what you once learned here, before you saw fit to speak ill of the glorious Empire."

The lessons. The school. The punishments.

Iden's jaw clenched, and she loosened it with an effort. "Perhaps I will," she said.

Gleb gave the Aqualish equivalent of a harrumph. "Do not think you will receive any special treatment."

"No, of course not." Iden almost snapped the words.

She was supposed to act as if she felt she should be cowed but wasn't. It was extremely easy, because Gleb was starting to irritate her.

Gleb gazed at her for a long moment—long enough, Iden thought uncharitably, to make sure that the Holo-Net cam droid could get a good close-up of her face. Then Gleb addressed her officers.

"Take her away," the Aqualish instructed, then turned and strode briskly toward the door.

The two officers, a Zabrak and a Duros, seized Iden's arms and all but shoved her to the entrance of the second waiting shuttle. Iden stumbled but caught herself, and glared at the Zabrak. *All for a good show*, she thought. She couldn't wait till this was over.

There was no chance to speak with Gleb in the shuttle to the J-Sec headquarters. As the shuttle settled into the hangar where the official vessels of Jinata Security were located, hundreds congregated outside there, too, held back by crowd-control droids. And there were HoloNet cam droids capturing everything while Iden was walked, the Duros and the Zabrak each holding one of her arms, through a gray durasteel walkway to the detached buildings that were Gleb's private living area.

Even then, the two officers who had manhandled Iden on the rooftop followed them into the gleaming, flat-topped metallic structures draped with long red banners adorned with the white cog of the Empire. "The instructions of your father," Gleb said, bridling slightly. It obviously displeased the Aqualish to be required to submit to anything that might make her look less than completely capable. "You see, Iden? You may only be under house arrest, but there will be no escaping."

Iden stayed silent.

"Iden will accompany me to my office," Gleb instructed the J-Sec guards. "I will brief her about what is expected of her during her . . . *stay*. Come on, girl."

Iden followed Gleb into her office. The door hissed closed behind them. "Do not worry," Gleb told her, "this place is entirely private."

As far as you know, Iden thought but did not say. She held out her hands to Gleb and looked meaningfully at them. Gleb unlocked them, glancing down at Iden's wrists.

"They did not use the right size," she said. Iden's wrists were raw.

"Tell me something I don't know," Iden said.

"I am not going to treat them," Gleb said. "An injury will help make everything more believable."

She's enjoying this, Iden realized, then wondered why she was surprised. When she was younger, she'd idolized Gleb for a short time. The Aqualish had stepped in to fill the void created by her parents' divorce. With her mother traveling the galaxy and her father home only irregularly, Gleb was the only adult authority figure the young Iden had.

It wasn't that Gleb was physically cruel. She was too smart for that. No, it was the subtle things. She liked to be in control—of everyone and everything. And now she was going to oversee not just Admiral Versio's only child, but Admiral Versio's grand plan for Inferno Squad.

"Have you watched any of the coverage?" Gleb inquired. Iden sank into one of the chairs. Elsewhere in Gleb's life, she espoused the austerity of the Empire. But here, in her own residence, it seemed she enjoyed her creature comforts. She went to a sideboard and opened it, taking out a bottle of golden-brown liquid and a glass.

"No, I wasn't allowed to," Iden replied.

"You should. It is glorious. Everyone hates you." Gleb poured the beverage into the glass, one specially designed to accommodate her tusks, and drank. It was an ugly, slurping sound. Both sets of her scarlet eyes were bright.

"Thanks, I'll pass. I had my fill of that at my court-martial. I just hope it's enough to attract attention. How in the hell are the Dreamers going to get to me if you've got me locked up, anyway?" The thought of this farce dragging on for more than a few weeks was too unpleasant to contemplate.

"I do not think you understand quite how unpopular you are. All you need to do is keep that up. Make everyone around you believe that you do not *really* regret what you said about the Empire. That you are tolerating this only because there is no way out for you. The Dreamers are hungry, and they are angry, and they are desperate. They will come for you, all right."

Iden leaned back in the sofa and rubbed her eyes. Those involved in her court-martial and sentencing had gone easy on her because of her father, who, even though he was supposedly "outraged," had gone on record as being convinced that his daughter would change. She knew what was usually done to prisoners—especially traitors. She had been present at interrogations. But even this seemingly lighter sentence was draining.

"In the meantime," Gleb continued, "you will be sharing my quarters. You will have a small area to yourself, including a private courtyard. You have a couple of messages waiting for you." She hesitated, then added, "From your parents."

Iden stiffened. She'd expected to receive an update and instructions from her father upon her arrival in Gleb's house. But her mother . . .

It hadn't been that long since she had seen her mother; when Iden had returned as one of the few survivors of the Death Star, Zeehay had contacted her as soon as she'd been notified. It had been a good talk, though brief. As her illness progressed, Zeehay tired more easily. But Iden wasn't looking forward to this one. Loyal Imperial and respected artist Zeehay Versio might be, but Iden could count on one hand the people outside of Inferno Squad who had the security clearance to be told the truth, and her mother wasn't among that number. Iden had urged her father to reconsider. "Mama's not doing well, and she should know," she had said, but her father shut her down at once.

"This is top secret, Iden. She doesn't have the clearance. I'm surprised you'd even suggest such a thing." The words had stung, because she knew she shouldn't have asked. But she wasn't sorry she had tried. Zeehay Versio's condition would not be improved by her daughter's court-martial.

She nodded at the decanter of brandy. "Don't suppose there's one of those in my room?" She didn't drink often, but some liquid courage might help her handle what she was about to face.

"Of course not," Gleb replied, annoyed. "This is supposed to be something resembling work release, Iden.

You have been found guilty of sedition. You are lucky to even have a bed rather than a cot in the local prison."

Can't risk anyone smelling alcohol on me, Iden thought. *And I bet she loved turning me down.*

"Thought so. Are we done here?"

Gleb took another slurping, dribbling pull on the beverage. "I think so, yes. Up at oh five hundred. You can exercise in the courtyard, and there is a fresh uniform for you in your room. Be ready to go by oh seven hundred. And the work will not be pushing datapads, either. Dismissed."

The rush of resentment at hearing Gleb uttering the order surprised Iden. She greatly outranked the Aqualish, and for a moment she was tempted to remind Gleb of that fact. But Gleb was a key player in this scheme, and in her own way was performing a valuable service to the Empire.

Iden would be gone soon enough, her attention taken up with the meat of the mission. She could afford to let Gleb have a momentary sensation of superiority.

Her room was surprisingly pleasant, if not as luxurious as her former—and present, she supposed—boss's was. There was a small, neatly made bed with a nightstand and an adjustable lamp, a table with a datapad—and a holoprojector.

Rather cowardly, she thought, Iden decided to hear from her father first. It had been deemed too risky for him to contact her during the arrest and court-martial phase, but this particular recording had been earmarked for Gleb.

His image was only about the size of her hand, but even in miniature his presence came through. "If you're watching this, then you have arrived successfully and are in your room at Gleb's residence. This means that we've navigated everything smoothly, and you are now reduced to waiting. I trust, though, that you will rise to the occasion and persevere.

"You have, of course, been isolated from current events, even public ones, until now. Gleb will be able to fill you in on many things, and I've sent along a few bottles of brandy to, ah, lubricate the flow of information and to show the Empire's appreciation of her cooperation."

Iden snorted. So that's where the bottles had come from.

"The others have already embarked on their own journeys to the rendezvous point," Admiral Versio continued. "I have been in irregular contact, so largely they, like you, are on their own. I have confidence, however, that shortly all of you will rendezvous at the Dreamer base of operations and proceed as planned. In the meantime, I suggest when possible without further incriminating yourself that you maintain the façade and keep yourself in the public eye. Gleb will assist in that."

I'll bet she will, Iden thought sourly.

"If there are further developments that you need to know, she will inform you." The hologram disappeared. *Not even a goodbye or good luck.*

Iden had been concerned that her father might say something best not overheard, so she had chosen to view Versio's message inside, away from any prying eyes. But she realized as she looked about the small room that she had not been outside—at least, not without the company of three or four stormtroopers—since the events had begun. Gleb had mentioned a courtyard, and suddenly Iden felt the need to escape even a pleasant confinement.

She took the holoprojector with her. Even if it was overheard, this second message would not harm the mission in any way.

The earlier overcast skies had cleared, and the courtyard was surprisingly pleasant. There was little greenery, admittedly; there was little "greenery" anywhere on the planet, though it was not an ecumenopolis like Coruscant. Not yet, anyway.

But there was a shin'yah tree. As was traditional, it had been planted so that its branches overhung a small stone pool. The water was not completely still, but it flowed, slowly, over an unlipped edge into a second pool. From there it drained so that, out of sight, it would be quickly and efficiently purified and cycled back into perfectly potable, clear liquid. The blue sky and the bright leaves were reflected in the pool, and as Iden watched a breeze rustled the tree. A single scarlet leaf detached itself from its branch and wafted its way down to land in the water.

A thin, crimson curl twisted languidly as the water leached the leaf's pigment. Another curl joined it, and a third, then a fourth. The impression one had was that the dying leaf was bleeding out. Folklore had it that the tree had once been a young woman who had slashed her wrists when forbidden to marry the suitor she had loved.

The water bore the fallen leaf and its billowy scarlet trail slowly toward the edge in a funereal manner. Iden watched it hover there, then gracefully tip over the edge, out of her sight.

The trees had survived, amusingly enough, because of her father, who praised them as a symbol of the planet's devotion to the Empire. Displaying the trees had become a popular pastime for those wanting to stay on the Empire's good side—which was anyone and everyone among the planet's nonhuman populace who had the room to plant them.

This had happened before Iden's birth, but she had watched the holos of his speech—the one that had gotten a red stone statue of him erected—often enough to remember almost all of it. Certainly the most famous lines: "Once the Maiden of the Shin'yah let her life's blood flow, drop by drop, for a great love. And so, too, we of Vardos, the people of the Shin'yah, let our life's blood flow in heroic battle, for love of our Empire."

It amused Iden that while they were a symbol of Vardos's patriotism, the trees were purely ornamental. They yielded no fruit, and the wood did not lend itself to carving or for use as firewood. They were, quite literally, good for nothing—other than propaganda and looking pretty—but that small detail seemed to have escaped her father. They had become a symbol to Versio, and that was sufficient to grant them amnesty when the rest of the planet's vegetation succumbed to the march of duracrete.

Iden was, nonetheless, glad they had been spared. She had a dim memory of a house full of paintings of the white trees and their weeping red leaves, and a mother and father who smiled and spoke kindly to each other.

She grimaced. She could put off the task no longer. She sat on the gray stone side of the pool, carefully put down the holoprojector, and activated it.

She gasped softly.

Her mother—her beautiful, radiant, always smiling mother, who was never unkempt despite her slow decline—looked terrible. Her large, expressive eyes were bloodshot, and her hair was a mess. She stared seemingly straight at Iden as she spoke.

"I don't even know what to say," Zeehay said. Her voice cracked on the last word. "I had to find out about it through the HoloNet. I couldn't believe it, at first. I told Garrick that blond boy had set you up. That my darling Iden, who loved the Empire just as much as I did, would never, *ever* turn her back on it like that.

"But it wasn't a setup. I'm told you're going to be court-martialed. I want you to know I'm going to do whatever I can to help you. I can't bear the thought of losing you. Whatever you did, however you feel . . . it can be changed if they just won't take my baby."

Fresh tears filled Zeehay's eyes and trickled down her dark, sunken cheeks. She wiped them away and for a moment sat silently, pressing her full lips together hard.

"I don't know what happened to you. I don't know who got to you, or why you would say such horrible things. It's not true. The Empire is a force for great justice in this galaxy. It's the only thing that stands between us and the mindless, angry chaos of the Rebellion. What do you think I've been doing all these years? I have a gift, and I've used it to inspire others to join up, to support their Empire, so that we can finally help those who *need* our help!"

She'd done more than just use her gift to inspire others. Zeehay had traveled to planets all over the galaxy, trying to reach the populations with her art. It was on such a mission that she had contracted the disease that was slowly sucking the vibrancy, the good humor, the very life out of her. She'd fought it for four years, but Zeehay and her daughter knew that the time would come when she could fight no longer.

The medical droids had encouraged her to keep painting, to do what she enjoyed as long as she could. They cautioned Iden that undue stress would be detrimental.

One of Iden's hands drifted to the opposite wrist. She squeezed it, hard. Pain blossomed, bright and clear and sharp. Iden needed the pain someplace where she could control it. She was sure that there were no Imperial bugs in Gleb's house, and she was equally sure that Gleb herself had installed means of spying on her new houseguest. And Iden was not going to give her former teacher the chance to gloat over Iden's suffering.

"Baby, I want you to know that whatever happens, I'll always love you. You're my daughter, Iden. You'll always be my daughter. And I'll always be your mother. Whatever you do, whatever you say . . . I can't ever not love you."

Zeehay took a long, quivering breath. "But . . . I have lost my respect for you."

A soft, hurt sound struggled to escape Iden. She bit her lip, hard, and squeezed the cuff injury harder.

"I am . . . shocked, and disillusioned, and—Iden, you didn't just betray the Empire or the Emperor. You betrayed your father. You betrayed *me*. And I'm not sure I can ever forgive you for that."

Mama, no—

Years fell away. Iden stood beside her father, who towered so tall over her then, watching the shuttle lift off the ground, bearing her mother far, far away. Iden wouldn't see her again for years, and never again on Vardos.

It's all right, her father had said. *It's best for all of us that she's gone. She's a Versio in name only. We—you and I—are true Versios, and Versios don't cry, do they?*

No, sir, her five-year-old self had replied in a voice thick with unuttered shrieks of grief. *Versios don't cry.*

Iden gritted her teeth and jabbed her thumb into the raw flesh.

The holographic image smiled weakly through her tears. "But I will try to forgive. Once you understand what you've done, and how wrong you were. But you've got to get to that place. So you get there. And you get there fast."

Zeehay seemed to want to say something more, but she changed her mind. She shook her head and wiped again at her wet face. Then she reached out toward the holorecorder—and was gone.

You get there. You get there fast.

Iden's pain dissolved, replaced by grim determination. Oh, she'd get there, sooner than any of them ever expected. Because once they had found the source of the information leak—once they had ground the Dreamers into the dust and returned victorious as Inferno Squad— Iden would be able to be a captain again. She would be able to tell her mother then that everything she'd said had been a lie, and it was only love of the Empire, not hatred for it, that had given her the courage to get through these awful days.

She lowered her gaze and saw that the pressure on her wrist had caused the wound to reopen, and a drop of red blossomed in the water, then drifted away.

CHAPTER 12

Iden felt like a leashed pet.

She was allowed some liberty, but only under proper Imperial supervision. If Gleb was not in residence at the same hours Iden was, three guards remained on duty. Gleb had warned Iden to always assume she was being overheard when they were present. Iden had assured her that it went without saying, even as she swallowed her anger at this blatant assumption of her stupidity. Meals were taken in Gleb's presence, and everywhere Iden went she had an armed shadow walking a few paces behind her.

What hurt most of all was not being able to fly solo. Iden missed the cockpit of her TIE fighter so much that she ached when she thought about it. She craved the comforting blackness and circular enclosure; the glint of red lighting, the efficient controls that responded with ease to her touch.

It had been ten days since her arrival, over a month since her "act of treason," and despite Admiral Versio's assurances that the Dreamers were actively searching for a figurehead, there had been no hint that the terrorists were aware of her presence here. No cryptic messages, no attacks on Gleb's house, nothing out of the ordinary. The only notice anyone had taken of her had been some of Gleb's students, who had shouted "Traitor!" at her while she was being escorted to her ship three days before.

Maybe the Dreamers simply thought that justice had been done. Maybe they didn't believe Iden. If only her mother hadn't doubted her, too . . . but Iden couldn't allow herself to dwell on that. She would complete her mission, sniff out the source of the leak, recover the dangerous information, and return to a hero's welcome and a parade. Or, perhaps, be quietly reassigned. Either way, her mother would, one day—hopefully soon—discover that her daughter was not, never had been, never *could* be a traitor.

She couldn't shake the memory of the holorecording, though. Zeehay had looked so frail. Iden's mood and thoughts were dark when she stepped into the starfighter and settled into the pilot's seat. A moment later she heard the footsteps of her copilot, Azen Novaren, on the ramp.

Her first assigned copilot—or "watchdog," as Iden knew she was meant to be—had been a woman named Semma Waskor. Captain Waskor had been judgmental, but at least she also had been taciturn, which meant that Iden was not going to be subjected to lectures. They had nodded to each other, Iden had gotten in the pilot's seat, and that was pretty much that other than what was absolutely necessary for Iden to complete her patrol circuit over various Vardosian cities. It had suited her fine, and she was saddened to hear that Waskor had been badly injured in a tram accident, along with several others. At first, Iden had hoped the tram accident would herald contact from the Dreamers, but no such luck.

Instead, she'd been saddled with Lieutenant Azen Novaren, an older man with graying hair and lines etched in his face from too much sun. He'd been entirely forgettable, and the last two days had been more boring than irritating.

"Good morning, Iden," he greeted her as he boarded.

She sighed. *Iden*. "Good morning, Lieutenant Novaren."

She heard the door slide closed behind him as he replied, "I really hope it will be. We're going on a little trip together."

And Iden felt the press of a blaster muzzle between her shoulder blades. Her pulse leapt and she practically cheered.

Finally!

She went very still. "What's going on, Lieutenant?" she asked quietly.

"I already told you. We're taking a little trip. Now, very naturally and calmly, I'd like you to get out of your seat, sit in the copilot's chair, and strap yourself into your crash webbing. And don't attempt to summon help. I won't hesitate to kill you."

Through the viewport, she could see other pilots in the hangar going about their business. Bored looking, all of them; dull-eyed, doing their duty, going home in the evening to spouses and families or a night alone watching holovids and drinking what alcohol their credits could purchase. They had all watched Iden like shirrhawks at first, hungry for novelty, but that had worn off by the fourth day. Now no one noticed that Iden Versio was sitting in plain view with a blaster pressing into her back, and that was just fine with her.

She obeyed, easing into the copilot's chair carefully, keeping her hands where he could see them, and strapped herself in.

"Hands behind you," Azen instructed. When she complied, he snapped a pair of stun cuffs onto her wrists. "Now. Be a good girl and don't make any noise, and I won't have to hurt you."

"Hurt me? I thought you were ready to kill me."

"Oh, don't think I won't if I have to, but you're much more valuable to us alive."

"Who's *us*?"

"All in good time. First, we need to get clear of this awful little planet and out of the Jinata system." Casually, Novaren flipped switches, pressed buttons, and went through the precheck. Then he said, "J-Sec Patrol, this is Lieutenant Azen Novaren piloting the *Brightstar,* 4014B, requesting permission to take off."

"*Brightstar* is scheduled to be piloted by Iden Versio, Novaren," came a voice.

"Copy that, but there's been a change of plan." His voice was calm, bored; the voice of a pilot doing a job he didn't particularly like and had been doing for too long. Iden found herself admiring that. "She's copiloting today."

"I'll need verbal confirmation of her flight code from Versio."

Azen looked at her expectantly. He indicated the blaster he held at his side, out of sight of the other security members milling about outside. Iden hesitated, then said, her eyes locked with Novaren's, "Versio here, confirming my flight number is 18104."

"Copy that. You're cleared to go."

Novaren flipped the radio off. "You agreed rather quickly," he said.

"You didn't leave me much choice. Your blaster wasn't set to stun," Iden said, nodding at the weapon.

He didn't reply, focusing instead on lifting off and hovering for a moment before heading toward the open doors. "Sharp eyes. No, it wasn't," he said, reaching down for it. "But it is now."

He fired.

By the time Iden blinked into consciousness, slightly nauseous and aching, she and Azen were surrounded by stars. "What happened?" she asked.

"Nothing much," her kidnapper replied. "Just a jump to hyperspace."

"There's a tracker on this ship."

"Not anymore."

Iden regarded him with a hint of admiration. "You're good," she said. "Let me guess . . . you were behind the tram incident. You needed to get my minder out of the way."

"Guilty as charged," Novaren replied.

"A lot of people died on that tram."

"A lot of people died on Alderaan." He gave her an appraising look. "Or had you forgotten that?"

Iden winced with feigned pain and looked away. "No, of course not. Not forgetting about it is what got me court-martialed. I'm . . . a little surprised it was this easy. I would have thought there would be some excitement around stealing a J-Sec vessel."

"Plenty more where we're going."

"And where is that, precisely? You never told me who *we* is. Am I being kidnapped? Held for ransom? I should warn you, my father's pretty put out with me these days. Won't be all that lucrative."

He actually chuckled at that. "No, that's definitely not the plan. You're a pretty cool customer, aren't you?"

She shrugged. "TIE pilots who survive the destruction of the Death Star don't get rattled by much."

"Good point." He was quiet for a moment, then said, "We're far enough away that I'm not too worried about pursuit. So here are some answers. *We* are a group of individuals who hate the Empire and all it stands for. And we're willing to do whatever it takes to bring it down." He glanced at her. "We thought you might want to help us do that."

"You're with the Rebel Alliance?"

He made a face, as if he'd just bitten into something extremely sour. "Hell no. Until they got their nerve up and stole those plans from Scarif, I'd have said the Alliance would rather meet with the Emperor for tea and politely ask him to consider surrendering, if it wouldn't bother him too terribly much."

Despite the situation, Iden smiled. That was precisely

the impression she'd gotten of the Alliance. "Then—who are you? Or don't you want me to know?"

Oh, he wanted her to know, all right. He was arrogant, and he wanted to brag. If all of them were like Azen, this mission was going to be over before it had barely begun.

"We," he said, giving the words weight, "are Saw Gerrera's partisans."

Iden feigned surprise. "What? Saw was killed at Jedha. I thought they—you—all died with him. That's what they told us."

"The Empire thought so. But they were wrong. You can't kill an idea, Iden. No matter how many of us die to bring down the Emperor and his corrupt, brutal regime—even if *all* of us die—that idea will live on after us."

A terrible thought seized Iden. "So . . . are you going to kill me? To send a message to the Empire?" How was it that none of them had considered that? Her father was so very certain this would work—

"No, you're safe with us, as long as you'll work with us. We went to a lot of trouble to get you off Vardos. We want to use you, not kill you. And hopefully, you'll convince everyone that you will, indeed, be of use."

"I hope so myself," Iden said. "Where are we heading?"

"Dreamer home base," he replied. "The Shadow Side."

Iden asked her abductor-rescuer questions as they traveled, trying to get more information useful to her mission and to the Empire. As she had expected, he didn't reveal much.

"The Shadow Side" turned out to be exactly that—an area of a planet named Jeosyn. Azen explained briefly that this was a world with an extremely slow rotation, which made for long, hot days and long, cold nights. The dawn and dusk cycles, which the planet was currently experiencing, lasted about three months. "We live in the narrow band of the planet's dusk, which is temperate," Azen said.

"I've never heard of this planet," Iden said.

"Galaxy's a big place, and the Empire isn't interested in anything it can't use."

"No occasional visitors?"

"Let's just say we're not overly concerned with Imperial discovery," Azen replied as he brought the ship down to the planet for landing. This area of Jeosyn was almost frozen in time at that moment right after sunset, when the light was almost but not entirely gone, and twilight had claimed the landscape. Everything was lavender and purple and blue. This world had no moon to cast potentially revealing illumination over its surface, and as the ship skimmed below the helpfully concealing canopy of dense trees, Iden realized many of the rocks were limned in faint shades of green, white, blue, and purple.

"Lichen?" she guessed.

"Yep," Azen replied. "Between the lingering light, the lichen, and night goggles, you don't even have to turn a ship's lights on."

"This really is perfect for you, isn't it?" she said, adding, "I suppose I should say *us* now, shouldn't I?"

"Not yet," he replied. He threw her a glance. "You've got an uphill battle, Iden Versio."

She disliked the familiarity. Hardly anyone addressed her as Iden. Only her mother and Gideon had done so, and even Gideon called her by her rank and last name except on clearly informal occasions. Not bridling when strangers—enemies—used it was going to take some getting used to.

"And yet," she said, unable to suppress her irritation completely, "you were the ones who abducted me."

"Don't look at me," Azen replied. "This whole thing was the Mentor's idea. So just . . . be aware."

"The Mentor?" Iden asked, alert. Did he refer to Staven? "Does everyone have a code name?"

"Some of us do. Some don't care. You'll find out which is which."

They continued, flying nearly as close to the ground as a landspeeder before finally "docking" in a large cavern. Azen settled the ship down and, positioning his body so that Iden couldn't see what he was doing, entered something on the console.

"You won't be able to operate this without the code," he said, "so don't get any ideas."

"You think I want to go back to Vardos?" she retorted.

"Can't be too sure," Azen replied. He unfastened her stun cuffs; she rubbed her wrists when her hands were liberated, then accepted a pair of night goggles he handed her.

"Most of us don't need these anymore, and most of our light and heat sources don't disturb night vision. We know the area and our eyes have adjusted." He smiled. "We usually need dark goggles for the first hour or so after we leave, actually."

Another thing to mark me as an outsider, Iden thought, but she accepted them and put them on. *Better this than tripping over everything.*

She fell into step beside him as they left the cavern and set out across a flat area shielded by trees. Up ahead, the terrain again offered jagged, jutting rocks and tumbled boulders. Azen began to climb and she followed, trying to place her feet and hands where he did as they scrambled up the rocky surface. He waited for her at the top, making no move to assist her.

She clambered up and stood. "First test?" she inquired.

"Try about the twenty-seventh," he said. "You don't yet appreciate how well we've been monitoring you." That was unsettling—if it was true. "Come on," Azen continued. "It's not far now."

They walked along the ledge in single file, and Iden was particularly grateful for the goggles. A fall from here would be nasty indeed. Eventually the ledge widened onto a plateau where several overhangs and caves offered shelter. Inside the largest cave, she could see a light source and figures moving around.

They had reached the Dreamers' encampment.

As they drew closer, Iden removed the goggles. This was obviously the central gathering spot. The scent of cooking wafted to her nostrils, making her mouth water and her stomach growl. Iden had been "kidnapped" in the morning, and she assumed the appetizing aroma was emanating from the midday meal—not that she could reckon the time of day by the unchanging light.

She heard friendly conversation in Basic, but it went silent as Iden and Azen approached. By the time they reached the cavern, all the partisans were staring at her.

"Everyone," Azen said, "this is Iden Versio."

CHAPTER 13

Iden straightened, barely stopping herself from snapping to attention. She was as thick into enemy territory here as she had been on Yavin's moon. The wary tension in her body ebbed slightly as she realized that the rest of Inferno Squad's members had successfully negotiated their own paths to the planet as planned. It had been over a month since Iden had seen them. And while she had expected them to look different out of uniform, she was startled at how much they appeared as if they already belonged.

Seyn, with her healing, deliberately caused wounds, looked small and wary as she spooned food into her mouth quickly, as if someone were about to take it from her. She glanced furtively at Iden, then back down at her meal.

Del, his clothes smudged and well worn, seemed as

if he'd lived here forever, and even spit-and-polish Gideon lounged comfortably beside his "brother." Neither had bothered to shave in the—two weeks? three?—since they'd been there. Both regarded her with curious but wary expressions.

While she was glad to see them, they only made her feel yet more out of place in her stiff maroon-and-blue J-Sec uniform. She looked around, silently assessing the group.

The only one that the datachip had mentioned was the leader, Staven. She recalled the two images that had appeared in his dossier. One was that of a young, attractive man with a thick head of dyed-blue hair. He had what Iden was starting to think of as "the Look"—that righteous, firm, certain expression worn only by young males who had been captivated by the "ideals" of the Rebellion. The second one was an official image after he had been captured. He looked older; the naïve, hopeful young rebel had given way to the hardened warrior, but despite bruises on his face, the man in the image had stared back defiantly.

The man she beheld now had the same blue hair—though it was difficult to see the exact shade in the shadowy green light cast by the heater—but was otherwise quite different from either image she had seen previously. Imprisonment had changed him; had given his once-open face lines of anger and weariness. He stood away from the rest, leaning against the curving stone wall of the cave, arms folded across his chest as he regarded her expressionlessly.

"You got her," he said. "Good job, Azen."

Closer to the cooking cube, finishing their own meals,

was a family that initially looked very human. Their pink eyes, startlingly visible in the dimness, gave them away. Though Iden had never seen the species before, she recognized them as Kages, and in full daylight she would have been able to tell that their skin was gray as stone. The Kage homeworld was Quarzite, where they dwelled beneath the surface in constant semidarkness illuminated only by the soft purple glow of the crystals that gave the planet its name. Iden was willing to bet she was looking at former members of the elite Kage Warriors, individuals who had likely already been rebels before they had joined the partisans. The Kage Warriors waged constant war against the Belugans, the dominant species on their world. With that background, it was not surprising to see them among the number of Dreamer partisans.

The father was in his early forties, all lean muscle under his tunic and cloak. The woman next to him was slender but wiry and lithe, and her face was pretty, but hard. The boy, presumably their son, looked to be in his mid- to late teens. Their expressions and body language were openly hostile, and even as they sat beside the heater, Iden suspected they would be able to leap into action in a heartbeat.

She noticed that they had blasters within easy reach. So did almost all the others.

Perched on a boulder a bit away from the heater, his dark clothing and gray fur melding with the shadows, was a Chadra-Fan. Like the others, he was peering at her, and she could see the green illumination reflected in his large, bright, shiny eyes.

The silence became uncomfortable. It was the Chadra-

Fan who finally broke it, with a shrug and a surprisingly cheery "Hello! I'm Piikow!"

Iden gave him a faint smile. "Hello, Piikow," she said. No one else volunteered their names.

"Some of us are offplanet right now, but they're due back soon," Azen said. "I'm starving. Are you hungry?"

"A little, yes."

He took a bowl and went to ladle something stewlike from the pot that bubbled on the heater. He thrust it at her. Iden accepted it and stood for a moment, then awkwardly sat down on a leveled rock near the heater. She forced herself not to look over at her fellow Inferno Squad members, instead allowing herself a quick perusal of the cavern. Most of it appeared to be a natural formation, but the Dreamers had made some alterations, such as the stone upon which she now sat. Other boulders had been leveled as well, serving as tables and chairs. Lasers had cut several different-sized alcoves in the curving walls, which they used for storage. She caught a glimpse of a large one farther in, swathed in shadow. There was enough light from the lichen to catch the outline of a blaster. A weapons cache, then. She moved her eyes from it quickly, lest she be noticed staring at it.

Staven now stirred from where he had been watching her. "So. Iden Versio. Daughter of Admiral Garrick Versio, survivor of the Death Star. Hero of the Empire. Now universally despised. What did Azen tell you about us?"

He was an attractive man, but his scorn was ugly. Iden didn't rise to the bait. "Not a lot," she said, which wasn't entirely true. "That you're Saw Gerrera's partisans, and you hate the Empire and all it stands for. That you're willing to do whatever it takes to bring it down, and you think I can help you with that."

Staven nodded. "Sounds about right. Can you?"

"It depends on what you want."

Staven's face clouded suddenly. "This isn't a game," he snapped. He gestured at Del and Gideon. "These two? They sought us out after everyone in their cell sacrificed their lives trying to buy them that chance."

Both supposed brothers managed to look uncomfortable. Staven turned to the Chadra-Fan. "Piikow here had his family taken from him and held hostage, so that he would work willingly in a dangerous environment. It turns out his family was murdered within an hour of his arrival at the factory, because that's how the Empire likes to do business. He'll be joining them at some point soon, because he's had too much exposure to toxic chemicals. But he's going to help in every way he can, as long as he can."

Iden hadn't noticed it before, but she saw now that there were bare patches on Piikow's head and the backs of his hands where gray-blue skin showed through. His expression at Staven's words made clear that the Chadra-Fan did not like being singled out.

"Seyn's an escaped slave, whose master helped the Empire negotiate on the black market. Ru, Halia, and Sadori Vushan are Kages—members of a subjugated species that's struggled against oppression for generations. Nobody here has come from a life of privilege and power."

"Not directly, at any rate," came a warm, pleasant male voice. The form of what Iden guessed to be a human man moved into the firelight. He was lean and a bit taller than average, clean-shaven with thick, shaggy dark hair that was streaked with gray. Iden couldn't tell what color his eyes were—some light shade. His face was lightly lined, but the crinkles around his eyes indicated more smiles than scowls. He was smiling now.

"I was born into a life of power and privilege some thirty-odd years ago. But I've had neither for quite some time. You and I have a few things in common, I think, Iden. That's why I suggested to Staven you'd be willing to help us."

"What's your name?" Iden asked the newcomer.

"Call me the Mentor," he said. Which was an answer, and also wasn't.

Despite her hunger, Iden allowed the bowl of stew to cool in her hands as she regarded first the alleged leader, then the one who had managed to push through a request to kidnap her. She looked back at Staven.

"I'm guessing you're the leader. Tell me how I can help you."

The Mentor's smile widened. At that moment, Iden heard voices approaching the encampment, talking softly with the sort of suppressed, relieved excitement that Iden recognized as the sound of people who had returned from a successful mission.

"I smell tikktikk stew!" came a bright female voice.

"I'm gonna eat it all," the Kage boy—Sadori—called in warning.

"Only if you want to get pummeled," came another female voice, husky and warm. A man laughed.

A Twi'lek, followed by a human male and female, strode into the ring of firelight. Immediately the energy shifted. The Twi'lek was welcomed with hugs, and for a moment the smiles and laughter made the encampment feel less like an outlaw hideout than a weekend "roughing it" with friends. It was an odd transition.

The newcomers noticed Iden right away, of course. "So," the human female said, keeping her eyes on Iden as she went toward Staven. "Well done, Azen, you got her. Those months spying on Vardos paid off. Good times ahead, now that you're back!" She gave Azen a friendly clap on his back and turned to Staven. The partisan leader opened his arms to her, and she slid into an easy embrace. He kissed her forehead and she leaned against him as they both returned their attention to the gathering.

Iden's parents had never demonstrated any kind of physical affection in front of their daughter, and Iden found that this, almost more than the abduction at gunpoint or being the center of suspicious attention, made her uncomfortable.

"She going to work with us?" the human male asked. He was the youngest, other than the Kage boy, lean and scruffy looking and suspicious. He had startling green eyes and good features beneath the layer of stubble.

"Yes, she is," Iden said, unable to bite her tongue in time.

"We arrived right before you did," Azen said. He pointed his spoon at Iden. "Water's still a little icy."

The Twi'lek's lekku twitched as she regarded Iden with an appraising gaze.

"How did it go?" the Mentor asked the Twi'lek, clearly attempting to divert attention from their Imperial—guest? new member? prisoner?—Iden still didn't know what they thought of her.

"Very well," the Twi'lek said. "They were clay in my hands. And in Kaev's," she added, throwing a glance and an exaggerated, theatrical wink in the human male's direction. He pretended to swoon, threw her a kiss, and smiled, revealing startlingly white, even teeth. Everyone laughed. "It never ceases to amaze me what people in power will say—or do—when presented with something they desire and can't have."

Staven alone didn't smile. "One of these days, Dahna," he warned, "you're going to get in over your head."

Iden expected more laughter and banter, but instead Dahna grew serious. "Not happening. You learn all the tricks of survival when you're owned."

Iden, who had taken a bite of stew, paused in her chewing for an instant in surprise, automatically glancing at Seyn before she realized what she'd done. A shock went through her—dammit, had she betrayed herself already?—until she remembered that Seyn had already been introduced as a slave. Anyone watching her closely would simply assume she had made the connection between the two women. Iden had to tamp down a sudden rush of anger at the slip. She was uncertain about convincingly living out the life of an undercover spy, and the thought bothered her.

I am a Versio, and Versios excel.

"Is she clean?" the Twi'lek—Dahna—asked. "No recording devices, no transmitters? Nothing?"

"Oh come on," Azen said, exasperated, "you think I'd bring her here if she wasn't? The ship's clean, too."

Iden froze as the significance of the statement registered. She lifted her head from the bowl of stew and looked Azen straight in the eye.

"Azen?" she said, her voice ice. "*How* did you search me?"

His gaze slid away. "Scanners," he said.

"*Just* scanners?" Iden challenged him. Azen scowled and didn't reply, jabbing at his stew with his spoon.

"Azen, did you touch me?"

"Well, I had to be sure, didn't I?" Azen shot back.

Iden flushed in outrage, and her hands gripped the bowl tightly. She'd expected to be searched, but to discover it had been done without her knowledge, while she was *unconscious*—

She started to rise.

In an instant, the tenor of the gathering turned. All three Kages were on their feet, blasters or vibroknives in their hands. Judging by the clattering sound, others, too, had drawn weapons. Staven had surged toward her, and Iden turned to face him, shaking with fury.

And then, faster than Iden would have given him credit for, the Mentor was between them. "Back off, Staven! Everyone else, *sit down*!" He glanced over his shoulder and said in a quieter voice, "You too, Iden."

Slowly, her eyes on Staven, Iden sank back down onto the stone. Her body trembled with unleashed kinetic energy. Staven didn't move, but after a few seconds the others complied with the Mentor's request—some more graciously than others.

"Staven," the Mentor said again, quietly. "She has a right to be angry."

"She's an Imperial captain, daughter of an Imperial admiral!" Staven spat. But he did take a step backward.

"And nothing is more certain in life than that parent and child will disagree," the Mentor said. "We all agreed to bring her here. We believed she could help our cause. And this is how we inspire her to join us?" His eyes sought out Azen. "Azen, you owe her an apology."

"Yes," said the Twi'lek, harshly, "you do."

To his credit, Azen looked deeply uncomfortable. "Okay, I'm sorry. But you have to understand. We were taking a risk in bringing you here. The last thing I wanted to do was to jeopardize the group. Gleb's people might have put something on you, to track you in case you tried to run away. It's not like you were a guest at her place."

It was a reasonable assumption. Iden knew that had the roles been reversed, she wouldn't have hesitated to search him just as thoroughly. War was, after all, war. But she wasn't going to give them that. She had the moral high ground now, and wouldn't yield it until doing so would serve her.

"I'm not exactly an invited guest here, either," she said.

"No," said the Twi'lek, "and once, you were our enemy. We hope that's not the case any longer. So, for now, we're going to give you the benefit of the doubt."

"After you've *searched* me thoroughly, of course."

The former slave lowered her head in acknowledgment. "After we've searched you thoroughly, yes. We must protect our own. There are so few of us left to do the work. I'm willing to bet you understand that."

Iden waited a moment, but then sighed. She'd made her point. Time to appear gracious. "I do understand it. And I'm willing to bet you understand that I'll punch the next person who touches me without my permission."

To her surprise, the Twi'lek's face lit up with a knowing grin. "And I'll be right behind you to take my own swing."

"All right," the Mentor said, looking around at the group. "Let's try this again."

Everyone settled back down. "We call ourselves the Dreamers," Staven said.

"Dreamers? Azen said you were Saw Gerrera's partisans."

"We can't be him. We're just following in his footsteps. We're keeping alive the Dream. Saw was the face, the voice, of our cause. It was a hell of a blow. And we lost a lot of people on Jedha along with him."

His eyes flickered to Iden as he spoke, and they were hard as stone. *Does he know that the Death Star was responsible for Jedha, too?* she wondered. *And if so, how?*

"Since his death, we've been actively recruiting, so there're lots of newcomers. Del, Gid, Seyn, Kaev, and now you, Iden. On the plus side, the more the Empire arrogantly shows off how far they're willing to go, the more people are growing outraged. They want to fight back while there's still time. This is good, this is *great*— but we lost Saw. We lost the man who gathered the people, who inspired them. The Empire is doubling down on any rebel group . . . and we're all prepared to die if we need to. Which means we'll need those others, those people who are filled with anger and want somewhere to direct it."

He looked over to Kaev. "They hit us hard, with Alderaan." The younger man nodded, solemn. "But *we*— the Rebel Alliance, with help from Saw right before he was martyred—hit back by destroying something the

Empire values much more than lives: their perception of their own infallibility. And they're still hurting. Aren't they, Iden?"

"Yes," Iden replied at once. "No one will admit it, but they're all shaken. Even at the highest levels. You're absolutely right. Now's the moment. We need to keep hitting them, hard, before they can recover."

"And if anyone can help us with that, you can," the Mentor said to her. He gave her a kind smile.

"Once we're sure we can trust you," Staven said pointedly. "People are inspired. They're ready to fight now, because there's a chance that we can win. Many didn't believe that before. But we've got to be smart about who we bring into our midst.

"This group is new. But a lot of us have worked either directly with Saw or with one another over the years. Rebel groups aren't tidy like the Empire, Iden. People wander in and out. But you forge bonds when you've fought beside someone. Kaev here has already gone on five missions with us. He's done well." Kaev beamed under the praise.

"He needs to follow orders better," Dahna said, but softened her words with a friendly wink.

Kaev laughed and nodded self-deprecatingly. "I'm learning!"

"We haven't found the right mission for Seyn yet, but she's already proven herself invaluable with her forgery skills. Del's been assisting Piikow to work wonders on getting some of our older ships up and skyworthy, and both he and his brother Gid have flown with us on separate missions."

Iden felt the old familiar, easy sensation of friendly

competition stir when Gid's name was mentioned. "If you know about me, you know I'm an exceptional pilot," she began. "I'll be able to—"

"Pilots are commonplace, even good ones," Staven interrupted her bluntly. "We risked taking you from Vardos for a completely different reason. If you can't help us, if you don't earn our trust, you'll be gone. And by *gone* I don't mean given a ship with a full fuel tank and a farewell party. You're here now, and you can't be allowed to leave."

The sudden turn from the lighthearted teasing to the reality of how brutal the partisans really were at their hearts was startling—as, no doubt, Staven intended. He smiled. It was the first time he had done so since Iden had arrived, and she didn't like it. It was cold and predatory, and she realized that he wasn't at all happy to have her here, and he wanted very much for her to fail.

CHAPTER 14

In the past two days since Azen had brought her here supposedly against her will, Iden had been interrogated by Staven, the Mentor, and Dahna. Anticipating this, she and her father had discussed what she was to reveal: enough to make them believe her when they verified the information, but nothing that would seriously harm the Empire. And so she was free with her information. But despite Staven's gloating near-threat on the first night, none of the Dreamers told Iden very much about anything at all.

As she sat inside the cave with a pile of old, battered, mismatched armor they had set her to mending, Iden was beginning to recall her time at Gleb's with fondness. There, at least, she had been granted privacy and permitted to fly. Here, she was not allowed out of the company of at least one of the veteran Dreamers. When she left to relieve herself, someone came with her, and everyone slept together in one of the caves. They even made sure that when she prepped her bedroll, she never slept next to Kaev or any of the other new recruits.

She looked up from her tedious task as Azen and Sadori walked over to her. Both bore sacks of something that created angular bulges in the bags. Clearly, it was more armor for her to mend.

"Ru and Sadori just got back with these," Azen told her. "Staven wants you to clean them up." They dropped the bundles at her feet. One of the bags opened.

A white plastoid helm rolled out. It was spattered with still-wet blood. Iden could smell the coppery reek, but forced a pleased reaction.

"One less stormtrooper to worry about," she said.

"Fourteen less," Sadori said, a hint of pride in his voice, then walked away without another word. Azen still stood, and now he thrust another, smaller bundle at her. "Del and Piikow are over in the third cavern working on one of the ships. Take some food to them."

The sweet smell of a ripe fruit mixed with the stench of blood. Iden stared at him for a moment, then pressed her lips together against a scathing retort. On her way, she passed Piikow returning to the encampment. He leaned heavily on a walking stick, but his pace was steady. "Is everything all right?" Iden inquired.

Piikow waved a small hand. "There was something I wanted to show Del," he said. His breathing was labored, but his eyes crinkled in a smile. "I'm fine. Just takes me a little longer these days to get from one point to another."

She gave him a look of concern. "Don't push yourself," she warned, but inwardly she was practically turning cartwheels. Finally, a chance to talk to one of her team alone. She picked up her pace but resisted the urge to break into a jog. She didn't want to attract any attention.

He looked up from his work as she entered. "We have a few minutes," she said without preamble, thrusting the sack with fruit and hard-boiled, black-shelled eggs at him. "You have to find a way for us to communicate, and you have to do it immediately."

Del took the sack and set it down. The ID10 droid hovered about a meter away, two of its four appendages grasping tools. Del had done his best to alter its stark Imperial appearance with a paint job in shades of white and blood red. It reminded Iden uncomfortably of the stormtrooper's helm.

"I know," Del replied. "I'm working on it, but Piikow is usually around."

Iden stepped away slightly, pretending to examine the vessel herself. She stole a glance over her shoulder. No sign of Piikow, though she spotted Halia and Staven engrossed in conversation.

"We've all got minders," Iden murmured. "But I think mine are the worst." She yanked her thoughts back to business. "We need to get this mission going. Ru and Sadori came back with bloody stormtrooper armor for me to fix. Next time I'm afraid they might just leave the head inside and stick it on a pike."

Del looked grim at the image that conjured up. "It's nothing compared with the numbers we lost on the Death Star, but for a small, newly formed group, the Dreamers are sure making their presence known."

"Have any of you had to—"

"No, not yet," Del replied. "Just some supply runs that put us against basic security. Nothing big, and nothing Imperial . . . yet."

"It's just going to get worse. Have you overheard anything useful?" Iden asked. "Any idea as to how they're getting their intel? Nobody's going to let anything slip around me."

Del wiped his hands and cracked open a shell. "I cannot get used to purple eggs with blue yolks," he said, then, "Nothing. I haven't been able to talk to Seyn alone yet, but I think she may know something." He gestured at the ship. "Obviously, they're making use of my technical skills. I do know that Staven's been talking with Gideon—" He grimaced. "—*Gid* about piloting, but so far they haven't trusted him enough to test his skills. Once they let me work unsupervised, I might be able to bug the ships."

Iden fought back impatience. "By the time they trust *me,* the war will be over," she said.

"Hey," he said kindly, "it's only been a couple of days. We've all been here much longer. They'll come around."

"That doesn't help," she said, casting another casual glance back toward the encampment. Halia, who did not look happy, was stalking toward them. "Dammit, here comes Halia."

They were discussing purple eggs by the time Halia reached them. "Over my objections," she said before they could even greet her, "Staven has decided to give you a comlink."

That was a step in the right direction. "Thanks," Iden said, accepting it. Del fished out his and tossed it at the

ID10, but the droid made no move to catch it. The communication device landed on the stone floor of the cavern and rolled a bit.

Del sighed, rising and picking up the comlink and handing it to the droid himself. "I need to work on that," he said to Iden and Halia. Addressing the droid, he said, "Hold this," and it reached out one of its slender arms and grasped the proffered tool. "The droid will take care of it while I work. I'm trying to make sure this little guy can help out in all kinds of ways!"

Iden kept her face neutral, but inwardly she rejoiced.

Del had just told her to keep an eye out for the droid.

But another day passed without any contact from Del. Iden was impatient, but she had faith in Del, so until he figured out how to reach her, she focused on learning everything she could about the Dreamers.

She was almost certain that Staven was the one who had obtained and was acting on classified information. After all, he was the group's leader, seeking out devastated partisans and pulling them in to become Dreamers. He had known Saw personally and had obviously cared about him. But he was proving to be frustratingly tight-lipped—at least when she was around. Iden had to hope some of the others were getting more information than she was.

Azen had revealed nothing more to her about how he, a partisan who had known Staven for some time, had managed to infiltrate J-Sec. He, too, was high on her list. If he could infiltrate J-Sec, he likely had valuable contacts in other areas as well.

The human girl Staven had welcomed so warmly was Nadrine. She was, apparently, an explosives expert, and the mastermind behind the "bombs as jewelry" design. Her hair was long and she usually wore it in a utilitarian braid. Even in the lavender light of constant dusk, Iden could see that she had quite a lot of freckles. If Staven trusted her with information, she might be a good person to get to know.

Dahna, the escaped slave, was second in command. Iden had initially assumed that role belonged to the Mentor, but while everyone seemed to have respect for him and even Staven was willing to defer to him on occasion, no one treated him like he gave orders. Both Dahna and the Mentor seemed to be well disposed toward all members of the team; perhaps they would be useful.

Iden found the Chadra-Fan, Piikow, to be the most approachable Dreamer next to the Mentor. He was already chatting comfortably with Del, which interested Iden; she caught snatches of their conversation and realized they had bonded—or, in Del's case, pretended to bond—over the droid and other technology. Staven had said Piikow had once been employed by the Empire. It was possible that he had some contacts who still were; she could easily see him having friends who remained fond of him.

Iden realized with chagrin just how much they would have to contribute to the Dreamers if they were going to maintain the façade. She took comfort in knowing that, eventually, the terrorist group would be destroyed— along with their knowledge. They were angry, and angry people did not share information if they didn't also share beliefs, so there was little risk that the Rebel Alliance would learn anything of value that could be laid at Inferno Squad's feet.

The Vushan family was among the most reclusive of the group, and Iden highly doubted they were the leaks. But Iden had noticed the son, Sadori, sneaking glances at Seyn, who responded by catching his eye, smiling shyly, and looking away. Good, Iden thought; another possible useful connection.

As Staven had mentioned, Kaev was also a relative newcomer to the group. At one point, when Iden and a few others were cleaning and inspecting the recent cache of weapons the Pantoran pirate had delivered—along with Del and Gideon—to Jeosyn, Kaev had taken her aside.

"I know people are suspicious of you, and I know you understand why, but . . . I wanted to thank you in person," he said.

She gazed at him, confused. "Thank me?"

He nodded, his green eyes intense. "Yeah. See . . . I had family on Alderaan."

"Oh," she said sympathetically.

He nodded. "When I heard you talking about it in that recording . . . how it bothered you that so many people died who hadn't even lifted a hand against the Empire, it gave me hope that other people will understand what you do."

"Other Imperials?" She looked at him doubtfully.

"With luck, yeah. But anyone who might take a minute and look beyond all the flag-waving. Who might decide to stand beside us as we tear down the Empire." He shrugged, suddenly embarrassed. "Who knows, right?"

She had given him a grateful smile. It would be nice to

have an "ally" among the Dreamers in addition to the Mentor.

"Right. Who knows? The Empire is rotting and corrupt. It *must* fall as quickly as possible. Doesn't matter who goes down with it." As she spoke the words with what she hoped was earnest conviction, she wondered how long it would take to get used to saying such lies.

Since they had been here longer than Iden—and were perceived to be less of a threat than a known Imperial TIE pilot—the other three were doing much better. As they had all expected, Seyn, with her delicate and deceptively open, innocent appearance, had won over most of the group. Nadrine and Dahna were demonstrably fond of her, and young Sadori looked to be feeling emotions a bit warmer than that. The Mentor, too, seemed sympathetic toward her. In fact, the only ones who still seemed cool toward Seyn were Staven and Azen. That wasn't unexpected. Staven, as the leader, would be the most suspicious of the group, and Azen was—well, Azen.

Del, too, was well on his way to being accepted. That, also, didn't surprise Iden. Del had a calmness and a self-deprecation that put people at ease.

Unfortunately, it was Gideon who seemed to be stirring the most resentment. She was fond of him, but she knew better than anyone how arrogant and competitive he could be, and it seemed like something he'd done had already irritated several of the Dreamers.

Iden sighed as she continued to work on repairing armor and even mending flight suits. *Come on, Del,* she thought. *Where the hell is that droid?*

"Goodness, you're industrious," came the pleasant voice of the Mentor.

Iden glanced up at him and shrugged self-deprecatingly. "I don't want to be taken out and shot," she said.

"Neither do I, but I've got something you might enjoy more than fixing old uniforms."

Her smile widened. "I'm in."

The Mentor took her on a ride of about twenty minutes along a narrow, serpentine path through the gnarled trunks of ancient trees, leaving the speeder beneath the overhanging canopy. "Come on," he said. "It's just a brief walk from here, but it's safer not to leave the speeder out in the open."

"Do you anticipate visitors?"

"No. There's nothing remarkable about this place to attract them. But when you're hunted, and you're few, it's always best to be safe."

"Even if they don't see you, if someone got close to you they'd be able to detect your—our—ships and equipment," Iden said. "Don't you worry about that?"

He chuckled. "No. We're safe."

Even for someone who had lived her whole life on a "need-to-know" basis, the cryptic nature of the Dreamers rankled. Iden thought it was because this attitude contrasted so vividly with the extreme casualness and friendliness that had been on display earlier.

They fell into step together, Iden wearing her night-vision goggles, the Mentor apparently not needing them. "As Staven told you, until Jedha," he said as they walked, "Saw Gerrera was the face and the voice of the partisans—such as they had. He wasn't overly fond of the spotlight, nor did he have the sort of inclusive personality of his sister, Steela." He smiled a little. "She was astonishing. So much was lost when she died." The smile, too, died as he spoke.

"You sound like you knew her," Iden ventured.

"I did. I knew Saw, too. So did my goddaughter." He shook his dark head ruefully. "The entanglements among me, people I love, and the partisans runs deep, despite diverging paths."

He turned to her. "You strike me as being a lot like Steela. Your bearing, your unwillingness to be pushed around. Staven doesn't like to admit it, but he sees it, too. You'll be a good face for the Dreamers, but unless you're a secret thespian, you'll probably have to practice first."

Iden felt relief wash through her. She was finally going to become the "voice of the Dreamers," as her father had expected. Maybe now she'd be privy to the missions the others were departing on so frequently, and discover where Staven was getting his information from. But she had to pretend she was still in the dark.

"Hang on a minute," she said. "I'm not sure what you mean. Good face?"

"You're Iden Versio," the Mentor said. "You're recognizable. In the past, the Rebel Alliance has had good luck countering Imperial propaganda with the truth of what the Empire truly is. And *that* was even with mysterious, faceless rebels. When Mon Mothma and Princess Leia became identified with the Rebel Alliance, it gave it a legitimacy it had never had before. Think what the impact will be if you were to speak to the galaxy—you, who were once so firmly an Imperial, now a member of Saw Gerrera's Dreamers."

Iden shook her head. "That's not what I came here for. I'm not some politician, or a holovid star—I'm a soldier. A pilot. And I'm top-notch at that, too, you can try me!"

"Of course you are. As I said, your career is public knowledge, Iden. We know how good you are at that. And we'll put those skills to use, too, but not until we've got the Empire good and scared, and those who secretly want to overthrow it ready to stand up and fight—maybe die."

"I have to say, I don't think this is one of Staven's better ideas," she said.

"Actually," the Mentor replied mildly, "it was mine. As I said—I've seen this tactic used before, with excellent results. It could be said that Saw wasn't the real first rebel leader. That was Steela. It's worked before. And with someone as significant as you, it can work again."

It had been implied when she first arrived that bringing her here had been the Mentor's idea. And now he was confirming everything. Why had Staven listened to him? She had been certain the blue-haired man had been the one in charge, calling the shots . . . using leaked information. Was she wrong about that?

They reached the lip of the depression. "Wait here," the Mentor said, and hurried down the sloping canyon walls with the loping grace of a younger man. He reached the bottom, seeming to her eyes now only a centimeter tall.

He turned and faced her. "This place is a natural amphitheater," he said. Iden gasped a little, and a smile touched her lips. She could hear him perfectly, and he wasn't even shouting.

"That's amazing!" she yelled back.

"Isn't it, though?" he said. "I'll coach you on your body language and extemporaneous speaking. Won't do to have you read from a script. Now you come down and try."

She descended to the bowl where he stood, and he retreated to the top. Once he had settled in, she began.

"Citizens of the Empire," she began. "I—I mean—"

Her comlink vibrated. She clicked it. "No, that's fine," came the Mentor's voice. He apparently didn't like to shout. "Right now these people, unfortunately, are citizens of the Empire. Continue."

Iden took a breath. "Citizens of the Empire," she yelled.

"No, speak normally," came the Mentor's voice again.

"Citizens of the Empire," Iden said in a normal voice, "it's not what you think it is. The Empire, I mean. Isn't." This . . . she had not anticipated.

She was absolutely horrible at public speaking.

Somehow, that possibility had not occurred to her or her father. This had been the sole reason that the Dreamers had taken her from Vardos. Staven had said in no uncertain terms that her life depended on how well she served them. Sudden anger—not at them, not at her father, but at herself—choked her and she couldn't speak.

Then she heard: "Hang on."

The small figure at the top headed back down again. When he reached her, he gestured that she step away from the "stage." "Take a seat. No, no need to run back to the top. I just want to show you the sort of thing I'm looking for."

She obliged, her face growing hot with commingled

embarrassment and anger, striding away a bit and then sitting down on the ground. The Mentor settled himself, then struck a pose, standing perfectly straight and lifting his head high.

"People of the galaxy!" His voice was strong and vigorous, laced with passion. "For too long, we have labored under the brutal yoke of the Empire. Under the guise of offering aid, it has dragged us, world by world, system by system, on its hideous march of narcissistic greed, promising opportunity and instead sucking us dry. Instead of improving our livelihoods and our lives, it has destroyed them both—even stooping to the depravity of wiping out entire planets. Alderaan—you are not forgotten!"

Iden leaned forward, her own worry eased by the power of the performance unfolding in front of her, settling her elbows on her knees and her chin in her hands. She couldn't tear her gaze away from the slim, elegant figure and his impassioned words.

"We remember you, too, Jedha City. The Empire has shown us that no place in this galaxy—not a world full of defenseless civilians, or an ancient sacred site—*no place* is safe from the malice of the Emperor's dark heart, or the greed of those who grow rich and fat by plundering worlds! This *must end*!"

The hairs on the back of Iden's neck lifted. Not just from the power of the words, propaganda though they were, or the sonorous voice wrapping them in melodic tones from a heart that bled with genuine loss. She realized now why the Mentor used a false name. And now she understood why he was not the leader—why he stayed behind when the others ventured forth, facing danger.

Iden was listening to someone who knew how to give speeches. Someone who likely had once been known. He wanted Iden to do what he couldn't do for some reason she didn't yet understand: to speak out against the Empire, inspiring with words and passion and presenting a strong, certain mien.

He was a man in hiding. He was someone important.

Iden was going to find out who.

CHAPTER 15

Del had definitely harbored reservations about the "going undercover" aspect of the mission, but he found it easier than he had anticipated. He'd always communicated better with his hands than with words, and once they'd cleared the cover story hurdle and Staven had agreed to let Piikow show him a few things, it got much easier.

He'd never met a Chadra-Fan before. Although he had grown up on Coruscant, which was home to many species, he hadn't really interacted with many nonhumans. Certainly not once he was part of the Imperial war machine. It took a little while for his ear to get accustomed to Piikow's high voice, but once it did, he felt right at home—in a way, even more than he did with his fellow squad members. Because Piikow's first language wasn't chittering and cheeping—it was mechanics.

Just like Del's.

Under the Chadra-Fan's watchful eye, Del had been entrusted with the repair of certain vessels. So far, they were minor issues, mostly maintenance. Piikow promised him that soon they would start repair work on what he called "a very sad starfighter."

Everything had emotional resonance for the Chadra-Fan, who had an insatiable curiosity and loved to tinker. Nothing, not an eating implement, not a bolt or screw or metal scrap or brightly colored stone, was overlooked. How he managed to find half of the things he collected was a mystery. And it was nothing short of unbelievable to watch him diligently turn these found bits and pieces into emergency replacements for certain items, new inventions, and sometimes just some kind of gizmo that whirred, blinked, and moved and did nothing but amuse. And then he'd turn to Del and grin, his lips pulling back from sharp little teeth.

When he wasn't being supervised, Del turned all his attention to the droid and the comlink. He'd sent the droid out for various things several times already: an extra bottle of water, or a tool, or a piece of fruit. The Dreamers had gotten accustomed to it wandering about, humming a little to itself. Very soon, they'd cease to notice it as it went about its duties.

Iden, of course, was the leader, and should be the first person Del sent the droid to once he'd accomplished his goal. But Seyn was the one who appeared to be the most accepted, and therefore the most likely to be permitted some solitude. Besides, she had given him some nonverbal clues that made him feel she had discovered something significant. Iden would just have to understand.

. . .

Seyn had been the one to advise against wearing communications devices of any sort, no matter how cutting-edge or cleverly disguised. "If this group has access to the sort of information we think they do, they may be aware of the latest technology," she had said. "They'll be alert, at least at first, until they trust us."

Now Seyn was kicking herself. She had learned something very important and very disturbing when Iden had arrived on Jeosyn, and over the last couple of days she had tried, and failed, to find a way to speak with Inferno Squad's leader. Iden—and the rest of the team—needed to know what their intel specialist had discovered.

Seyn had been the first to arrive. She'd been questioned, of course, as Del and Gideon had been when they arrived. Iden was being interrogated and examined, too, but the deep suspicion with which the Inferno Squad leader had been viewed troubled Seyn. Iden was enduring much more scrutiny than Seyn had expected, and she wondered if Staven had already made up his mind about the admiral's daughter. She'd been relieved when the Mentor had said something to Iden, and the two had left together earlier. Someone at least was reaching out to Seyn's commanding officer.

Seyn had noticed that while the Mentor often went on jaunts by himself, either on foot or in a small shuttle, he was never included in any offworld missions. She wondered why. He was trusted, obviously, and seemed to be liked by most of the Dreamers, though sometimes Staven seemed exasperated by him. She had never seen the Mentor before, she was sure of that. With her memory, to see once was to remember forever. He puzzled her.

Seyn knew she herself had been lucky. Dahna had taken her under her wing from the outset, and now the Twi'lek was the main partisan who worked with Seyn. She'd passed all their tests with flying colors, demonstrating a believable level of familiarity with computers and forgery, and turning out high-quality faked documents.

They still weren't ready to explain what the forgeries would be used for. When asked if she knew how to pilot a vessel, she claimed ignorance, but she did ask if they would teach her to shoot. She explained that with her steady hands and sharp eyes, she might be good at it. Staven had said he'd think about it.

It was a skeleton crew at the moment, as most of the Dreamers were currently offworld. Del was off tinkering with Piikow, and Staven and Gideon were heating rations and discussing piloting when Seyn entered the main cavern. Or, more precisely, arguing about piloting.

"When are you going to let me really show you what I can do?" Gideon was saying.

"All in good time."

"You're paranoid," Gideon said. He looked thoroughly exasperated, and Seyn knew him well enough to know it wasn't entirely a performance. Gideon loved flying, and he was starting to push for more than the blue milk runs that Del had referred to. Somewhat to Seyn's surprise, the tactic seemed to be working.

"Saw taught me to be paranoid" was Staven's reply. "It's kept us alive."

"Yeah, well, it's keeping me grounded, and you're wasting a valuable resource."

Staven smiled, almost indulgently. "I'll tell you what. When the others get back, I'll take you up. You can show me what you can do."

Gideon pressed a hand to his heart. "Don't toy with me, Staven," he said, and both men laughed. They smiled a greeting at Seyn as she entered and helped herself to some fruit, milk, and hard-boiled prevva eggs.

"Seyn," Staven said, rising, "just the person I wanted to see. I've got another job for you." He motioned her over and she obliged. "It's pretty simple, compared with some of the others we've asked you to do. Identification cards for students at a small university." He handed it to her. The image of a young human male about Sadori's age stared back at her. Seyn wondered how they had obtained the card, and if they had eliminated its owner. *Acceptable casualties,* she reminded herself. She examined the card, thinking.

"That doesn't look too difficult," she said. In reality, it would be almost pathetically easy. This obviously wasn't a military school, which eliminated all kinds of challenges. "For Sadori?"

Staven gave her an odd smile. "We'll need two, actually. One for Sadori. And one for you, if we decide you're ready when the time comes."

She was genuinely surprised and pleased. "Me?" she said, allowing the emotions to charge the word. "Thank you!"

"Don't thank me," Staven said. "Thank Sadori."

Seyn ducked her head in a gesture of shyness. Sadori hadn't yet said anything to her other than the occasional greeting. This was an excellent development on many levels. "I'll thank him as soon as he gets back. Do—do you think I'll be ready?"

"You'd better be," Staven said. "You two are the only ones the right age. Even Kaev's too old for this. But don't worry. We've got time yet to train you."

"Is it all right if I take my breakfast back with me?" she asked. "I'm anxious to get started on this."

Staven hesitated, then seemed to reach a decision about her. "Sure, why not," he said. "Just don't get any yolk on the document."

She laughed and left with her food, the ID card, and a lighter heart. When she entered the sleeping area, she was surprised to find someone—or rather, some*thing*—waiting for her.

It was Del's droid.

Seyn glanced around to make sure she was alone, then put the food down, turned to the droid, and pressed a button on the hovering machine. A small hologram of Del appeared. "Give your comlink to the droid. When it gives it back to you, press the second button and say my name."

The hologram vanished. *Second?* Seyn thought, confused. The comlinks used by the Dreamers had only one. Shrugging, she handed it over to the ID10. It immediately went to work on the device, its limbs moving so quickly and deftly they were almost a blur. Once, it even produced a tiny chip. After a few moments, it booped to signal completion and handed the comlink back.

It now had two buttons on it.

Seyn clicked the second one, very carefully. "Del?" she said.

"It worked!" Del's voice was relieved and delighted. "But from now on, we need to be careful. Always start by using the name of the person you're comming, and if it's safe, they'll say clear. If not, just pretend you were reaching out for some other, Dreamer-approved reason."

"Copy that. What did you do?"

"Essentially, you're now holding two comlinks. One that everyone can access, and one that only the four of us can."

"You're a genius," Seyn said.

"Well, best of the best, right? I'm going to have the droid hook us all up as soon as I can."

Her pleasure faded. "Listen up, before anyone walks in on me. There's something I have to tell you."

CHAPTER 16

Gideon had spent the last few days doing his best to sell himself and his piloting skills to Staven. He had tentatively probed for information as to how much—or, preferably, how little—the Dreamers knew about the other cells. Staven had said that no one had mentioned the brothers, but Sadori had helpfully chimed in that people often drifted in and out, so it looked like the Brothers Farren were safe from discovery, at least for the moment.

He hoped the hostility that was being shown to Iden would ease up. It was understandable, of course, and not unexpected, but if they continued to keep her at arm's length, Inferno Squad's job would be far more difficult.

Even as he thought of Iden, she and the Mentor entered the cave. They were talking very intently, their heads close together. Iden met Gideon's eyes and nodded a greeting. They went to one of the food alcoves, unpacking pieces of fruit as they continued their conversation.

Gideon turned back to Staven and noticed that the other man was still watching the retreating figure of Seyn. There was a softening on a face prematurely hardened.

"Rough life, that one's had," Gideon ventured.

"No one's had it easy," Staven replied.

"No, but she's got it harder than most. She seems to be coming out of her shell."

"Yeah. I'm glad. She . . . reminds me of someone."

Gideon wagged his eyebrows. "Oh really? Does Nadrine know?"

"No, not like that. This kid. She was presented as Saw's adopted daughter, but—well. She was very good at forging things. A little younger than Seyn is now, similar name, even. I'm glad Dahna brought Seyn back with her."

Staven had struck Gideon as being one of those very tough, angry young men who always seemed to pop up when rebellion was in the air. He was reminded that many such young men—even partisans—were terribly idealistic. It was sad, really. But it was something that Inferno Squad could use.

"What happened to the other girl?" Gideon inquired.

It was the wrong question. The softness hardened again. "Dead," he said. "In the end, everyone's dead. Some just sooner than others."

He rose abruptly and went out. The Mentor and Iden fell silent as he passed them without even an inquiry about what they'd been doing. The silence was awkward. Finally, the Mentor spoke.

"Staven is hard because he's been hurt," the Mentor said. "He's lost a lot of people he loved. The only way you can get through that is if you really believe they died making a difference. The destruction of the Death Star came at a pivotal moment for the Rebellion, and at a not inconsiderable cost. But I truly believe that the Rebellion will succeed."

"We'll see if you're right, old man."

The Mentor sighed. "I suppose I am, to you two. I *do* feel old sometimes, when I think back on all I've witnessed. But I have faith. Regardless, even if it fails, tyranny cannot stand forever. It is an ugly beast that must feed. Eventually, the Empire will devour everything it has, and will turn on its own."

"Have *you* lost people you've loved?"

There was the twinkle of a much younger man in the Mentor's eye as he replied wryly, "I'm old, remember?" More seriously he added, "Yes, of course I have. My parents were killed, back during the Clone Wars. And my goddaughter was killed, too. She was a partisan." He nodded in the direction of Staven. "He loved her."

That took Gideon by surprise. He wanted to ask more, but he heard voices outside and realized that one of the ships had returned. The Mentor smiled. "You'd better get out there and hold Staven's feet to the fire before he puts you off again."

The moment had passed. It was unfortunate, but the old man had a point. And Gideon *was* anxious to be flying again.

"You're right about that," Gideon said to him, nodded at Iden, and went out to greet the returning Dreamers.

The Vushan family, Kaev, and Nadrine were obviously in high spirits. Nadrine's face lit up as she saw Staven, and she quickened her pace. So did he, and he pulled her to him for a deep kiss.

Gideon believed the Mentor when he said Staven had loved his goddaughter. But it was also clear that the Dreamer leader cared deeply for the freckled girl with the laughing eyes. If anything were to happen to her, it would certainly affect him and possibly destabilize the group.

Gideon gave the Kages and Azen his friendliest smile. "How'd it go?" He didn't expect to hear many details; it was just another supply run. So he was surprised when Halia said, "We brought back a present for you, Staven."

"For me? You shouldn't have," Staven said. "I've had my eye on the latest blaster model."

"Better than that," came Azen's voice. "We brought back a hero."

Iden and the Mentor were talking about how to project without losing one's voice as Gideon entered. "Speak from here," the Mentor said, placing a hand on his mid-belly. "From the diaphragm."

"Iden."

Gideon's voice sounded . . . off. She turned to look at him, but his expression was unreadable. "Staven wants you."

"I'm coming," she said, but she didn't need to. The Vushans, Azen, and Staven entered the main gathering cavern, and they had someone with them.

The stormtrooper had lost his helmet and the rest of his upper body armor at some point. His face had been beaten and bloodied, and the black body glove he wore beneath his uniform was torn. Azen hauled him in by one of his arms; the other dangled limply at an angle that ought to have been impossible.

Iden's breath caught, but she forced herself to appear calm.

"Mentor," Staven said, "how did your first session go with our budding new star?"

"What?" asked the Mentor, astonished. It seemed like the strangest query, with a bleeding, half-conscious stormtrooper not three meters away.

"Let's have Iden do a first audition," Staven said. "Sadori, get a holorecorder." While the youngest Kage raced off to obey, Azen threw the trooper to the stone floor of the cave. He cried out and lay there, panting. His uninjured arm quivered as he tried to push himself up.

"This man fancied himself a hero of the Empire. Tried to stop us stealing supplies in an old storage area no one cares about. So we'll feature him in your first speech."

Iden stared, appalled. This man had only been doing his duty. He'd been harming no one, and he was far from any position of power. "Anyone can beat up a guard," she said, grasping for something, anything, to prevent this from happening. "This won't look good. We'll just look like bullies."

"I want to see what you can do." His voice was jovial, but his eyes were cold.

"Staven, this is foolish," the Mentor said. "Iden's right. We won't inspire anyone if we record this."

Sadori returned to the cavern carrying the requested holoprojector. Staven placed it down and turned it on.

"Go ahead, Iden," he said. "Let's hear what kind of a Voice of the Dreamers you are."

She couldn't. But she had to try. Had to do something, or else she'd be on the floor, beaten, bloodied, and broken, just like the unlucky stormtrooper was. So, stiff-legged, Iden Versio, TIE fighter pilot, Death Star survivor, daughter of Admiral Garrick Versio, went to the sprawled figure on the ground and stood over him, her hands on her hips.

But she couldn't think of what to say. Couldn't come up with the phrases of hatred and justification that Staven wanted.

The stormtrooper unwittingly saved her. As Iden frantically tried to speak, he coughed violently, spewing up blood, twitched, and lay still.

"That was uncalled for, Staven," the Mentor said quietly.

"I think it would have sent a powerful message," Staven said.

"Oh, I'm not disagreeing with you on that. It would just have been the wrong message."

Staven glared angrily at the Mentor for a moment, then his gaze slid over to Iden. "We'll never know now. I'm not sure our Voice was up to the task."

"Don't worry about me," Iden snapped.

"But I do, you see, and that's the problem." He shook his head, the anger visibly draining from him to be replaced by a look of exhaustion. "I need either a drink or a flight."

"Well," Gideon said, "how about you let me show you what I can do flying, and then you show me what you can do drinking."

Iden continued to stay silent, but was profoundly grateful for the distraction Gideon was offering. She had no desire to be around Staven right now. In fact, she had no desire to be around anyone. She needed to run, to clear her head, to erase the image of what had just happened. Even though she knew that this was likely just the beginning of what she would be asked to do in the name of the Dreamers.

Asked to do for the Empire, she reminded herself.

"You know what?" Staven said. "Let's do it. Put on something you want to fly in, and let's head to the scrap heap. Then show me what you got."

"The . . . what?"

"You'll see," Staven said. "And comm Del, I want to take his droid along, too. I'll meet you at the ship."

"What about him?" Gideon asked, gesturing to the body on the floor. Dahna and Seyn had wandered in, drawn by the commotion, and Seyn was now talking in hushed tones with Sadori and Halia. The two Inferno Squad team members did not make eye contact.

"Ru, Azen, take him out to the usual spot."

Iden felt her stomach clench at the words and their significance.

Gideon had rejoined Staven wearing the outfit in which he'd arrived, complete with the battered brown jacket. Iden had suggested he wear it frequently, to further cement his connection to the now extinct cell in the Dreamers' mind; it was the same outfit he had worn at Tellik IV, and, as Seyn had thought he might, Staven had indeed seen the altered footage of the explosion at Singularity.

"I thought they outfitted pilots better at Nebula," he said, referring to Gideon's alleged old partisan cell.

"Hey, if you have something better, I'll gladly wear it," Gideon replied. He thought it was a pretty good sidestep. He was starting to get used to this whole undercover thing.

"We'll find out if you're worth wasting a flight suit on," Staven retorted. "Let's go, flyboy."

The scrap heap to which Staven was referring was a cache of stolen ships housed in another one of the seemingly ubiquitous caverns that riddled the landscape. It indeed looked like a large-scale junkyard.

Everything from landspeeders to droid parts to starfighters was here. Staven had brought a light and led Gideon past ship after ship, taking him deeper into the cavern's sloping chamber. Gideon unfastened the droid from his back, casually thumbed a concealed button, and let it explore. It would record everything it saw—and that could be very useful at some point. Del had hoped that, once the Dreamers dropped their guard, the droid could be utilized for eavesdropping, but for now it wasn't yet welcome everywhere.

As they moved back, the droid emitted a few noises of discovery. They sounded sad to Gideon's ears—but that was probably him anthropomorphizing. It was just a machine. He turned, curious—and his eyes widened as his gaze fell on a damaged TIE fighter. He felt like he'd been kicked in the chest and stared too long at it, drawing Staven's attention. If the droid had indeed "felt" sad, Gideon certainly shared the emotion.

"Yep," Staven said, stepping beside him and gazing at the black vessel, "we managed to steal one of those and bring it back. Somewhat the worse for wear, unfortunately. Ever seen one of these babies up close before?"

Gideon shook his head. "Nope," he said, glad his voice didn't betray him.

"The Empire makes good ships, I'll give them that. I want to get it fixed up one day and use it against the bastards. I guess everyone has a dream, right?"

A cold, slow anger began to simmer inside Gideon, along with the urge to strike the rebel leader. "Right," he said instead. "Maybe you should get Del on that."

"Right now," said Staven, "I'm getting *you* in *that*." Gideon tore his eyes away from the TIE to see what Staven was pointing to and did a double take.

It was a very beat-up, very sad-looking A-wing.

"You're kidding me."

"I never kid."

"That piece of junk would make Del cry. Hell, it would make his droid cry." He put his hands on his hips and sighed. "Well, it takes a sense of humor to ask me to fly that, or have you lost that completely?"

Strangely, Staven smiled. "I had one, once. We win this war, I might have it again. But for now . . . let's just say if you can put this old rattletrap through its paces and make it look good, you pass."

Gideon almost started laughing as the droid moved from one end of the ship to the other, conducting a cursory inspection. It was almost more than his life was worth to even get in the thing, let alone do acrobatics with it. But then again, his life was indeed on the line. At last the droid came back.

"Is it flyable?" Gideon asked it.

The droid beeped. Del was better than anyone at deciphering its sounds, but after several days alone with it and Del in the close quarters of the *Fast Friend*, he'd come to understand it pretty well. The droid was giving him the equivalent of *I think this might be safe*. Hopefully, it would be better inside.

It was not better inside. "What do you even *use* this for, anyway?" he asked Staven. The vessel had two seats—one for the pilot, one for an instructor. Staven settled down into the instructor's seat.

"Target practice," Staven replied, fastening his crash webbing.

"That's not even funny," Gideon said, taking time to familiarize himself with the controls. He'd never been in one of these before and did not want to make any rookie mistakes.

"I'm not joking," Staven said. He kept his face straight for about ten full seconds before a sly grin got the better of him. "Your face," he said, chuckling. "But seriously, the A-wing's spaceworthy. And if it turns out not to be . . ." He patted the chair. "Both of these are ejectors."

The droid, hovering behind Gideon, suddenly booped and attached itself firmly to Gideon's shoulder.

"Listen," Gideon warned as he slowly moved the ship toward the cave entrance, "if you want me to show you what I can do, I'm going to put this ship through its paces. It may rattle your teeth a bit. You sure it can handle that kind of treatment?"

"Bring it on," said Staven.

"Your funeral," said Gideon. "Well, mine, too, but I'm game."

As soon as they were cleared, he narrowed his eyes, his heart speeding up in gleeful anticipation. "Here we go," he said. And the ship exploded into action.

Staven swore loudly as he was slammed against the back of the seat. With barely a meter of clearance, Gideon maneuvered the ship like he would a speeder, zipping along the flat stone and then veering hard to the right to plunge into the overhanging canopy.

"What the hell?" Staven said, turning to stare at Gideon with wide eyes.

Gideon ignored him. "This is what you do to shake pursuit," he said. He could hear the thumping and scraping of tree limbs against the ship's hull, but he'd assessed it well—there was enough space here for him to bring the ship through with little to no damage. It cleared out up ahead. He tilted the nose up sharply. Again, he and the partisan leader were flattened against the backs of their seats. He could feel the little droid tightening its grip, could hear its soft, long beeps.

Up they soared, almost completely vertically, then Gideon leveled it out. Time for some impressive moves. He pulled backward and the A-wing made a tight loop— and two more for good measure.

Staven had fallen silent, and Gideon was grinning like an idiot. This was a rickety old bucket, and it might yet kill him, but if it did, he'd die doing what he loved.

Back down again. He'd found the weapons controls now, and fired the laser cannons at that rock formation there, that clump of trees there, then soared up and over the butte that was suddenly right in front of them, up, up, piercing the cloud layer into a sky dotted with stars against a still-purple field of frozen dusk.

There was silence. Gideon turned to look at Staven.

The leader of the Dreamers looked more alive, more fully present, than Gideon had yet seen him. Gone was the stone-faced, humorless man who had stared coolly at him and Del, who had given Iden a look of almost pure hatred. That armor had been falling off him piece by piece as he welcomed his—partner? girlfriend?—back. More had been shed as he had shown Gideon a place that the former TIE pilot believed Staven thought of less as a junkyard and more as a treasure trove. Now it was as if the armor were completely gone. This was Staven as he might once have been.

"I've never seen anything like that in my life," the Dreamer said. "And I've seen a lot."

Pride surged in Gideon, then it abated almost at once. Even at his best, Iden had always been able to fly rings around him. And once Staven had seen Iden fly, Gideon would again be relegated to second best in someone's opinion.

The thought cooled his excitement but didn't erase it entirely. For now Iden was persona non grata, and Staven was impressed with him, and he would content himself with that.

"Shall we head back?" he asked.

"Not just yet," Staven said. "I think you still have a few more boulders to strafe."

CHAPTER 17

Iden forced herself to watch as Azen and Ru stepped forward, picking up the stormtrooper's body between them and half carrying, half dragging him out of the cave. She wondered if anyone was going to clean up the blood and vomit. Even as she had the thought, Kaev and Nadrine entered with buckets of water and cloths.

Iden couldn't help it. She looked away. The Mentor sat with her for a moment longer, then excused himself. "I'll be in the sleeping cavern if you want to talk, Iden. Or practice some more."

"Sure looks like I need it," Iden said. What Staven had done had been intended to shock her, to catch her off guard, and she was angry with herself that she had let the ploy work.

"You'll be fine. I have absolute faith in you." He patted her shoulder comfortingly, then rose and left.

Dahna, leaning against the cave entrance, watched him go, then turned to look at Iden. She seemed to make up her mind about something and strode forward, sitting on the flattened rock beside the admiral's daughter.

"Bet you miss the feel of a blaster in your hand," Dahna said.

Iden looked at her in surprise. "You read my mind," she said.

Dahna chuckled warmly. "No need for that. Our ways take some getting used to, and to be honest, that was a dirty trick Staven pulled on you."

"Thanks," Iden said uncertainly. "But it sounds like this has happened before, if you have a 'usual place' to put bodies."

"It has," the Twi'lek said. "We have scavengers here—big ones. We call them Crunchers. They're like big rodents—and I mean big—and they'll eat anything, and all of it. They'll take off what we can use of the trooper's armor and leave the rest for the Crunchers."

Which meant that the armor Iden would next be mending and cleaning would be the trooper's. Everything about this was ghoulish. She couldn't think of anything to say to that.

Dahna smiled kindly. "I know this is hard for you. These people used to be allies. But they aren't, and I believe you understand that. You'll get used to it, but until the Empire is overthrown, it has to be done. Come on. Let's go shoot something."

A quick ride in a speeder took them to an open area with scattered boulders and the occasional lone tree. Some of the boulders obviously had been part of much larger ones at one time, and the black scoring on them told Iden that this was a popular site for target practice. Iden took the blaster that Dahna handed her. It was an older model but well maintained, and it could kill just as efficiently as a newer one.

"You're letting me shoot. Thanks," Iden said. Both women knew that there was a chance Iden would simply use the blaster on Dahna, and Iden appreciated the trust. "Now I just need to get Staven to let me pilot."

"You sound like Gid," Dahna said, casually flipping off the safety of her own blaster. "Never saw a young man so in love with the sky. Staven's taken quite a shine to him."

Iden was pleased that Staven had finally agreed to test Gideon's piloting skills. While she was better than her friend, she knew Gideon was superb. They were TIE-fighter pilots: They had to be. She knew Gideon must miss being at the controls as much as she did, and she was glad he was getting the chance to fly again.

"Watch my pattern and duplicate it," Dahna said. Casually, her blaster on minimum power so as not to reduce her targets to rubble, the Twi'lek took aim and fired seven times in what seemed like a random pattern, even whirling around after the fourth blast to shoot at boulders that were behind them. Iden watched like a shirrhawk. It felt good to drop into that place of laser-like focus. To not think about a stormtrooper being beaten to death for protecting a warehouse, or gigantic ratlike creatures devouring his remains. To not worry about letting some damning truth slip accidentally. She liked her world when it was just target, weapon, and her.

"Your turn," Dahna said, bringing Iden back into the present, where every word was a potential grenade.

Iden nodded. "Good for Gid," she said as she aimed her blaster. "After this last fiasco I'm beginning to think that the only way I can get on Staven's good side is to single-handedly take down the Emperor."

She emulated Dahna, hitting the boulders in the precise order demonstrated.

"Good shooting," Dahna said, the words casual although the Twi'lek was clearly impressed. "I think if you did get a shot at the Emperor, you just might be able to take him down. And don't be too hard on Staven. He'll come around. Now—see that cluster of trees?"

Iden saw some burned trunks that were on their last legs—or maybe their last roots. "If you want to call them that, yes," she replied. These were much further off, and Dahna switched out her handheld blaster for a rifle.

"There's seven of them, total. Some are harder to see than the others. Again, memorize my order." Dahna fired, then handed over the rifle.

And again, Iden completed the exercise perfectly. Unlike Seyn or Del, or even Gideon, she didn't have to pretend to be less experienced than she actually was. The Dreamers knew her reputation, and now all that skill and training was on their side—or so they thought.

She and Dahna had turned one of the trees into nothing more than kindling by the time they were done. "How long have you been with the Dreamers?" Iden asked. She figured she had plenty of time to ask innocent-sounding questions and, hopefully, get a lead on which Dreamer was the one with the intel.

And while it wasn't flying, it felt glorious to be shooting a weapon again.

"The whole group is new," Dahna said. She holstered her blaster and began walking, waving for Iden to follow her. They were heading toward another cluster of boulders. "We were bits and pieces of other groups. After Saw's death, we . . . kind of crumpled. Some went off on solo missions that were really just suicide-by-stormtrooper. Others disappeared—maybe turning themselves in."

Like Bokk, Iden thought, but did not say.

"Staven and the Mentor connected, somehow. They won't even tell us. They're a strange pair, but they loved Saw, and they love liberty, and they hate the Empire. Staven's the boss, but he values the Mentor. We're doing things now that the old partisans never could do. And I am so glad to be a part of it." She glanced over at Iden. "And I'm glad you're here, too, Iden. To see someone who was once so deep in the Empire's heart and know she understands . . . you're going to inspire a lot of people. And you'll make a difference. But first . . . we're going to try to shoot each other."

Iden's body grew taut. Then Dahna laughed. "I'm just joking!" she said. "I just want to test your reflexes. We're going to use these boulders for cover and fire at each other. First one to get stunned loses. And," she added, "do make sure your blaster isn't on kill."

When she and the Twi'lek returned about an hour later, the bloodstains on the stone cavern floor were gone. Staven and Gideon had returned, and the Dreamer leader looked much more relaxed. He even nodded politely to Iden as she entered.

"Your codes," he said. "We're going to try them next trip."

Iden blinked in surprise. "Great. I hope they haven't been changed. It's been four days."

Staven scowled. "Yeah. That one's on me." Gideon was indeed being a good influence; that was as close to an apology as Iden thought she'd ever get from the blue-haired young man.

"Some of us are going on a supply run later this afternoon. You're welcome to come if you like," Dahna said as Iden reached for a bottle and filled it from a water container. "We're going over to the sun side. Might be a nice change for you."

Iden was about to open her mouth to agree when Del's droid, which had been hovering beside Gideon, turned its red photoreceptor in her direction. Slowly, it "blinked" three times as it looked directly at her.

Del's words came back to her: *I'm trying to make sure this little guy can help out in all kinds of ways!*

"Thanks for the invitation, Dahna, but I think I'll try to go find the Mentor. Anyone know where he is?" If he was onsite, she'd talk to him briefly, then go for a "run" and get somewhere safe to talk to Del through the droid. If not, she could go "look" for the Mentor.

"He went off a while ago," Kaev said as he entered and headed straight for the food alcove. "He does that a lot. Never sure where he goes, just says that he has to go sort out his his thoughts."

Convenient. "Staven . . . you're right. I need more practice."

He looked as surprised at her words as she doubtless had earlier, then he nodded. "Good" was all he said.

The droid floated out of the cavern. "And off it goes back to Del," Gideon said. "I'm jealous of him and that little contraption. He needs to make me one."

"He needs to make all of us one," Iden said, then left.

Seyn was in the common sleeping cavern and looked up when Iden entered. "Are you all right?" Seyn asked quietly.

"Are you?" Iden replied.

"Staven likes to shock. We should expect things like this from now on." As Seyn spoke, the droid entered, humming. "Oh good, finally. Give your comlink to the droid. Del has installed a second button and a second channel for us." She filled Iden in on the security around this method of communication while the droid went to work.

Iden clicked the second button and as instructed, said, "Del?"

"Clear," Del's warm voice replied, and the two women exchanged relieved glances.

"You're brilliant, Del," Iden said.

"Remember you said that when we finally get debriefed," Del said. "The three of us have been in communication for a while via this channel. Gid's still with Staven, but since no one questions our talking privately together I can catch him up later. Captain, I know you have things to share with us, but I think Seyn's got the most pressing concern."

Curious, Iden looked at Seyn.

With a somberness that belied her young features, Seyn stated, "I recognized Azen Novaren. He's an Imperial agent. His real name is Lar Kantayan."

Stunned, Iden managed, "Did he recognize you, too?"

"We've never met or worked together. I'm lucky that at one point his file crossed my desk, and I took a brief look at it. I wished I'd seen more, but I can tell you what I know."

Iden was profoundly grateful for Seyn's eidetic memory as the former NavInt agent continued, "He was a less than stellar ISB agent. He had a couple of formal censures, and there was talk of termination." She didn't elaborate as to what type of "termination" had been discussed. "You will recall your father said that there had been an attempt to infiltrate the partisans before. That was Lars Kantayan—though I guess we should call him Azen Novaren now. He and Staven have worked together before—but Novaren was acting as our agent. ISB recalled him, which is why he and Staven hadn't seen each other in a couple of years. Novaren was reassigned to Vardos."

"Vardos?" Iden asked. "Why Vardos?"

"It was definitely a demotion. The Empire always likes to keep an eye on things, and there were apparently rumors that Gleb might not be as trustworthy as one would like—skimming off the top, making her own deals, that sort of thing. The document didn't go into specifics, and investigations like this happen all the time. However, because it was Vardos, Admiral Versio was not informed that she was under investigation."

Iden rubbed her eyes. "One hand didn't know what the other hand was doing then. All right, so he was reassigned to Vardos, and my father didn't know. But why did Azen bring me here? Would they have reassigned him?"

"No," Seyn said firmly. "Not back to the partisans with that kind of record."

"So he's acting on his own."

"In my opinion, yes. From what we've heard here, he and Staven were in contact while he was on Vardos. He knew Staven was looking for a mouthpiece, and then you appeared."

"Is he acting as a partisan or as an Imperial agent?" There was silence, from both Del and Seyn. "Let me re-phrase that. Seyn, what would be your best guess?"

"It's hard to tell. He wasn't pulled out because anyone felt he was becoming a true believer, but rather that he wasn't accomplishing anything. My best guess would be that he's either become a double agent, or he's trying to get back into ISB's good graces by handing them a real coup."

"The last true leader of the partisans, me, and who-ever the Mentor is," Iden said.

"The Mentor?" It was Del. "What about him?"

"That can wait, but essentially, I have reason to be-lieve that once he was a public figure of some note. I'll have plenty of one-on-one time with him to see what else I can get him to tell me. I do know that, like Staven, he worked with Saw early on, and knew and respected Saw's sister, Steela."

"Gid said that the Mentor's goddaughter was in-volved with the partisans—and that Staven was in love with her," Del offered.

"That's . . . a pretty major connection," Iden said. "They seem so different, Staven and the Mentor. On so many levels. Dahna says that the two of them formed the Dreamers together. They've both got ties not to just Saw but to each other. They're both determined to honor his memory by destroying the Empire. I had suspected that he or Staven would be our target—but now I have to wonder if our leak is Azen. He's the only one we know for certain once had access to classified Imperial information."

"I'd agree about Azen, and I'm surprised to hear about the Mentor. I didn't recognize him," Seyn said. She looked annoyed.

"Seyn, you can't have seen pictures of everyone in the known galaxy," Iden said. "Don't worry about it. We'll figure all that out later. Right now, what I want to know is, is Azen going to be a problem? Does he suspect us?"

"I think he would have let us know if he did," Seyn said.

"No wonder he searched me so carefully," Iden said. "He was trying to find out if I was acting on behalf of the Empire. That certainly would have thrown a wrench into the works. Good to know my cover passed an ISB agent's inspection. Del, any way you can set up a bug on him?"

There was a silence, then he said, "I can try. But if the partisans are paranoid and double-check everything, you can bet that a double agent would be worse. It'd be awfully risky, and if he found out about us—"

"We can't let that happen," Iden interrupted. The thought of being at Azen's mercy, or revealing anything about what they were doing—no. Inferno Squad had a purpose far beyond one man's greed, and there was no way to tell where his loyalty really lay. If he had any at all. "Dammit. This was the last thing we needed. We don't have time to play a long game against two enemies."

"So, what do we do?" asked Del.

Seyn hesitated, then said, "My instincts say we can't

trust him. The reason he was given black marks was, and I quote, 'agent failed to provide sufficient support for fellow operatives.' I think if he finds out about Inferno Squad's mission he'd use us to get the intel for himself, then turn us over to Staven right away even if he isn't a double agent. He won't want us stealing his thunder if or when he betrays the Dreamers.

"If you were working with him in the field, would you trust him? And if you were his superior, would you send him out in the field again?"

"No. To both. Not in a million years."

"Del?"

"I don't have Seyn's insight, but I certainly don't like him. Gideon says he'd like to punch him, but while that would be entertaining I don't think that would help."

Iden smiled a little. Del always knew what to say and when. "I'm with you all. I hate to say this about a fellow Imperial, but I don't trust him. And we can't risk this mission."

"What are your orders, Captain?" Del asked. Seyn looked at Iden expectantly.

"We have to find out if he's our leak, and recover what we were sent here to find if so. Regardless . . . we take him down. And here's how we're going to do it."

CHAPTER 18

Seyn was impatient as she returned to the main cavern. It was a new sensation for her. Since her graduation from the Academy and even before, she had been capable of deep focus for extended periods of time. While she had heard some of the others complain about how much they disliked "living in half-light" all the time, Seyn didn't mind this aspect of the mission. She had spent almost all her time in a small room, alone with the comfortable glow of computer screens.

Then, her role had been passive: a translator, an observer. But now she was interacting, and in ways quite different from those she had anticipated.

The subject of one of those ways was waiting for her, his strong, chiseled features drawn with worry. Sadori had noticed her reaction to the stormtrooper's murder, and they had talked about it a little bit, but he was still concerned about how she might be feeling. It was touching, and strange, and Seyn was conflicted.

If she was smaller and looked younger than her age, then Sadori was the opposite. Well built and graceful, he looked older than Kaev, who had four years on him. The Kage in general were regarded as uncommonly beautiful among humans and near-humans, and Sadori was a fine example of that. How was it that this kind young man, who was so fierce when he fought and so gentle when he did not, found it so easy to reconcile the level of violence that the Dreamers advocated?

"Are you all right, Seyn?" he asked solicitously.

"Yes," she said. "I've had some time to think." To remind herself of why she was there, and to have a new goal to focus on. "Sometimes hard choices are necessary ones. Is this something you had to learn, too?"

"My people are born into lives of deprivation," he said. "I knew how to fight almost before I knew how to walk." The fighting ability of the Kage Warriors, it was said, sometimes evoked comparisons to the Jedi. They were physically powerful and phenomenally agile. "We've fought together as a team—well, forever."

"Does your family still go on missions together?" Seyn inquired. As she listened to the response, which could be valuable, she also listened to conversations going on in other tongues.

—*changed the security code at*—

"We used to, until Saw's death. Now, when I go on a mission, one of my parents always comes with me while one stays behind."

She looked at him askance. "I don't understand. Why don't they want to fight together any more?"

He looked embarrassed. "It's silly," he said.

—*excellent place for a drop and run*—Ru, Sadori's father, was saying quietly to Azen.

"If you were trained so young, you obviously know how to take care of yourself."

"It's not that. Since Jedha, things . . ." He hesitated. "We're dedicated. All of the Dreamers, not just my family. You've seen it, we all go in with bombs on our bodies, and we're ready to use them. But I'm their only child, and if something went wrong—they want someone there to protect me, and someone back here if . . . so there's one of them left for me to come back to."

Something inside Seyn softened unexpectedly. It was such a strange juxtaposition, this calm discussion about bombs strapped on bodies and parents not wanting to leave a beloved child an orphan, even as their actions could make orphans of others. Impulsively she reached out and squeezed his arm.

"Don't be ashamed of that," she said. "They love you. They know what we do is dangerous, and they want to minimize any risk you might have. I'm sure it's not because they don't respect you as a warrior."

His normally guarded face lit up with surprised pleasure, then he gently placed his own large, strong hand over her small one.

"I think . . . I finally understand how they might feel that way. I'm glad you're coming on a mission with me, but I wish you weren't, too," Sadori said. "I wanted to ask you first, but I didn't think I should get your hopes up in case Staven said no. I thought it would be a good opportunity for you."

"Do you know the details?"

Sadori shook his head. "Staven hasn't shared them yet. He likes to keep things close to his vest." Seyn had noticed. "You can say no if you want to."

"This is important," Seyn said. "I want to be part of it."

Gideon was holding forth about flying. Staven was laughing and had his arm around Nadrine, who snuggled into him with a soft, contented smile.

"It *is* important," Sadori agreed. "Since Jedha, just like Staven said, there's been a fresh urgency. I'm glad we're in a unit with two people who actually knew Saw. I trust them to know what they're doing—how to make everything we do count. We need to strike and not hold back, no matter what the mission or the target. My family is fighting for something that's even more important than our homeworld. We're fighting for a future that *doesn't* involve fighting," Sadori said, his voice soft. He gazed at her intently, and his hand on hers was warm.

—if he'd just tell us more—Ru continued.

"There you are." Azen's voice. He was addressing Iden and the Mentor, who apparently had just returned. Sadori sighed, squeezed Seyn's hand, and let go as they both turned to the newcomers. "Where have you two been? More rehearsals?"

"As many as it takes," Iden said before the Mentor could speak.

"I'll help as much as I can," the Mentor promised her.

"How about now?" Iden suggested.

"I like how you think!" exclaimed the Mentor. "Let's go!"

Seyn watched them leave. "Do you need to get back to work, too?" Sadori asked her.

Yes, Seyn thought. *I do.* She knew Del needed information about Azen in order to conduct an efficient search of the ship's databank.

But there was other work to be done, too. She turned to Sadori and took his large, strong hand in hers, curling her fingers about his.

"I'd rather stay here and talk," she said. "The Mentor seems so nice. How long have you known him?"

Piikow had been resting, which had given Del the time he'd needed to upgrade Iden's comlink and discuss Seyn's discovery. After the conversation, Del took advantage of the fact that he had his droid but not his minder and went to the cavern where Iden's old J-Sec starfighter was being kept.

His first thought had been to access the computer. Iden had replied that, unfortunately, she would not be of help in this case. During her time under "house arrest" on Vardos, she had not been permitted to have access to the ship's computer for anything other than routine flights. Only her copilot, most recently one Azen Novaren, also known by a host of other aliases, knew that.

So Del had to rely on the droid.

He kept one eye on the entrance to the cavern while the droid hummed and beeped as it attempted to bypass security protocols. Seyn had offered to compile a list for Del of everything she knew about Azen, so soon he would have a list of keywords to look for.

They were all bringing their best game toward this abruptly urgent task, but Del never quite realized just how alone they would be if things didn't go according to plan. The mineral composition of the planet's rocks, which helped conceal the Dreamers' vessels and technology, also made any contact impossible unless it was local or the communication equipment was out in the open. There was no way for Inferno Squad to contact the admiral that wouldn't be detected. The hope was that soon at least one member of the team would be deemed trustworthy enough to fly solo. Then, whoever it was might possibly be able to get a message out.

If the mission went well, that moment might arrive sooner rather than later, but it sure as hell wasn't now. Del simply had to hope they'd get lucky. Because if they didn't, it would only be a matter of time before a trained Imperial agent—double or not—would sniff them out.

He had barely started when Piikow commed him. "Come back to the cavern," he chirped. "There's something I want to show you."

Frustrated, Del asked, "Are you sure? I can keep working on my own if you want to rest some more."

"I'm certain," Piikow replied, "and there's plenty of time to sleep when you're dead, so come on back!"

Curious as to what this was all about, Del obeyed. Piikow had a sly, satisfied look on his batlike face as he bustled Del into a speeder that he himself, naturally, had revamped to suit his small stature as driver. "Staven gave me this one in exchange for my promise to quit trying to, ah, *improve* the others without express permission," he said, in all seriousness.

"It looks terrific," Del said politely. Actually, it looked slightly insane. Piikow had completely gutted the interior. The entire console had been redesigned, with all the buttons and the steering wheel sized to the Chadra-Fan's smaller fingers and much shorter reach. They were also much prettier than standard, utilitarian buttons and glowed like tiny gemstones. Piikow's seat was designed to accommodate his size and was luxuriously padded, and the crash webbing was decorative as well as efficient. The overall effect was that the small furred driver was snuggled in securely, wrapped almost like a baby in a blanket. It would have been funny, except that Piikow looked so pleased and content with the results.

Del didn't know what his friend had done with the ship's engine, but when he climbed in and Piikow took off, it was a startlingly smooth and swift ride. "Where are we going?" he asked as the speeder zipped along.

"Did you know," said Piikow, answering with another question, "that there used to be a sentient species on Jeosyn?"

"I did not," Del admitted.

"Since I'm not able to go on any missions, I've spent my time here learning about this world. These long dawns and twilights, and the even longer days and nights—everything had to evolve to accommodate that. The animal life, for instance. Nearly everything that's not rooted down either migrates or hibernates. And because the dawns and dusks are so long, there's a whole variety of species that live just in those windows! It's fascinating!"

Del wasn't a scientist, but Piikow's enthusiasm was contagious. It *was* kind of interesting. He settled back in to listen.

"And the plants!" Piikow crowed. "Incredible! They alternate between the sun and volcanic activity for their energy. There's so much to learn here, so many different examples of ways to think creatively. For instance, you already know that one of the reasons we're so safe here is that there is a unique combination of minerals in the planet's surface that prevents anyone from scanning us. Isn't that helpful? What we could do with that, if we had the resources to understand the combination."

Del realized that Piikow had been squandered laboring in a factory. If someone in the Empire had reached out to him and his family and given him a place in research—but that was a dark road to go down, and a futile one. What was done, was done.

He redirected Piikow back to the original topic. "Tell me about the sentient life," he said.

"Oh, right . . . well, I can't."

Del blinked. "What?"

"Well, I can't, because we've no idea what happened to them. I've read up on the archaeological expeditions, and they all are laced with extreme frustration. The most recent one happened more than a century ago. Everyone washed their hands of this place because there's just not anything to explore. The species left no remains, no buildings, very few tools, no writing or art that's recognizable as such, and no technology. Except for one thing."

"What?"

Piikow, who had been diligently keeping his eyes forward and his hands on the tiny wheel, now gave Del a devious glance. "*That's* where we're going."

Del frowned. "Give me a hint."

The Chadra-Fan, clearly delighted with Del's reaction, shook his large-eared head. "Nope. You'll see!"

Resigned, Del settled back into his seat and closed his eyes. And then the next thing he knew, Piikow was poking him with his clawed, stubby fingers and saying, "We're here! Wake up!"

"Here" seemed to be yet another cavern. Piikow climbed out of the speeder, retrieved his walking stick and a lantern, and moved toward the yawning entrance. Del swung his long legs out and caught up quickly.

"I found what I'm about to show you quite by accident a few years ago," Piikow said, a bit sheepishly. "When I first arrived. I'd built my little speeder and was doing some exploring on my own . . . not the wisest idea, considering I fell and crashed through an extraordinarily thin layer of rock into a second cavern below! Fortunately, I was able to get out—and in the meantime, I discovered something wonderful. Come on!"

He ambled farther inside the cavern. Del followed, and then he stopped. "Is it my imagination or is it getting lighter in here?"

"It is! Er, isn't. I mean it's not your imagination. The light is coming from the hole I made when I fell through."

The two continued on, the light growing stronger—a cool, indigo illumination. Del could see the aforementioned hole in the stone floor now—and a ladder poking up from it. Another lamp and various tools and a length of rope sat at the ready beside the mouth.

Piikow went to the ladder and plunked down his lamp. Carefully he began to descend, pausing only to wave Del forward. "Come on, come on!"

Del didn't need much more urging. Other than pausing to ascertain whether the ladder would bear his weight, he followed willingly. Like darkness made visible, the indigo radiance wrapped around him as he descended. When his feet touched solid ground, Del turned around.

And started back, gasping.

They were huge, and they were stone, and they were

still. And they stretched back as far as the eye could see. They had heads and arms and legs, and the beautiful, eerie purple light was shining from what passed for eye sockets.

"Statues," he murmured. "They're beautiful."

"And a trifle alarming," Piikow said. "I must confess, I was scared to death for a moment when I first saw them."

Del wasn't going to admit to having the same reaction. If the creations before him had been crafted to resemble their long-dead, mysterious creators, the beings had been near human, though the faces—save for those eerie, radiant eye sockets—were a complete blank. The heads didn't even have hair, or a realistic shape—just a perfect orb perched atop a surprisingly detailed form. The figures had cloven feet and hands that had two opposable thumbs. They were even modestly dressed, with artfully carved, draping folds and breeches covering forms that appeared to be androgynous. Was this how they had actually looked? Del wondered. Or were these completely imaginary beings constructed by ancient crafters?

"Why so many?" Del wondered aloud. "And why were they all locked away down here?"

"Ah, if we only knew," sighed the Chadra-Fan. "But someday we might. I do know one thing, though."

Piikow seized Del's hand and tugged him farther down the cavern. One of the statues had fallen, and Piikow had covered it with a blanket. It presented a curious image, as if the Chadra-Fan had been concerned that the statue might catch a chill.

"This one toppled down, for some reason. Look!" With a flourish, the Chadra-Fan pulled off the blanket.

The simply carved orb that had served the statue for a head had cracked open, revealing purple crystals. Clearly, the ancient denizens of Jeosyn had used crystals to mimic glowing eyes. But there weren't simply two crystals inside the hollow skull. There were three—two small ones and one much larger one.

Del's gaze wandered down the body from the head. Piikow had taken tools to the the statue, opening it up further, and now Del could see that it was not, as he had thought, carved of solid stone.

It was as hollow as the head was. And inside the ceramic torso, arranged in all the places that one might expect to find organs in living beings, crystals of different sizes and shapes were positioned. These, too, had been carefully carved. Tentatively, Del reached out and touched one of the crystals.

It was polished to perfect smoothness and it was warm.

Stunned, he looked over at a gleeful Piikow.

"You see, don't you? These figures—they weren't pieces of art or architecture," the Chadra-Fan said, his high voice hushed with awe. "These were *machines*."

Del sank back on his heels, wonder flowing through him. "But why create them just to put them down here? What was their purpose?"

"Maybe," Piikow said, "if we could get one working . . . it could tell us."

Del looked back at the tumbled-down . . . droid? He supposed that was what it was, technically: a droid made of stone and crystal instead of metal, plastoid, and wiring. "Do . . . do you have time to work on this?"

"Rarely," the little tinkerer replied, sighing. "You're aware of how few of us know how to fix things when they break. Especially since most of the things we get are already broken, in some way. They have me working for hours on end. There's always something to keep me busy."

He turned from gazing raptly at the droid to peer conspiratorially at Del. "But, if another talented technician just happened to show up . . . who could speed up those regular repairs by working with me as a team . . . maybe both of us would create some free time to work on these stone fellows down here."

Del was torn. He was here with a mission: to recover the lost information that had revitalized the Dreamers. And now there was a secondary one—investigate Azen. He should stay as close to as many of the cell members as possible, so that he could overhear or observe anything that might be useful.

But he'd never even imagined stumbling across anything like this. Inhabitants of the galaxy, over the millennia, had utilized crystal energy as fuel. And the Death Star itself, of course, had been so awe-inspiringly deadly because it drew its energy from kyber crystals. But these crystals just seemed to . . . sit there. He knew it would drive him crazy to walk away from this.

Maybe there was a way to make it work out so he could do both. Piikow was a chatty little fellow. If Del could direct the Chadra-Fan's attention properly, Piikow might unwittingly reveal information he wasn't supposed to. And it wasn't as if he wouldn't be able to spend as much time as he needed working for the Squad before heading down here.

Inferno Squad was first, always. But this could be second.

Del made his decision. "Maybe we could," he said. And smiled.

CHAPTER 19

A few hours later, Dahna, Kaev, and Halia returned from a supply run with containers filled to the brim with a fruit that smelled like the very best kind of hot summer day. Just a whiff made Iden, who had returned moments before with the Mentor, smile and her mouth water. Everyone crowded around and helped themselves, peeling the fruits deftly and popping the tangy-sweet sections into their mouths.

"What is this called?" Iden asked, wiping her lips as the juice trickled down.

"No idea," said Sadori. He snagged one of the largest of the bright-yellow fruits and presented it to Seyn with an awkward but somehow endearing little bow. She smiled and took it, laughing as she peeled it.

"We call it Dahna fruit, because she loves it so much and it makes her happy," his mother said. Iden was surprised that the female Kage had even acknowledged her, let alone answered her question so cheerfully. Apparently, Dahna fruit not only tasted wonderful, but also brought out the best in people.

Then, without warning, Dahna grabbed Piikow's hand and tugged playfully on it. "Come on," she urged, and led the Chadra-Fan out toward the front of the cavern.

Iden was completely confused. "What are they doing?" she asked the Mentor as he came up beside her. He, like everyone else, was smiling.

"Why, they're dancing," he said.

And sure enough, the Twi'lek was stamping her feet on the ground, her graceful body moving in time to an unseen melody. Her lekku danced, too, undulating and twining. Seyn was watching with great interest. *Studying what Dahna is saying,* Iden thought. Then Seyn looked startled as she had her own hand taken and Sadori led her out onto what now had to be thought of as the dance floor.

Piikow was thoroughly enjoying himself, chittering with laughter and moving as much as his frail body would permit. Iden was confused. The Kage couple smiled at each other—Iden had never seen that before—and went to dance as well, holding each other's hands and swaying together.

"I see that," Iden said, annoyed, "but why?"

"Why do people dance?" the Mentor asked, and this time she realized he was teasing.

She was still annoyed. "A Twi'lek," she said. "I know enough about slavery to know that Twi'lek female slaves are very popular with . . . with people who own slaves. Their masters make them dance for their own entertainment. So why would Dahna *want* to dance?"

"Let's ask her!" the Mentor said. Then he called out, "Dahna! Our newest member wants to know why you want to dance, since you were forced to as a slave."

Iden expected everything to come to an awkward, if not downright hostile, halt. Instead, the teal-skinned woman threw back her head and laughed.

"Because I *can*, child," she said. "Not because I have to. Because I want to. Because I can dance, or sing, or not do any of those things if I don't feel like it. I dance because I'm happy, here, with my family. I dance because I am *free*."

A roar of approval went up. "This is what you're helping bring about, Iden," the Mentor continued.

"Partying?" Iden said, only a little sarcastically. Dahna's simple joy in her movement was infectious. Piikow, though still enjoying himself, had started to tire, and then Del had darted in, gently carrying the elderly Chadra-Fan to one of the flat-topped rocks where he could recover from the exertion.

"No," the Mentor replied, choosing to take the question seriously. "You're helping to bring freedom to the galaxy. So that one day, everywhere, people will be safe to express themselves. To enjoy, without fear. That's what the rebels want, in the end. That's all we want."

Del caught her eye and gave her a warm grin. Surprised, Iden smiled back, a bit awkwardly.

"This makes you uncomfortable," the Mentor observed.

Yes, it does. Because what I'm seeing here now couldn't be more different from what happened here this morning. And it's hard for me to know that these hearts that are so full this moment can turn so cruel.

"It's certainly not the Empire," she said. "And . . . that may take some getting used to."

The next morning, if the term could even be used in a place that was constantly twilight, Inferno Squad was scattered as usual when they were sent for. Staven was waiting for them in the common cavern. Gideon was already there, sitting beside him, cleaning a blaster. He nodded at his "brother" in greeting, but largely ignored the rest of them.

"I hope you're ready to get to the real work," Staven said. "Because I've got jobs for all of you."

Finally, Iden thought. She, Del, and Seyn quickly expressed their willingness. Gideon looked as though this was not news—which it probably wasn't. He and Staven appeared to have bonded after Gideon's test flight.

Staven waved them all to sit while he outlined the plan. "The Empire has begun mining operations on Affadar, and we all know what that means."

Iden knew a little about Affadar. It was a largely undeveloped world, with a relatively small population of humans and an indigenous amphibian species called the T'Laeem. The T'Laeem were sentient but primitive. Mining operations there couldn't be beneficial to them, but the human population would likely benefit from a new prosperity. And, of course, the Empire would have access to resources necessary to continue the war. The Empire was often faced with such difficult choices.

"For a change, the worst thing about this situation is not the Empire," Staven said. "It's the local government in the designated mining province that has chosen to work with them. Specifically, the ephor, Emoch Akagarti. He's personally profited from the alliance at the expense of not only a beautiful world and the likely extinction of a sentient species but the health of his own people—or so rumor has it."

He smiled that edgey, cruel smile. "In three days, we're going to pay him a visit. We're going to use the J-Sec ship that Azen so nicely brought us when he kidnapped Iden. Del, we need you and Piikow to spruce it up, make it look more Imperial at first glance. We'll also allow you access to our databanks so you can figure out how to hack the security for the ephor's residence." Iden forced herself not to smile. An ephor was not a moff, but if Del could hack into a moff's home, he could definitely handle this.

"We don't want to kill this man, necessarily. We want to ruin him. Destroy him. Show his people what kind of slime he really is. So here's how I think we can do that."

The more Iden listened, the more she liked the plan. It could solve several of Inferno Squad's problems in one fell swoop.

The downside was, their schedule for eliminating Azen just got bumped up. Way up.

Del was delighted that he could work on the J-Sec ship for both the Dreamers' mission and the one for Inferno Squad, and Seyn's timing couldn't be more perfect.

"You've got the list?"

"I do," Seyn said, and handed him the datapad. "It's all on there. Everything I could remember. Code names, alternate identities, the wording of his censures, everything. It should be of use."

"I'm sure it will be of very *great* use. Thank you. It's going to be tricky, but I think this'll work. I'm going to use these as keywords. I'm also going to see if I can find his logs in here."

"Where's Piikow?" she asked, looking around.

"He's not been feeling well. Kinda worries me."

She turned, surprised. "Worries you? He's a Dreamer, Del. He's the enemy."

"He is," Del said. "And he's a smart, funny, imaginative little fellow who didn't deserve what happened to him or his family. I can hold both in my head."

"Just make sure it's in your head, not your heart," she said. "Good luck."

Seyn was heading back to the communal cavern for a bite to eat when she heard Sadori softly calling her name.

"Sadori! Hi," she said, stammering a little. He'd caught her by surprise, and she rebuked herself. Then again, Sadori was quiet and lithe, moving with the grace of a big cat. The combination of his naturally gray skin and his dark clothing rendered him almost invisible in the dusk, but his pink eyes glowed brightly. He was calm, poised, and precise in everything—except when he was around her.

He fell into step beside her. Back at NavInt, her size had been completely irrelevant. Her companions were coworkers, whom she spoke with mostly in passing, and she spent almost all her time in her dark room watching vidscreens. Not only was her work detached emotionally, she was also physically removed from it. But here, and especially when she stood next to Sadori, she became acutely aware of her physical self: she barely came up to the middle of his chest and had to take almost two strides to his one.

Sadori cleared his throat. "I was just wondering if . . . if you might like to walk with me? It's pretty quiet tonight, and there's a place I go that I'd love to show you."

Seyn was hungry, but everything was so tentative with Sadori that she was afraid of crushing him if she declined, and the team couldn't afford to close any doors right now.

He noticed her hesitation. "We won't be long, unless you decide you want to stay. I think you'll like it. But we can come right back if you want."

Warrior from birth Sadori might be, but there was a gentleness about him. She need fear no harm. Besides, she knew a thing or ten about dropping an attacker who was twice her size. So she smiled. "I'm a bit hungry, but why don't we take something to eat with us?"

His expression brightened. "A . . . picnic? Yes, let's do that." He smiled down at her, then said, "Oh . . . by the way, do you know how to swim?"

Seyn looked at him askance. Would a slave have been taught this? Possibly. "I do," she said. "Are we going swimming?"

"We'll be in water. Only if you want, though."

She was wearing one of Dahna's outfits, a sleeveless tunic that fell to midthigh on the Twi'lek and midcalf on her, and leggings she'd had to roll up twice. She could stand getting wet if the occasion warranted it. "We'll see what I think when I get there."

"Then let's pack our picnic and go!" He held out his hand.

Seyn looked at it for a moment. Del had to deal with a chatty Chadra-Fan. Iden was forced to endure barely civil discourse from the Dreamer leader. Gideon, lucky bastard, got to go flying. *And I have to pretend to be romantically interested in a teenage boy.*

She smiled up at Sadori as she took his extended hand. They walked into the cavern, wrapped up some fruit and raw vegetables and two prevva eggs in some fabric, then went out into the constant twilight. She raised an eyebrow at the sight of a speeder bike awaiting them.

"Ever been on one of these before?" Sadori asked.

What was the right answer for a slave? "No," she lied.

"I'm very good at it. You'll be safe, I promise. Hop on and make sure you hang on tight."

Hoping she would not regret this, Seyn climbed onto the bike behind the large Kage youth, slipped her arms around his narrow waist, and held on.

Mindful of Seyn's supposed lack of experience, Sadori took it slowly, navigating through a maze of trees for about fifteen minutes until they had reached a semi-grassy area. When the night phase of Jeosyn arrived, the grass would die, to return at "dawn." But for now, it was thick and lush, a pleasant contrast with the stone areas where the group made camp.

Sadori powered down the bike and held out his hands to help her off. She allowed him to do so, looking around curiously. There were the usual lichen-covered rocks, and starlight. The grass was a nice change, but it wasn't exactly special. She looked up at Sadori in inquiry.

"Not here," he said, and pointed to what was a dark smudge against a sloping hill. "There's a grotto in there. That's the place."

Seyn took a step in that direction, but Sadori hesitated. "Seyn," he said, "do you trust me?"

She tensed, but she was more curious than afraid. "Why do you ask?"

"I want to surprise you," he said, his voice warm and eager.

She glanced again toward the grotto, then said, "Yes. What do you want me to do?"

"Take my hand and close your eyes," he said. "I'll make sure you don't stumble. I promise."

Seyn closed her eyes. She was still tense and knew he could tell that, and when he touched her his hand was gentle and respectful. He instructed her when to step forward, and warned her when there was a stone or uneven ground in her path. He kept his promise; she did not have a single misstep.

She could feel it when she entered the cave. The air was moist and cool. She heard a soft lapping sound—the promised water for possible swimming. It smelled like rich dirt and growing things, a comforting scent. Sadori put his hands on her shoulders, turning her to face in a certain direction, and then she heard him moving about the area.

There were a few soft splashes and then he said, "Okay . . . open your eyes."

She did so—and gasped.

Magnificent indigo crystals jutted up from the floor of the cavern, providing light enough to see but little more. Sadori had removed his tunic and stood waist-high in the water. He kept very still, hardly even breathing. In his hands, he held a large bowl that was carved from another type of crystal, also purple, but lighter, more magenta in color.

"Sadori, this place is beautiful," Seyn said honestly. She found herself smiling.

"It is," he agreed, "but this isn't why I brought you here."

He lifted one hand from the crystal bowl with a flourish, then dipped it into the water with a sweeping motion.

Soft blue light appeared, trailing after his fingers like liquid blue flame.

It was nothing unique in the galaxy. The scientific phenomenon of bioluminescence, the emission of light by a living organism, appeared on multiple worlds. But here, in the cool, slightly damp darkness, it looked ethereal and mystical.

Sadori beamed at her pleased reaction. "You can stay there if you want," he said.

"Oh no," Seyn said. "I'm coming in." She kicked off her boots, but before she stepped into the pool, she paused and looked at him. "But . . . I'm curious . . . why have you brought me here now?"

His expression turned pensive. "We'll be going on our first mission together very soon. Anything can happen. I wanted to share this place with you before—well, just in case something goes wrong."

Seyn realized that not even special forces like Inferno

Squad lived on the edge as much as the Dreamers did. They put their lives on the line with every mission, of course, but they didn't wear bombs strapped to their bodies. No wonder they danced, and laughed, and drank, and *lived* while they could.

She stepped forward into the pool. With each splash of her feet, there was a blue rippling reaction as the tiny living organisms in the water responded to movement. The bottom of the pool leveled out quickly, and she stood facing Sadori as he held the bowl.

He set the bowl down into the water. A sudden flare of blue around it continued as the crystal bowl floated, bobbing gently. Sadori picked up a small stick about as long as his hand that had been resting inside the bowl.

"This bowl came from my homeworld of Quarzite. It was one of the few things we took with us when we left. As long as there have been Kages, it's said, there have been these bowls. And as long as the bowls sing, the Kages will continue."

Very gently, he struck the bowl's rim with the stick.

A haunting, bell-like tone issued forth. Another blue flare blossomed in the pool, fading with the sound.

"The vibrations," Seyn said, her voice soft with wonder. "They can feel the vibrations."

His pink-hued eyes glowed like the tiny sea creatures. "Magical, isn't it?"

It was not magic. But at the same time, it was.

"Yes," Seyn said. And she stood there in the cool water, shivering but unwilling to leave, not thinking about the past or the future, but fully here in this place, with this beautiful boy, listening to the haunting tones of the singing crystal bowl while Sadori played the music of ancient stones, and the glowing blue creatures danced to the sound.

The Mentor offered encouragement during Iden's repeated practice sessions with him at the amphitheater. She was improving, she could tell, but the Mentor was constantly trying to make her even better.

"Don't shout," he would tell her. "You don't have to." Or, "Don't let your eyes dart around. You want to look full into the holorecorder. You can't possibly tell me you've never done that before."

Iden felt a stab of pain as she recalled her mother's message. It reminded her that she needed to finish this mission and get home, and tell her increasingly frail mother that her daughter had never once swayed from her loyalty to the Empire. She would need to deliver a few "speeches" on behalf of the Dreamers, but she hoped fiercely that it would be no more than that. She also hoped, probably futilely, that her mother might not be informed of the speeches. It had been hard enough on Zeehay to see the footage shown at Iden's court-martial. If she saw this—

"Of course I've done this before," Iden said. She could not allow herself any distraction from the task at hand. "But this feels different."

"You're getting better. I know I'm pushing you."

"Don't apologize," Iden said. "I don't want to be better, I want to excel. Staven brought me here for this and I want to prove myself to him."

"You and I have so much in common, I suppose I simply assumed you'd take to this as easily as I did. I know it's not something you're used to, but it's hard to overestimate how helpful to our cause it will be. You'll be saving lives, too. It is always better to reason with people than to kill them."

"Some people just can't be reasoned with," Iden said. She went to sit beside him on the ground. He seemed to be in a reflective frame of mind; maybe she could use that. She grasped a nearby stick and began scratching lines in the hard-baked dirt.

"And that knowledge grieves me," he said. "But it doesn't mean I can deny it."

"You're an odd partisan," she said.

"I know. Staven and I . . . disagree on how to go about many things. But we both agree that the Empire must be defeated."

Scritch. Scritch. Keeping her eyes on the lines emerging from the tip of her stick, Iden said, "What do you mean, we have so much in common?"

He was quiet for a moment, then spoke. "I came from a famous family," he said. "During the Clone Wars, I was . . . confused. Seeking answers, with all the fire and folly of a young teenager." He smiled a little. At the gesture, Iden glanced at him. She could see the boy inside him still; if the years had not been kind to his spirit, they had been gentle with him physically. "I ended up with the wrong sort of rebels, and then what I thought were the right sort."

"Saw and Steela," Iden said.

"Saw and Steela," he confirmed. "But we lost Steela,

and Saw forged his own path with the partisans. My goddaughter joined him. I didn't. Not then. It seems like over the course of my life, I've been on every side imaginable. The Confederacy, the Republic, the Empire, the Alliance, and then back to the partisans. I worked with Saw again for a time—not physically, but we were in communication. Then came Jedha, and now Saw's gone. I was angry, and sorrowful, and I wanted—I want—this war over."

"You don't approve of the level of partisan violence." It was a statement, not a question.

"No," he said. "Never have. But I do approve of Saw and Steela's passion, and I don't want to overthrow Staven. I just wish he would listen."

An idea was forming, hot and exciting, inside Iden's mind. This could be the way to complete the mission. She had already observed that some of the partisans did what they did because they felt there was no choice. Others seemed to thrive on the violence, the slaughter. She understood that. She'd never felt as alive as when she was firing on the rebels, blowing them out of the sky.

Every member of Inferno Squad was a soldier. They'd all been involved with combat. Taken lives.

Some in ways more brutal than others—

This was the answer. Each team member was already focused on one or more of the partisans. Staven was not leading a unified band. Names easily came to mind of those who were either as unshakably loyal or as bloodthirsty as he—Azen, the adult Kages, Nadrine. Then there was Piikow, and Dahna, who did what they did out of duty, not delight.

She paused and looked at what she had absent-mindedly sketched in the dirt: stick figures with blasters. Some were scowling. Some were smiling.

Divide and conquer.

An ancient strategy in warfare, perhaps as old as warfare itself.

CHAPTER 20

Iden had wondered why she was always mending and polishing armor. Most of the time the Dreamers didn't use it, preferring their nondescript gray flight suits. Iden thought perhaps they stripped the corpses of their clothing simply to have trophies. But now, they would prove highly useful.

Because she was the most familiar with stormtrooper armor, at least as far as Staven knew, the Dreamer leader wanted her suited up for the mission. It would help her avoid recognition, which was unlikely but possible, until such time as she wanted to be recognized. And the HUD would be invaluable. Rebels might call them "bucketheads," but stormtroopers wore armor that was extremely functional.

Her codes for Imperial space identification—as she had known they would be—were accepted. She was glad that Staven had finally decided to test them; if they continued to be "good" for too much longer, it would be suspicious.

All was well as they set out. Their first stop—Akagarti's residence. The J-Sec shuttle was brought in at night, flying dark and landing a safe distance away. It was large enough to contain a speeder that carried four, and Iden, Staven, Kaev, and Nadrine made their way to the perimeter fence. A pair of EMP grenades made short work of it. They waited to see if the crackling display triggered any reaction, but there was nothing.

"To the house," Staven ordered.

"I can't believe we're just walking up to the front door," Kaev muttered.

"Backwater worlds rely pretty heavily on specific types of technology," Iden said. "Once you know what they use, you know how to counter it."

They were not challenged when they approached the house. Iden had brought a bigger weapon into the fray—a DEMP, or destructive electromagnetic pulse ion carbine. She used the highest setting. It discharged with a burst of blue filagrees of electromagnetic radiation, chasing one another over and around the residence, destroying any recorders, force fields, or other security devices.

The other three targeted the door and fired, creating a burning hole. Cradling the DEMP in one arm, Iden reached out a hand for a blaster. Staven gave her one. She walked forward cautiously, blaster at the ready, then fired again and again through the gaping hole. When at last she stepped through, she saw four stormtrooper bodies sprawled in the entry foyer.

It was possible they weren't dead. Stormtrooper

armor was designed to dissipate blaster shots. Iden couldn't risk them recovering and attempting to stop the Dreamers' plan. There was only one way to be sure.

I'm so sorry, Iden thought as she placed the blaster muzzle at the vulnerable juncture of torso and shoulder on each stormtrooper. *You die for the Empire.*

She straightened. Her HUD revealed no immediate threat. "Clear," she called back. The other three climbed carefully through the still-smoking entrance, and Staven said, "Kids first, then the parents," as they raced inside.

The house, not quite as large or as lavish as Moff Pereez's, was dark and quiet. There was no other security in this area, and Iden suspected that if there were troopers or guards in the house—and it was possible there weren't; that the EMP attack might have drawn them all—they'd be locked in whatever rooms they found themselves in. No automatic doors would be working anywhere in the house.

"Stand back," Iden called. She fired at the door, then kicked it in.

Akagarti's daughter, seven years old, was standing away from the door as Iden had advised, fists clenched, her tears betraying her bravado as she stared up at Iden.

"Trooper?" she asked. "What's going on out there?"

Iden felt a pang. This child was an Imperial citizen, one who did not fear stormtroopers but saw them as a source of protection.

"Come with me," was all Iden said. She reached down and grasped the girl's arm, ready to clamp down if the child panicked or bolted. She did neither, accompanying

Iden obediently as they left the child's room and went
into the hallway.

A sudden high-pitched shriek of terror told Iden that
Staven had retrieved the little three-year-old boy. The girl
tensed but didn't pull away. It was only when she saw the
door to her parents' bedroom open with Nadrine standing guard, cradling the large blaster in her arms with
easy familiarity, that the girl put the pieces together and
tensed to flee. But Iden dug her gloved fingers into the
soft flesh of the child's upper arm and dragged her into
the bedroom despite her struggles.

Ephor Emoch Akagarti and his wife, who looked
to be in their early forties, wore sleeping clothes of
comfortable-looking white fabric. They sat bolt upright
in their bed, stiff as if they were made of stone, only
their eyes darting about in helpless, hunted terror.

But when they saw their children, the stillness shattered. The mother let out a wailing sob and surged forward, and Emoch cried, "No! Please! Whoever you are,
please don't hurt my family!"

Nadrine whipped the blaster around and pointed it
directly at the woman, who froze, trembling, while Kaev
seized Emoch and hauled him out of bed.

"Room's clear, by the way," Nadrine said to Staven.
"No bugs."

"Good." He leaned over the child and said calmly,
"Run to your mother." The boy scrambled to obey, racing to the bed where his mother scooped him up and
clung to him tightly. To Iden, he said, "Let the girl go,
too."

The girl wrenched herself free, turning her small face
up to Iden's helmeted one with a look of bitter disillu-

sionment before she hastened to climb onto the bed. Her mother pulled her close as well.

Staven turned to Emoch. "How your family fares in the next half hour is entirely up to you. And 'whoever we are' happens to be Saw Gerrera's partisans."

Emoch gaped at him. It was not an attractive expression. "I . . . that's not possible, Saw G—"

Staven backhanded the man savagely. His wife gasped and the little boy whimpered.

"You're not fit to speak his name," Staven said, his lip curling with disgust. "He's gone, but the dream he had is alive and well. I hope your family will be able to say the same of you. Come on."

Staven dragged the cowering ephor to his feet, snapped a pair of stun cuffs on him, and shoved him forward. "Where are you taking me?"

"We're going to pay a visit to the water purification plant."

The man blanched, and the mark Staven had left now stood out even more. Iden waited for the lies, the protests, the explanations, but all Emoch said was, "I'll do whatever you want, but I beg you, please don't hurt them."

"Good little dog," Staven approved. "Now my friend here is going to wait here with your family. If any of your guards tries to come in here, he'll happily kill them. If any of your family tries to escape, he'll happily kill them, too. Everyone clear on this?"

The three on the bed nodded silently.

"Good. Now. You three are going to have a front-row seat at what we'll soon be showing to the rest of the galaxy." He placed a palm-sized holoprojector down at the end of the bed.

"Are you going to kill us?" the girl asked. She had been crying, but her flushed face was composed now.

"Possibly," Staven said. "It all depends on what Emoch does. Fair warning—you might learn a few things about your husband and dear old dad that you won't like. You'd better hope I'm happy with what happens in the next fifteen minutes or so."

He jerked his head toward the door. "After you, trooper," he said, mockingly. Iden stepped back out into the hallway. She, Staven, Nadrine, and the hapless Akagarti would rendezvous with the J-Sec shuttle outside. Akagarti would direct them to the water purification system's entry and, hopefully, cooperate by continuing the façade that all was well.

Staven drove the speeder while Iden sat beside him. In the back of the four-person speeder, Nadrine pressed her blaster to Emoch's temple. Iden's HUD continued to allow them to easily navigate the area.

They met with no resistance. "Backwater security is a joke," Iden muttered.

They arrived at an area marked by large, blocky buildings: the treatment plant for the mine's runoff. "Which one is the last in the process?" Staven demanded. "Where the purified water is kept?"

"That building, on the far right," Emoch said. "The cisterns are in there."

They got out of the speeder and approached the building. Staven and Nadrine each carried a multifrequency spotlight glowrod. They entered the building the same way they had entered the house, and Iden swapped out her DEMP for a blaster. Once inside, their glowrods revealed a gargantuan plastoid container about five stories high. Pipes led into it and away from it. The top was flat, and affixed to the side was a simple two-person lift. Each of the four walls of the vast room had a door large enough to permit machinery to pass in and out. "Where do those lead, Emoch?" Staven asked.

The man swallowed. "Different rooms where processing occurs."

"What kind of processing?"

"Screening, coagulation, sedimentation—"

Staven cut him off. "I think we should have a look at that, too, then." He smiled at Nadrine. "Can you take the speeder and handle that while the trooper and I conclude our business with Emoch?" The ephor cringed, very slightly, at the turn of phrase.

"I'm on it." She turned to Akagarti and showed him another holorecorder, waggling it playfully. "And the galaxy is going to see everything that I do."

Emoch actually stumbled. Iden wondered if he was going to faint. She could almost smell the sour reek of fear. She thought back to Inferno Squad's first mission, where they had crashed the wedding of Moff Pereez's daughter and recovered blackmail material, and asked, "You don't have a bad heart, do you?"

He turned to her and, to her surprise, gave her a sad smile. "No," he said, "but I'm sure you all think that I do."

"Well," Staven said, with that awful brightness that

presaged something dark and dangerous, "then let's head on up to the top and take a look around, shall we?"

He removed the stun cuffs and nudged Emoch with his blaster. "I'll be right behind you," Staven told the ephor as he started to climb. Iden went to the one on the other side and ascended the great tank.

Staven and Emoch had reached the top shortly before she had. Still keeping his weapon trained on the ephor, Staven strolled to the side of the vat and peered over.

"That's a long way down," he observed. Akagarti bit his lower lip at the comment.

The top of the cistern was completely flat, with a trapdoor in its center. "Locked," she said. "Do you have a key, Emoch?"

He shook his head, and the apprehension on his face was obviously genuine. "N-no," he stammered. "I . . . to be honest, I've not been here since the plant was formally opened. I've not been anywhere in here since then."

"Well, then," Iden said, and fired her blaster at the lock. To her surprise, Emoch cried out. "Scare you?" she asked.

"Y-yes," he said, staring at the smoking hole she'd blown in the door. She frowned and gazed at him searchingly. He was growing more agitated. Though that wasn't surprising, really. He had to suspect that whatever Staven intended, it would be happening shortly.

As if to confirm her thoughts, Staven angled his glow-rod in her direction and said, "Start recording."

Iden was ready. They'd discussed the sequence of events, and she'd even rehearsed it with the Mentor. While Staven kept his blaster trained on the ephor, Iden set down the holorecorder on the level surface. She gazed into it and began to speak.

"Citizens of the Empire," she began. "For we all are, still, citizens of the Empire. You have been tricked. Lied to. Betrayed. Murdered. If you defied the Empire, you were killed, and even if you acquiesced and obeyed, kept your heads down, you were still killed. I know. I once believed in the Empire. But I know better now."

She lifted her hands and removed the helm, shaking out her long hair, and gazed directly at the unnamed audience. "My name is Iden Versio, and I'm a member of Saw Gerrera's partisans. I believe in the dream."

It was hard to believe, watching the strong-voiced, confident woman proclaiming her hatred of the Empire, that a few days ago Iden was intimidated by public speaking. *But that is Iden,* Gideon mused. She never met a challenge she couldn't bend to her will.

"I've got to say," Azen said, sitting beside him at the ship's console, "she's absolutely fantastic. I really didn't think she could pull it off."

Obviously you don't know her, Gideon thought but didn't say. Instead, he watched, silently, as Iden, still clad in her stormtrooper armor except for the helmet—a theatrical touch suggested by the Mentor—continued.

"I am here on the planet Affadar, with Ephor Emoch Akagarti. He is the leader of the southernmost continent of Pammur, which is rich in forests, rivers, and mountains . . . and in minerals the Empire wants. Emoch has assured his people that their water supplies won't be affected by the mining runoff. And I am here, standing atop a cistern supposedly full of purified water, to hold him to that promise."

Iden reached a gloved hand through the hole she'd blasted in the hatch door and pulled the door open, holding the holorecorder so that the viewer could see what she saw. The water was about two meters from the top. Gideon could hear it lapping quietly.

"It looks clean," Azen said. "I wonder if we're on a wild caranak chase."

"The water certainly looks clean enough, and there's no smell," Iden was saying. "But there's one way to find if this water is potable."

She removed a bottle from her utility belt, fastened a cord securely to it, and then lowered the bottle into the water. Once it was filled, she pulled it up and presented it to Emoch.

"Here you go, Ephor," she said. "Prove to us that this water is clear. Take a nice, long drink." Emoch stared at the proffered bottle blankly.

At that moment, Gideon heard Nadrine speaking on her comlink. "You won't believe this," she said. "We're still recording, right?"

"Yeah," Staven said. They were not live; Staven wanted to hedge his bets in case Iden froze up at a crucial moment. "What have you found?"

"Nothing, is what I've found."

"I don't follow." But Gideon did. He started to grin.

"Water needs to be processed at several levels before it's potable," Nadrine was saying. "I found cisterns full of fresh runoff, and the first few layers of processing— eliminating solids, removing anything that clouded or colored the water, that sort of thing. But then there are two rooms where the cisterns are empty. The pipes completely bypass them."

"So you're saying that there are levels of processing that are simply not happening?" Iden said, trying to get clarification for the hologram's future audience.

"That's exactly what I'm saying. Half of this plant is just for show."

Iden turned to Emoch. "Those filtration systems must be expensive to purchase and maintain," she said. "Much easier to just produce water that *appears* to be filtered. Who's going to know the difference, Emoch? Not your family. I'm willing to bet they drink water brought in from the north, or maybe even offworld."

Emoch didn't answer. Again, Iden thrust the bottle at him. "Drink. Or we'll kill you where you stand."

He extended a hand, wrapped his fingers around the white bottle. "I'll be happy to drink," he said, and true to his word, he took several long gulps.

"Dammit. Stop recording, Iden." Staven was annoyed.

But Iden wasn't about to listen. "One of the chief dangers of this runoff is the fact that it contains a large amount of dangerous heavy metal and bacteria. Not enough to harm someone in a single serving. But children are advised not to drink it, because they're much more susceptible. Isn't that right, Ephor Akagarti?"

"I don't know what you mean," the man replied, not meeting Iden's gaze.

"The hell he doesn't," Gideon muttered. "Iden, you're brilliant."

"So you're saying this is safe for children? I hope

you're right. Kaev—you are with Emoch's family. How are they doing?"

"So far, so good." Kaev was trying to play along, but he had no idea what Iden was doing.

"Good. Make sure the boy has a nice, refreshing drink of the filtered water his father says is perfectly harmless."

"Handing the bottle to him now," said Kaev, catching on.

There was no bottle, of course. There hadn't been time or opportunity to stop off here, fill up a bottle, and then break into the house to kidnap the ephor's family. But Emoch didn't know that.

"No!" Emoch shouted. "No, Taryai, don't drink it! None of you touch it!"

And there it was. To save his family, Emoch might drink a few mouthfuls of the obviously toxic water. But he wouldn't put his vulnerable child in jeopardy. It was almost noble. Almost.

Azen couldn't tear his eyes from the riveting drama that was unfolding . . . as Iden had banked on.

While the ISB agent stared at the man begging for his children's lives, Gideon feigned a stretch. His right arm extended upward and back, locating and touching a button on the hovering droid. It slowly, soundlessly, moved away to another part of the ship to do what Del had programmed it to.

There was still plenty of time to escape. Time enough for Gideon to enjoy Emoch's unraveling.

"You took the credits that were intended for the water treatment and kept them yourself," Iden was saying. "You blamed the outbreak of bacteria on a particularly rainy season. Your mansion, with its soft beds and lavish furnishings, was bought with the blood of your people! You don't want *your* children poisoned, but you'll poison thousands of others!"

She turned to Emoch. He was on his knees now, one hand on his stomach. Whatever he had drunk wouldn't kill him, but it was clearly making him sick.

"Can you swim?" she asked him. Before he could answer, she had grabbed Emoch and flung him into the water. He screamed in protest and made a wholly satisfying splash. Iden closed the door. Gideon could hear his voice, muffled and unintelligible. If he couldn't swim, he would die. If he could, he might be able to manage long enough for rescue to get there.

Staven began a slow clap. "Nice work, Iden," he said. "Throwing him in was a great touch."

"Thanks," she said. "We should get out while we can, though."

"Not just yet. I'm going to record the other rooms, too," came Nadrine's voice.

"Come on back, Nadrine," Staven ordered. "Iden's right, we should get out. We have enough to make a hell of a message."

"I won't be long; just hang on," Nadrine replied. "You'll thank me when you see this stuff. It's . . . it's like the set of a holodrama. It's completely fake!"

"Okay, okay, but make it quick!"

Gideon stiffened slightly. This was not a good development. He and the rest of Inferno Squad had worked the timing out to the minute. He rose and went to the restroom. He needed to make sure that, later, he could honestly say that Azen was unsupervised in the cockpit for a few minutes.

As Iden's father had taught them, the best lies had truth in them.

CHAPTER 21

"Call her back, Staven," Iden urged. "We're on borrowed time as it is."

"Have you ever tried making Nadrine do something she doesn't want to do?" Staven said. He meant it as a joke, but she could tell he was growing increasingly worried.

Another minute ticked by. Two. Sealed inside the cistern of poisoned water, Emoch was still shouting out pleas. *Well, we know he can swim,* Iden thought.

"Okay, I'm in the speeder and heading back," Nadrine said. Iden relaxed, ever so slightly, and put her helm back on.

"Good. Let's get the hell out of here." Staven clicked on his comlink. "Azen, Gid, head down and pick us up where you dropped us off."

"Roger that," came Azen's voice. "Kaev, do you copy? Stun them and head on out to the rendezvous."

"Got it."

Iden stamped on the closed door of the cistern before she left, climbing down the ramp affixed to the huge container.

"Nadrine," said Staven as he dropped the last few rungs, "where the hell—"

Blasterfire screamed through the door.

Dammit, Iden thought as she and Staven fired back. If it hadn't been for Nadrine wanting more images, they'd have been safely in the shuttle by now, able to flee just ahead of the pursuing security vessels that would be sent out.

The plan had been so perfect. And yet, even as she had the thought, she heard her father's voice in her mind: *There is no foolproof recipe for success. There is only the best* chance *of success.*

"Azen, Gid, get yourselves here *now*!" Staven shouted into his comlink over the sound of blasterfire. "Nadrine, meet us at the rendezvous. Look sharp, we've got troopers!"

"I'm coming as fast as I can!" Nadrine cried. "No pursuit so far!"

"Staven," and Kaev's voice was high with tension, "I stunned the family, but somehow security's been alerted."

"We'll come get you," Staven said. He and Iden kept firing, and then there was silence from outside.

But Iden still heard the sound of blasterfire—coming through Staven's comlink. "You can't," and Kaev was now shouting to be heard above the shriek that was starting to drown out his words. ". . . five of them . . . troopers . . ."

Another shot, then silence. "Kaev," said Staven. Then, louder, *"Kaev!"*

Staven pressed his lips together in a grim line. Their chances had been good, but Nadrine just might have doomed them all.

Gideon ground his teeth in frustration as the shuttle headed toward Staven's coordinates. Damn Nadrine, anyway. Everything would have been fine. The Dreamers had gotten what they'd come for, there had been no need to dawdle over fake cannisters. He'd instructed the droid to activate the homing beacon Del had placed on the shuttle before they left with plenty of time to both escape and put up a fight.

With Nadrine's delay, security would be here at any—

The vessel rocked violently from a glancing hit.

—minute.

"What the hell?" Azen shouted. "How did they find us?"

"No time for questions," Gideon yelled back. "I fly, you fire, got it?"

The J-Sec security vessel was responsive as such things went, but it felt like he was piloting through mud. He brought it up as fast as he could. The good and bad news was that the three Imperial ships firing on them were TIEs—good, because Gideon was so familiar with them he could mount a good defense, and bad because, well, they were *TIEs*.

It felt odd to line up the familiar vessel in his sights, but he did so. Azen apparently had no qualms about firing on an Imperial starfighter, either. He blasted it to pieces and shouted, "Give me another!"

Considering the TIE pilots were trying to kill them, Gideon obliged as fast as he could. He banked hard to the left, almost but not quite escaping bolts of green laser energy. The ship shuddered again. The console started to smoke.

"Droid, get on that!" Gideon ordered, and the droid immediately set to work. Gideon completed the maneuver and swung back around to see the TIE that had hit them clearly preparing for a second shot.

"Get it!" Gideon shouted, and grunting with anger and effort, Azen did so. It was strange, to be happy to see a TIE fighter explode.

"Another coming in on your right," Azen warned. Gideon swerved hard in that direction, going under and up from beneath the one remaining ship.

Both men cheered as Azen got it in his sights and fired. Grinning, Gideon glanced down at the console. "All clear," he said. "Let's get to Staven."

And hope we're not too late.

Iden and Staven stood outside in the deceptive quiet. Sprawled on the ground were two scout troopers, their speeder bikes a few meters away. "Nadrine," Staven said into his comlink, "where are you? There are biker scouts out there, so be—"

"I think I found them," came Nadrine's voice. She was barely audible over the sound of the roaring speeder and the shrieks of blasters.

Staven looked at Iden. For the first time, there was

nothing cold, or sullen, or mirthful in his face. His emotions were naked and on display, and he was terrified for someone he loved.

"I got one of them," came Nadrine's voice. Then a sudden volley of blasterfire. Then nothing.

"Nadrine," Staven said. The hand that held the blaster trembled. "*Nadrine!* Answer me!"

"We've got company," Iden said. Her HUD had alerted her to an incoming vessel—and it wasn't the J-Sec security fighter. Staven didn't reply. She turned to look at him. He was staring, frozen, at his comlink, straining to listen. To hear the voice of someone who would never speak again. "Staven!" she said again, sharply this time. "Snap to it, soldier!"

He blinked, as if coming out of a trance, and looked up. The comlink fell from his fingers.

The very familiar shape of a *Lambda*-class T-4a shuttle was now visible with the naked eye.

This wasn't how it was supposed to end, Iden thought. But life—or death—rarely unfolded as it was supposed to.

She grimly lifted her blaster—a feeble and utterly futile gesture against a ship armed with laser cannons. Beside her, Staven did the same.

Calm in the face of her death, Iden found herself wondering whether the vessel would land and disgorge its contents of twenty stormtroopers, or just take them out in a volley of cannon fire.

She would never find out.

A green streak sliced through the night sky. Fire blossomed on one of the T-4a's wings. More laserfire, and the ship began to wobble, imbalanced, as it tried to loop around to return fire. Another strike, at its wings, and then again at its engines. The shuttle got off a laser-cannon volley, but it came nowhere near its target. The J-Sec vessel dove beneath it, fired up, and got out of the way as the ship, its engines and wings both damaged, crashed into the landscape about half a kilometer away.

Iden could hardly believe it. She half laughed, half gasped as the familiar ship settled down and the ramp extended. Ten seconds later, Iden and Staven were on board.

Azen looked back at them. "Where are Nadrine and Kaev?"

"Gone," said Staven, his voice a harsh rasp. "Get us out of here."

"We may have company very soon," Gideon said. "Get in your crash webbing."

They had barely done so when the ship lifted off, soaring almost completely vertically upward, breaking through the wisps of clouds up to open space. Then the stars turned into white streaks.

Iden exhaled and closed her eyes for a moment, preparing for the next step.

"What happened?" Azen demanded. "What went wrong?"

"No idea," Staven said. He still looked disoriented and disconcertingly blank. He pressed the heels of his hands against his temples, as if physically forcing himself to think, his mind to clear.

"Could someone have put a homing beacon on the ship without us knowing?" Iden said. The next step in springing the trap.

"Impossible," scoffed Azen. "We were both here in the ship the whole time."

"Never left this console except when I hit the restroom," Gideon said. He feigned a look of concern. "Still . . . hell, it's worth checking, at least. Droid—check the ship for any tracking devices." The droid beeped acknowledgment and hovered off.

There was silence for a while, as Gideon checked the ship for damage and the droid went about its inspection. Staven rose at one point and went back to the ship's galley. Over the quiet hum of the vessel, she heard the distinctive clinking sound of a bottle against a glass rim, and the sloshing of liquid.

Staven returned, carrying both bottle and drained glass, and poured himself another shot. The sound of the droid beeping shrilly startled all of them. It sped back, moving anxiously, holding something in one of its pincers.

"What the—" Gideon said, as the droid dropped the item into his hand. He lifted his head and turned to look at Azen. Pure loathing contorted his handsome features. "You lying sack of—"

He lunged for the startled Azen, wrapping one hand around the other man's throat and keeping his other hand clenched around the object the droid had found.

"Gid, no!" Iden shouted. Staven sprang into action, dropping glass and bottle as he inserted himself between the two now-fighting men. He shoved Gideon backward and forced open the pilot's hand.

Staven stared at what Gideon held. "It's . . . it's a homing beacon," he muttered.

Iden rose and went to look at it. "Not Imperial," she said.

"No," Staven said. "This is one of ours."

The droid made several beeping and chirping noises. "The droid found it on the *inside*," Gideon said. "Which means that *he* planted it!" He stabbed an angry finger at Azen.

"Me?" yelped Azen. "Why would I want to do that?"

"He was alone when I used the restroom," Gideon said. "He could easily—"

"Iden," Staven said, "give me your blaster."

She did, and he lifted it up so that it was trained on her. She blinked. "What—"

"Go get three sets of stun cuffs. Put one on Gideon, and one on yourself, and give the third to me. All I know right now is that Nadrine is dead, and Kaev, too, and one of you three is responsible."

"I was with you the whole—" Iden began.

"You might not have planted it yourself, but I've never really trusted you, Iden. So Azen will take us home, and you and Gid will sit in cuffs until we get there. And then we'll find out who did this. And once we do . . ." His lips curved in that ugly, cruel smile. "The Dreamers are going to have some sport."

Iden stayed calm. This was all playing out as expected. The only thing they hadn't accounted for was that Staven appeared dangerously unstable from grief. Fortunately, he refrained from killing anyone before Azen had brought the damaged ship down.

He extended the ramp and Iden, Gideon, and Azen, now also in stun cuffs, preceded him. Staven had alerted his people to meet the shuttle, and now they all stared with various expressions of shock and anger as he explained what had happened.

"Piikow, Del," he shouted, his voice ragged with pain. "Check the ship for sabotage. Iden, Azen, Gid— On your knees, hands behind your head."

Dahna glanced at Iden. "Staven—"

"Do it!"

This was not the time to protest, and clearly Dahna recognized that. Staven looked like he was clinging to sanity by the thinnest of threads, and his fingers clearly itched to blow the "traitors" away. Probably the only thing that restrained him was a desire to know what they had done that had made things go so horribly wrong.

Iden knelt and placed her hands behind her head.

"We don't leave till we've checked out the ship," Staven continued. "None of us."

Someone had brought extra glowrods. Del, more mobile than Piikow, began to inspect the vessel itself, while the Chadra-Fan analyzed the ship's computer. Iden was glad of this; it would be much better if Piikow came across what Del had labored first so hard to create, then to conceal it until the time was right.

No one said anything. Dahna handed out water to everyone. Staven waved his away, his attention fixed on Gideon, Azen, and mostly Iden. Time passed. Iden's legs and arms began to cramp, but given Staven's twitchy fingers, she didn't dare move.

Finally, Piikow appeared on the ramp. "Staven," he said, "please come here."

Iden's heart sped up. Something was about to happen that might well see her dead within the next three minutes.

"Ru," Staven said, "keep an eye on them."

Ru nodded, taking Staven's blaster and training it on the captives. The Kage's eyes were cold, despite their warm tint.

The seconds went by. Then a minute. Then two.

Staven appeared on the ramp. Swift as a snake strike, he snatched the blaster from Ru's grasp, closed the distance between himself and—

Azen!

—and slammed the butt of the weapon against his head.

Iden sagged forward, the relief making her feel weak. Dahna extended a hand to help her up. She accepted, wincing at the stiffness as life rushed into numb limbs. Beside her, Ru assisted Gideon as he got to his feet. Dahna unfastened their stun cuffs, her purple eyes wide with shock.

"What the hell—" grated Azen, hand clapped to his bloodied skull.

"Tell them!" shouted Staven. "Tell them what you found, Piikow!"

More subdued than she had ever seen the lively Chadra-Fan before, Piikow obliged. In a low voice that conveyed his shock, he spoke of listening in disbelief to what he fully believed he had heard; what anyone without access to highly complex equipment would have believed they heard: recorded conversations Azen had conducted with "someone" in Imperial Intelligence. And finally, he listed various identities "Azen" had utilized in these conversations; conversations that Del had cobbled together from bits and pieces of the logs Azen had recorded over the months he was at J-Sec with a bit of creative doctoring. Then, his ears drooping, Piikow returned to the cockpit.

There was stunned silence. "So what this tells me," Staven said in an unnaturally calm voice, "is that the *entire time* I've known you, Azen, you've been planning to turn us over to the Empire."

"It's not true!" Azen looked around frantically, still bleeding, finding no sympathy in the eyes of people who had trusted him. "I would never betray you!"

His wide-eyed gaze fell on Iden, and he spat out blood and a tooth in her direction. "You," he growled. "You did this to me!"

"Me?" Iden did her best to look shocked. "Why would I want to do this?" She turned to Staven. He was shaking, his fists clenched, ready—eager—to take another swing at the traitor. "Staven, I've given you several codes. Pieces of intel. And all of them—*all of them*—have been successful. And just now, I'm the one who got what we needed out of Akagarti. Some of these missions have had a high Imperial body count. Why would I participate in that if I were working for the Empire?"

Still reeling from the revelation, Staven grasped at the straw Azen offered. "Maybe . . . maybe *you're* a double agent," Staven spat at Iden. "Maybe you set this up, and it's all a trick!"

"I don't even have the code to that ship's computer! I was under house arrest when I flew it," Iden replied. "You've all watched me like a shirrhawk. When the hell did I have time to do anything? If I were that brilliant, I'd be the damned Empress."

At that moment, Piikow again appeared at the top of the ramp. "It took me a little while, but now that I've been able to get into the databanks I've uncovered an entire sublevel of Imperial intel."

Intel that is all false—except for what it says about Azen, Iden thought. She bit the inside of her cheek so that she didn't smile. Del and Seyn had outdone themselves— and in so short a time. "I've run some checks on the code names. Staven—there are even *pictures*. It's him. It's true."

All the color drained from Azen's normally florid face, until his skin was a sickly, milky shade.

Iden rejoiced fiercely. He knew he was beaten.

"How did you do it?" he whispered, turning to look at her through the drying mask of blood on his face. "You couldn't possibly know *any* of this. What did you do? *What did you do?*"

She scoffed in disbelief. "Me? Not a damn thing. But you"—she smiled, cruelly—"you just doomed yourself."

He sagged, then lifted his head. He knew better than to look to Staven; there would never be forgiveness there. So he looked to a gentler man.

But even the Mentor, it seemed, had his limits. His brow was knotted and his blue eyes blazed in righteous anger.

"So many in this galaxy are born into their fates," he said. "They labor, and suffer, and die, unable to alter them, unable sometimes even to hope that something will change. I've lost people I loved fighting for those who couldn't fight for themselves. Who couldn't choose. You were one of the lucky ones who could, Azen. And you chose the Empire. You chose to betray those who believed you to be a friend. Don't you *dare* look to me for mercy. I've stood in both places of this war, too. But I made a decision. And I will live or die by my choice.

Kaev and Nadrine *did* die for theirs. You—you will die for *nothing*."

Azen looked like a trapped animal who felt the net closing in. But it was too late for any escape, any appeal for sympathy. He'd never been a pleasant person, not to anyone.

"Tell us what you know," Staven said. His voice was flat, dead, which was somehow more sinister than his fury.

"And you'll make it quick, is that it?" Azen shook his head, recovering some composure, some little shred of dignity. "No. I refuse."

Now, at the end, he was finally behaving like an Imperial, Iden thought.

A sort of energy went through those gathered. They knew what that meant. Iden did, too. She'd seen reports about what partisans did for information. The Empire performed torture as well, from time to time as necessary. But it was more elegant. It caused pain without damage. Well, physical damage, at least.

The Dreamers would not be so scrupulous.

"You're going to have to work for everything you get from me," Azen said.

"Don't worry," said Staven. "We will."

They did.

It took seven hours for Azen to die.

CHAPTER 22

The mood was somber that night at the encampment. Work would begin on the shuttle, but not yet. Everyone needed to process what had happened. Staven had ordered that Azen's corpse be put "in the usual place. Though even Crunchers might well choke on such putrid meat," he had added.

Upon his return to the encampment, he'd wordlessly taken a speeder bike and roared off by himself. No one seemed to notice or care when the members of Inferno Squad did the same thing, one by one.

Iden had directed them to a specific spot she'd found during her daily runs. Although they'd all grown largely accustomed to living in near-darkness, they'd brought their night-vision goggles to keep alert for predators—both the two-legged and the multilegged kind.

"It's good to see you," Iden said.

"It's good to see you and Gideon at all, considering what happened on the mission," Del said. "And Staven wasn't very stable when he got off the shuttle, either. I thought he was going to blast you first and figure things out later."

"You weren't the only one," Gideon said, then added lightly, "although I'd have made a fine leader if that had happened."

"Not yet," Iden said. She looked at them and squared her shoulders. "A good day's work for sure, but we still haven't made inroads on where the partisans have been getting their information." Nothing they had been able to obtain from Del's investigation into Azen via the ship's logs indicated he had anything of note. It did look like he had hoped kidnapping Iden would be the "big score" to restore his favor in the eyes of ISB.

"I guess either Staven has his own informant off-world that he's being extraordinarily tight-lipped about, or else your friend the Mentor is sitting on something he's doling out sparingly," Seyn said.

"He's not my friend," Iden said, quicker than she intended. "There's tension between those two, and we need to start pushing that. Hard," she said. "Gideon, Staven seems to have taken to you. He's going to need a friend right now after Nadrine's death and Azen's betrayal. Plant some doubt in his head about the rest of the group. Even me if you have to, but especially the Mentor and those who seem to think like him."

"I will be the absolute best friend Staven's ever had," Gideon promised.

"How are things going with Piikow?" Iden asked Del.

"Fine. He seems to like everyone, and everyone likes him."

Iden shook her head. "Not good enough. Piikow appears to operate on an even keel. Convince him that Staven isn't a trustworthy leader anymore.

"Seyn." She turned to the youngest member of the team. "So far, you've done a fine job ingratiating yourself with the Vushans. Keep up the good work. I'll continue trying to get information from the Mentor. Does anyone have any questions?"

There were none. "All right. We'd better wander back toward the encampment. It's all right for us to be seen together now, I think—we're all welcome here at this point. But I'd rather it not happen too often. Comm me if you learn anything or you think there's trouble."

Gideon punched Del in the shoulder. "Come on, brother mine. Let's head on back."

"Hey, quit punching me," Del said good-naturedly. "I'm your big brother, remember?"

"Ah, but I am the witty and dashing younger brother who flies the ship and gets to have all the fun."

Their voices faded. Seyn started to head back, too, but Iden said, "Seyn? I need a word."

"Of course," the other woman replied promptly.

"We've all been making 'friends' here. But you're the only one who's involved in . . . well, I suppose it's a romantic relationship."

"Not to worry, Captain. I don't love Sadori any more than Gideon is Staven's best friend."

"If there *is* something between you two, I need to know. Things like that can get tricky."

"Permission to speak freely?" At Iden's nod, Seyn

said, "I've worked with literally hundreds of agents. Many in deep cover. I'm well aware of the peril of getting emotionally involved. Besides, he's just a teenager."

"He's eighteen, you're twenty," Iden said. "It's not that big of an age gap, but your point is well taken. I'm sorry I questioned your judgment."

"It's understandable, Captain. Will that be all?"

"Dismissed."

On impulse, Iden decided to climb one of the trees. She was feeling stifled under the deep canopy. When she stuck her head out of the leafy cover, pulled off her night goggles, and beheld the glittering starfield, she felt a tug of homesickness. How she wanted to be out there, in the *Corvus.* Wearing her uniform again.

She had asked Seyn not because she doubted the other woman's resolve, but because she herself was surprised by how the deaths had affected her. It had been part of the plan, of course, and at the time the idea had been conceived she had felt nothing. But Kaev and Nadrine had been easy to like, and seeing the anguish in Staven, and how it had affected all the partisans . . . she didn't like where her thoughts were going.

"Permission to come aboard, Captain?" Del called.

Despite her somber mood, she was smiling as she said, "Permission granted." Within a few minutes he was on a branch beside her.

"Thought you headed back to camp with Gideon."

"Couldn't help but notice you wanted to talk to Seyn." He pulled off his goggles and looked at the stars, as she had done, then turned to her. "You okay?"

"We got rid of Azen and cemented our position in the group. Why wouldn't I be?"

"I just wanted to make sure you weren't too rattled by what happened today," he replied. "We chat with, laugh with, eat with, and fight alongside these people. We even sleep next to them. But they're still the enemy. This is harder than combat. It's easier to kill someone whose favorite color you don't know, or who hasn't trusted you with their dreams." He paused, then said, "Gideon told me Staven cried."

"Really?" Iden asked, surprised.

"He did. It shook him. It's the second time he's lost a woman he loved."

"I suppose we can use that," Iden said.

There must have been something in the tone of her voice, because he turned to look at her.

"They're rebels, Iden," Del said, kindly. "They're not people. We can't think of them like that. If we do, we can't finish what we came here to do."

"Who are you trying to convince, me or yourself?" Iden asked.

"Both of us, I guess."

If Gideon were here, he'd say, "Thinking about them as people makes you soft. And Versios aren't soft."

And he'd be right.

Wouldn't he?

Iden was more than ready for another mission to happen, and glad that Seyn, who had done so much without complaining behind the scenes for so many others, was going to finally see some action. As long as Seyn returned safely, Iden didn't even care if the mission was a success or a failure. Success would buoy Staven and distract him from his moodiness that so often seemed to be directed her way. Failure would make him more unstable, and give the Mentor something to point to.

It was a fairly straightforward mission, though it relied heavily on Sadori and Seyn being convincing in their roles as two teenage schoolchildren. The event was a public-relations stunt. The relatively calm world of Anukara was opening a munitions factory. Anukara's moff, Rys Deksha, would be playing host to General Ivel Toshan for a public ceremony to open the plant. Students from a nearby school would be given a special tour and get to meet their moff and the general. Afterward, there would be a luncheon for the dignitaries.

The idea was for Seyn and Sadori to blend in with the students and plant a bomb at the final stop of the tour—the great hall. It would kill the moff and the general and in Staven's words, "Send a strong message about how far we're willing to go to stop the Empire."

Dahna frowned a little. "You'll delay the opening, and that'll cost them a lot of credits, which is good. But while Toshan and Deksha are public figures, they're not very highly placed," she said.

Iden and her team, of course, had offered no objection to the plan. This was as her father had warned her—sometimes her own people would have to die. She thought of the stormtrooper, beaten bloody, who had died still trying to rally and fight. The assassination of a moff and a midlevel general would be a black eye to the Empire, but Dahna was right. This wasn't a statement about "how far they would go."

"No, they're not, but you see . . . they're not the real targets."

Iden had a terrible suspicion. He couldn't possibly be suggesting what she thought he was. Not even the Dreamers would—

"It's the children."

Several people spoke at once, most of them sounding as stunned as Iden felt.

"We're not child murderers!" snapped Dahna.

"There's nothing more innocent than a youngling, Staven," Piikow pleaded.

The Kages said nothing, but Sadori looked stunned, his gray face paler than usual. Her team was struggling to keep their composure, and Iden herself felt cold sweat gathering at her browline and under her arms.

"Absolutely not!"

The voice was deep with anger, resonant, and brooked no disagreement. The Mentor, who usually sat quietly and seldom even offered an opinion when the missions were being assigned, was on his feet. His fists were clenched, and his eyes were bright with righteous fury.

Staven didn't rise. He stayed seated atop one of the flattened boulders, meeting the Mentor's hot fury with cold eyes. "This isn't your group, Mentor," he said. "You have no voice here."

"I will not allow this, Staven," the Mentor continued, as if Staven hadn't even spoken. "This is too far. I told Saw, and I will tell you, there are limits to what you can do. If you exceed them, you are on the side of hate and cruelty, and that's the side of the Empire. If you want to sit next to them at the table, killing children is the quickest way to do it!"

"I've given *everything* to fight the Empire!" Now Staven did rise and took two steps toward the Mentor.

"Everything! I've got nothing *left* but hate and cruelty, and I will shove that down the Empire's throat every chance I get until they choke on it!"

"The Mentor's right," said Staven's second in command. "We can't kill innocent children."

"Dhana, these aren't 'innocent children,'" Staven said. "They've been robbed of their innocence because they're children of the Empire. They're already rotting on the inside. They might be young, but their family, their friends, their culture is our enemy. And they'll grow up to get into stormtrooper uniforms and kill us and our loved ones."

Iden swallowed hard as the words of her father came back to her: *The child of a rebel may be a child yet, but we must look to the future. It will grow up to be an enemy. And our enemies must be destroyed.*

"Our enemies must be destroyed." Iden wasn't aware that she had spoken until all heads turned to her. The Mentor looked startled. Her jaw tensed, but she didn't deny the words. She had to communicate to her team that no matter how brutal or personally devastating the task, they had to complete it. They couldn't risk the mission.

Iden made a vow then and there. This would be the last mission in which they would participate. Her team would set the Mentor and Staven against each other, just like they were now, their own codes and morals, like sharp teeth, rending one another. Inferno Squad would determine who had the intel, where it was hidden, and take it. And let the tiny handful that remained of Saw Gerrera's partisans see their "dream" drown in despair and discord.

The beast would devour itself.

. . .

Del had been able to hack into the system and obtain the codes that permitted them to land near a school shuttle filled with nearly four hundred excited human children ages fourteen through eighteen. Dressed in matching school uniforms, Seyn and Sadori walked over to board the shuttle. Only humans were admitted into the school, so Sadori was disguised: He had spent over an hour having his pale-gray face and neck covered with concealing cosmetics; he wore contacts that turned his naturally pink eyes brown and hid their soft glow. Fortunately, the school permitted gloves, as long as they were black.

"We do this all the time," he had told Seyn. "This is a weapon that's every bit as important as a blaster or a vibroblade. Kages aren't commonly seen outside of Quarzite, so if we don't want to attract attention, on this stuff goes."

Seyn, who had supervised so many undercover agents, was impressed. Each Kage had their own palate. While all three had had gray skin, their shades varied, and the cosmetic hues were selected to match the tone as much as possible. Halia, for instance, would apply warm, darker colors that made her resemble Iden, whereas paler Sadori's human color was closer to Gideon's. This school was not a military one, so Sadori was able to keep his long, black locks and thus conceal his Kage ears. If someone took the time to examine him, they might notice the flaws. But Seyn knew from experience that people generally saw what they expected to see.

Sure enough, the harried teachers glanced cursorily at the two "students" and then at the IDs Seyn had so carefully crafted, and waved them through without pause. Sadori was proud of her; Seyn had expected nothing less.

"Go all the way to the back and fill in all the seats!" one of teachers instructed. Sadori went first. Seyn followed. Then: "Wait." Seyn tensed. The teacher, a tall, slender man with sharp features and a dully pained expression, peered at the droid affixed to Seyn's back. "You can't take the droid with you."

"Check the card," Seyn said, as if she was tired of reminding people. "I've got a medical condition that it helps monitor."

He looked at her skeptically, then reread her ID card. "All right. You can bring it, but it will have to go into the compartment at the rear during the flight."

Seyn rolled her eyes and then said, "Okay, okay." She looked over her shoulder and addressed the droid. "You heard him," she said. "Go on. I'll wait for you outside when we get there."

The droid booped its acknowledgment, detached itself, tucked up its limbs, and flew over the heads of the excited students as it made its way to the rear of the shuttle. Sadori had already found a seat and waved her over.

"Are you nervous?" His voice was pitched low as he reached for Seyn's hand and squeezed it.

She squeezed back. "A little," she said, and it wasn't entirely a lie. How many agents had she monitored, how many more had she sent into the field, in situations nearly identical to the one she was experiencing now? She could do a count if she had the time, but knew it numbered in the hundreds.

And how many didn't make it back? She pushed the thought aside. She had to focus on the job at hand.

She settled back into her seat, making no effort to remove her hand from his gloved one. It helped with their cover: two teenagers more engrossed in each other than anything else. No one looked twice.

Beneath their uniforms, as always when the partisans went on a mission, they both wore patches of the malleable explosives. The material was difficult to detect, and while the Empire did have the technology to do so, such scanners were still new, prone to breaking, and very expensive. The intel that they had on the plant on Anukara was that such equipment had not yet been installed. Seyn hoped that was still true. If not . . . the droid would be able to disable the scanner.

The flight to the weapons factory was filled with the loud sounds of rambunctious students, and completely uneventful. When they exited the shuttle, Seyn waited, and the droid emerged and immediately settled again onto her back.

"Let's go," Sadori said. He leaned over as if to kiss her cheek but instead whispered, "You're going to do great!"

She smiled at him and fished out her comlink. "Hi, Dad!" she said brightly. "We're here, waiting to get in. I'm so excited!"

"Stop making me feel old," Del said. "Will you get to keep the comm? Your . . . mother and I worry, you know." She could imagine Iden's eye-roll.

Sadori, so much taller than she, craned his neck to look up ahead, and nodded at her.

"Looks like," she told Del.

"We'll be there to pick you up when you're all done. Just let us know when you're ready."

"Thanks! I'll talk to you soon!"

Garrick Versio had been right. The trick in deceiving someone was to mix as much truth as possible into your lies, and be relaxed about what you were doing. Seyn agreed completely. If you behaved as if you belonged, people usually overlooked you. Some, in fact, could smell fear, and sweat droplets or quick breathing were dead giveaways among human and near-humans, as had been the case at the Singularity bombing.

So she held her "boyfriend's" hand, and looked excited, and obeyed instructions as the river of students was shuttled through. She had to rely on Sadori's height advantage for information about what was around them. He told her everything he noticed that was of import, couching the information in ways that sounded completely innocuous, such as "Wow, there must be at least twenty-five stormtroopers here. They're lined up on both sides of the gate!"

He was extremely good at this. If his parents had the same skill level, then Staven was squandering them by only using the Kages in a fight.

They gathered outside the main entrance, where an exaggeratedly large red ribbon draped across the huge door to the building. A stormtrooper stood rigidly at attention, his gloved hands closed about the hilt of a lengthy vibroblade that would shortly be cutting the ribbon.

The ceremony was open to the public. The intel that Staven said he had obtained indicated that this would be the most heavily secured area. If anything was to go wrong, it would most likely be here.

While they waited, Seyn went over the plan. At approximately oh nine hundred local time, the local moff, Rys Deksha, and the visiting dignitary, General Ivel Toshan, would emerge to formally open the factory. Speeches and posing for the cam droids was expected to last twenty minutes, and then the students would be admitted for their tour of the facility. Their IDs would be checked once more, but security was expected to be relaxed as this was a contained, previously screened group of local teenagers. They would begin moving through the factory at oh nine twenty, and the two-hour tour would culminate with a half-hour meet and greet at eleven thirty in a receiving area that had been laid out for a banquet.

There the students would be permitted to interact with the general, the moff, and their aides. At noon, the students would return to their shuttle, and the dignitaries would be served luncheon at the same site at twelve thirty.

Except that wasn't what would happen. At eleven fifty-five, everyone in the room would be dead.

The ribbon-cutting ceremony went off smoothly, with Deksha and Toshan keeping their speeches brief and to the point. Seyn knew of Toshan, and was aware that he, like so many moffs, had a preference for the finer things in life. She wondered if someone in a position of authority was unhappy with his performance recently, and had sent him out to this backwater world as a reprimand. He certainly didn't look like someone who was happy to be here.

After the speeches, each of the two men placed one hand on the vibroblade's hilt and together cut the ridiculous ribbon, which fluttered prettily in a sudden breeze. Everything was captured by the cam droids. It was intended to be what was called a fluff piece, but later, Seyn knew, it would be regarded as hard news.

Something fluttered inside her, and she frowned, quelling the sensation. Iden had made it clear that Seyn was not to interfere with the execution of the Dreamers' plan. Seyn was an Imperial agent, a member of an elite team, and casualties happened in war. And what was happening now, as cheerful, excited students clogged the main doorway eager to get in, was as much a battle as any that was fought between starships.

She was, of course, stopped when they reached the initial main scanner, and she had to explain to the tired-looking guard that the droid was medically authorized. As proof, she produced her fake ID. The guard waved her through.

So far, so good. Time to check in.

CHAPTER 23

"I really hope Seyn's ready for this," Staven said. He and Iden were piloting the vessel while Del monitored Seyn and Sadori through the eyes of the droid.

"Me too," Del replied. "She seems pretty sharp, though. And Sadori seems to have it under control." It amused him to see Staven worried about a professional NavInt supervisor handling an undercover mission. So far, Seyn was blending in better and learning more than any member of the squad. And to think they all originally thought of her as the rookie.

They had backup plans, of course. They always did. But even as Staven expressed his reservations, he didn't seem overly concerned.

"Hi, Dad!"

"Hi, uh, sweetheart," Del said into the comlink. "Did they give you any trouble with your med droid?"

"No, I'm okay," Seyn said. "Feeling great! So much to see here!"

"Can't wait to hear all about it," he said. "Keep me posted!" He clicked off his comlink. To Staven, he said, "They're in. Got the droid through no problem, and they've assembled the bomb."

"You know," Staven said, "the Empire is enormous and complex. Sometimes they're very, very clever. Sometimes, they're just stupid and miss the obvious things. Can't even catch a pair of teenagers smuggling in a bomb."

That hadn't escaped Del's notice, either. When the team had completed its mission, they would have an earful for Admiral Versio about how much tighter some security needed to be.

But then again, by the time they returned the Dreamers would be no more, and the Rebel Alliance was too crippled by its own moral code to push a similarly violent agenda. Its leaders would be as horrified about what was about to unfold as the Empire.

As, if he admitted the truth, Del himself was.

Staven hadn't really warmed up to anyone from Inferno Squad other than Gideon, and ever since they'd lost Nadrine and Kaev, he'd just gotten grimmer. There wasn't much chitchat to pass the time while they waited for the school trip to run its course.

So Del leaned back in his chair, laced his hands behind his head, and closed his eyes, trying to focus on something other than the slaughter about to come.

In his mind's eye, he saw glowing purple crystals.

. . .

The factory was clean, shiny, bright, and utterly Imperial. The students were appropriately impressed. They seemed thrilled to be here today, chatting, laughing, and taking vids in areas where they were permitted to do so. There were no more stormtroopers, just guards and a few engineers on the site to answer questions.

Seyn again attracted unwanted notice because of the droid. A couple of the students exclaimed over it, their envy turning to sympathy when Seyn explained that it was for her medical condition.

"Oh, I'm really sorry to hear that," said a girl who reminded Seyn uncomfortably of Nadrine. "Can you have chocolate? I got some for my birthday."

Chocolate was a rarity in this part of the galaxy, and Seyn demurred. "Oh no, I couldn't take that."

"You must be new at school, and that's never fun. Especially when you're—well, if you need a medical droid . . . I'm Anice," the girl said. "Go on, have a piece, or else my kid brother will eat it all when I get home."

Seyn went very still. Anice would never get home.

"You eat one for me, right now, and tell me how delicious it is," she said, forcing a smile.

"Twist my arm," Anice joked, and popped one in her mouth. "Mmmm . . . it really is *so* good! You sure you don't want one?" she offered again.

"It's more fun watching you," Seyn said. She hung back as the group filed into the next room. She didn't want to make any more idle conversation with the fiery-haired, freckled Anice.

After what felt like forever, their guide said, "Well, that's all for today, kids! It's time to go into the reception area, where you'll get to meet and chat with General Toshan and our own Moff Deksha!"

Up at the far end of the room was what was obviously the main table for the visiting dignitaries. It was set with fine linens, plates, and dining utensils. Exquisite decanters sat at the ready for a luncheon that would never come, and for a wild, nearly hysterical moment Seyn wondered if they contained Toniray wine. It would be macabrely ironic if so.

"Do you think you can get there safely?" Sadori whispered.

She considered. The droid might be able to, but even as she had the thought, two other serving droids came out from side doors, bearing various nonalcoholic libations and appetizers.

"No," she said. "But I can probably get near the end of one of the regular tables. That will more than suffice. I'll go get everything ready."

Toward the beginning of the tour, she had asked to visit the restroom to "get my medication" from the droid. There, she had retrieved all the necessary material to affix their personal bombs. She'd attached hers to her chest, and given the components to Sadori, who'd headed off to the restroom to attach his own bomb.

Now she politely asked a guard where the restroom at this end of the building was. Once she was alone, she quickly opened the droid's casing, removed the parts for the deceptively small third bomb, and assembled it quickly.

She paused as she prepared to set the timer.

She went over everything the bomb's detonation was supposed to accomplish.

Delay the factory opening? Yes, that troubled her not at all.

Kill the moff, the general, and a handful of aides? That was a difficult one, but Admiral Versio had warned Inferno Squad that such deaths were acceptable in the name of eliminating the partisans and preventing future attacks.

But Moff Deksha and General Toshan wouldn't be the only Imperials dying. Seyn thought of Anice, with her artless and complete generosity. Of her unknown brother and her parents; of nearly four hundred other noisy, laughing, fascinated students. Who were just kids.

Seyn stayed in the restroom for a long, long time, thinking.

She made her decision. And then she set the timer.

Sadori threw her a relieved glance when she emerged. "I was worried," he said, slipping his arm around her briefly. "You okay?"

"Yes," she said firmly. For the first time since the mission had started, she really was. "The timer's set."

"That gives us five minutes from when you activate it. It looks like everyone's here. Let's head over. I'll distract people."

They took glasses of sweet, bubbly beverages from the serving droids and sipped as they made their way to the end of one of the far tables, within two meters of the head table where the dignitaries would be celebrating their luncheon. With Sadori's frame blocking her from view, Seyn slipped the bomb—carefully—out of her sleeve and passed it to the droid.

"Hey, Dad," she said on her comlink. "Not feeling so good. Can you come pick me up?"

"Be right there."

Seyn took a breath. "Under the table, in the center, set for fifteen minutes, then get on my back," she whispered to the ID10.

The droid booped, dipped until it was level with the table, and did as it was told. Then, its mission accomplished, it resettled itself on her back.

"Now!"

She and Sadori moved through the crowd as quickly as they could without drawing attention, pointedly not making eye contact. Sadori was like the prow of an old-fashioned water ship, parting the cluster of teenagers with Seyn following, gripping his hand hard, her heart slamming against her chest.

They reached the hallway, heading toward an exit door, and then they were outside, putting distance between themselves and the building as fast as they could. The shuttle would be here at any minute.

And then Sadori slowed. Confused, he looked back at the factory. "It should have detonated by now," he said.

Detonated. Killing everyone in the banquet hall. Killing nearly four hundred innocent Imperial subjects, who'd done nothing other than be born on this planet and attend school here.

Seyn reached for his hand. "I'm sure it's okay," she said.

He hung on to her hand, but still looked back. She tugged. "They're landing," she said. "Sadori, come on, let's go, the bomb's still going to go off!"

But he was shaking his dark head. "Something's wrong. The bomb's a dud."

It wasn't a dud. It was functioning perfectly. Functioning with a fifteen-minute delay, not five, so that the excited students would have the chance to pile into their shuttle and talk the whole way back about what they'd seen.

So that Anice's brother could steal her candy.

"Sadori," she said, begging.

The young Kage turned to her and gently grasped her upper arms. His eyes were wide, and it was strange, so strange, to see them brown and not their warm, softly radiant pink.

"Seyn," he said, and his voice trembled. "I've been fighting my whole life. So have my family—all my people. I fought so that one day, I wouldn't have to fight anymore. I fought for that future. I believe in it. And I have to do everything I can to make sure that future happens."

He couldn't be saying what she thought he was. Frightened in a way she'd never been before, Seyn reached up and put her hands on his cheeks, smudging the cosmetic peach tones and revealing his pale-gray skin. Wanting to see *his* skin, *his* eyes.

"Sadori, it's fine, it's fine. Stay with me." Her voice cracked on the last word.

Stay with me ten more minutes, and those children live.

Stay with me ten more minutes, and you live.

Stay with me.

"I don't mind," he said, softly, sadly. "I just wish . . . I wish that future could have been with you."

And then he pressed his lips to hers, kissing her first

tentatively and then passionately as she returned the kiss with urgency. She clung to him, absurdly thinking she could hold on tight enough to keep him there, but then the cool air rushed in to fill the sudden space between their bodies and he was gone, racing faster on those strong, long legs than she could ever hope to run.

Futilely, stupidly, Seyn tried to catch him, shouting his name, until she tripped and hit the ground hard and was scooped up by Del, who had seemingly materialized out of nowhere.

"What the hell happened?" screamed Staven, his face flushed a deep, angry red, both fury and fear in his eyes as Del rushed into the ship with Seyn in his arms.

The bomb was defective, Seyn should have lied. *Sadori went back to fulfill the mission.*

Instead, she couldn't speak. Her hand went to her chest, where her own last-resort bomb was affixed. Where Sadori's was.

Sadori—I'm so sorry—

The ship took off right as the factory exploded.

Less than a minute later, the bomb Seyn had delayed also detonated. Through eyes blurred with either grief or joy or perhaps both, Seyn looked down through the viewport as hundreds of tiny figures escaped to safety.

The next few days were a blur.

Seyn had never seen Sadori's parents display much emotion. And at first, when the ship had returned to Jeosyn and Staven had to tell them the unthinkable, they had seemed stunned, and only nodded. They were composed and even kind to Seyn, wrapping her in a blanket and sitting her down by the heater to prevent her from going into shock even as they themselves quietly, unobtrusively, did so.

The debriefing was stunningly calm. Later, Seyn realized why. There was no shock of betrayal around this death, as there had been with Nadrine and Kaev's. There was no fury or graphic violence to inflame darker, baser emotions, as there had been with Azen's interrogation—or, more properly, execution.

Sadori, the joy of Ru and Halia Vushan's lives, he whom they loved so much they seldom let him out of their sight, had died a courageous death, completing a vital mission when equipment failed. In the eyes of a Dreamer, he was a hero.

It made something inside her, something Seyn had never even known was there, retreat, like a small animal hiding in its burrow.

She stuck to the story. Yes, she had been careful. Yes, she had instructed the droid to set the timer for five minutes. No, she hadn't noticed that anything was wrong with the timer or the bomb. Yes, she had tried to dissuade Sadori from sacrificing himself, and yes, that had been wrong of her, as it wasn't the Dreamer way. Yes, she was proud of Sadori and would always remember him.

Yes, Sadori Vushan was a hero.

Seyn was not sure which was worse—that Sadori had died, or that he had done so trying to ensure that four hundred students had died with him.

Then Del and Piikow were grilled about their preparation of the bomb. They had done everything right, they claimed, and had double-checked each other's work.

Staven was frustrated, but he did not blame anyone for what had, in the end, simply been a horrible disaster. "No one owns luck," he said. "We've had some good. And we've had bad. This wasn't anyone's fault. Simply . . . bad luck. We just have to make sure that Sadori didn't die in vain."

Iden arranged to meet Seyn for a walk as soon as possible. The two women walked off from the encampment, arms folded, heads close together. Iden felt the sympathy from the others as they watched them, close enough to observe, not close enough to hear what they said.

"What really happened out there?" Iden asked in low voice. "Del is afraid he missed something."

"No," Seyn said. Her voice was flat, and her eyes stared out into the distance, but her voice sounded calm and in control. "I take responsibility."

"What do you mean?"

"I made a decision on the spot to delay the timer. It would still explode—still kill Toshan and Deksha, and do some serious damage to the facility—but it would go off after the students were out of the building."

Iden felt for her. Gently, she said, "We discussed this. It was a necessary sacrifice."

"I thought so, too, until I was there," Seyn said. "These were innocent children of the Empire. Almost four hundred of them. The Dreamers still made their point. I didn't stop the event, just . . . altered it."

Iden started to piece it together. "And Sadori didn't know you'd delayed the timer. He went back."

"He activated his own bomb." There was no trace of emotion on Seyn's face.

Iden groped for words. She'd seldom felt so helpless. "It's not what was ordered. But I can't say that I'm sorry the students survived."

Seyn pressed her lips together, then, to Iden's shock, buried her face in her hands.

Iden felt a frisson of apprehension.

For the first time, Iden felt a real worry that Seyn might not be up to this. The rest of the team had all had up-close-and-personal combat experience. Seyn had sat in dark offices watching vidscreens, listening to multiple different conversations in multiple different languages, and studying dossiers. Most of her field experience had been in simulators. She'd never been forced to make the hard choices. Like whether to save four hundred students, or watch someone you knew—maybe even genuinely cared for—run headlong away from you to blow himself up.

And she'd been the one to order Seyn to pretend to be romantically interested in Sadori.

"He kissed me." Seyn said it bluntly. Another shock rumbled through Iden, like a groundquake tremor of emotion. "Right before he ran back in. I tried to stop him from going, but he was just—*faster* . . . I'll never be able to stop seeing it," Seyn said, her voice soft, almost a whisper.

Iden's jaw clenched, trying to find a place of common ground. "We all know a little something about that," she said, kindly.

Seyn's head came up. There were still tears in her eyes, but she was angry. "No, you don't."

"Seyn, I've—"

"I don't care what you've experienced, or what anyone else on the team has experienced. You're not me."

Iden tried again. "Seyn, I—"

Seyn waved a hand to silence her. "Shut up. Just *shut up.* You, Del, Gideon—you'll forget what you've seen, eventually. Not all of it. But time will soften it, and it'll lose some of its punch. You'll forget some of the details. But I won't. I *can't.*"

Sudden sympathetic horror filled Iden as she understood what the younger girl was trying to say.

Seyn had an eidetic memory.

If Iden or Hask or Del relived something awful that had occurred in their lives, it would, eventually, fade, at least somewhat. Not so for Seyn. Whenever she thought about the events of that day, Seyn would see them—not through the softening gauziness of distant memory, but as if it were all happening right in front of her, all over again. All because of her choice.

"Oh, Seyn," Iden said. "I'm sorry."

She was, but there was nothing she could do. Seyn would have to bear this burden alone.

For a long moment, they stood, their faces rendered different silvery shades of gray-white by dusk's light and lichen-light. Iden looked at her team member—her friend—and in her mind's eye, she saw the kind, gray face of Sadori.

They stood there a long time.

CHAPTER 24

When the two women returned, Halia was waiting. The Kage Warrior merely nodded to Iden, but she approached Seyn and placed a hand gently on her shoulder.

"I know you may not be hungry," she said, "but we have prepared a meal. It's as close as we can come to making Sadori's favorite. Will you join us?"

"Thank you," said Seyn, her voice heavy. "I would be honored."

Iden watched them walk away.

It wasn't supposed to be this hard, she thought. *We were just supposed to find the intel and then get out. And I don't think we're any closer to doing that than when we first got here.*

The Mentor walked up to join her. "Most of us have seen death in battle before," he said. "Lost someone. Seyn hasn't. She'll be all right. She's strong."

Find the intel and get out. She turned to the Mentor, nodding. "I hope so."

"The Vushans have asked her to share the shun-rai—the funeral meal," he said. "To remember the dead, the Kages eat their loved one's favorite food, and set a place for their spirit to join in."

"Some people have favorite foods I wouldn't like to eat," Iden said, trying to lighten the conversation.

The Mentor chuckled. "That's true," he said. "I was once at a dinner where, if it wasn't squirming as you chewed it, it wasn't fresh enough."

"Where was that?" Iden asked.

He waved a dismissive hand. "Far away from here" was all he said.

"Everything's far from here."

He chuckled again, and made as if to go back to the cavern.

She grasped his sleeve. "Mentor?"

"What is it, Iden?"

"Can . . . I talk to you?"

His kindly face furrowed in concern. "Of course," he said. "Let's walk for a bit."

They fell into step. Iden was silent, wondering how best to begin the conversation. "You said that we had a lot in common," she said at last.

"I did, but I'm sure there's much we don't have in common as well. People want to believe that people they like or admire are just like them, when it really isn't so."

"You admire me?" That surprised her and she stopped for a moment, staring at him.

"Well, yes," he said. "Look at you. You're, what, twenty-one? Twenty-two? And look what you've accomplished. Top of your class, TIE pilot, survived the Death Star. And then after all that, you had the courage to question your convictions. See if they really held up. Some people never get that far in self-examination. I regret that I didn't know that Azen, or whatever his name was in the end, was an Imperial agent, but I'm glad he brought you to us at least."

Iden was bombarded with conflicting emotions. On the one hand, the Mentor, a man completely unknown to her until very recently, saw her achievements—although one of those was a lie—and praised them freely. How was it this stranger thought more highly of her than her own father did?

"You mentioned a goddaughter," she found herself saying. "Did you ever have a family yourself?"

Sorrow settled over his aquiline features. "I was not very lucky in love," he said. "Or rather, I was fortunate to meet many remarkable women, but nothing seemed to last. But yes. I did have a family, once upon a time. An Imperial family. A wife whom I loved, and her daughter who—well, for me, the sun rose and set with her smiles. So now you know that I have some idea about leaving loved ones behind. Turning your back—or, in our cases, our coats, as it were. But now"—he gestured back toward the encampment—"the Dreamers are my family. We're all we've got now. So I have to take care of them, as best I can."

"Share what you've learned," Iden said.

"Just as you do. Just as the Kages do, as Staven does. We're a family, and whatever our differences, we stick together, and we pull together."

· · ·

"There are times," Staven said, taking a long swig from the bottle, "when I would just as soon stick the Mentor on a ship and send him off on a wild caranak chase." He handed the bottle to Gideon.

Gideon drank. Earlier that evening, he'd watched Iden go off with first Seyn, then the Mentor. Seyn had returned and was now flanked on either side by a Kage Warrior, almost as if the family had adopted her. She seemed to be holding up fine. Del and the Chadra-Fan were off doing whatever it was they did.

Iden had looked at Gideon before walking off with the Mentor, and he'd taken it as a sign to keep cozying up to Staven. Which was fine. He found Staven's intensity appealing, and it was fun simply hanging around him. And, as now, directing the conversations.

"Why don't you do just that?" Gideon asked, handing the bottle back to the partisan leader.

"Can't, more's the pity," Staven growled.

"Aren't you the leader?"

"Hell yeah, I'm the leader, which is why I see to it that he doesn't go on any missions that could get us into trouble."

This was the third bottle they'd shared tonight, and while Gideon could hold his liquor, it was still affecting him. Fortunately, it was hitting Staven harder. His words, slightly slurred, were flowing much more freely than usual.

"How could he get you in trouble?"

"Someone might recognize him, and then everything would get shot to hell," Staven said with a trace of annoyance, as if that ought to be perfectly clear to Gideon.

So Iden had been right. Gideon had to admit that she usually was. The Mentor was, or had been, someone important. *Everything would get shot to hell*. What did Staven mean by that?

"Well, he doesn't appear to be doing much to earn his keep," Gideon said with a shrug. "Everyone else does all the work and faces all the danger. Three people dead—four, if you count Azen—and he just sits around the fire lecturing everyone."

"It's a trade-off," Staven said with a sigh, and took another long drink before passing the bottle back to Gideon. "But if I could get rid of him and the Imp woman, I'd do it in a heartbeat."

Gideon almost choked on the alcohol, spitting out a mouthful as he laughed. "Imp woman?" Oh, that was a keeper. He couldn't wait to try it on Iden.

Staven grinned. "Iden," he said. "I don't know, Gid. I mean—it turns out that it was Azen who was an Imperial agent. We know that now. And she didn't have anything to do with the bomb being a dud. But I wonder if Azen was acting alone, and I can't shake the feeling that Iden's not trustworthy."

That was an issue everyone on Inferno Squad was painfully aware of. Gideon took a breath, trying to launch into yet another subtle defense of his commanding officer. Then he paused. Iden wanted to set one group against the other. Gideon shouldn't be defending her—or Dahna, or Piikow, or Del.

He should be attacking them.

So he did. "Yeah," he said. "I know what you mean. I get the feeling she could turn on us at any minute."

"Really?" Staven asked.

"Yeah," Gideon said. "And where are Del and Piikow? Weren't they supposed to be repairing the shuttle?"

Staven frowned. "They were," he said. "I should talk to them when they get back." He took another drink, looking thoughtful.

"Us" versus "them."

Works every time, Gideon thought.

"How long have you been working on these things?" Del asked. He and Piikow were in the caverns with the statues again. Under the Chadra-Fan's watchful eye, they had deliberately opened up a second statue, removing it piece by piece, measuring and recording everything in scrupulous detail. With the stylized humanoid shapes of both the external shell and the internal components, Del felt more like he was performing an autopsy than disassembling a machine. As he spoke, he lifted a rounded crystal. It felt almost hot in his hands and pulsed, as if it were indeed the heart it had possibly been crafted to resemble.

"About six months," Piikow replied. "I'm not very mobile, nor can I move heavy things, so I'm quite thrilled that you're here and interested. Until now, any research I've been able to do has been solely with the damaged one."

"And that's obviously a limited experiment," Del said. They'd already seen a difference between the two. The crystals inside the fallen statue had been duller than the ones they had seen in the newer one. And these were much warmer.

Del shook his head. "I gotta admit, these things are starting to unnerve me."

"In a good way, though, yes?" Piikow's ragged ears were pricked forward hopefully.

"Yes," Del said, and it was the truth. "If we go on the idea that these were active machines, and these crystals were fuel cells . . . why have so many? And why did they carve them in different shapes? Did each one have a unique function?"

Del was seated on the stone floor, Piikow next to him. The Chadra-Fan had just used a hammer and chisel to break open the crystal that corresponded to the liver, provided their hypothesis that they had been crafted to represent organs was correct. There was nothing inside it. It was just a solid crystal, though it did not like to be broken. The pulse and the glow faded.

Piikow emitted a growl of annoyance. "Well, that just destroyed it."

Del laughed, gesturing with a tool toward the line of statues that trailed off for, seemingly, forever. "We have a few spare parts."

"We do at that!" his companion agreed cheerfully. "If only we had as much time."

Del looked up, his brow furrowing. "What do you mean?" Were the partisans planning to change camps? He found that he really hoped not.

He'd noticed that the Chadra-Fan's moods were mercurial. Now the ears drooped. "Our lives here are always on the edge. At any moment, another one of us could die on a mission. Or the Empire could find us. Or . . ." He lifted his large eyes to Del's. "I don't know how much longer I have. Melodramatic, I know, but it's true. I suppose that's true for everyone, though, isn't it?"

Del refocused on the crystal he held in his hand. "Yeah, I suppose it is. Us more than most. Just got to use that time well."

"I think this is time very well spent," Piikow said, his normal buoyant optimism reasserting itself.

"Me too," Del answered, forcing himself to smile. He glanced over at the "skull" he'd opened earlier, and the brain-shaped crystal it housed.

Brain. If he could convince Iden—or, really, Admiral Versio—that Piikow's odd, dancing brain was worthwhile, that he was of value to the Empire . . . maybe they wouldn't kill him. Piikow's condition was currently going completely untreated. The Empire had no end of resources at its disposal . . . if it chose to use them.

"We're going to figure this out," Del said firmly. "And we're going to start by understanding how the hell we tell these statues what we want them to do."

Piikow squirmed happily and applauded, grinning almost from ear to tattered ear.

We all have a job to do, Seyn reminded herself about a week after the disaster at the factory. Iden was spending most of her time in the company of the Mentor and those he appeared to be closest to—Dahna, Del, and Piikow. Gideon, on the other hand, seemed well on his way to usurping Dahna as second in command in Staven's eyes. The two often stayed up into the night drinking and talking. And Del kept leaving with the Chadra-Fan. They were up to something, but in their increasingly infrequent four-way conversations, Del had told them that he was simply trying to extract as much information as he could about the limits of partisan knowledge and technology.

Since Sadori's death, his family had moved more toward Staven's hard-line, bloodier way of looking at things. Of course they had; they were hurting, and they wanted revenge. And violence was what they had been raised on.

Seyn found herself sitting with them, eating with them, and one night Halia had opened up and spoken about Sadori as a child. The family was so grim most of the time that Seyn was honestly surprised to hear funny stories. She found herself smiling, and then wishing that Sadori were here to be good-naturedly teased by those who cared for him.

Seyn reminded herself that she was *not* Sadori's love, that she was a member of an elite squadron, and that she had a duty to perform. She needed to pull herself out of this confusing melancholia. Sadori was dead. She didn't need to flirt and pretend anymore.

What she needed to do was return to the person she had been before this mission.

What she needed to do was listen.

So she did. Eventually, Staven had more work for her to do. It was comforting to fall into the old habits: focusing on the forgeries and eavesdropping on conversations.

*—I heard Staven arguing with the Mentor—*Halia speaking to Ru in their own language, in a voice of concern. Good, Seyn thought. Hask was fanning the flames.

*—running out of Dahna fruit, better make a run!—*Piikow, teasing Dahna in an attempt to lighten the mood.

The Twi'lek chuckled slightly and replied in the same tongue that he was the one eating all the Dahna fruit.

—*does not trust her.* That was Ru, replying to his wife. *Nor do I.*

Seyn kept her eyes on the Dahna fruit she herself was eating. This could be important. Whom did Ru not trust?

She is the daughter of an Imperial, but she left, Dahna was saying. Her command of the Kage language was crude but comprehensible.

Staven still has it in his head that she is Imperial, Ru replied. *He said he wants her dead.*

That was a bad development, but not unexpected. Their divide-and-conquer plan ran the risk of veering into real danger, and they all accepted that.

Gently, Piikow said, "We have lost so many. Too many. Here I am, old and sick, and I live while Nadrine and Kaev and Sadori are gone."

"I love the Vushans, but it was wrong to raise a child as Sadori was raised," Dahna said in a soft voice. "Growing up with all this so commonplace. He probably never even thought there might be another way to complete the mission."

"Ru and Halia loved him! They did what they thought was right, and so did Sadori," Seyn said, angry that Dahna thought so poorly of the Kages and keeping her voice quiet so the Vushans wouldn't overhear.

Everyone was staring at her. And too late, Seyn realized that Dahna had not been speaking in Basic. Piikow had spoken in his own language, and the Twi'lek had responded in the same tongue.

As had Seyn.

Dahna said, very quietly, "Seyn . . . how do you know Piikow's language? You told me you only knew Basic and Huttese."

"I must have picked up some of it," Seyn said.

"You don't 'pick up' Chadra-Fan," Ru said, in the Kage language.

"You . . . lied to me." Dahna, in Twi'leki.

The Kages went very, very still. Their faces were hard and unreadable, like doors that had slammed shut. Piikow's black eyes widened and he looked at Seyn in shock. Seyn kept her face blank, still smiling a little as if in embarrassment at having caused a fuss and perhaps a touch confused about what was going on.

"Staven keeps saying he thought Azen wasn't working alone," Dahna snarled. Then, in a tone that shook with anger and pain, she added, "But we *never* suspected it was you."

It's just a guess, Seyn thought wildly. *She'll have to convince everyone else.* Even as she clung to the thought, deep in her heart Seyn knew that it was a futile hope. A week ago, she'd have been safe in that assumption. Even if Dahna had noticed her reaction, she wouldn't have thought anything of it. No one would have; Seyn the Slave was the darling of the camp. But now that the factory mission had gone so terribly wrong, everyone was angry and looking for someone to blame.

Seyn had been the last to see Sadori alive. The Kages had practically accepted her as a future daughter-in-law, and even Staven liked her. It was Iden they had distrusted, never her, and Seyn saw again the Twi'lek putting her life, the lives of everyone on her team, at risk in order to save an escaped slave.

Like Sadori, Dahna had cared about her. And now Seyn had just shattered her heart.

"I just . . . I seem to be good at languages," she said. "You know what it's like. When you're a slave, you have to be able to adapt quickly."

Dahna's hand shot out and closed around Seyn's wrist as tight as stun cuffs, and the Twi'lek hauled the much smaller woman to her feet.

"Staven!" Dahna shouted, her voice ringing through the quiet camp. "*Staven!*"

She marched toward the gathering area, dragging a stumbling Seyn behind her. Seyn knew at least three ways of breaking Dahna's grip. She could escape into the nightscape. She'd studied the terrain and knew several places where she could hide; she had learned enough about what was safe to eat and what wasn't to survive.

But Seyn knew she wasn't going to flee. She'd just messed up, terribly, and had to fix it. She had to face the Dreamers, convince them that Dahna was mistaken.

She started crying, fearfully. "Dahna, what's wrong? What have I done? You're hurting me!"

Piikow was scurrying to keep up with the Twi'lek's long-legged, swift strides. "Dahna, are you sure?" he said. "You need to be sure before you accuse her of this!"

"Piikow, you know how long it took me to speak your language. And let me ask you this—why did she lie about it? People lie when they have something to hide. And I intend to find out what Seyn's hiding."

By the time Dahna had closed the short distance between the sleeping cavern and the main gathering space, everyone was assembled.

"Dahna, what's happened?" Staven asked. Gideon Hask stood beside him.

Her teeth bared in an angry snarl, Dahna flung Seyn down hard onto the rock by the heater, where Iden, Del, and the Mentor had been sitting, talking.

"You thought Iden was a traitor. But I think it's this one."

"Wait, what?" the Mentor said, staring at Seyn, his blue eyes wide with shocked disbelief.

"Piikow and I were talking. In his language. Not only did she understand what we said, but she answered back. And she's constantly maintained that she only knows *two languages*. Who lies about knowing languages when joining freedom fighters?"

"Someone who wants to eavesdrop," Staven said.

Seyn saw the emotions flit across the faces of the partisans—confusion turning to disbelief, then suspicion. But not certainty. Not yet.

"Oh, Seyn!" Piikow's warbling, slightly squeaky voice was heavy with pain. "The second blast."

"What?" asked Halia, sharply.

"You all reported hearing a second blast, not long after Sadori's bomb went off." To Staven, Del, and Iden, he said, "It was a weapons factory, so you all assumed it was just the weapons exploding. But it wasn't." He turned his enormous eyes back to Seyn. "It was you, wasn't it? You were the one who set the timer. You said you told the droid to set it for five minutes . . . but I don't think you did. I think that second explosion was also one of our bombs . . . set to go off later." He gulped. "Sadori . . . he died for nothing."

These people did not believe in second chances. They

had only just been betrayed by an Imperial agent, someone they'd thought they could trust.

And now—it had happened again. No, Seyn could not look for any kind of mercy now.

She didn't dare risk making eye contact with any of her team. What could they do? If they tried to speak up for her, they would only bring suspicion on themselves. But she saw the horror on their faces out of the corner of her wet eyes.

They stood, not saying anything, her friends; they couldn't, and Seyn blamed them not at all. They shouldn't draw any attention to themselves.

"Give her to me," came a cold voice. It was Halia. She had already drawn her vibroblade, and it sparkled and sizzled with dark-purple hues in the dim light. Her husband stood beside her, his arms folded across his broad chest. His eyes burned with anger, but he would give the kill to his wife.

"Wait, we need to get to the bottom of this," the Mentor snapped. "This could all be a misunderstanding."

"Stay out of this, Mentor." Ru's voice held a note of cold warning. "You've not lost a child."

"No. I *didn't* lose a child of my body. But a woman I loved was killed right in front of my eyes because she fought against injustice. My goddaughter died in service to the partisan cause. And I've betrayed my own family, most likely forever, because of actions I've performed, *also* in service to the partisan cause. I know you grieve, Ru. But don't presume I don't know suffering."

He turned to Staven and said darkly, "I don't think you've forgotten, Staven. Or have you?"

"You know I haven't," Staven snapped. He stabbed a finger in Seyn's direction. "But if she's an Imperial agent, she's dead."

"*If* she's an Imperial agent. *If*," said the Mentor. "It's a small word, but it has a great meaning. I've come to accept that sometimes we must kill people just because they're in our way. And if it does turn out she's a traitor, then yes, I will kill her myself. But we *don't* turn on one another!"

He looked from Staven to each of the others in turn, his arms open in a gesture of appeal. "We, the Dreamers—we're all that's left that we know of. We've lost three of our own in the past month! We can't afford to just cut her throat and move on!"

"So what do you want to do with her?" Dahna asked. Seyn realized that despite everything she'd seen, Dahna desperately wanted to be proven wrong. Seyn suddenly found herself unable to look at the Twi'lek.

"To start, we could check the droid's databanks," the Mentor suggested.

No. Seyn couldn't let them do that. There was no telling what they might find.

"That won't be necessary," she said. "Piikow is right. I delayed the timer. I could not participate in the murder of nearly four hundred students."

"Are you an Imperial agent?" Staven said, his voice icy.

"No," she replied.

"As I said," Halia stated, "give her to me. I'll get the truth out of her, even if I have to flay that pretty skin off her in tiny little strips!"

"Stop!" Staven's voice brooked no disagreement. Ru reached and gripped his wife's arm, shaking his head.

Staven strode over to Halia and took the blade from her hand. She relinquished it to her leader, and she and her husband stood, holding each other, burying their faces. The pain radiating from them was palpable, and Seyn thought that hurt worse than the knife would have.

So much she would never be able to erase now, even if she survived this. If Staven would let the Mentor conduct the interview, she might be able to convince him she was just too soft-hearted and had acted impulsively. The Mentor—and Dahna, and Piikow, too, she realized—were searching for reasons to believe her.

The others were looking for excuses to kill her.

Staven regarded the blade for a long moment, turning it this way and that, gazing at the purple sizzling blade as if it held answers. Then he went to where Seyn stood, her wrist still gripped by Dahna's strong fingers. He towered over her by a full thirty centimeters.

He stood so close to her, she could smell his sweat and feel the heat of his body. *Go ahead,* Seyn thought. *Lose your temper. Strike me down before I tell you anything. Make it quick.*

CHAPTER 25

Every instinct in Iden was screaming at her to defend Seyn, her crewmember. Her teammate. Her friend. They were four against six, and Piikow wasn't a strong fighter. They could take the partisans, and save Seyn. Perhaps, when the Dreamers were dead, Inferno Squad would recover the data they had been sent to find somewhere among their belongings.

Perhaps.

But they would fail in every aspect of their mission. Iden knew her father, and unlike the situation back on Tellik IV, he would not be predisposed to giving them yet another chance. This was it. Everything they'd been working toward had led to this moment.

Seyn had put the mission in danger. She had messed up, had let herself be discovered. And if anyone other than the Mentor was going to question her, Iden knew that *question* would be simply a nicer word for "torture." Seyn would break under that. Anyone would. Iden, along with the others, had just witnessed a man twice her age, who had been an experienced Imperial agent, break under the Dreamers' questioning. Seyn, so new to all of this, newer than Iden had fully comprehended, would hold out as long as she could. But they would break her, and learn everything, and then they would kill the rest of Inferno Squad.

No. Iden couldn't let that happen to her team. Not Del, or Hask—

Or Seyn.

All this flitted through Iden's head in less than a second.

Staven turned to Iden and threw the blade in her direction. Her attention snapped back into real time and she caught the sizzling blade by its hilt.

"I say we kill two birds with one stone," Staven said. "You've been under a cloud since you got here, Versio. Let's clear the air a bit. We'll watch *you* question the girl. Shouldn't be too hard. We've already shown you how it's done."

All the attention was on Iden now. She realized that the vibroblade she held was the only weapon that any Inferno Squad member held at the moment. Not that they weren't quite capable of dispatching others with their bare hands—it was part of their training.

But the rest of the Dreamers had drawn their own weapons. Iden and her team might be able to take down only a couple of them before the Dreamers killed them. But take them down, they would.

She tightened her grip on the weapon and looked directly at Seyn. *See it in my eyes,* she pleaded silently, then looked away from the girl to glance at the partisans and her team. They nodded, ever so slightly.

Seyn was a member of Inferno Squad. She was one of them, and they were in.

If they all attacked at the same moment, they stood a better chance.

Iden squared her shoulders and prepared to turn back to face Seyn. But even as she started to move, there was a flurry of movement and a horrible wailing sound of fury.

The Dreamers had beaten them to it.

No! Iden whirled, stabbing forward with the glowing blue blade, impaling—

Seyn.

Her dark eyes were wide and her mouth was open in a soundless O. For a moment that stretched like an eternity, the two women stared at each other. Seyn's mouth moved, murmuring a single, soundless word.

Yes.

Then, raggedly, she said in a defiant but rapidly weakening voice, "For the Empire!" To Iden's horror, Seyn pulled the blade deeper. She gasped, then, slowly, all tension leaving her slim body, she crumpled to the ground.

Seyn . . .

The blade was released from her flesh with a wet sound. Suddenly furious, at what or whom she didn't know, Iden shouted, "Lying traitor!" She dragged her gaze away from the appalling sight of Seyn's body and found herself staring directly at Staven. "I'm sorry," she told him. "I didn't expect a rush like that."

The words came easily, swiftly to her lips, and some part of her marveled at that.

His eyes searched hers, and he pressed his lips together, creating a hard, thin line. His hands clenched and unclenched, as if he wanted to seize and shake her but knew better.

"Give the blade to Halia and come with me," he said, turning on his heel and striding out into the darkness. Iden obeyed, returning the weapon to its owner. Halia's face was cold and hard as stone. Iden felt all their eyes boring into her.

"Staven—" the Mentor called after them.

Staven stopped and regarded the older man. He lifted his hand, fingers raised in warning. "My people. My decisions."

There was nothing the Mentor could do. The Dreamers called Staven their leader. Iden had no doubt but that the mysterious diplomat could still fight very well indeed; he was lean and fit, the only hint of age showing in the gray at his temples and the laugh lines on his face. But Staven was right. The Mentor looked at Iden and tried to give her a reassuring smile. He didn't succeed.

There was nothing her people could do, either. Iden turned and followed Staven.

He said nothing as they walked. Iden wished he would speak. Without distraction, she could feel the emotions threatening to close in on her. She could still see Seyn's upturned face, the awful wound in her flesh.

Iden thought she had made the decision for the team. Seyn had had other plans.

When they were so far away that the cavern opening

was but a small orange smudge, Staven halted and turned to her. They were a meter apart.

Staven's blaster had been in a holster at his hip. Now it was in his hand. Iden wondered if it was set to stun. She didn't think so.

"Convince me."

"What?"

He shrugged. "Convince me why I shouldn't just kill you where you stand. I've been a partisan for years, but suddenly I have not one but *two* Imperial agents in my group. Oh, excuse me—two Imperial agents, and one supposed Imperial defector. Seems a bit of a stretch of the imagination to think they're not all connected. Don't you think?"

Iden was silent.

"So." He shrugged, as if they were having a normal conversation. "Go ahead. Here's your chance. Convince me."

Iden was suddenly utterly and completely drained. She was tired, so tired. Tired of pretending, tired of probing, tired of being sidelined and suspected. Tired of constantly striving, and never reaching.

"Why would I team up with them? Seyn had everyone fooled, and Azen—he abducted me, put cuffs on me, and searched me when I was unconscious!"

The best lies have a grain of truth in them.

"Or so the two of you claimed," Staven said. "I've no idea how real any of that was. Think about the lengths the Empire went to get Seyn here—giving her injuries, putting her in a locked cuff. That's a lot of prep. All you needed to do was lie a little. And I know, and you know, Imperials are very good at that. I don't for a moment believe your story about Alderaan suddenly thawing your icy cold Imperial heart. Kaev once told me he did, but look where it got him."

"I had nothing to do with Kaev and Nadrine's deaths!" Suddenly, for some stupid reason, it was terribly important that she made Staven believe the one thing that was real. Then she said, quietly, "There's nothing I can say that would make you believe me." As she spoke the words she realized that they were the unvarnished truth.

Seyn. I'm so sorry. You died to keep the mission alive, and I can't even think of anything to tell him.

"*Convince me!*" He screamed those last two words, his voice raw and harsh. The hand that held the blaster trembled. She could take it and—

Fail. Again. As she had been failing.

We're Versios. Versios don't fail.

She suddenly felt a great pain in her chest, as though she had been kicked by one of the great hooved beasts that migrated, following the Jeosyn dusk. She gasped.

"My father," she said, thickly. She was trembling, as if she stood in a strong wind, and instead of snatching the weapon from Staven she wrapped her arms around herself. Like her mother had held her, when she was a child.

Her mother now thought she was a failure, too.

Iden moaned softly.

"What about him? *What about your father, Iden?*"

He laid no hand on her, but he battered her with his words. An image of her father rose in her mind. So stingy with anything resembling kindness, or approval. Always pushing. Pushing her to succeed, to excel, to be the best of the best.

And she was. She *was* the best of the best.

And that would still never be enough for him. Nothing would be enough for Garrick Versio.

The best lies have a grain of truth in them.

Iden dropped to her knees, the hard rock bruising them, her whole body sagging.

"I hate him," she whispered.

Silence, long and frightening and infused with portent, hung between the two—the daughter of the admiral, the leader of the rebels.

"I hate him," she said again, and then again. She lifted her face up toward Staven, who stood over her with the blaster muzzle pointed at her head. "You don't know what it was like. You can't. Nothing was good enough, nothing. And I wanted to hurt him. So I did."

You didn't just betray the Empire, or the Emperor. You betrayed your father. You betrayed me.

"I spoke against his beloved Empire. I sympathized with the rebels. I brought disgrace on the family name he was so damn proud of. And I joined the partisans—the bloodiest, cruelest, most hate-filled of all the rebels." Her vision swam with tears, but she blinked them back. She was a Versio, and Versios didn't cry. "You're right, Staven. I *don't* care about your cause. But I care that he cares. And that's why I'm here."

Staven stood as if rooted to the ground. His eyes were wide, his breathing rapid and shallow as he listened.

Quick as a thought, Iden sprang to her feet. She seized the muzzle of the blaster and pulled it to press directly against her head. Her eyes blazed as she stared into Staven's.

"You want to kill me? Go ahead. But if you don't, you'd better *never* doubt me again. Are we clear?"

A slow smile curved his lips. He pulled back the blaster, held up his hands in a shrugging, whatever-you-say gesture.

"We're clear," he said. He took a step back, regarding her with a peculiar expression on his face.

Iden didn't dare let herself believe it. "Why? Why now?"

"The Mentor thinks that rebellions are built on hope, but I don't believe it. Rebellions are built on hate, Iden Versio. And now I know you've got plenty of that burning in your belly. Come on. Let's get back to the others. Some of them might even be glad to see you're alive."

Her team—what was left of her team—was.

While she and Staven were gone, the remaining partisans had removed Seyn's corpse. Iden didn't inquire; she would ask one of her team later. She forced herself to laugh and make jokes, to join in the anger and the unkind words they hurled at Seyn, the traitor. Seyn, who for all intents and purposes had murdered Sadori, a boy who had done nothing wrong except fall for the wrong girl.

Through the horrific hours that stretched out until she and the others could reasonably depart to speak on their comlinks, one thing thudded through Iden's mind with every pump of her scorched heart: The thing she had feared and avoided at all costs—the thing that caused nightmares that woke her up, sweating and trembling—had happened.

She had failed, and others had paid the price for that failure.

Iden wanted to see her team, look into their eyes, read the messages of their bodies that their words weren't revealing, but she had to content herself with the comlink.

"What happened to Seyn's body?" was the first thing she asked.

"We—they—we all went—" Del took a deep breath. "The usual place. The Kages took it out in a speeder a short distance away. Piikow, Dahna, and I followed."

Iden felt her stomach knot as if twisted by an unseen hand, but she had to know.

"Did . . . was she buried?"

"No." That was Gideon, his normally bright voice somber. "They dragged her out and just tossed—"

"That's enough, Hask," Iden snapped. Her voice was harsh, hard. "We can't mourn her yet. We still have a mission to complete. Seyn gave her life to make sure we could do that. To save us. And we . . ."

Iden grasped the comlink so hard her knuckles turned white. She took a deep breath. "I failed her. I failed the team."

"Iden, don't blame—" Del began, but she cut him off.

"I'm not blaming. I'm taking responsibility for my failure, with her, and with you. We should have coordinated better. We should have watched out for one another. She was the rookie when it came to things like this. And we weren't there when she needed us. We were chasing our own goals, focused on our own assignments when we should have closed ranks around her so that she didn't slip up. And I let that happen. The failure is mine."

It was awful, and liberating, and cold, and cruel. She embraced it all.

"That won't happen again. We are a team, and we will act like a team, and we will find the source of the partisans' information and start the inevitable final toppling of them as any kind of a threat to the Empire. No more long games. We act, and we act decisively, quickly, and with complete coordination.

"The beginning of the end starts *now*."

CHAPTER 26

Del wasn't sure how to behave around Piikow anymore. He had orders from his commanding officer that it was time to close the net. Del had a small part to play, but not a major role. That was fine with him. He'd grown content to stay in his engine room over the years, and while he had quickly readapted to a field assignment, the clandestine nature of the operation had chafed. He'd gotten around it by focusing on the shared project with Piikow. But now his main task was to unobtrusively get everything ready for a fast getaway once, as Iden had grimly phrased it, "All hell breaks loose."

So he found he had to force himself to behave normally around the Chadra-Fan while making excuses as to why he couldn't go down into the crystal cave with him today. "I've got some work to do I've been putting off," he said, which was the truth as far as it went.

"I understand," Piikow said. "All of us were shocked by Seyn's disloyalty. It's a difficult thing to grasp. Sometimes, it's good to be alone for a bit. Just tinker—do something with your hands and let your brain stop running everything."

Dammit, the little guy understood. "Thanks," he said. "That's exactly how I feel right now." He cocked his head, as if he had an idea. "No one else knows about the statues, right?"

"I didn't think anyone else would be interested."

"I'd feel better if someone accompanied you today," Del said. Piikow's normally bright eyes were dull with sorrow. He looked thinner, frailer, than he had before. Seyn's "betrayal" had been a blow. The words were very true—and also had a purpose. "Why don't you let the Mentor in on it? He seems like a pretty smart person. He might have some suggestions that techies like us wouldn't even think of."

Piikow brightened. "He might at that. It could be a good distraction for him, too. Those statues will yield their secrets yet!" he chirped, shaking his small fist in pretend defiance. Then he turned and went back toward the sleeping cavern.

Del made his own way toward the ship Iden had chosen. He had taken a few steps, and then he stopped dead in his tracks.

Let your brain stop running everything, Piikow had said.

"Hey! Piikow!" The Chadra-Fan paused and turned around. Del jogged back, catching up to him, and beamed down at him. "You figured it out! How the statues worked!"

Piikow blinked. "I did? Well, how clever of me. What exactly did I figure out?"

"Brain waves," Del said triumphantly. "The original creators must have had some form of telepathy. The crystals must be able to somehow detect brain activity. They're not connected with one another inside the statues in any physical way, so it has to be nonphysical connection."

"Brilliant!" Piikow clapped his hands excitedly. "The Mentor is, as you say, very knowledgeable. Perhaps he has run across something similar."

Del gave what felt like the first genuine smile in ages. There was a lot he couldn't do for Piikow. A lot he shouldn't even want to do. But at least he'd been able to make some contribution toward solving the mystery of row upon row of still, silent statues with organs made of glowing purple crystal.

He turned back to the task at hand. When he was a safe distance away from the main gathering cavern, he clicked on his comm.

"The Mentor will be with Piikow for a while," he said.

"How long?"

"Not sure. At least an hour, I would think." The Mentor seemed to be a highly educated and well-traveled man. He probably would be thrilled with the discovery, and might be gone all day.

"More than enough time. Good job, Del."

He clicked off the comm and took a deep breath. He could focus, now. Del Meeko wouldn't let the other two remaining members of Inferno Squad down.

. . .

Everyone but Del, Piikow, and the Mentor was in the main gathering cavern. Staven, with Hask, as always, called out a greeting to Iden, and she replied pleasantly. *What a difference,* Iden thought bitterly. *All it took was Seyn's death.*

The partisan leader must have shared something about the previous night's discussion with Iden, because Ru, Halia, and Dahna all seemed comfortable with her presence. They were wrapping up food items and tucking them into a small crate. "We're going to go looking for some more Dahna fruit," Halia explained.

"I need to get out of here," Dahna said simply. Of course these three wouldn't want to spend more time here than necessary, right now. Iden refused to look at the spot on the floor where Seyn had died. Someone— she didn't know who—had cleaned up the blood. "I can't take this constant semidark right now," Dahna continued. "I need to have sun on my face and eat something fresh from a tree. Want to come with us, Iden?"

She gave them a wan smile. "I think I'll just go for a long run. I need to move. Just make sure you bring back enough for me, okay?"

All of them understood that, too, and Dahna, looking old and very tired, said, "There'll be enough for everyone, I promise. We ready?"

The Kages nodded and walked off. The despair in the air was so thick, Iden fancied she could smell it.

"That's not a bad idea," Staven said.

"You are *not* going to pick fruit," Hask said.

"No, but I can sure as hell go for a flight. Get out of here for a while."

"Go. Clear your head," Hask replied. "Iden and I will

see if we can't go give Del a hand." Staven nodded a quick farewell, then he strode out.

For a moment, the two sat quietly, making sure no one would return unexpectedly. Then Iden asked, "Who cleaned up the blood?"

"Dahna," he said. "She was crying."

Iden nodded. She was silent for a moment, not wanting to think about Dahna crying over Seyn. "Okay," she said at last. "This is working out better than we had hoped. Del got Piikow and the Mentor out of the way, and now the rest are gone for a while."

"We don't know how long."

"Dahna and the Kages will be gone for a good chunk of time, and I'm willing to bet Staven won't be back for at least an hour. Just keep an eye out and comm me if anyone returns so I can head out on my 'run.'"

"Yes, Captain."

Iden couldn't recall when she'd begun calling Gideon by his surname. It was before Seyn died. And now he was calling her Captain.

Another casualty of this mission. The thought saddened her, but she didn't dwell on it. She rose and headed out to the sleeping area and went to where the Mentor's bedroll was, neatly tied up and put away. What few personal items he had were contained in a single over-the-shoulder bag. Like all the partisans, he traveled light.

Iden expected a flicker of guilt, and when it rose to the surface she quashed it quickly and set to work.

She was becoming convinced that the Mentor was the leak. She could believe that the older man would keep Staven around, even let him stay the leader, if the Mentor was the holder of vital information. But she couldn't see the reverse. Even if Staven had loved the Mentor's goddaughter years ago, even if they had both respected Saw Gerrera, Iden knew that Staven's dislike ran deep. If he didn't need the Mentor, the Mentor would not be here. Maybe not dead, but with another cell. No, Staven was the leader, but the Mentor had something he wanted. Staven was being forced to dance to the other man's tune, and he hated it.

There was a good chance—better than good—that the Mentor was smart enough not to leave important information with his bedroll. He probably had it on him at all times. She would, if she were in his position. But the search she was performing was twofold. She wanted to know if he were the leak . . . and who the hell he *was*.

There wasn't much. Some ration cubes and nutritive milk for snacks. No comlink; he'd taken that with him. There were a few trinkets whose significance would be known only to him.

And there was a datapad.

Can he really have been so stupid? she thought. It would make things so much easier if he had, but she would lose all respect for the man. The datapad was locked, of course, but it was a token attempt, and it was the matter of a few moments before Iden was able to slice in.

Quickly she began to skim, then, after a moment, she paused, realizing what she'd come across.

The Mentor had kept a journal.

All of those times when he'd gone off alone, claiming to want to be with his thoughts—it made sense. He'd wanted to chronicle those thoughts, record them in a considered manner. She checked the chrono. She had time.

Maybe this wasn't what it seemed to be. Maybe it was a code.

Iden settled down to read.

There was no code. But there was information, none of which pertained to the team's current mission, and all of which stunned her. After half an hour, reeling with what she'd just discovered, she put the Mentor's things away, taking care to leave the impression that someone had gone through them and tried to cover their tracks.

She got to her feet and commed the team. "Nothing here we can use," she said. "We'll have to rely on plan B. I'm going to change and head out for a run. Hask, you were with me this whole time, and you saw me leave."

"Copy that," Hask replied.

"Del, how's that ship coming?"

"She'll be ready for takeoff when we are," he said. "Going to grab some rations, too."

"Negative on the rations. Either we'll get out and they'll shoot us down and we won't need them, or we'll soon be in Imperial space and can make contact with the admiral. We don't want to tip our hand before we need to. Anything you need from here?"

"Nothing I can't live without," Del said.

"Same," Hask said. He and Del each carried a hand-held blaster, and there were more within reach in the cavern's alcoves.

"Okay then. We just need to be ready. I'm betting things will start moving fast after that."

She clicked off the comlink and set off for a run as she had said, trying to process everything she'd learned. Part of her wanted to tell her team, but she needed to hold on to this particular card in case she needed to play it.

One thing she had been completely truthful about—things would very soon be kicked into unstoppable motion.

Staven returned about an hour later. Hask commed Iden, who turned around and headed back. By the time she arrived, sweaty, flushed, and much calmer than she had been before she left, Staven had already started drinking. Good. That would help.

Dahna, Ru, and Halia returned from their own trip about an hour after that, looking noticeably better and bearing delicious fruit. Del drifted in at some point, smudged from working on the shuttle, and Piikow and the Mentor arrived, talking animatedly, right before dinnertime.

"Del!" the Mentor exclaimed. "I can't get over what you and Piikow have been doing. He tells me you theorize that the crystals responded to brain waves."

"Crystals?" Halia asked sharply.

The Mentor turned to the Kages. "I've just visited an underground cavern lit by crystals. Similar, I believe, to the ones on your world. More astonishing than that is that hidden away in this cave are perhaps thousands of ceramic statues with crystals inside them that correspond to human organs. Piikow thinks they aren't statues, but machines—droids, if you will. And Del believes that their creators might have been telepathic."

"Well," Staven said, "haven't you all been busy."

"We have," Piikow said, apparently not noticing Staven's sneer, "but it's nothing of use to us. Yet," he added, looking at Del.

"If it's of no use to us, then it's of no use," Staven said. "Unless the Mentor here wants to write a paper to present to some university somewhere, you need to quit wasting your time on this. We still have work we have to do, don't we, Mentor?"

The Mentor's enthusiasm bled out of him, and Iden watched as he almost visibly put on armor against Staven. She was having a hard time looking at the older man, now that she finally knew who and what he was. But she had to keep behaving normally. *But not for much longer.*

"Our fearless leader is quite right," the Mentor said, his voice clipped and calm. "We'll talk about our future plans after dinner. In the meantime, I'll be back in a few moments. I want to jot down some notes on these statues while it's fresh in my mind."

Jot down some notes in your journal, Iden thought. Her heart sped up, but she got up and prepared her plate as if everything was normal. When she caught Del's and Hask's eyes, she gave them a slight nod.

Be ready.

Not five minutes later, the Mentor stormed back in. Iden thought she had seen him furious before, but that was a pale imitation of the anger that radiated almost palpably from his slim frame.

"Staven," he said, and his carefully controlled voice held a cold edge, "a word with you?"

Staven paused in his eating and scowled. "Mentor," he said, "after dinner."

"No. Now."

The leader rolled his eyes and put another forkful of meat into his mouth. The Mentor closed the distance between them in three strides and knocked Staven's tray out of his hands.

A gasp went up. Everyone was suddenly on high alert. Apparently, this had never happened before. Staven was on his feet, his face flushed. "What the hell do you think—"

The Mentor seized Staven's tunic and brought the leader's face to within centimeters of his own. Between clenched teeth, he growled, "I said *now!*"

He let go of Staven and turned, marching outside.

Staven's hand dropped to the blaster at his belt, then he clenched his fist and followed the Mentor.

Thus far, all had gone according to Inferno Squad's plan. But now, there was no plan. They just had to be ready to react to whatever happened between the two men.

Everyone was silent. Iden caught snatches of conversation when one or the other raised his voice.

—went through my personal property. You had no right to—

—Nobody went through your things . . . care enough about—

—any more missions until—

—damn well better, that was part of the deal for—

Finally Staven stalked back in. He ran his fingers through his blue hair even as he swore—the epitome of someone who'd been bested. Then he planted his hands on his waist and calmed himself. He looked up at his companions.

"So . . . Things are going to change around here. Just letting you know. Gid—walk with me."

Hask rose obligingly, and the two men left. Dahna

stared after them, her mouth open. She was supposedly second in command, but Staven hadn't even looked at her. He'd asked for Hask. It looked as if things had already changed, Iden thought.

"I'm going after the Mentor," Iden said. She paused to grab a blaster from the supply area. At Ru's expression, she said, "Just in case."

"He did look pretty upset," Del volunteered.

"Do you know where he's going?"

"I . . . have an idea."

CHAPTER 27

"I need you to do something for me," Staven said.

"Name it," Hask said.

Despite his urgency, Staven seemed not to be able to utter the words. He pressed his lips together for a moment and took a deep breath. "I need you to kill the Mentor."

Hask wasn't surprised. This was a risk Inferno Squad had taken when it had chosen to pit the two against each other. "Why me?"

"Because the others might hesitate. They've known him awhile, and you've never really liked him."

"No, I don't," Hask agreed. "Can I ask why? What the hell was he so upset about, anyway?"

"I kept him around this long because he had information I needed. He's been the one, other than Azen, to provide us with targets."

Iden was right, Hask thought. "And now you don't need him anymore?"

"I need what he knows, but I don't need him. He was upset because he was convinced that someone had gone rummaging through his things today."

Hask shook his head. "Nope. I was here all day while you were out. Nobody touched anything. Why would we, anyway? We had no idea he had information he was holding out on."

"I tried to tell him that, but he wouldn't listen. You need to take him out. He's starting to get paranoid."

And you're not? Hask thought but didn't say.

"And you need to do it quick. He might just take off and take the information with him."

"I'm on it," said Gideon. He held out his hand. "Give me your blaster."

Iden had hopped onto a speeder bike. Her comm chirped when she was about halfway to her destination.

"It's me," Hask said when she responded. "Seems the Mentor's been holding out on Staven with regard to some very important information. I'm to recover that info and kill him."

"I'm halfway there. Where are you?"

"I had no idea where to find him. You sure you can?"

"Yes. I need you to tell Staven you'll do it and then get to the ship. Tell Del to make an excuse and join you there. This shouldn't take long, and then we can finally get off this wretched dusky world."

"You've got a blaster, then?"

"Yes."

"Well . . . all right then. I was looking forward to putting a hole in that prig myself."

Anger swept through her, but she tamped it down. "That's an order, Hask. Not a request."

"Of course, Captain."

"I'll let you know when I'm heading back." Iden clicked off the comm and crouched low over the speeder's bars.

She was not looking forward to what she had to do next.

Iden took a back route to approach the amphitheater indirectly. She knew that the Mentor would come here, and having read his journal, she now understood why. She dismounted several meters away, unholstered her blaster, and moved toward the place where she had "practiced" so often with him.

With her night-vision goggles on, she could see him clearly. There was one stone in the center of the basin where he liked to sit, and he was perched atop it now. He held something in his hands, turning it over and over. He had no night goggles on, which was foolish, but somehow he looked up in her direction. He couldn't possibly see her, but Iden froze anyway.

"Did Staven send you?" The Mentor spoke in normal tones, but his voice carried perfectly.

Iden stepped forward and shouted back. "No. I came of my own accord."

"Join me, Iden," he said, waving her down. She paused. She could take the shot from here and be done with it. But there was so much she wanted to know. And he didn't appear to be armed. Except, of course, with information that she wanted.

Slowly, keeping the weapon trained on him, she made her way down into the amphitheater, stopping about four meters from him.

He smiled at her sadly. "I thought it would be you. I assume you found my journal."

"Yes," she said. "Now it all makes sense. How you knew Saw and Steela, your education and political knowledge. My father wasn't very fond of senators, so I don't think I've ever met one before."

"And you still haven't," he said. "I'm just plain old Lux Bonteri now."

Plain old would never accurately describe him. He was the son of a senator of Onderon, and he'd been a senator representing that world himself. In his youth, he had loved both a Jedi and the original partisan rebel leader. He had fought against, and for, the Republic, and then against the Empire, before going into hiding, having somehow acquired confidential information. Rebel or no, Lux Bonteri was quite possibly one of the most impressive men she had ever met.

But she couldn't tell him that.

"The information," she said. "Hand it over."

"I can't do that, Iden, you know I can't." He looked at her regretfully. "You'll have to kill me if you want this."

"I will."

Lux nodded. "I know" was all he said.

Even so, Iden didn't fire. Not yet. "Where did the information come from?" she demanded.

"My daughter."

It was probably the last thing Iden would have expected him to say. There had been no mention of this in the journal. "Your . . . you mean your goddaughter? But you said she was dead."

"Maia? Yes. She's dead. I don't have a biological daughter. I told you I was married once, and my stepdaughter is as close as any blood-bonded child could be. She's a little older than you. You'd like her."

"I don't understand."

"You know," the Mentor—Lux—said, as calmly as if she weren't standing a few meters away with a blaster aimed at him, "no one really likes showing themselves in a bad light. We all want to think we're doing the right thing, all the time, in every situation."

Iden swallowed. She thought about Seyn. Of the determined look in the girl's eyes as she had lunged toward her commanding officer, forcing Iden's hand. Forcing Iden to kill her. Seyn had done the right thing in that moment. And Iden had, too.

But Seyn should never have been placed in that position. Never. That was all at Iden's feet, and she could never, ever undo that.

"You're right," she said. "We do want to think that."

"But we're so far from perfect it's almost absurd," Lux continued. "I think of some of the things I did when I was young; how fortunate I was that I had people to pull me out of it when I got in too deep, was being far too stupid. I've loved, and I've been loved, Iden. And I used that love as a weapon to get what I wanted. I'm deeply ashamed of that, but I'd do it again in a heartbeat."

"So . . . your stepdaughter obtained vital information and gave it to you."

"Yes. She isn't highly placed herself, but she has access to a lot of classified documents."

"You convinced her to turn on the Empire? Is she a mole?" Iden realized now Lux had seldom mentioned his stepdaughter—not even in his journal—because he was protecting her.

"No. Never." Lux was completely firm in his response, and she believed him. "She's as Imperial as they come. She takes after her mother in that respect. But— she loves me. Well . . . she did." Regret filled his voice as he spoke. "I can't help but wonder if, now, she despises me."

Iden knew she ought to kill him right now, but she didn't. This story intrigued her, pulled at her in a way she couldn't fully articulate. She told herself she merely hoped to add another feather to her proverbial cap— to have the name of another traitor to pluck from an important position, the way one plucked a weed from a garden.

But she also wanted to hear more about this. About someone who was, if Lux was to be believed—and she didn't have cause to doubt him—*as Imperial as they come* but who could still do something to betray the Empire.

She needed to understand.

So, mindful of everything in her environment and her blaster still leveled squarely at his unarmored chest, she said, "Go on."

"You know why I joined the Dreamers, unlikely a fit as I am. But after Saw was killed at Jedha, before I reached out to them—I reached out to her first. I told her that Saw's death upset me more than I could ever have imagined." He gave her a sad smile. "The best lies are the ones that have truth in them. Aren't they?"

Iden didn't answer. Lux continued.

"I said that it was obvious that the Empire's power could not be denied. That the only true peace could be bought with its victory. I told her I'd give them everything I had on the operations of the Rebel Alliance—but I wanted amnesty. I asked her to give me specific places and times where it would be safe for me to turn myself in—someplace public, where I'd be on record. I told her I knew that some people in the Empire weren't as honorable as she was, and I was afraid I might be taken, tortured, and then killed. It . . . upset her to think about anything like that happening to me."

Iden swallowed hard. *End this now*, she told herself. *He won't tell you her name. He'll die before he'll do that. He has nothing more of import to say. Kill him, take the chip, and get your team home.*

But she did not pull the trigger. Instead, she licked her lips and forced her voice to be calm. Icy.

"So she gave you names of people she thought you could trust to be honorable when you surrendered," she said.

"More than just names," Lux replied. "Detailed information on where they would be. What events would be going on. Security codes. Eleven major public events spread out over three months. Eleven different options for me to surrender to the Empire."

"One of them was the trip to the factory," Iden said, putting it all together.

"Yes. Both of those men, whatever their failings, were not the hard-liners that so many others are. They'd have honored my surrender. Three other events had already happened before you arrived."

"I know about those." They were the ones her father had mentioned—the ones that had caused him to send in Inferno Squad. In an effort to revitalize the Dreamers with new, important victories, Lux Bonteri had doomed them. She was certain he knew that now. "Obviously you didn't surrender."

Lux shook his head. "No," he said. "Though at one point . . . I thought about it. But then I remembered: This isn't the Rebel Alliance. This is the *Empire*. And you have more cruelty in common with the partisans than you'd like to think."

Iden wanted to deny it, but she couldn't. It was true. Even Hask had said as much at one point. Instead, she said, "I'm not your confidante."

"No," he agreed, "but you *are* the last person I'm going to see before I die, and I want someone to know— well, know at least as much as I'm willing to tell."

"So tell. Then die."

He shrugged, and continued. "I didn't turn myself in. Not just because I'm not keen on torture, but because, eventually, I'd betray my stepdaughter, too. They would figure out her part in this—and they wouldn't understand why she'd done it.

"So instead, I tracked down Staven—someone else who had worked personally with Saw. I told him some of what I told you—that I had a onetime source of information, and I was willing to share it with him—but not all at once. Staven didn't like that, but what was he going to do?"

Iden thought. "And so far, you've hit four of the targets. And no one's made any connection."

"There's no connection to make. They've so little in common it looks random—except that the Dreamers somehow got the information. There's nothing at the present time to trace it back to my daughter." His eyes bored into hers. "Except you, now. And I don't think you'll do that."

"Why wouldn't I?" Iden challenged.

"First, because after my disgrace years ago, she changed her name. It would be difficult to track her down. Second, because as I said—she's a loyal Imperialist who loves her father despite everything he's done. And . . . I don't think you believe that she should die for that."

The blaster wavered. Then Iden leveled it again. "Chitchat time's over. Give me the chip."

He shook his dark head. "No."

"Lux . . . You just said the Dreamers were no different from the Empire. You don't agree with how they handle things. You didn't just destroy weapons or shipyards, or kill off Imperial soldiers—innocent people died in those attacks. Civilians. *Children* would have, if not for Seyn. The people the Dreamers are supposedly fighting for!"

"I never would have told Staven about the school tour had I known they would target the students. You know that." His eyes flashed angrily.

"And you should have known that wouldn't matter to him. You were never going to get them to change."

Strangely, his pale-blue eyes brightened at that. "Ah, but you see, that's something that the Empire doesn't understand. There's always hope, Iden. Hope that if you speak truth long enough, the right person will hear it, and *know* it to be the truth."

Something inside Iden snapped. Her icy calm exploded in a burst of white-hot rage—against what, she wasn't exactly sure.

"You're not making inroads, you're just making enemies!" she snarled, trembling with fury. "Let me tell you something about that hope of yours. Right after you left, Staven took Gid aside and ordered him to follow you. To get the information about the rest of the strikes, and then to kill you. Staven. Your *leader*. He's not listening, Lux. None of them are."

He seemed shocked to hear that, and for a moment he looked smaller to her—and older, as if the years had suddenly caught up to him. Then, oddly, he began to smile, and that abrupt aging fell away.

"No," Lux said, "obviously, *he's* not listening. And maybe none of the others are, either. But answer me this. If, as you say—and I do believe you, by the way—if Gid was ordered to follow me, get the information, and kill me . . . why are you here?"

"Because I told him that you trusted me, which might mean you would show me where you hid the information. Much faster than killing you and randomly searching."

"That's a reasonable explanation. And it's true, as far as it goes. I do trust you, and I don't trust Gid. But I think there's something else—some other reason why you didn't want him here. Why you wanted to come yourself."

When Iden didn't answer, he continued, taking a cautious step toward her. "And you know . . . that gives me almost more hope than I had before. You can't quit hoping, Iden. Cling to it like a lifeline, because it is. Hope that something you do, or say, will make a difference. Look at what happened with the Death Star. One man hoped, for years, clutching an awesome, tremendous secret close in his heart, that somehow he'd be able to reach someone and let them know that abomination had a weakness. The rebels who stole the plans at Scarif died, but they hoped that they had transmitted the signal in time. Leia hoped the plans would reach the rebels. *Hope,* Iden. It's at the root of everything we believe. Without it, we're nothing."

"If hope is all you have, then you already *are* nothing," Iden said quietly. "And you know what they say. Live in hope . . . die in despair."

She fired.

CHAPTER 28

Iden was wrestling with her emotions, shoving them down to be dealt with later. How could you be confident in your decision and still question it? How could the same thing be both wrong and right?

It doesn't matter, she told herself. *You did what you were ordered to do.* Nestled snugly inside a compartment of her utility belt was the precious chip. The partisans would never recover. They would never threaten the Empire again, in any way, large or small.

"I'm on my way back," she said to Hask.

"It's done? Did he have the chip?"

"It's safe in my pocket. All we have to do is get out of here and head home."

"Copy that. But I have a little surprise for you first."

Iden frowned. "Did something happen? What's going on?"

"Everything is completely under control, and it wouldn't be a surprise if I told you. Del's got the ship out and ready to go."

"I don't like surprises, Hask, and I'll be there in ten."

Del and Hask were waiting for her when she brought her speeder up to the shuttle. So were the Dreamers.

Del was leaning against the ramp. His head rested on one arm, cradling his face. A blaster dangled limply from the fingers of his other hand. His body was taut, as if he were in pain.

Hask had a blaster, too, but he was grinning, waving to Iden as she pulled up.

The Dreamers lay sprawled on the ground.

Iden stared at the crumpled forms. She couldn't breathe.

Staven, an expression of shock still on his face. The Kages, lying beside each other, reunited with Sadori. Dahna had fallen in an oddly graceful position, her lekku fanning out beside her, a dancer even in death.

And Piikow, his little body looking even smaller and more fragile, now that it did not house the energy of his enthusiastic personality.

All bore the unmistakable marks of blaster burns. All were quite dead.

"See? I told you it was a surprise," Hask said. "Shockingly easy. We should have done this a long time—"

Iden was on him, grabbing his tunic and shoving him, hard, against the ship's bulkhead. He made no move to stop her and simply stared, as if she'd lost her mind.

Breath came back to her in a rush. "Why?" she shrieked. "*Why?*"

"Easy, Captain," soothed Hask, "you're getting carried away here. All I did was—"

"This wasn't necessary!" Iden continued to rail. "We're cleaners, we're not assassins! We're not murderers! We got what we needed, the mission was over, they were toothless. You had your orders, dammit, and you disobeyed them. You disobeyed *me*!" She took a breath and said again, more quietly, "This wasn't necessary."

She stepped back, the anger receding like a wave from the beach, leaving her feeling weak and achingly tired. Wisely, Hask didn't say anything else. Iden forced herself to turn and look at the bodies.

"There's no rush to leave now," she said. Her voice sounded flat to her own ears, as if she were speaking in a room that muffled sound. "We'll bury them."

"The Dreamers just left Seyn to be taken by—"

"We're not the Dreamers, Hask!" she snapped. "We're supposed to be better than they are, remember? Or have you gotten so caught up in Staven's bloodlust that you've forgotten you're an Imperial officer?"

Hask drew breath to speak, but Del interrupted him. "Captain, Lieutenant . . . we've got company."

Iden followed Del's wide-eyed gaze and gasped.

Moving toward them were huge, lumbering forms, humanoid except for perfect round heads out of which stared two spots of dark, luminescent purple.

The sound of blasterfire rent the air, and one of the forms shattered like a clay pot. The pieces fell to the ground, revealing more crystals contained within. Del reached over to Hask and grabbed the blaster, preventing him from shooting a second time.

"I don't think they're going to hurt us," Del said, "but let's get out of their way."

The three Imperial agents stepped back, away from the bodies, and watched with a combination of astonishment and trepidation.

There were four now, moving toward the shuttle and the figures sprawled on the dirt. More movement farther off revealed that a fifth was approaching to join them.

"These are your statues," Iden said. She was whispering; she didn't know why.

"Yes," Del said, also softly. "They've been reactivated, somehow. But there are only four—wait, five of them."

"They don't seem hostile," Iden said.

"But they're coming," Hask said.

"There are a lot of them in that cavern," Del warned him. "They'd just keep coming. We'd run out of blaster power before half of them got here." He watched, almost reverently, as the clay creations continued their steady stride. "Something . . . *woke* them. And I have to know what."

They stood and watched. Closer the huge constructs came, calmly, with no hostile or rapid moves, until each of the five stood beside a fallen Dreamer. Then, in perfect synchronization, they bent and gently, oh so gently, took the limp forms in their arms. Iden watched in wonder, her heart suddenly, strangely, full, as the statues seemed to cradle the bodies, like a parent gathering up a slumbering child and bearing it to bed.

Then whatever had sent them here caused them to turn around, and as slowly and solemnly as they had arrived, they retreated the way they had come.

"I was wrong," Del breathed. "I thought they operated on telepathy. They *do* respond to sentient brain activity—but only when it stops."

So this was why there were no relics of the ancient civilization. They had created guardians who tended to them when life was extinguished, bearing their bodies away out of sight, bearing away perhaps all remnants of their existence.

"Was this all they were meant to do?" Hask asked. Even he pitched his voice low as they watched the retreating guardians, carrying their precious burdens, disappear into the distance.

"It could be," Del said. "But what better way to address the end of a civilization?"

"This was what happened to the stormtrooper—to Azen and Seyn," Iden said. "It's why we didn't find their bodies. These . . . guardians sensed the end of sentient life, and took care of them." She paused. "I'm glad."

"Me too," Del said.

Hask said nothing, but he looked more serious and thoughtful than Iden had ever seen him.

Her anger with him fell away, as if the guardians had borne that away with them as well, and she was glad of that, too.

"Let's go home," said Captain Iden Versio.

The debriefing was as rocky as Iden had expected it to be.

They were grilled, separately, by an Admiral Versio who made little effort to hide his disappointment that they had lost one of their members. Iden remembered sitting in her father's office with Del, Hask, and Seyn, her stomach in knots, burning with the desire to be the one to lead the team. The best of the best.

Now she folded her hands and regarded him as he fired question after question: When did she know that the mysterious, nameless Mentor was the informant? How did they spot Azen? What did Seyn do to reveal herself? Why did Iden not notice that Seyn was in distress?

He kept hammering at her as if she were a rebel ship and he were a TIE fighter, using words instead of a laser cannon. She took a breath before answering each question, calmly and completely. Finally, he asked the one she knew was coming.

"Whose fault is it that Lieutenant Marana died?"

"It was my fault, and mine alone," she said.

He raised his eyebrows at that. "You don't think she brought it on herself? That it was her own carelessness that caused her death?"

"No, sir. She was my crewmember. She was my responsibility." And then, the words. "I failed her and my team." She might not have Seyn's eidetic memory, but Iden knew that she would never forget the look on Seyn's face, the silent *yes*. "Lieutenant Marana wasn't just my squad member. She was my friend. I can only hope that I can be as courageous and selfless as she was when one day it's my turn to face death. I myself am prepared to accept any discipline you suggest."

Her father leaned back in his chair, scrutinizing her. "You yourself? What about your crew? From the sound of things, they, too, failed Lieutenant Marana."

"I would argue against discipline for them. I will point out that in a single mission, we stopped a potentially disastrous leak before its final target was attacked and turned the Dreamers against one another—sooner rather than later, they'd have been fighting themselves, not us. Hask's activity was significant in dividing the Dreamer membership, and Meeko's technological mastery enabled us to communicate and interfere with the Dreamers on a regular basis."

"So you are saying the agents obeyed your orders to the letter?"

"Negative, sir, but no harm was done." The Dreamers had been living on borrowed time. If Iden was brutally honest with herself, she had to admit that death by blaster bolt was preferable to other ways they might have met their ends—particularly if the Empire had come to do so. "Lieutenant Hask eliminated the Dreamers of his own volition. It is my opinion he believed he was adhering to the larger scope of the mission, which had as part of its goal the eventual elimination of the entire partisan resistance movement."

"We could have gotten information out of them first," Versio said. "I've included that in my report on Lieutenant Hask."

Iden suddenly realized how very much she would not have wished that on Dahna or Piikow . . . or even on the Kages or Staven. She made no reply.

"Debriefing of Captain Iden Versio concluded," her father said into the holorecorder. "Recommend no further investigation into the death of Lieutenant Seyn Marana. Recommendation for Posthumous Black Laurel for Service to the Empire issued. Commendations are also recommended for Commander Del Meeko and Lieutenant Gideon Hask, and also for Captain Iden Versio." He turned off the holorecorder.

Iden was surprised. "Thank you, sir," she said, rising. "Permission to speak freely?"

"Granted."

"When can I talk to Mama? I assume she's been told about—"

"Iden."

The usage of her first name stopped Iden cold. Words suddenly lodged in her throat. Something had happened. Something bad. She couldn't even find the words to form a question, simply looked up at him mutely, silently begging that whatever he had to say would not be the thing she imagined, the thing she feared.

"Why don't you sit back down," he began.

The words escaped. "No," she said. "I'll stand."

He searched her eyes, then nodded. "It's as you wish. I wanted to tell you this earlier, but we had no way to easily and safely communicate with Inferno Squad until your mission was completed," Versio said, his voice quiet. "We couldn't risk jeopardizing the mission. And I didn't . . ." He paused and cleared his throat. "I wanted to tell you in person."

No.

No . . .

Voiceless, helpless, her ramrod-straight posture all that was left to her, Iden waited.

"Her illness was more advanced than either of us knew. Three weeks after you left, it claimed her life."

Iden continued to stare at him, her fists clenching, still unable to speak.

"Zeehay never much cared for Vardos, so we had her

interred on Svaaha, where she had her last assignment. There's footage of the ceremony, if you'd like to see it. And I can arrange for you to visit her grave if you wish to do so."

Iden wanted to rage. Scream. Claw his face. Claw her own. Zeehay's bright smile, her warm eyes, her joyfully unselfconscious belly laugh, those long fingers covered with old-fashioned paint—gone, all gone.

"She died thinking her daughter was a traitor." Her voice was a whisper, a breath.

Her father said nothing for a moment. Then, in a quiet voice, he said, "No. She didn't."

Iden gasped softly, her eyes burning with tears. She stared at her father as if at a stranger, trying to reconcile all she had known her entire life with those three simple words. The mission was top secret, and he had violated all manner of military regulations to do what he had done. Her heart was full, so beautifully full, and yet it was broken, because this moment meant everything, and changed nothing.

"Thank you" was all she said. He nodded.

They stood for a moment.

"You're a strong soldier, Captain Versio," he said at last.

"Thank you, sir," she replied.

He squared his shoulders, and the moment slipped into memory. "Rest up. I've arranged for all of you to have private lodgings for tonight. Thought you might appreciate some solitude after living with those . . ." Versio couldn't even come up with a word vile enough to describe what he felt about the Dreamers. "*Them,*" he finished. "You and the rest of your team will report here at oh nine hundred for your next assignment. I know it's soon, but it's always best to get right back into the thick of things. Not to dwell on them. And the Empire needs your help."

"I serve at the pleasure of the Empire, sir."

"I know you do. You're a Versio. It's how I raised you." He paused. "Good night, Captain. Dismissed."

She was still at the Diplomat, but this time she had her own room, on one of the regular floors. There was no guard at the door, for which Iden was unspeakably grateful. She entered the code for the door, stepped inside, and let it close behind her. As it did so, the room lit up automatically.

Iden's bag fell from nerveless fingers to the carpeted floor. She took a forced breath and muttered, "Off." She couldn't bear the light, too bright, showing things too clearly. She needed darkness, quiet, anything that wasn't harsh or cruel. Even her skin felt hypersensitized, as raw against the brush of her gaberwool uniform as if the first few layers had been removed.

Outside, myriad colors flashed, bright splotches in the never-quite-dark night. Iden turned around, staring out the window, then made her way, stiff-legged, to the bed. She felt a thousand years old as she sat down, staring at nothing but seeing everything.

She smelled her mother's scent, light and sporty and clean, felt those strong, comforting arms slip around her small child's body before Zeehay, with a reassuring smile, went into the shuttle.

She saw Seyn in her crisp white NavInt outfit, her impossibly young face a carefully controlled blank. She saw the scars marring that face, and then the expression of calm resignation in the young woman's eyes even as she snarled in false rage.

She saw Seyn fall.

Iden closed her eyes and shoved the heels of her palms into them, but closed eyes did nothing to halt the parade of images. She thought of Piikow's bright eyes, of how beautifully Dahna moved when she danced, just for herself. Of Sadori's shy smile when he looked at Seyn, as if she were all that was wonderful and beautiful in the galaxy encapsulated in the slender form of a petite young woman. Of how, sometimes, Iden had seen that same expression in Staven's eyes when he looked at Nadrine.

She saw again Azen's torture, the limp bodies that Hask had offered as a "surprise," and the enormous and silent guardians who so tenderly gathered them and bore them to rest. She saw Lux Bonteri, the senator from Onderon, giving a speech to a single audience member, in a natural amphitheater light-years away, his voice still strong, still filled with hope and determination despite all that he had seen. She saw Tarvyn Lareka looking at her with concern in his eyes as they walked the floor of a Star Destroyer.

It's best for all of us that she's gone. She's a Versio in name only. We—you and I—are true Versios, and Versios don't cry, do they?

No, sir, her five-year-old self had replied in a voice thick with unuttered shrieks of grief. *Versios don't cry.*

But the tears did not care that she was a Versio. They came at last, racking her body, scalding her eyes and face, hoarsening her throat, an outpouring of grief not just for Zeehay Versio, who was the last soft thing Iden ever remembered, but for everything that had ever been hurt, or destroyed, or ruined. Everything she had lost, from the woman who bore her to the childhood she'd never really had.

And when at last her sobs were spent and the tears had dried, their salty crust on her face evidence of grief made manifest, the world was the same as it was before. The lights still dipped and dodged in the window. The bed was still soft, the sheets still crisp, although her pillow was damp.

Iden's breathing slowed. It was the first time she had wept since the night her mother had left Vardos, when a little girl had curled up and, muffling her sobs in the pillow, wept for the mother who had never really returned, and now never would. But she had passed peacefully, and somehow, Iden knew that everything would be all right.

Despite her aching certainty that she would never, ever sleep again, sleep stole over her.

In her dreams, the shin'yah trees wept over water, and their leaves bled crimson until it was washed away.

EPILOGUE

Inferno Squad's next mission was a simple one. A moff on a distant world was being blackmailed. The team was to locate and neutralize the blackmailers and recover all evidence of the moff's indiscretions. NavInt had a dossier they could peruse while they were in transit.

Straightforward, clear. Iden was glad of it.

She'd arrived early, and now climbed aboard the *Corvus* with a half smile on her face. She examined it from bow to stern, with renewed appreciation for its sleek, efficient lines after so long spent with junkers.

She went to their quarters and removed a bottle from her bag. It was expensive, but she didn't begrudge a credit. She placed it on Seyn's bunk. *You'll always be with us,* she thought. *You'll always be a member of Inferno Squad.*

"Oh, sorry, Captain. Didn't realize you were aboard."

"At ease, Agent," Iden said. "Come on in, Del."

"It's good to be back." He sighed, looking at the ship as if it were an old friend. For him, she supposed it was. For all of them, honestly. His eyes fell on the bottle—and on the bunk on which Iden had placed it.

"It still hurts," he said, quietly.

"It probably always will," Iden replied.

He sat down on his own bunk, elbows on his knees. He looked down for a minute, then up at her. "May I ask you a question? Unofficially? You don't have to answer."

Iden stiffened instinctively, then forced herself to relax. This was Del. Her friend. Her teammate. Who had never let her down, and was always kind. "Go ahead," she replied.

He scratched his nose. "It's more of a statement, actually—"

"Del."

He turned his warm brown eyes back to her. "When you came back . . . that night when we left. I saw your blaster as you went up the ramp." He paused. "It was on stun."

Iden said nothing.

"You didn't kill the Mentor, did you?"

She didn't reply. He waited for a moment, then nodded, brushing it off. "I did say you didn't have to answer, didn't I?"

"I think you know," Iden said.

He nodded again. "I . . . a few days before we left . . ." He lifted his gaze to hers, completely serious. "I was trying to think of a way we could get Piikow treatment."

Iden felt something inside her soften. She gave Del a smile, then lifted her finger to her lips. *Shhhh.*

"Permission to come aboard, Captain!" Hask's voice was strong and cheerful.

"Permission granted, Lieutenant!" she called back. He strode in briskly but, like Del, paused at the sight of Seyn's bunk.

While Hask sank down in his own bunk, Iden uncorked the Tevraki whiskey and poured shots for each of them. As she handed them out, she said, "I know we all remember that night in the suite where we had our first toast. We didn't know what lay in store for us. We didn't know what and, more important, who we would lose. But we finished our mission. The Dreamers are no more. Seyn Marana gave her life to make sure that happened. And we honored her sacrifice by seeing to it that it did."

There was a pause, and then Del cleared his throat and squared his shoulders. From his mouth came a cacophony of ugly sounds—gibberish, and yet somehow familiar. They looked at him, quizzically, and he smiled, a little embarrassed.

"That was Seyn's toast," he said. "About rending the flesh of our enemies. The one she made that night. I asked her to teach it to me. Boy, she was right—it *is* difficult to pronounce Ahak Maharr if you don't have tusks."

They laughed, and it felt good. Seyn would have approved. The three knocked back their shots, and Iden refilled them and lifted hers.

"To the best team the Empire has ever assembled," she said, certain of the truth of her words.

"To Inferno Squad!"

ACKNOWLEDGMENTS

No book is birthed in a vacuum, and that goes doubly for a media novel, and this one in particular.

I'd like to extend my heartfelt appreciation to my marvelous editor, Elizabeth Schaefer, who was so patient with me during the writing of this and so excited about every draft I turned in to her. I owe her a case of Tevraki whiskey.

Also deep thanks to the many hardworking *Star Wars* people, from longtime friend and Editor-at-Large Shelly Shapiro, Senior Production Manager Erich Schoeneweiss, Assistant Editor Tom Hoeler, Designer Liz Eno, Production Editor Nancy Delia, to Deputy Director of Publicity David Moench at Del Rey.

Enthusiastic appreciation to those at Lucasfilm: Executive Editor Jennifer Heddle and the marvelous Story Group folks Pablo Hidalgo, Leland Chee, Matt Martin, Steve Blank, Douglas Reilly, and James Waugh.

Last but not least, thank you to all those at EA, Motive, and DICE, who were as excited about this book as you are about the game, and a huge shout-out to Walt Williams and Mitch Dyer, for their fabulous script that birthed the members of Inferno Squad.

Many, many thanks. I'm honored to have been part of this.

Read on for an excerpt from

STAR WARS: PHASMA

By Delilah S. Dawson
Published by Del Rey Books

Phasma and her warriors began making preparations the moment they saw the explosion high overhead. As the ship's remains streaked across the sky, Phasma tracked it with her quadnocs, taking careful note of the direction in which it fell. At the very least, ships like this could be pillaged; at most, there was always a hope that they could be salvaged and used to get offplanet. No one alive had seen such ships do anything but fall and crash, but they were evidence of the larger galaxy beyond Parnassos, of a future that had been denied them. It was painful, living on such a treacherous planet with so many reminders of the ease and technology that had once been taken for granted. At the very least, there would be metal, tech, clothes, medicines, food, and possibly working blasters scattered around what was left of the ship. These were the greatest riches in Phasma's world.

But they had to hurry. Other groups in other territories would also be watching and preparing for the journey. Falling stars, as they called them, were rare, and this ship was the shiniest thing the Scyre had ever seen—so bright that they had to shield their eyes as it arrowed down toward the planet. Part of the ship popped off and floated down separately, headed for the area where the Scyre lands bordered the enemy Claw clan's, which made it all the more important to hurry.

The journey was not easy, for no journeys on Parnassos are. The Scyre territory was mostly spires of black rock, jagged cliffs, ledges, caves, and occasional tide pools when the ocean was at its lowest. Within their accustomed living area, they maintained a series of ziplines, rope bridges, tethers, nets, and hammocks, and even the least nimble Scyre member could get from place to place without too much trouble. But beyond their nesting place, along their border with the Claw, the terrain grew even more dangerous. The bridges weren't sturdy, and one never knew when a support spike might be rusted through or a stone spire crumbling away to nothing. Phasma's warriors were lucky that the ship had crashed during a time of low tides, so they were able to traverse the terrain far more easily than if the tides had been high, not to mention that during high tide, the ship might've been swallowed by the sea—or a monster in it.

When they reached the line of flags delineating the borderlands between the Scyre and the Claw, Phasma called a halt and pulled out her quadnocs. Five figures were being pulled up onto the plateau from the land below. Using the lenses, Phasma followed the footprints and drag marks back to where a metal machine waited, half submerged in the sand and beside a huge, piece of fabric. It was the part of the ship th popped off and gently floated down. The Scyre had never seen so much fabric in one piece in all their lives, and it was clear why several Claw members were down there, busily cutting the long lines that held the fabric to the machine so that they might claim it for their own. The downed ship was nowhere in sight, but far, far away, across the sands and yet more rocks. Phasma tracked the thin line of white smoke that feathered up into the sky, marking the path to true riches.

A cheer went up from the gathered Claw as the first strange figure was dragged to standing on top of the plateau. It was a man, and for Parnassos, he wore very little, just finely woven clothes of a smooth, uniform black and tall, shiny boots speckled with sand. He was the oldest person the Scyre folk had ever seen, with pale-white skin and red hair going gray at the edges. Although his limbs were slender enough, his belly was big, and he had dark circles under his eyes. He smiled blandly at the whoops and whistles of the Claw folk but was clearly not celebrating, personally.

Without a word, Phasma urged her people forward, motioning for them to be quiet and quick. When they stood on the edge of the plateau, behind the crowd of Claw folk so mesmerized that they hadn't even noticed the interlopers, Phasma and her people finally saw the miracle occurring.

The Claw's leader had pushed the man gently aside and reached for the next figure, a warrior wearing white armor streaked with gray sand over a thin suit of black. A gasp went over the Claw folk, and Phasma's warriors,

.oo—such armor would've given anyone on Parnassos a huge advantage over the elements, and the solid helmet seemed an improvement over their light leather masks. Two more white-armored soldiers followed, and lastly came a droid. It was shaped vaguely like a human and made of matte-black metal, and it took the longest to haul up, due, most likely, to its weight and its inability to climb. The people of Parnassos had seen the component parts of hundreds of droids and even used droid metal for their weapons, but no one living had seen a droid stand of its own volition and hold up an indignant hand, as this black droid did when the Claw attempted to touch it.

The droid spoke to the man in black with a mechanized voice. It was hard to hear on the plateau, surrounded by whispering and the sudden gusts of wind, but the language seemed both familiar and different. The man in black spoke back to the droid, and the droid spoke again, this time much louder, its voice projected by some sort of strange machinery.

"My name is Brendol Hux, and I'm afraid my starship was shot down by an automated defense system over your world. My language is a little different from yours, so this droid will translate to your more primitive dialect.

"My emergency pod has landed very far from my ship. I have lost several of my own people in this horrible tragedy. But if you are willing to help me, I can offer you the kind of technology and supplies that your world has lost. I come from a powerful band called the First Order that brings peace to the galaxy. I am tasked with scouring the stars for the greatest warriors, that they might join our cause. Our people are well cared for and well trained. Ask my soldiers, here. Troopers, is that not so?"

The three soldiers in white nodded and barked, "Yes, sir!"

"Each of these warriors was selected from a distant planet and trained to fight for the First Order. If your people help return us to our ship, I will take whoever wishes to join me back to our fleet. These soldiers will live in glory and wealth, never suffering for want again. Now, who will help me?"

The Claw people stood to cheer, but a new figure appeared beside Brendol Hux, a warrior wearing a fierce red mask.

"I am Phasma, and I am the greatest warrior of Parnassos." Removing her mask, Phasma faced Brendol and waited for the robot to translate. "I will help you find your ship."

EXPLORE THE WORLDS OF DEL REY BOOKS

Read excerpts from hot new titles.

Stay up-to-date on your favorite authors.

Find out about exclusive giveaways and sweepstakes.

Connect with us online!

Follow us on social media
Facebook.com/DelReyBooks
@DelReyBooks

Visit us at UnboundWorlds.com
Facebook.com/UnboundWorlds
@unboundworlds

DEL REY